Inspired by the handwritten journals and letters of the author's great grandfather, Ira Seeley, Henry's Pride is the story of men and women on both sides of the Civil War. Writing nearly in real time 150 years after the events, from 2012 to 2015, Greg Seeley takes us on a journey behind enemy lines, onto the battlefield, to the neglected farms back home, and inside the prison camps during this divisive period in American history. Meet Henry Hancock, a prideful Union sergeant and later captain, who faithfully performs his duty while trying to make sense of what he calls "the nation's nasty business." Meet his brother Jonas, injured, mustered out of the army, yet still traumatized by his experiences in an artillery battery. Meet Theodore, a runaway slave too young to join the Union Army, who becomes a hired worker at their Minnesota farm. You'll also meet Darius, the young heir to a Georgia plantation, fighting for the Confederacy to protect his inheritance while Hamilton Stark, his overseer back home, goes to extreme lengths to prevent runaways and head off a slave insurrection. Mr. Seeley, a loyal student of history, interweaves these very compelling and realistic stories with letters to and from home, describing a world so vivid and human you will be instantly transported.   -Victor A. Davis

For Dad and Mom

HENRY'S PRIDE

GREG SEELEY

Printed in the United States of America

First Printing, 2016-10-27

ISBN 978-1-537-53438-1

ISBN 1-537-53438-6

Edited by Katie-bree Reeves of
Fair Crack of the Whip Proofreading and Editing

Cover design by Paul Copello of Designistrate.com

ACKNOWLEDGMENTS

A special thank you to all of the friends, relatives, and colleagues who have contributed their time, support, effort, and talent to this endeavor. To my great-grandfather, Ira Seeley, whose letters home while serving with 29th Iowa Infantry Regiment in the Civil War inspired me to create the fictional Henry Hancock and his family. Thank you to my grandparents and my parents for preserving those letters for over 150 years - keeping them part of a family heritage that makes the Civil War very personal and intensely real.

Thank you to my editor, Katie-bree Reeves, whose keen eye and sense of style helped turn an idea and a raw manuscript into a finished project worthy of readers' time and attention. To my cover designer, Paul Copello, for his care in creating a design depicting the real essence of my story. To my friend and fellow writer Victor Davis, whose work I admire - thank you for your editorial critiques and plot suggestions that helped bring my characters to life and give them depth.

Most of all, thank you to my wife Carolyn - for your love, support, patience, and understanding as I pursued one of the significant items on my bucket list, writing a novel. Thank you also for taking the photograph of our family heirlooms that provided the basis for Paul Copello's cover design magic.

AUTHOR'S NOTE

This is a work of historical fiction. Names, characters, places and incidents are products of the author's imagination. Any resemblance to actual persons, living or dead is entirely coincidental.

The letters and their format included within and all of their grammar or structural compositions (including spelling) are purposely written as they appear. This is necessary in order to replicate as closely as possible the style and vernacular of actual letters written during the period.

To the best of the author's research and knowledge, the slave dialect presented is authentic and accurate for the period in which the novel is set. It is intended to be nothing other than genuine and reflects only the lack of education afforded to Black Americans during the time.

Other Books by Greg Seeley:

The Horse Lawyer and Other Poems (2014)

Principal Characters

Minnesota

Phillip Hancock – Henry and Emma Hancock's grandson

Henry Hancock – A tenant farmer originally from Ohio.

Emma (Em) Hancock – Henry's wife.

Jonas Christian Hancock – Henry's older brother who shares in the farm work and builds furniture in a shop in the nearby town of Thayer.

Ellie Hancock – Henry's youngest sister

Albert and Lucille Anderson – Henry's landlords and neighbors.

The Britt family – Charles and Margaret (twin sons are Thomas and Will) – Neighbors of the Hancocks.

David and Mary Alice Weinberg – (husband and wife) neighbors of the Hancocks.

Leland Atlee – An army friend of Henry's from a nearby town of Crestville

Georgia

Andrew Morgan – Owner of Pine Hill Plantation at Milledgeville, south-east of Atlanta.

Darius Morgan – Andrew's son.

Hamilton Stark – Overseer at Pine Hill.

Celia, Dahlia (sisters) and Toby (no last names) – slaves at Pine Hill

George and Harold (no last name) – a pair of brothers and Confederate Army deserters.

Adam Kendrick – a Georgian private and reluctant Confederate veteran.

Susan Kendrick – Adam's mother.

Keela – a young slave girl abandoned as her owners flee the advancing Union Army.

Taylor Adams – Andrew Morgan's Presbyterian Minister and close friend.

Mississippi

Isaac – a slave at Angus McManus' Riverview Plantation north and east of Vicksburg

Theodore – a runaway slave from a plantation near Corinth

Massachusetts

Reverend Joshua Gibbons – A recent Methodist seminary graduate from a prominent Boston family.

Doctor Sean and Katherine Gibbons – Joshua's parents

Illinois

Rose (Hancock) MacDonald – Henry's sister, married to Robert, an army physician posted at Rock Island.

Hosea Billings – Captain of the Guard – Federal Prison Camp, Rock Island

Kansas

Shelby Hancock – Cousin to Henry, Ellie, Rose and Jonas

PROLOGUE

Phillip Hancock slowed down and pulled off of the highway. For the first time in many years, the retired Dallas, Texas trial lawyer heard the once-familiar sound of gravel underneath his tires. The turn-off was unmarked and barely visible now. The county no longer bothered to trim the trees over and around the opening and the fences on either side had not seen new posts or wire in decades. The gravel itself extended only a few yards and even that had yielded mostly to native grasses.

He had rented the 1995 Ford Taurus in Minneapolis and spent last night at the Holiday Inn in Albert Lea. This morning, he had made a brief stop in Crestville before turning north, then west. It was here that the great wheat- and corn-growing prairie began to give way to the forests. It was here that it had all begun.

He continued up what had once passed for a road. It was now not much more than a wide path. Waist-high grass rustled against the side of the car. Occasionally, he could hear the sound of heavier brush scratching along the door and underneath the car as he drove over small saplings. It didn't really matter. He could well afford to pay for any damages that the rental company might decide to exact from him. In only another few years, he pondered, the grass and brush would consume all signs that the road had ever been there.

He himself had nearly completed his seventy-sixth year, and all who remembered the place would soon be gone. It would be as if the once-thriving little community called Thayer had never existed.

He had driven perhaps a mile when the road disappeared into a pasture. It now consisted of only the built-up roadbed, which itself was beginning to settle into the fields. Occasionally, it traversed a ditch where the bent and rusted end of a galvanized culvert poked through the weeds. Soon, he reached the creek and knew that he would have to make the remaining mile and a half or so on foot. A few large timbers of the bridge that he had crossed so many times in his youth lay rotting among the willow trees and were barely visible. He pulled the canvas rucksack from the back seat, sprayed himself liberally with bug repellant, put on the green safari hat, and walked into the grass.

Presently, he reached the edge of what had been the town. He stopped briefly and gazed up 'Main Street' toward the weathered clapboard ruins of the Methodist Church. On either side of the street were rows of intermittent brick facades – most one-story but some two-story, now reduced to one by time, snow, wind, rain, and vegetation. Between the buildings were overgrown lots – some empty and some containing piles of brick where the structures had succumbed to the inevitable and fallen in on themselves. One, he speculated but could not be sure which, had once housed his great uncle's furniture-making shop.

There was nothing left to identify what each of the buildings had been but Phillip knew some of them off by heart – Britt's Mercantile, Warden's Lumber and Coal, Hardee's Drug, the Walker House Hotel, and so on. At the blacksmith shop, part of the forge remained, rusted but still there. Had he walked closer, he would have noticed the anvil lying on the ground – its oak-stump base having long since returned to nature.

A block to the west, a grove of mulberry trees and various species of brush surrounded what had been the brick public schoolhouse where he, along with many of his family, had either studied, taught, or both. He recalled that the one building had housed all grades from one through to high school. He knew that, for most generations before his own, studies had stopped as early as the sixth or seventh grade. He noted that, on his last visit, some twenty-five years ago, some of the glass windows had still been in place. All of them were now either gone entirely or broken. Pigeons and other assorted birds flew freely in and out. Twenty-five years ago, there had been a roof. In the interim, it had fallen into the classrooms and the small gymnasium. Poplar trees now grew up behind the walls.

He strolled leisurely up the street, his ears filled with the sounds of horse hooves clopping over the now-crumbled brick streets and the voices of merchants greeting each other as they swept the steps of their stores and began preparing for the day's business.

It shouldn't have ended this way. He let his mind toy with the idea of what might have been had fate not intervened. First, the railroad had been extended from Albert Lea, but routed through Crestville rather than Thayer. Some businesses had relocated while others that might have established themselves in Thayer opted for Crestville instead. Then, there were the lean, dusty years of the thirties. Many farmers, unable to keep up with their debts, had simply quit trying and left. Merchants, now with fewer customers, were forced to leave also. There was also the great tornado of 1946 that had destroyed the sawmill. The mill that employed about one-third of the town's workers was never rebuilt. Finally, there was the new highway that bypassed the one he had just been on, leaving it only as a secondary county road.

He reached into the rucksack, pulled out his camera, and began taking pictures at various angles up and down the street. Satisfied with what he had done, he walked on up the hill, gazed briefly at the remnants of pews still lined up in the church, took a couple more pictures, and kept going. Climbing over a couple of falling fences, Phillip realized that he was technically guilty of trespassing but figured that no one would really mind.

After another mile or so, he reached his destination. He was pleasantly surprised to see that someone had taken the trouble to mow down the little cemetery and even trim around the stones. Some of the more recent ones (he guessed that there had been no new burials in a least forty years) looked pristine. Older markers appeared moldy and weathered to the point where the inscriptions were barely visible. Some stood as straight as if they had just been set. Others were tilted at odd angles and appeared ready to fall over. The iron fence surrounding the yard was largely intact with only a few gaps where the welds appeared to have been broken and the unsupported iron knocked over by cattle seeking to scratch against it.

He started by taking a photograph of the entire cemetery and then began to walk about shooting photos of each stone, especially trying to capture the faded inscriptions. Some of the names he knew well – obviously, the Hancocks. Others, he recalled hearing his parents speak of but they were entirely foreign to him. Yet most had one thing in common – their struggles and hard lives spent in carving out a community in southern Minnesota and their commitment to leaving something greater than themselves behind.

It was a perfect autumn day. The sun was bright, not blinding. The air was crisp, not cold breezy, not windy. The leaves on the maple and oak trees had just begun to turn. Placing the camera back in his bag, Phillip began again to simply stroll around.

P. Henry Hancock Jr.
Minnesota Infantry
Civil War

Emma Hancock
His Wife

Jonathan Hancock
Infant Son

Jonas Christian Hancock
Minnesota Artillery
Civil War

David Weinberg
Mexican War

Mary Alice Weinberg
His Wife

Rev. Joshua Gibbons
Major and Chaplain
Massachusetts Volunteers
Civil War
Medal of Honor

Ellie Gibbons
His Wife

Edward Kaler
Minnesota Infantry
Civil War
Buried - Tennessee

Mona Kaler
His wife

Albert Anderson
Pennsylvania Cavalry
Killed in Action – Fredericksburg
Buried – Baltimore, Maryland

Thomas Britt
Minnesota Infantry
Civil War
Killed in Action – Shiloh

William Britt
Minnesota Infantry
Civil War

Sarah Britt
His Wife

There were many others. One, in particular, had always intrigued him. While most of the markers consisted of simple slabs primarily of marble, this one, which stood near the back of the cemetery, was much more opulent. The seven foot high granite obelisk was topped with a copper finial that had long-since aged to green. While the inscription in the granite should have appeared much as it had the day that it was carved, it was nearly illegible. Either time and the elements or something else had long ago obscured most of the name and there was no indication that the man had been in the army. Phillip could make out only a few of the letters. 'Da … M … n.'.

The second inscription read only 'Charlotte. His Wife.' Any burial records had long ago disappeared.

Careful to make certain that it was securely in place; Phillip sat on the ground and leaned against one of the posts supporting the fence. He pulled from the rucksack a small, stainless steel coffee thermos. He poured a cup about half full, drank a couple of swallows, and set it on the ground beside him. From his jacket pocket, he removed a pair of reading glasses and a small leather pouch, which he had carefully wrapped in brown paper and tied with string. From the pouch, he took an aged leather-bound book and gently turned to the first page. He gave the first notations only passing notice. When reading them before, he had found them to be interesting though not particularly absorbing. He skimmed them briefly and devoted his attention to what followed:

Patrick Henry Hancock Jr.
His Journal.

In the intervening days, some have begun to call it the Battle of Shiloh. Others are referring to it as the Battle of Pittsburg Landing. I think that what it is called matters little. I believe it will be remembered largely as two days of unspeakable slaughter that, in the end, resolved nothing.

15

My great fear is that the battle, as fearsome as it was, will be only one of many yet to come before this nasty business is finished . . .

CHAPTER I

First Sergeant Henry Hancock crouched behind the stump and tamped another ball and wad down the muzzle of the Springfield rifle. Moments before, the stump had been an apple tree with the promise of fresh, sweet fruit in the fall. Now it was shattered by canister fired from one of the Rebel's guns across the lane and only jagged splinters reached above his head.

Henry wondered if he hadn't been dead since his early moments in the line. Perhaps this lowest circle of hell into which he had descended was to be his eternal punishment for the killing he had committed shortly after arriving here. Henry knew he might have killed men at Fort Donelson in February, but that seemed different. He had not really seen those men in the confusion and the smoke and the rain. This time he had seen the man – a man just like himself, who didn't want to be here either and who would never go home to his wife and little ones – had seen the man and had shot him squarely through the head. He had watched him crumple lifelessly from the ranks only to be walked over by another man who also didn't want to be here.

Yes, this had to be Hell. There was nothing else it could be. He had never seen, nor could he imagine, anything this awful in life. Nothing in the Sunday sermons he had listened to as a boy in Ohio or as a young man in Minnesota had prepared him for what he now heard and saw going on around him in this place. The constant roar of the cannonading was greater than the worst thunderstorm he had ever heard. It went on and on. And it wasn't followed by a gentle rain; it carried in the breeze the rank smell of sulfur that burned the nostrils and sickened the stomach, making it difficult to breathe. Every blast was followed by the awful shrieks and screams of both men and horses, raked with shot and now writhing through their last moments.

The hell seemed different for each. Around him, some were curled up on the ground, covering their heads and sobbing – their weapons lying uselessly at their sides. Others were running for what they thought to be the safety of the rear – some with their weapons and some without – some reaching the rear ranks only to be scolded by their officers – others falling as they were shot in the back. Some charged almost mindlessly forward into the fight – some falling as soon as they emerged from the ranks and others nearly reaching the Confederate lines. Here was a captain – shot dead before he could completely raise his sword. There was a lieutenant, suddenly without his left arm, and a colonel, slumped lifelessly in the saddle of a terrified horse.

It took only seconds to load the rifle but to Henry it felt like forever. It was hot for the seventh of April – stifling hot. But then this wasn't Minnesota. It was southwest Tennessee and only a short distance away was Mississippi. He reached to wipe the sweat from his face to keep it from stinging his eyes. As he pulled down his hand, he could see that the sweat was blackened from smoke and powder. He swung around from behind the stump and quickly found a target. Not wanting to see his ball hit its mark, he aimed the rifle, closed his eyes, and squeezed the trigger before throwing himself back to the ground.

****

Like his father, Patrick, and his younger brother, Henry, Corporal Jonas Hancock had fervently hoped and earnestly prayed that this day would never come. With every letter received from the brothers' cousin, Shelby, in Lawrence, Kansas in 1859 and 1860, the hope had seemed to grow dimmer and the prayers seemed less likely to be answered. When the Rebels had fired on Fort Sumter a year ago, this day and the horror that he was now seeing and hearing around him had become a certainty.

The Hancocks were not Quakers, though many from the neighboring farms around his boyhood home in Ohio were. They were not pacifists, but neither were they war hawks like many of their Minnesota neighbors, who saw war as a necessary and inevitable means of ending slavery. Such a man was their landlord, Albert Anderson, who had left Minnesota even before Sumter to return to his native Pennsylvania. There he had organized a cavalry regiment now attached to George McClellan's army fighting back east.

With Jonas, it had little to do with the issue of slavery. Minnesota was solidly set in the Union as a free state. Like Shelby, he was sympathetic to the plight of the slaves but, unlike his cousin, he did not see their freedom as something worth going to war over. He knew in his heart that slavery was wrong but hoped that, within a few years, the institution would simply die on its own.

Things had changed after Sumter. Now it had become a matter of preserving the Union. Jonas had enlisted in an artillery regiment being formed in Albert Lea and trained to handle horses and equipment for a field gun. Over time, he had advanced from being one of the 'spare' men to being in charge of the caisson and its ammunition chests. In February, he had been at Donelson but had seen little action. This time it was different. The thunder from the cannons was more violent than any he had ever heard in a thunderstorm back home. And here there was smoke so acrid and dense that his eyes felt like they were on fire. It was nearly impossible to breathe. Even more foreign to him, there was shouting everywhere – not just men shouting to be heard above the roar of the guns but shrieks of pain as canisters from Rebel guns exploded and both men and horses were torn apart. And there was the dying.

19

Everywhere around him, men were screaming and dying. He prayed to be deaf so he couldn't hear it.

The noise wouldn't stop even for a moment. All up and down the line, the batteries were continuously firing – one after the other. It left no opportunity for the enemy to advance. Jonas was in charge of the gun limber. His job was to prepare the charge and set the fuse time. At this moment, he had just prepared a charge and handed it to Private Harris, who was designated as crew member #7, to be carried to the gun and loaded. He turned back to the caisson to prepare the next charge.

Jonas never heard the canister that landed and exploded just behind the gun. He only felt the force from the blast behind him. The pain was immediate. He pulled up his hands and covered his ears to keep it out but it was too late. It was already there. It rolled into his head from each side, searing hot and relentless as it converged in the middle of his brain. He could not hear himself scream as it became too much to bear. The force of the blast threw him to the ground but he did not feel himself fall. His prayers for peace had not been answered, but the prayer for deafness had. Jonas Hancock's eardrums had ruptured. Not only had the noise of battle ceased for him but he would never hear another sound.

Had any of Jonas' battery mates been alive to see it, they would have observed him writhing on the ground in pain, still covering his ears with his hands. They would have seen his legs thrash about as if trying to run but going nowhere. But they were *not* alive and they did *not* see. Jonas lapsed into what should have been merciful and restful unconsciousness. The sleep overcame him but the rest did not come. Instead, he watched himself struggle to his feet and begin to run. His legs grew heavier with every step. The rain spattered his glasses and his rain-soaked clothing felt plastered to his skin. He didn't know what had become of his forage cap but his hair stuck like paste to his scalp. And the noise – the awful noise. It was impossible to separate the lightning and thunder of the storm from the fire and roar of the guns. He covered his ears with his hands, hoping to make it go away. But it didn't. It just never did!

The mud caked on his boots making it increasingly harder to move and he felt as if it might eventually swallow him entirely. He slipped and fell face first into the awful muck. He managed to get to his feet, went a few faltering steps, and fell again. He pondered that might be better to just quit and let the mud cover him over. But there was the noise – always the noise. Perhaps if he could run far enough, the noise would stop. Maybe, with more effort, he could outrun it. He had to keep going.

A few yards farther and he stumbled again. But he hadn't slipped this time. He had tripped over something – perhaps a tree root. As he tried to pick himself up, he realized that it wasn't a root at all. It was a leg. But that was all. There was no body to be seen – just part of a leg sticking out of a boot – covered with mud and blood. Jonas got back to his hands and knees, vomited, and managed to regain his feet. "Have to keep going. Have to get away from the noise."

Ahead of him was a small stream. If he could manage to get across, perhaps it would be quiet on the other side and he could rest. He kept covering his ears and continued to slog through the mud. But the stream drew no closer "Have to get to the stream." With each step he took, he seemed to retreat another step away. "Have to reach the stream."

Something else knocked him to the ground. It wasn't just the noise now. There were shells flying and exploding above him. Trees, that moments earlier had been blowing and swaying in the wind, were now being shredded into

21

splinters before his eyes and fragments were flying everywhere around him. The roar of the guns seemed to come from behind him as well as from ahead. Had he gone the wrong direction? Had he run into the barrage instead of away from it? Where to go? Perhaps if he could still reach the stream, he could lie down between its banks and maybe be safe from the shells. He was incredibly thirsty. "Have to reach the stream." He got to his hands and knees and began to crawl. He could no longer cover his ears with his hands but it seemed to make no difference. The noise – the God-awful noise!

When he could no longer crawl on his hands and knees, he lay down on his belly and pulled himself forward through the mud with his arms and legs. "Have to reach the stream." At last, so close – only one more obstacle. He reached to push it out of his way. "Almost there." But the noise, the terrible pounding, unrelenting noise!

He tried again to push it out of his way and realized that it wasn't a log at all. It was a body – a body with a gaping hole in its chest. The body's knees were grotesquely bent. Jonas looked into the wide, open eyes of Private Harris who was staring, unseeing, at the rain. "Oh God, No, No! Oh God!" He let out a piercing scream that he could not hear and rolled down the embankment and into the stream.

****

Henry stayed on the ground as he dropped another ball into the barrel of the Springfield and replaced the percussion cap. It was a bit harder than doing it while standing but it made him a more difficult target. He would have preferred to fire from this prone position because it was easier to steady the rifle. But there were other comrades in his line of fire. Also, he needed to be able to either move ahead or fall back on a moment's notice as the situation required. At this moment, it appeared that the entire line was about to fall back to a more defensible position.

The smoke seemed increasingly dense and choking. The noise of the rifles and cannons grew ever louder. It was now impossible to pick out individual soldiers from the gray wave that lay ahead. The enemy moved closer as they trampled over both their own and the Union's dead. It was more a matter now of simply loading, firing into the smoke, reloading, and firing again. In an odd way, that relieved him. He was simply another among hundreds doing his duty. He only hoped that, when this was over, whether he was alive or dead, somehow a forgiving God would understand.

****

Colonel Davis Pope, M.D. walked among the cots at the hospital. The din of the battle days earlier had subsided. Those who could not be saved had died on the field. The burial parties were already going about their grisly work of trying to identify bodies and digging shallow graves. Though he grieved for the dead, the doctor's attention was now fully devoted to the living now under his care.

He would pause and speak with an orderly or a nurse about the condition of a patient. Once in a while he would smile but, more often, his countenance was simply grave. Occasionally, he would stop and speak to one who could hear him, put his hand on a shoulder and try to provide a measure of comfort. For others, there was no comfort to be provided and the best he could give was to call for a chaplain to give the last rites. Here and there, a nurse or orderly would be bent closely to a patient, writing a letter home for one who either did not know how or whose wounds prevented him from doing so. Some would be the first of many letters. Others would be the last.

There were rows of men with bandaged heads and faces or now missing legs, arms, hands or feet. There were moans but many of the soldiers were silent, benefitting from laudanum generously distributed to ease their pain until they had healed enough to be invalided out and sent home – their war ended. But, at least, some of these would live.

From a cot near the end of the enormous tent came an ear-piercing scream, "Oh God, No, No! Oh God!" Pope rushed to the man's bedside and spoke with an orderly who had been busily attending another patient nearby. "Dreaming," he said to the orderly. "It's dreadful. I've seen it in other patients. Sometimes it stops. Sometimes it doesn't. He gently shook the man in an attempt to arouse him. "Wake up, wake up." There was no response. There was only the flailing of arms and thrashing of legs.

"Don't think he hears you, Sir," said the orderly. "We tried talking to him when he first came in but he wouldn't talk back. Wonder if he's deaf. The litter bearers from the ambulance party told us he did the same thing when they picked him up on the field– said he was thrashing about, screaming, and then got quiet like whatever was bothering him had suddenly stopped. They told us he opened his eyes and looked at them but didn't act like he heard them. Hasn't responded to anyone else either.

Dr. Pope had seen it before as a young field surgeon in the war with Mexico – men who looked otherwise healthy but whose ear drums had been ruptured by the concussion from cannons, either their own or from enemy shells which landed nearby and exploded. Though he was fortunate to never have experienced it himself, he could only imagine the excruciating pain that such a wound must cause.

"We don't know who he is," the orderly told him. "If he had his name sewn in his shirt, it must have torn loose. They found a Testament near him but there were other men around – all dead. The Bible could have belonged to any of them but we brought it with him. The name written in it is Jonas Hancock."

"Give him more laudanum. Let him rest."

The shelling had stopped and that was some comfort. Had it been moments, hours, days? Jonas didn't know. He was too tired and in too much pain to care. He half-opened his eyes but could see only ghostly figures who appeared to be standing in a fog. They must be talking, but he couldn't hear them. His head felt as if it were about to break open. He tried to open his eyes a little further but couldn't. One of the figures bent over him and put something that felt like a spoon into his mouth. It was harder to keep his eyes open now, but the pain in his head seemed to ease a bit. He gave up on opening his eyes and let the laudanum do its work. Soon it again began to thunder and lightning. He tried to run but his legs felt so heavy. "Got to make it to the stream."

****

Camp near Corinth, Mississippi

April 1862

Dearest Mona,

We are in camp now. We have just returned from supper and the boys are resting. I thought I would write you a bit. Oh, Mona, this letter is so hard to write! I have been avoiding it because I didn't want to worry you. However, I must tell you about our action last week for I know you will hear

25

of it from letters that others write home or perhaps even read of it in the newspapers. Our battle was the most terrible thing I have ever seen and I hope never to see such a thing again. I fear though that there be many more before the Rebels are finished and we can come home to our loved ones and go on with our lives in peace.

The fight took place near a place called Shiloh Church and it was so loud that I almost think that even those already resting in the churchyard could have heard it.

In the end, our troops carried the day but, oh! my dear Mona, the cost was so high! Captain Hinton, along with Lieutenants Richards and Jacobs are dead. So are John Wilson, Seth Roberts, Leander Smith, and Thomas Britt. Will Britt lost his leg and is now in a hospital and I assume will be invalided out when he is well enough to travel home. I grieve so for the widows and for the children who will never see their husbands and fathers again. I pray, but am not confident, that this terrible thing will soon be done and I can hold you in my arms again.

We don't know what will be done about the leadership of the company – whether some will be promoted or whether replacement officers will be sent whom we do not know. We are all hoping it will be the former. Nearly all of the boys hope that Henry Hancock will become one of our lieutenants or even captain of the company. All respect him as both a man and a soldier. He does not want to be here anymore than we do but he knows that our cause is just and that it must be carried on if the Union is to be preserved. I think the boys would follow him into Hell itself if asked. We have taken to calling him 'The Lion' and ourselves 'The Pride.' When the Rebel line finally looked as if it were about to bend and the order was given to advance, he let out a tremendous roar that we could actually hear above the other noise, "Come on boys! Let's end the war right here!" he yelled, and charged into battle with the company behind him. Such courage have I rarely seen before!

I must close now. Corporal Jeffers has just come into the tent with some tobacco he has managed to obtain. We have determined to enjoy our pipes and visit for a bit before taps sounds.

Keep yourself well. I will be home as soon as I can.   Love as always,

Edward.

****

Hamilton Stark was not from Georgia or, for that matter, from the South. No one in the area of Pine Hill Plantation knew him well. Those who knew something of him saw him as a cunning man who lived by two guiding principles alone – his devout cowardice and his firm belief in the subservient role of the African race. The first had brought him from Indiana where he had fathered a child with a neighbor's daughter and fled the wrath of her father and brothers. Andrew, the plantation's owner, and his son, Darius, had first met Stark in Atlanta and hired him as overseer for their field hands. The cunning, they thought they could handle. They had quickly seen the cowardice and had found in him a flaw that would make him easy to manipulate and control. His sufficient disdain for the field hands would allay any concerns about hiring a northerner.

What neither Stark's conversations with his employers nor his demeanor in the fields revealed was his extreme fear of the *slaves* on the plantation. It was easy to appear brave and confident while riding through the fields on a horse and armed with a whip and pistol. It was quite another matter after the sun set and the plantation was dark. Stark rarely left his quarters, located near the stable, after dark, and never without a gun. He had a large dog that he claimed was for companionship. In reality, he had trained it to share his disdain for the slaves. The dog, benignly named Jack, slept just outside his door and accompanied him nearly everywhere at night. When Stark slept, the pistol was always close by.

In addition to being a coward, Stark was incredibly vain. Tall, whitish blonde, and strikingly handsome, he always wore gloves and a brown, wide-brimmed felt hat to protect his fair skin from the hot Georgian sun. He kept three pairs of identical boots, two always freshly polished. He constantly chided the stable boy, whose job it was to polish them, if the shine fell short of his sense of perfection.

It was the same with his shirts. As with the shoe polishing, he had arranged with the Morgans that the services of the laundry girl would be part of his compensation. What he had *not* arranged with them was his use of the girl for his personal pleasures. He neither knew, nor cared, whether Andrew or Darius were aware. He suspected that Darius, before he had left for the war, had been using the house-cleaning girl in the same way. Andrew, he had decided, would probably look the other way as long as he remained effective as an overseer. What he did not know was that Annabelle Morgan would have sent him packing in spite of her husband's probable but futile objections. It didn't matter. She was lying in the family plot near her flower garden.

Stark doubted that either Andrew or Darius, if he returned home, would ever see him as a friend. Their arrangement was only business. Though he envied them the hunts, the grand parties, the fine cigars, and the expensive liquor, he also realized how the plantation system worked. He would not change it. What he did not realize was the degree of their contempt for him and their view of him as just another piece of plantation equipment. He was of little more value than the slaves themselves. He continued to hope that, regardless of the outcome of the war, they would continue to find him useful in one way or another. Possibly that would someday enable him to create a modicum of wealth and power of his own.

Neither did Stark have friends away from the plantation. He rarely saw the overseers from neighboring plantations, except when they would occasionally run across each other in Milledgeville while running errands for their bosses. Even then, there was little more than drinks at one of the saloons and some idle talk. An ironclad rule was that they never discussed plantation business with each other. Poker, when it occurred, was not a social game but business – intended to supplement what all considered to be less than adequate wages.

The rare trips to Atlanta were much the same except that they were, for the most part, more anonymous. One might, upon occasion, run into an acquaintance, but such an encounter was rare. He preferred Atlanta because the city was young, vibrant and alive. The liquor was tastier, though more expensive, than that at the saloon in Milledgeville and the girls at the houses were prettier and fancier than those at the Portman House. Milledgeville was closer though, only a few miles to the north. It had been Georgia's capital since 1804. He considered it stodgy and snobbish. It felt old, populated by old people with old money and old ideas. The only bad part about Atlanta was that the poker players at the saloons were more skilled than those to whom he was accustomed. He rarely left with more money than he had brought to the table.

****

It was early April in 1862 and First Lieutenant Darius Morgan, CSA was bored. There were only so many card games to be played and there was little opportunity to sample Richmond's other pleasures. Then there was the constant drilling which drove him mad. He considered it a colossal waste of time, likening it to only playing soldier. He envisioned himself as one of the painted lead soldiers he had played with as a child on the veranda at Pine Hill. He had moved the little soldiers around for hours at a time but, in the end, nothing ever really changed. At the end of the day he simply put both armies in a wooden box underneath his bed.

Darius thrived on killing. It disappointed him that there had been none thus far as the army waited to see what

McClellan would do next. The talk was that he had landed his army at Fort Monroe and was going to try to take Richmond from the south. Perhaps there would be some action and a chance to kill more of the invaders. He eagerly awaited the opportunity.

Darius had left Pine Hill Plantation immediately after the Georgia Legislature had passed the Articles of Secession. The war, were it to come, was bound to be a short one and he hadn't wanted to miss the chance to be a part of it and show the arrogant Yankees that the South would damn well keep its slaves.

Growing up, Darius had always been fascinated by his older cousins' stories about the war with Mexico – how they had routed the Mexicans at Buena Vista and marched nearly unopposed to Vera Cruz. The only Yankee Darius had ever known was Hamilton Stark. The man was as incurable a coward as any he had known – all bluster and bravery on the outside, yet spineless on the inside. All of the Yankees, he assumed, were no more than a great number of Starks. It was the numbers that bothered him but there was little doubt that courage and skillful shooting could overcome the North's only advantage. It shouldn't be that difficult to march straight to Washington and force the illegitimate devil, Lincoln, to sue for peace. And that would be that.

Manassas had done nothing to change Darius' mind. The Yankees, full of themselves with their flags and drums and fifes, had come to the battlefield apparently thinking that Lee and Jackson's armies would simply cut and run for home. My God, they had even brought women and children and carriages and picnic lunches. During early afternoon, Darius' regiment had been brought into the line. Within moments, he had drawn his first Federal blood and relished in it. By late afternoon, the carriages were running back in a panic to Washington with the army, in some places, running *ahead* of them. The field had been littered with flags, drums, fifes, rifles, side arms, and cannons, which the south could put to good use. And there were prisoners – hundreds of prisoners, who had dropped their weapons and chosen to surrender rather than fight.

And then, to Darius' dismay, the killing had stopped. Disappointed, he wondered why Lee and Jackson had not pursued the cowards all the way to Washington. He would have happily shot them as they ran. He hoped that McClellan would try to march on Richmond soon. The killing would then resume.

****

Andrew Morgan sat at his desk in his library. The evening was chilly for early May and he had the need for a fire. He sat listening to the rain spatter against the window behind him and lit a cigar as he prepared to re-read the letter he had received from Darius earlier in the day:

Richmond, Virginia

April 10, 1862

Dear Father,

I hope all is well at home. I suppose all of the fields are nearly plowed by now and soon it should be time to begin planting the cotton.

There are still rumors that McClellan has left or is soon to leave Fort Monroe and try to capture Richmond in his delusional thinking that he can take the city. Even if that were to happen, which we will of course never allow, even he surely cannot expect

32

that such a thing would break us and allow him to win the war. This army is entirely capable of defending our land, our freedom, and our righteous cause. We will never succumb to Lincoln's tyranny.

There is no talk in camp that the regiment will be sent out to fight McClellan. It seems that we are destined to sit here and wait for him to come to us, which our army out on the peninsula will never allow him to do. He will never get one soldier across the Chickahominy River. In truth, I don't believe that we are even being kept here to guard Richmond, which appears to be entirely safe. I believe that we are only being kept here out of the action to be available to guard the hundreds of prisoners that our comrades in the field will soon be taking. I think that is an entirely wasteful use of a regiment such as ours. I think that, were we allowed to join the fight instead, we could back the sorry Yankees off the peninsula or maybe even end the war.

I must close now. It is nearly time to go out and drill the men some more in order to make them ready in case they are ever allowed to fight. They are getting a little lazy and I really can't say that I blame them. They feel that their time is being wasted here. Those who own few slaves or none

would especially like to be home tending
their tobacco crops or their little cotton
fields.

Do you have any coffee you can send to
me? We have all of the tobacco that we can
smoke but coffee is becoming a bit scarce.

Also, is there anything you can do at all
to get me into the field? I would rather die
killing Yankees than die of boredom
guarding their cowards that we have taken
prisoner. And I think I should have been
promoted to captain long before now.

Stay well,

Darius.

P.S. Be sure to keep a close eye on Stark. I think
he fears you and certainly can remain useful to
us but you need to be as attentive as always.

****

Bright sunlight streamed into the tent and across
Jonas' face. The sides of the enormous tent had been rolled
up in order to allow the breeze to flow through and
alleviate the late spring heat. He opened his eyes and
looked around. The night had been good to him. He felt
rested and more clear-headed. The wrenching headache
was annoying but no longer all-consuming.

Jonas could see figures moving from place to place
but was suddenly aware that he could hear neither talking
nor footsteps. Nor could he hear the birds that should have
been singing outside. An orderly appeared beside his cot

and seemed to be summoning someone else. He then handed him paper on which was written, "Can you read?"

Jonas felt himself speaking but could not hear the words come out. The words on the note were blurry, but he could make them out. "Yes, but better if I had my eyeglasses. Where are they?"

There was another note. "They didn't find any when they brought you in. Must have been lost when you went down. We'll get you new ones."

"Then I talked!" Jonas realized. "They heard what I said."

"What is your name?"

"I am Corporal Jonas Hancock. I ran." He began to tear up and his voice, weak already, began to quiver. "There was an explosion. I ran away."

Another note quickly followed. "You didn't," it said. "They found you right where you fell, next to the gun limber. You did not run." The word *not* had been underlined for emphasis. "Perhaps you dreamed it."

"What happens now?"

"Most likely you'll be invalided out and sent home. The war is over for you."

"What happened?" Jonas asked. Where are the boys? Why can't I hear you?"

"We'll talk later."

CHAPTER II

Andrew Morgan had owned Pine Hill Plantation for about ten years, having purchased his two older brothers' inherited shares at the death of their father. Edwin and Thaddeus had both moved to Milledgeville for a time afterwards and gone into partnership in a lumber mill. The two had been frequent visitors at the plantation along with their families before having a falling out with each other and with Andrew, whom each had accused of taking sides with the other. In the end, both had left the area. Thaddeus had gone to New Orleans to become an attorney. Edwin was now living in Chicago and working for a banking house. He had not communicated with Thaddeus since his leaving. Until the outbreak of the war had made it nearly impossible, Andrew had corresponded regularly with Edwin. Though there remained some hard feelings over the family dispute, they had been able to mostly reconcile. Their correspondence related, however, mostly to business. Edwin, though he represented northerners, 'Yankees' as Andrew called them, who were mostly investors in steel mills or shipping companies, had also, until the outbreak of the war, represented various cotton planters from Georgia to as far west as Mississippi.

Pine Hill Plantation sat on a large rise along the Oconee River at the edge of the Upper Coastal Plain. The farm had been established by Anthony Morgan who had immigrated to Georgia from Scotland shortly after the end of the War of 1812. He had arrived at Milledgeville, which was then on the edge of the frontier, with little more than a small inheritance from his father, a beautiful young wife, and a dream. The farm derived its name from the stands of old growth pine that flanked the lane reaching from the riverbank upward toward the house. Unlike the homes occupied by most of the area's cotton planters, the Morgan home was more in the style of those of prosperous farmers in Ohio and Pennsylvania. The house – it could barely be called a mansion by the standards of the Upper Plain – between the Lower Piedmont and the Blue Ridge Mountains– was a white frame structure. It had no great cupola on the roof and lacked a third floor with a great ballroom. The great white columns which defined the Greek revival style were notably absent, as was a grand second floor veranda. Instead, when the family wanted to escape the hot Georgian sun, they would sit in rocking chairs or benches on the large front porch, which spanned the front of the house and overlooked the front lawn. The grounds, though Andrew insisted that they be well kept, were simpler and lacked the variety of foliage and the elegant style that defined many of the others. While this was not a problem for Andrew or Darius, it had always been a concern for the late Annabelle Morgan, who had always been envious of her wealthier neighbors and had felt it necessary to keep up 'appearances.'

The inside of the house was comprised of four large rooms downstairs surrounding a large open staircase leading up from the entry hall. It had a kitchen annex with a bakery in a brick shed just outside the back door next to the smokehouse. To the left, upon entering the front door, were pocket doors leading to the woman's parlor, behind which were more pocket doors leading to the dining room. To the left of the entry hall was the man's parlor, behind which was Andrew's library. A concession that Andrew and his father had made to their wives was that, although unassuming from the outside, the home would be well appointed on the inside in a fashion similar to those of the guests who would be entertained there. The upstairs consisted of four large bedrooms – two of which had been used by Andrew and Darius before Darius had left for the war, and two that had been used in the days when Annabelle was still living and overnight guests were more frequently entertained.

When Annabelle was alive and the house had more family and guests to be waited upon and cleaned after, she had assigned each family member a personal slave to do their bidding during all waking hours. Since then Andrew had reduced the house staff to two. Dahlia, now nineteen, was responsible for baking, cooking, cleaning the house, and tending the vegetable garden. Her sister, Celia, eighteen, did the laundry and sewing and also helped in the vegetable garden. Andrew had always felt that the house was overstaffed and that the slaves were better used doing other chores on the plantation. It had come as a great annoyance to Darius when his personal servant had been sent to 'apprentice' with the plantation blacksmith.

****

Camp near Corinth, Mississippi

May 2, 1862

Dear Sister Ellie,

I have just returned from the sutler's tent and have purchased some pipe tobacco and a couple of apples.

I suppose, by the time you read this, that Em should have received my earlier letter regarding our great battle. I did not write it to worry her but imagined that all of you would either read of it in the papers or hear of it from others. I hope never to write such a letter again but I have a great sense of dread that this terrible thing will go on for some time. I fear that there will be many more battles both here and out to the east in

Virginia. Many more lives on both sides must be lost I think before the Rebels see the futility of their cause and decide to lay down their weapons and return to their homes.

War is such an awful thing. It is the most scurrilous and sinister enterprise ever developed by man to settle disputes. It is such a waste of lives and resources that could otherwise be put to better use. After it is over, nothing is left but devastation and I fear that the bitter feelings that have been created will last for generations to come.

I have not seen our brother since just after the fight at Fort Donelson this past February. I am assuming that he was at Shiloh. I have made some inquiries but have yet to learn anything about where he is or how he fared. I know that the cannonading was fearful and that many in the artillery batteries were lost. I pray that Jonas was not killed or captured and that he is well somewhere but fear that this is not the case. In an army so large, it is hard to find out much but I will try to keep inquiring and will let you know if I learn something. I think that if he were able, he would have by now written to you or to Rose. I know that you will let me know if you hear from him.

The regiment has not moved much since the battle. There is talk that Grant would like to move on Vicksburg before the winter (such as it is down here) sets in. My own feeling is that such an achievement is overly ambitious and likely will not happen. If true and if we were to be successful, it would be a great thing. Our forces then would control the entire Mississippi River through all of the rebellious land from Arkansas to the Gulf. We would cut off their western armies and deprive them of men, armaments, and supplies.

It is time to fix and eat our supper so I must close. Please share this letter with Em when you see her and let her know that I am well.

Love,

Henry.

P.S.

I am informed that I am to receive a field promotion to replace Dwight Richards as First Lt. of the company. It is not something that I have sought or even want as I much prefer that Dwight were still here. Sadly, that is not to be. I feel that duty requires me to accept and the few with whom I have discussed it appear pleased with the appointment. There are a couple of men in the company, whom I feel, when it is known, will be jealous and will have wanted it for themselves but I discount them. I will not say who they are but I believe they would not be good leaders and would want the position only to carry a sidearm, order others about, and perhaps get a little more pay.

****

Even for an early May evening in Mississippi, it was unusually warm and muggy. It was one of those evenings when the air was so close that one could hardly breathe and it felt nearly possible to drown on dry land. It seemed that someone had draped a hot, wet blanket over the entire camp. The damp, warm air brought out hosts of gnats, chiggers, and other such pests. Henry had long since discarded his uniform coat and was standing outside of his tent smoking his pipe. It soothed him somewhat and the smoke seemed to help keep the critters from biting quite as badly.

Henry remembered early summer nights when he would lie on his back on the grass in the front yard at home in Minnesota and watch the stars. Somehow, just thinking of home, made the mosquitoes back there seem less bothersome. In reality though, they had seemed at the time to be the size of birds. The stars were not as bright in summer as in fall and winter when the air was drier, but he always marveled at their numbers and the constellations that they created. He had studied charts of the heavens and often thought he should have been an astronomer.

Tonight, however, the stars seemed to sparkle less and it affected his mood. For as far as he could see, there were lights from thousands of campfires and from lanterns both inside and outside of tents. He likened it to being in a city where all of the lights obscured the night sky – not at all like what he was accustomed to at home. He wondered, with so many fires every night, were any trees, barns, or fences still standing anywhere in Mississippi? There were a multitude of voices but he could only make out a conversation a few feet away. Here and there men were playing harmonicas, mostly mournful songs recalling loss or a longing for home. He thought it interesting how one could feel lonelier among thousands than when actually alone.

****

Crestville, Minnesota

May 7, 1862

Dear Brother,

I have just received the most joyous news! I have received a letter from Jonas! As you assumed, he was in the great battle at Shiloh. Sadly, all others in his gun crew perished when an enemy shell exploded in their midst but, miraculously, Jonas survived. His eardrums were ruptured from the blast and he will never hear again but he is otherwise well. He is to be invalided out and may actually be on his way home by now. I can't wait to see him and hold him! He expects to come by river steamer to Minneapolis and, if possible, will let me know when he expects to arrive there. I hope it is not presumptuous but I intend to ask our friends David and Mary Alice to come from

Thayer to go there with me to meet him and accompany him home. They have been so good to help Em farm the rental while you and Jonas have been away. They will continue to help through the harvest and to put in the winter wheat. Hopefully, Jonas will be able to farm but that remains to be seen. I am just so happy to have him home and look forward to the day when we all can again be together and go on with our lives.

I must close now and work on doing the laundry but want to get this letter in the mail so that you will receive it as soon as possible. I know you will be much relieved. I think Rose is planning to come for a visit in June. It seems like so long since I have seen her. Now that Jonas is coming home, I propose, if you agree, that I might try to get a position teaching at one of the schools near the farm and stay there with Jonas and Em until you come home.

As always your loving sister,

Ellie.

****

The day was overcast, cold, and blustery with a chance of rain – unusual for June in St. Paul. It was very unlike the day a little over a year ago that the crowd, many of these same people, had gathered at this same pier. That day had been sunny, balmy, and full of hope and optimism. The city had gathered then to see the 'boys' off to crush the rebellion planning to welcome them home before Christmas. Now, they gathered for the arrival of the river steamer, *Alpaca,* with its cargo, consisting mostly of wounded, but also the coffins of some of the dead whose families wanted the bodies of their soldiers brought home for burial. There would be no more 'boys.' The hardships and violence had seen to that. Now there were only men.

On that sunny day there had been bright dresses, smiles, and brightly colored parasols. There had been a brass band playing rousing marches and dignitaries, including the governor, giving inspiring speeches about patriotism, the Founding Fathers, and saving the Union. There had been flags and laughter and even some picnic lunches. Everyone had expected the war to be glorious, easy, and short.

The crowd today was as somber as it had been exuberant such a short time ago. There were no bands or politicians. The parasols had been swapped for mostly gray or black umbrellas splattered by a fine mist that had begun to fall. For many women, the bright dresses had been stored away in wardrobes or trunks and replaced by black, befitting the mourning of lost husbands, sons, or brothers. Gone were the smiles and the laughter. Gone, too, was any talk of the war being glorious, easy, or short. The war would go on and there would be more boats and more mourning.

Ellie Hancock could not see over the heads of the people around her in the crowd and had to rely on David to tell her what was going on. "What is happening? Can you see the boat yet?" Like her sister, Rose MacDonald, who had married an army surgeon now stationed down the river in Rock Island, she was tiny and petite. She appeared even more so when standing beside her brothers, Henry and Jonas, in a tintype taken just before they had left for the war.

The brothers each stood just over six feet tall and towered above Ellie's barely five-foot frame. The two men so closely resembled each other that strangers often mistook them for twins. In fact, Jonas was two years older than Henry. Both had sandy brown hair that they kept cut much the same. Both had the family's same deep blue, piercing eyes. Jonas had chosen to wear both a mustache and a neatly trimmed beard. Henry, on the other hand, had opted for only a mustache and remained otherwise clean-shaven when possible.

Those who did not know Ellie well might think her frail and somewhat timid. Those who *did* know her were well aware that she was, in fact, neither. A word or a stare could easily intimidate even the largest and toughest of the boys whom she was charged with teaching English and mathematics at her school back in Crestville. No, one did not mess with Ellie Hancock!

Ellie considered herself fortunate not to be wearing a mourning dress as so many around her were. Today, she had chosen a modest, dark brown dress that she had made herself and often wore to school. She wore a matching hat and had draped a shawl over her shoulders as protection against the slight chill in the air. She could hardly contain herself, waiting to see Jonas, knowing that he would be, for the most part, healthy. She expected him to appear little different than when she had last seen him. Sensitive though to the feelings of those around her, whose loved ones would never be whole, she tried her best to conceal her excitement.

A low murmur wafted through the crowd. Someone had spotted the smoke from the steamer in the distance. Ellie again wanted to clap her hands but caught herself just as David gently tapped her on the shoulder and nodded toward Charles and Margaret Britt who were standing nearby. Will would be on the boat and would soon be with them but missing his leg. Thomas was home also, but in a pine coffin, waiting for the last leg of his journey. Charles appeared to be fighting back tears as he held Margaret who was openly sobbing. Ellie knew her as a vibrant, strong woman but today she appeared aged and frail.

David leaned down to Ellie. "I need to move toward the ramp. Jonas won't know where to look for us. He won't hear us call out to him."

"I'm coming with you," Ellie told him. I just can't wait to see him."

"You need to stay here with Mary Alice. I'll find him and bring him to you." David, in his younger days, had seen the cost of war. He wished now to shield Ellie from seeing it for herself but knew that she must already be aware. He had served under Robert E. Lee's command in the war with Mexico fifteen years earlier. He had seen, in an instant, men who were young and fit become maimed and crippled for life. He had seen men die only a few feet from where he stood. David had struggled for years afterward with the seeming randomness of the death and suffering, wondering how it was decided who would die and who would come home healthy. The idea of predestination was foreign to his Jewish faith but he fleetingly found himself considering the possibility. Was it luck? Was it Providence? Surely it had nothing to do with the type of life one had lived. If it were that, Thomas Britt, a deeply religious and caring soul, would still be alive. David had finally come to the realization that this was not for him to know – at least not in this life. His best hope was that, in the end, it would all mean something and that perhaps some good would come of it. Still …

David began to gently work his way through the crowd – asking to be excused as he went, explaining that he would not be heard. Others, he knew, would also have to be found by their loved ones rather than being able to come to them. Some would have their eyes wrapped in bandages and others would be carried on litters to be placed in ambulances and taken to the army hospital to continue their recovery.

Taller than most, David could just barely see over the dark sea of umbrellas. He reached the front of the crowd minutes after the gangplank had been lowered and the *Alpaca's* passengers had begun to disembark. It was just as he had expected. Personnel from the hospital had boarded the ship to assist the littered wounded. Attendants who had made the trip with them now aided them down the gangplank to help them find their families. Here and there a wounded but mobile soldier would help a now blind comrade. Some on crutches or missing an arm or a hand appeared to proudly make their own way. For each, the war was now a bad memory that would, in one way or another, control the remainder of their lives.

The parade of wounded seemed to go on forever. "Such a waste!" David told himself. Finally, after what seemed hours but was, in reality, much less, he spied Jonas. With his invisible injury, the man looked lean and muscular – no different than when David had seen him over a year ago. The notable difference was the absence of the wide smile that he had always carried. His face was nearly without expression – hollow, with the once bright blue eyes staring grimly without a hint of their former youthful glint.

Merely steps behind Jonas, Will Britt walked nearly seamlessly on crutches. He appeared particularly nimble, David thought, for a man who, only a couple of months ago, had lost his left leg just above the knee. Will's face, however, bore the same expressionless countenance as Jonas' but with tears running down his cheeks. David made his way toward them, not really knowing what to say to Will and knowing there was nothing he could do for Jonas

47

except to wrap his arm around his shoulder and take him to Ellie.

Ellie threw her arms around Jonas in a joyous and lengthy hug. "Oh Jonas!" she shouted, momentarily forgetting herself. "I'm so glad you're home!" Realizing what she had just done, she released him and covered her face with her hands.

"It's alright," Jonas assured her – sensing what she had done and her resulting discomfort. "Me too!"

Will walked to his sobbing parents who were at once glad to have him home but grieving that they would never see Thomas again. The Britts embraced each other and slowly made their way to the back of the now thinning crowd toward the wagon which would carry them back to Albert Lea and then on to their home in Thayer where Thomas would be laid to rest. Ellie wanted to go to them but Mary Alice held her hand. "Leave them be," she said quietly. "Go see them at their home."

They spent the evening with David's sister and her family, retiring to the guest parlor after dining on fried chicken and mashed potatoes. There was little conversation at the table with the rest feeling awkward about Jonas not being able to hear their conversation. There were smiles all around when Jonas commented on how wonderful the dinner was compared to hardtack, canned beans, and old coffee. The rest of the evening was quiet as hosts and guests gathered around the fireplace. Jonas and David played chess. The mist from earlier in the day turned to a steady rain and a wind began to drive it against the window panes. Jonas grew agitated. When asked if something was the matter, he lied. Later he lay awake, watching but didn't hear the rain beat against the windows. He closed the blinds and the draperies but it didn't help. He still knew it was raining and blowing. He fought sleep but the fatigue of the boat ride home and the emotional reunion were overtaking him. "Don't sleep," he told himself, but it was too much. He pulled the covers over his head. Presently, he was again running through the wind, the rain, and the mud. For the first time, Ellie along with David and Mary Alice and their hosts heard the haunting scream, "Oh God! No, No! Oh, God!"

****

Richmond, Virginia

July 3, 1862

Dear Father,

We are still here guarding prisoners and it appears that we will be for some time. There are more now being brought in every day. There was a fight a few days ago at a place called Gaines' Mill. It is said, though we in the ranks do not know, that our generals now believe McClellan is like abandon his efforts to capture Richmond and withdraw his army back down the peninsula. If that is true, that means that our company has again lost the opportunity to engage them and diminish their numbers. I fear I am destined to spend the rest of the war here doing nothing but playing jail keeper. We have managed to get our hands on an amount of coffee so we are well fixed that way for now. Have you had a chance to write any letters to see if I might somehow get promoted to captain? That might make no difference if all we are allowed to do is sit here day after day but I still hope to get into battle and have the opportunity to kill more of the invaders before it is done.

I will make my letter short as there is really nothing else to report. I imagine the cotton is getting tall by now and wish that, if we aren't being allowed to fight, I could be home.

I will write more later. Now, good night.

Darius.

CHAPTER III

Summer in Richmond faded into mid-autumn. The sky today was as dark as Darius' mood. The breeze was biting and blustery. The leaves were quickly disappearing from the trees, piling up like brown snow drifts on the ground below. No one bothered to rake them. It wasn't important.

Darius lounged on a chair outside of the guards' barracks smoking a cigar and reading his newspaper. He was seething. Again, he had missed out on the action. The Battle of Antietam had been fought without him while he sat guarding prisoners – now more of them than ever here at Libby Prison with many coming from Maryland. Once more he had missed out on the opportunity to kill Yankees. According to all southern newspapers, this had been a victory for his country. Why hadn't Lee pushed his advantage over that incompetent McClellan and marched to Washington? He could have so easily forced the invaders to sue for peace and go back to minding their own business.

And now the tyrant Lincoln, less than one hundred and fifty miles away, had the gall to issue a proclamation freeing all of the slaves in the Confederacy. How did he plan to enforce that?! He had no authority here and everyone knew it. Fortunately, the slaves, since they couldn't read, wouldn't know. Still, there was word of mouth. If they learned, there was bound to be trouble. The last thing needed, with so many of the men of his generation not being home to handle things, was a slave rebellion. At least his father had Stark. Stark would know what to do and, despite his faults, could be ruthless. That provided Darius some comfort. What provided less comfort was what Lincoln planned to do with slaves that his army might manage to steal – arm them? Even the simpleton Lincoln should have known better than that.

He pulled out his watch – time to go on his shift. He stamped out the short remnant of the cigar, laid the paper aside, picked up his rifle, and headed toward his station. "Damn," he muttered. "Damn it all to hell. I'm as much a prisoner here as they are. I need a drink!"

****

Andrew and his Presbyterian pastor and closest friend, Taylor Adams, sat in chairs on the front porch of the house at Pine Hill. The porch faced north-westward toward Milledgeville. The setting sun gave the sky an orange glow as it reflected on the clouds that hovered above the red clay of the fields across the river. Andrew puffed intermittently on a long-stemmed clay pipe while the Reverend enjoyed one of the now-precious Cuban cigars that Andrew kept on hand for guests. Andrew leaned back, placed his boots up on the porch rail, and turned to his friend. "They just don't understand benevolent slavery. Do you think they ever will or do you think the war will just settle it anyhow?"

"Who doesn't understand it? Them?" He nodded toward two of Andrew's slaves who were busy repairing a fence beside the lane that lead to the river.

"No, not *them*. My *friends*, except you of course. I know you do. Most of the congregation doesn't either though I know you've tried. I've talked to them so many times. We both have. Oh yes, they nod their heads and smile pleasantly enough but I think as soon as we turn our backs, they talk among themselves and probably sneer at us for bringing it up. Then they go on mistreating their slaves just as they always have."

"Yes, I imagine so," Reverend drawled slowly after taking a puff on the cigar. "And imagine they always will in spite of anything we do or say. I think we may have converted a couple though, particularly the Lawsons and the Millers. But the rest, well … and if the war frees the slaves, what will become of them then?"

"I just don't know," Andrew replied. "I just don't know. We know they are an inferior race but just because God has destined them to be the slaves and us to be the masters doesn't entitle us to treat them cruelly, does it?"

"No. I don't believe it does."

"I've always tried to do the right thing by them. It makes business sense because they are able to work better and are less likely to try and run off but I've always felt it's inhumane to own them if we don't treat them properly. I've always had Doctor Willingham look at them. He doesn't like it, if course, but he does it for me. I've given them shelter and made sure they have enough to eat. I've given them lighter work to do when they can't do the hard labor anymore. I've let them retire when they become infirm and have continued to provide for them. I've never knowingly bought or sold one of them when it would cause a family to break up. I just don't know. What more can I do?"

"There is nothing else," his friend replied. "It's just the natural order of things. You'll not change that. You are doing as much as any man can."

"I worry though. I will keep on as I have but I'm concerned about Darius. What will happen when he comes home and when I'm no longer around? I'm fearful about that."

Andrew and Annabelle had never been able to quite figure out how or why they had failed with Darius but both felt they had. Even as a child, Darius had displayed a temper and a mean streak. He would bully the children of guests who came to the plantation. As a result, most visitors had chosen to leave their children at home. Andrew had once caught him beating his pony when the poor creature failed to properly jump a hurdle, and a stable boy for being too slow in saddling the pony. They had hoped that, as a young man, he would outgrow his selfish tendencies. That hadn't happened. Within a year of being sent off to the University of South Carolina he was home – expelled for fighting, drunkenness, destruction of property, and generally unruly behavior. According to one college official, Darius had even challenged one of his professors to a duel after receiving a failing grade on an exam.

When he joined the army, Darius assumed that his father's connections at the state capital in Milledgeville would mean an immediate officer's post followed by rapid promotions. Andrew, however, did not see his son as a leader. He, in fact, used those same connections to ensure that Darius would never be placed in a position of real responsibility where the lives or well-being of other soldiers might be put in jeopardy.

Andrew had genuinely hoped that the discipline of the army combined with seeing the suffering that war inevitably brought with it would change Darius and that he would come home a mature and responsible man. That hope, however, seemed to dim with each letter that Darius wrote. ***"Why am I still here guarding prisoners when the rest of the army is in the field killing Yankees? Why am I not a captain by now? Why? Why?"***

****

Captain Joshua Gibbons was not given to anger. Like his father, a prominent Boston physician and surgeon, he admired John Brown's zeal to free the slaves but abhorred his violent tactics. Unlike the fiery William Lloyd Garrison, he sought no vengeance against the slave owners of the South. He had only prayed that one day they would see the errors of their ways – that they would obey the prophet Isaiah's words to 'undo the heavy burden and let the

54

oppressed go free.' Before Sumter, he had always hoped to see it happen in his lifetime. That hope vanished as quickly as the blue haze of the cannon smoke. To him, the whole idea of war was as vile as that of slavery itself. But a year and a half ago it had come to that. There would be no stopping of it until one side or the other either prevailed by sheer force or simply lost its desire to continue the killing, the maiming and the dying.

The Gibbons family was among the few of the new wave of Irish immigrants to Boston who were not Catholic. Joshua had just finished his training at the Methodist Seminary and been ordained when the war broke out. He had wished nothing more than to spend his life serving God and ministering to the needs of his flock here on Earth as they went about their daily lives. Now those serving in the army would have to be his flock. He knew that their needs would be far greater than he had ever anticipated having to meet.

The custom and protocol of the army dictated that Joshua was not actually an officer of the army and he had no command. However, he was treated as a captain and was afforded the accompanying privileges of which he cared little. His 'uniform' consisted of a plain black frock coat with a standing collar, a row of nine brass buttons, plain black trousers, and an army forage cap with neither insignia nor ornament. Though he did not like weapons, he had agreed to learn how to load and fire a rifle, praying all along to never to have to use one. He had yet to see a battle and had been so far assigned to an army hospital where he had seen only the awful results. He knew, however, that he would willingly go wherever God and the army decided he was most needed.

****

This was a bright, early fall morning and there was a slight chill in the air. Had Henry been able to see past the thousands of white canvas tents that surrounded him, he would have seen acres of cornfields waiting to be husked. Much of the corn, however, was untouched. The army had sent out foraging parties to take what was needed but there were parts of the fields that had been left alone. Most of the slaves who had done the spring plowing and planting had been taken as 'contraband of war' by the army during the summer advance. Most were not inclined to go back to the fields.

Henry sat on the ground in front of his tent and leaned his back against an empty hardtack crate. He enjoyed his Sundays. There was normally no drilling. Sunday services, which were not mandatory but which he usually attended, were followed by free time which could be spent relaxing, writing home, or playing checkers. Today, these things would have to wait. There was something more important that held his attention. He discarded the last remnant of a fresh apple and scanned the newspaper that lay spread before him over his long, outstretched legs.

PRESIDENT LINCOLN FREES SLAVES!

That on the first day of January in the year of our Lord one thousand eight hundred and sixty three, all persons held as slaves within any State or part of a State or designated part of a State, the people whereof shall then be in rebellion against the United States, shall be then, thence forward, and forever free… And I further declare and make known, that such persons of suitable condition, will be received into the armed services for the United States to garrison forts, positions, stations, and other places and to man vessels of all sorts in said service.

"What do you think, Sir?" First Sergeant Atlee stood over him and looked down at the paper.

"What I think is that he should have waited," Henry answered, "until we finish this business of putting down the rebellion." He knew that Atlee was an ardent abolitionist – much more so than he. Henry had joined the Army mostly out of his desire to preserve the Union. He had hoped to see slavery ended as a result of the war once it started and sympathized with those held in its grasp. But he had never seen abolition as a primary end worthy of so much suffering and death.

"If I may, Sir, I think it's a grand plan and long overdue in coming." Atlee and Henry were close friends. Though respectful of their difference in ranks, Atlee knew that he could speak freely in private and there was no one else within hearing distance. "And it should free up more of our men for duty on the front lines."

"Certainly, you're entitled to your opinion. I respect that," Henry spoke softly. "But I feel it will only make the war harder and perhaps longer. We already know that we won't be in Vicksburg by Christmas and that the war won't end next spring." He paused, picked up his pipe and filled it. "You're right that it will free up more men for duty but in the areas we haven't yet reached, slaves will still be slaves. And, in the areas we *have* taken, we are already freeing them. I don't see that it will make much of a difference until this whole thing has been settled. In the meantime, I also fear that any chance of a negotiated peace that might have preserved our Union has just vanished. I think the Rebels will now see that they have more to lose than before and will just fight even harder. Anyway, that's my position and I stand by it. But then again, *I* am not the President."

"Well, I think you're wrong," Atlee grinned. "But then *I* am not the First Lieutenant! Checkers?"

****

Andrew sat by the fire in the library and read the newspaper. "So, he did it," he muttered to no one in particular. A lot of good it was going to do him if he couldn't enforce it. As long as there were no Federal troops in Georgia, it wouldn't happen. But then again, the South was being drained of men, ammunition, and everything else that was needed to fight the war. It would probably be only a matter of time. If it were to happen, it would be because God had pre-ordained it. And one could fight God.

If his slaves were emancipated by force, it would, however, relieve him of a decision with which he had been struggling for some time. He had questioned for years what should be done with his own slaves when he was no longer around. Though he kept them here at the plantation, he truly cared for their well-being and had long ago decided that his actions were in their best interest. Darius, he knew, and this was becoming increasingly apparent to him with each letter that he received from Richmond, would be a hard and cruel master. His slaves' lives would become hell here on Earth. Such a thing, he could not allow to happen. But, what to do? He had considered setting them all free at his death but where would they go? How would they fend for themselves?

If the South were to lose the war, there would be nothing more to be done. Still, if Generals Lee and Jackson were somehow able to pull off a miracle, the dilemma would remain. There was nothing to be decided tonight. He let the fire die down to embers and went to bed.

****

Jonas sat in a rocking chair between the kitchen window and the range and pulled off his boots. The warmth of the stove felt good on his feet. He and David had spent the cold, windy day in the field husking corn. They had nearly finished David's field and would soon begin working on his own. There remained the fall plowing and the sowing of the winter wheat. Fortunately, they had already laid back nearly enough firewood to take care of both of their houses for the winter. Hopefully, winter would hold off long enough to get everything done.

They had finished dinner and Ellie and Em had done the dishes while Jonas brought in more wood to keep the stove going overnight. There was no heat upstairs where the bedrooms were but at least the kitchen could be kept warm.

Em was sitting at the kitchen table writing a letter to Henry.

Thayer, Minnesota

October 11, 1862

Dear Husband,

We have just finished our dinner and so wished that you could be here with us. I hope this letter finds you safe and as comfortable as one can possibly be in camp away from home. Today is Saturday so Ellie did not have to teach school. She and I spent the morning putting up the last of the apples and pears and this afternoon did laundry and hung it out to dry. I wish I could send you some fruit to have during the upcoming winter but I

59

don't know if the jars would reach you without being broken or if you would be able to carry them with you if the camp were to be moved. I also baked some bread and thought how you love it fresh and hot with butter. But enough talk of that. I am afraid that I will just make us both more homesick for each other.

Jonas has obtained a book from the School for the Deaf in Washington, which helps the deaf communicate with hearing people through signs that each represent words. He has been studying it with us and also with David and Mary Alice when they drop by to visit. We are beginning to become quite adept at speaking with him. He shows us signs and tells us what words they mean and then we practice. Sometimes we still forget and talk to him as if he can hear but he seems quite understanding and is starting to hear us by reading our lips. He is quite anxious to teach you when you come home. He can still sing even though he can no longer hear himself and readily learns new songs by reading the sheet music. Last Sunday, he sang a solo in Church that everyone really enjoyed. He hopes to someday have a piano and to play.

My, he is such a hard worker. He is up before dawn working on chores, spends all day in the fields, and then more chores. He has done several repairs around the house and still manages to find some time to go to town and tinker in his cabinet shop. It is such a blessing to have him home.

Poor Jonas, though, still has that awful dream at night, particularly if it has been raining or if there is lightning. Of course, he cannot hear the thunder but seems to sense when it is raining even if the curtains are drawn and he cannot see the splatters on the windows. I feel so for him. He won't tell me about the dream but I awaken in the middle of the night to hear him screaming. I go into his room to rouse him and find him curled up under the covers and sobbing. He says the dream will go away over time and I pray that he is right but I have not much confidence in that. Once in a while, he refuses to go to bed and sits up in the kitchen all night smoking his pipe and drinking coffee. I don't think he has taken to drink and I doubt that he will as he has always been so opposed to it but I fear greatly for him whenever he goes out alone. There are so many things that could happen to him without his having his hearing. I don't like to share such news but feel that it is important for you to know.

This is such a pretty time of year. The weather is cold but not yet bitterly so as in winter. The trees are so pretty all dressed up

*in their bright red, yellow, and orange colors!
However, I would enjoy it much more if it did
not mean that winter will soon be on the way.*

*I am afraid that I have some rather sad
news to pass on to you. Mona Kaler has died.
Last Saturday she was cutting up a chicken to
fry. Her knife slipped and she got a severe
gash on her arm. Instead of beginning to
heal, the wound became sorer and her arm
became quite swollen. By Wednesday, she
had developed a very high fever and was
bedridden. Thursday evening, Ellie was
sitting with her. According to Ellie, she was
talking but was delirious and making no
sense. Dr. Hanson tried more medication to
bring down the fever but it only became
worse. Last night, she stopped talking and
appeared to have trouble breathing. Later,
she began talking briefly, calling out to
Edward. Ellie says that Mona then sat up in
bed, reached out her arms, said "Oh,
Edward, my dearest, I knew you would
come," and then lay back down and died. We
all imagine that she saw him only in her
delirium but felt pleased that it may have
given her some comfort in her last moments.
May her dear soul rest in peace! If word does
not reach Edward before, I am afraid that it
might be up to you to tell him. Please let him
know she will have a fine and proper funeral.
Jonas is making her a nice coffin. He and*

David and our other neighbors will see that the crops are put up and the house taken care of.

That is all for now. Please know how much you are loved and missed.

Love as always,

Em.

As Em wrote, Ellie sat across from her at the table reading letters that her students had written to send to President Lincoln.

Lincoln,

I don't know for sure what a slave is but Momma says people in the South Dear President treat them really badly and make them do all of their work for them. I'm glad you told those people that they can't do that anymore. You are a great man.

Love,

Constance.

Dear President Lincoln,

Thank you for freeing the slaves. My Daddy told me he was going to war to free the slaves. Since they are free

now, can you please let him come home? Momma and Billy and I miss him.

God bless you.   Angeline.

P.S. How are Mrs. Lincoln and Tad?

Dear President Lincoln,

Momma is really sad and she cries a lot. She says Papa won't be coming home from the war. I'm glad you freed the slaves.

Tommy.

Ellie closed her folder containing the letters. "Time for bed," she sighed.

****

Camp in Mississippi
October 12, 1862

My Dearest Em,

We have just returned from breakfast. Since it is Sunday, there is no drilling today. As I have some leisure time, I propose to write you a few lines. I hope this letter finds our family and friends all well. The weather here is quite pleasant. If not for being away from friends and family, I would be content to be here for some time. The air is cool and there is a slight breeze – just enough to provide some freshness and rustle the leaves on the trees. The trees here have begun to turn only slightly as yet but I imagine that where you are the colors are already bright.

The men are, for the most part, well and fit for duty except for a few who are experiencing itchy eyes and runny noses. As we know from home, that affliction normally disappears with the first hard frost. Here, however, the frost may yet be quite some time in coming so they may have to be uncomfortable for a while yet.

I have some sad news to report to you. Edward Kaler has died. He came down with an unexpected case of pneumonia. I visited him in the camp hospital last Wednesday. As he was extremely weak, I offered to help him write a letter to Mona. He declined my offer, saying that he would soon be fine and didn't want to worry her. On Thursday, his condition took a turn for the worse. By Friday evening, the doctor had determined that he would probably not live long. A priest was called but one was not available. One of the corporals, who is Roman Catholic, gave him the Church's Last Rites as best he knew them and moments later poor Edward was dead. I know that the

*Captain will write to Mona and send her
Edward's personal things. If you receive this
letter before she receives one, it might be
easier for her if you were to tell her but that
is up to you.*

*I have little other news so will close.
The boys are setting up a horseshoes match
and I think I will join them. Please know
that you are loved and missed.*

As always in love,

Henry.

****

A mile or so north of town stood a small, grass-covered knoll topped by a copse of birch trees now decked out in orange and gold. One of the first residents of Thayer had donated the land for a town cemetery. That had not been long ago and one could still count on both hands the number of occupied graves. There were two adult men who had been the first to be buried there – one a young father and the other a man who was quite elderly when he first came to town. They had both died before the Hancock family arrived. There were two women whom the family had known only casually, three infants, a young boy, and a young girl. The newest grave, not yet covered with grass, belonged to Thomas Britt. All in all, the town had been quite fortunate that there had not been more deaths since its founding. Most of the settlers had been young and healthy and the town had so far not experienced any of the contagious illnesses that had plagued surrounding communities.

The bright and balmy day belied the solemnity of the occasion. Em, Ellie, Jonas, and many others of the town's residents stood under the shade of the birches near the coffin that Jonas had just completed the night before. Thayer did not have a Catholic Church but a priest from Crestville had consented to attend and preside over a service for Mona Kaler. He had, moments before, finished his closing prayer that had followed a short homily. Jonas and three others now began to carefully lower the coffin into the grave. That done, each person present stepped forward and tossed in a handful of what would now become sacred earth. Most of the mourners began to walk away but a few and the priest remained behind as Jonas and the other pallbearers completed their task of filling in the grave.

Em turned to Ellie as they were walking away. "It is so sad. She was so young and Edward was so in love with her. He's going to be devastated when he finds out. I hope he doesn't let himself get killed on purpose just to be with her. It's a blessing that they didn't have children. I wonder who would have taken care of them. It would be awful if they had children and they became orphans and had to go to an orphanage. I have heard such terrible stories of those places. What if they had been adopted by people who only wanted them for labor and didn't love them?"

"You can't worry about that, Em," Ellie tried to assure her. "They had no children so I guess, in a way, that's a blessing. But when Edward comes home, he would make a wonderful father and they would have been something special for him to remember Mona by."

"But what about the rest? What about all the poor children whose fathers don't come home and their mothers can't afford to keep them? Who will take care of them? Oh, Ellie, this war is such an awful thing!"

Em was sobbing now and her hands were visibly trembling. "I'm glad that Henry and I don't have children."

"Em, you shouldn't say that. I'm sorry," she corrected herself. "I didn't mean to tell you what to say. I just meant that I wish you didn't feel that way."

"But I *do* feel that way. If anything should happen to Henry, I don't know how I could take care of myself, let alone children."

"Em, nothing is going to happen to Henry and, even if it did, you have me and you have Rose and Robert and you have Jonas. We wouldn't ever let you be alone."

"I would never want to depend on your charity, Ellie. And Rose and Robert don't even live here. And if you and Jonas both get married, and if you both move away, then what would I do?

Ellie was running out of assurances. "We're family, Em, so it wouldn't be charity. Even if you and I aren't sisters really, we're just like sisters. I can't promise that I'll never get married and move away but you haven't seen anyone asking me have you? And I certainly don't know of anyone asking Jonas for permission. I don't think Jonas will ever move away. He has his shop in town and he seems really attached to this land even if he and Henry don't own it. And don't forget, you also have David and Mary Alice."

"But we don't *own* any of it. I don't think I'd be able to keep paying the rent and stay here. And if just Jonas and I were to stay here together, people would talk."

"I don't think they would, Em. And besides, the people who know you would understand. The rest really don't matter."

"I just can't think about it right now," Em continued to sob.

"Then don't. Let's talk about something else."

"Promise you won't tell Henry that I worry so much," Em asked.

"I think we need to go home."

****

Henry gazed upward at the clouds. It was nearing midday. What had started as a whitish overcast had quickly turned to a heavy gray blanket that appeared to be growing darker by the minute. A steady breeze blew a light but cold mist against his face. He had no doubt that, by evening, the mist would turn to a stinging sleet. But that would be later and by then he hoped to be back in the relative comfort of camp. Ordinarily, the canopy of oak and ash trees would offer some protection from the elements, but not today – or, for that matter, any day for perhaps a generation or more. What had once been a lush and serene setting had been viciously shredded and raked six months ago by cannon fire at the Battle of Shiloh.

The torn trees were only one reminder of what had taken place here on the 6th and 7th of April. The landscape was now covered with dozens of plots, each containing the still-fresh, shallow graves of thirty or more Federal soldiers – most hastily buried soon after the battle near where they had fallen. Each contained an earthen mound marked only with a small wooden slab, many with the inscription 'unknown.' The field was littered with other reminders – broken weapons that had been abandoned as no longer usable, remnants of wagons, and the skeletons of horses and mules whose remains had been left for scavengers and then bleached by the unshaded summer sun.

Henry's mind drifted back to the charge on the battle's second day. He did not have a clear sense of where that had been relative to where he now stood but hoped it was far away and he wished never to visit it again.

His thoughts were interrupted by the gentle intonations of the priest delivering the Catholic Rite for the Burial of the Dead. The words were in Latin and he understood only a few but hoped they would allow Edward Kaler to rest in peace alongside his fallen comrades. "I am the resurrection and the life …" The priest, a chaplain from another regiment, then sprinkled holy water onto the coffin. This done, Henry stepped forward and, along with the others from the company who had come with him, lowered Edward's coffin into the grave.

Henry could not help but reflect upon the coffin. Most in the field had not been buried in one at all but only wrapped in blankets. Some had been placed with only a cloth covering over their faces. For Edward, the company carpenter had fashioned a box using wood from a crate that had arrived in camp filled with new rifles. Henry had placed a rolled-up blanket under Edward's head for a pillow and covered the rest of the body with the man's gun blanket. In Edward's pocket, he had placed the last letter that he had received from Mona.

The priest stepped forward and, again, sprinkled holy water on the coffin. In unison all of those present quietly repeated the Lord's Prayer. Their heads still bowed, each listened as the priest continued. "Grant this mercy, O Lord, we beseech Thee, to Thy servant departed, that he may not receive in punishment the requital of his deeds who in desire did keep Thy will, and as the true faith here united him to the company of the faithful, so may Thy mercy unite him above to the choirs of angels. Through Jesus Christ, our Lord, Amen. May his soul and the souls of all the faithful departed through the mercy of God rest in peace."

Finished with his role, the priest stepped backward but remained as Henry and the others filled in the grave. Finished, Henry and two others loaded their rifles with only powder and fired a final three-gun salute.

****

Isaac could read. But he was careful not to let anyone know – even his family or his closest friends. For a slave to be able to read and write was illegal in Mississippi. It was punishable by the severest of penalties, not only for the slave, but also for anyone caught teaching him. As a young boy at Angus McManus' Riverview Plantation north and east of Vicksburg, he had caught the attention of the tutor who had been brought from Kentucky to instruct the owner's children. Isaac had been the personal servant to the man, a service provided as part of his compensation. They had rendezvoused secretly one night a week in a windowless shed behind the cotton barn long after everyone else was asleep. Isaac had been always cautious never to be seen with a book or other reading matter and to not practice his lessons aside from their sessions. The tutor had told him early on how disastrous the consequences could be for either of them were they to be caught. One could be whipped and possibly sold away to another owner, who certainly would not be told of his abilities. The other would be banished from the plantation or, more probably, jailed.

Isaac had never known his father though his mother had told him often how good of a man he was and how he had adored Isaac. The little family had been separated when Isaac was two years old and his father had been traded away to a neighboring plantation for some mules and some farm equipment. Isaac's mother had learned by word of mouth that her husband had been sold soon afterward at a slave auction in Biloxi.

As the McManus children had grown and the tutor was no longer needed, the lessons ended. Mr. Edwards had moved on and Isaac had been put to work cleaning horse stalls and later sent to the fields to work cotton. Ever since that time, he had dreamed of being free and of, perhaps someday, finding his father. For now, there was nothing to be done except to work, wait, and hope. Escape had always been out of the question. Freedom was too far north, the chance of being caught too great, and the consequences too severe

What Isaac saw today nearly made his heart stop. Checking first to make sure that no one was around, he sneaked a furtive glance at a newspaper that someone had carelessly left lying in the horse barn.

LINCOLN TRIES TO FREE SLAVES

The tyrant Lincoln, not content with unjustly sending his army into a South which has only asked to be left alone and in peace, has now maliciously and illegally issued an order for that invading army to steal our slaves and arm them against us. As he has no authority, the order will not stand and can never be enforced ….

"Maybe, just maybe," Isaac told himself silently. He left the paper untouched and walked out of the barn into the bright sunlight. He remembered that each Confederate victory he had overheard being bragged about around the farm had been further and further south. It was just a matter of time now. He wanted to tell everyone but knew he could tell no one. For now, it was time to fall-plow the fields for next spring's cotton that he hoped not to plant.

****

Stark was furious. "Who does he think he is?" The tyrant was acting as if he thought Georgia was still part of the United States and that he had some authority here. Not only had he ordered the slaves freed but he wanted to arm them. "Fine, let him do it in his own country. You can give a field hand a gun but that doesn't make him a soldier. It just makes him a field hand with a gun and that's a big difference." It wasn't going to happen here.

Still, he was worried. What if the slaves in Georgia were to get wind of this? Would they run off? Worse, would there be a rebellion? The last thing Georgia needed now, with most of her able-bodied men fighting in Virginia and Tennessee to keep the invaders out, was an uprising. Who would be left to keep order? Well, there would be no uprising here! He would make certain of that! The question that bothered him most was whether Andrew would have the spine to do what was needed. Could he prevent his own slaves from running off and joining a slave insurrection? He was not confident. It was time to begin working on a plan.

The cotton had been harvested and stored in the barns until shipment could be arranged. That might be a while. It obviously wasn't going north to New England. The warehouses in Savannah and Charleston were bursting at the seams with bales waiting to be loaded on ships able to run the Yankee blockade. The cotton brokers weren't interested in buying a crop that they couldn't ship. There was nothing to be done now but start plowing to get the fields ready for next year's crop. Stark watched the slaves work as he sat on his horse in the shade of a small grove of pines near the field. "A plan – I need a plan. Got to make them *afraid* to run off or rebel."

CHAPTER IV

Joshua stood outside his tent on the outskirts of Fredericksburg and surveyed the sparkling stars. He had always loved watching the heavens. Tonight was no exception. The clear night, however, caused the air to be much colder and he wrapped his frock coat more tightly around him to fight the chill. This chill, he surmised, involved more than just the temperature of the air around him. He was feeling a deep sense of dread for what he knew was soon to come. General Burnside had managed to get most of his army across the Rappahannock and occupy the town but Joshua was aware that Lee's army still held the nearby heights. Even without formal military training, he knew that neither army would simply walk away. There was going to be a fight – if not tomorrow then almost certainly the next day. Countless souls on both sides were about to perish. It saddened him that there was nothing he could do to stop it except pray. At the same time, he knew that prayerful leaders on both sides were asking the same God to bring them victory.

A quick glance at his pocket watch told Joshua that it was time. He and two other chaplains had spread word throughout the camp that they would hold a prayer service at 7:30 p.m. for any who wanted to come. Denomination didn't matter and they hoped that even non-believers would come and find God on what could be their last night on earth. That it might be his own was not of great concern, though he did pray as Christ had, "Father, if it be thy will, please take this cup from me." What bothered him more was the grief that his family would bear and the need for someone to minister to the needs of the soldiers if he were to fall. Well, he decided, it was all out of his hands. He left what little warmth that the fire provided and headed toward the natural amphitheater created by some ridges located near the camp. He wondered if his counterparts up on Marye's Heights were holding a similar meeting tonight. He guessed that they were.

****

"Blessed are you, Hashem, our God, and King of the Universe Who has wrought miracles for our forefathers, in those days at this season." David prayed in Hebrew and lit the third candle on the Menorah as Mary Alice stood silently by. "Oh mighty Rock of my salvation, to praise You is a delight. Restore my house of prayer and there will be a thanksgiving offering. When You will have prepared the slaughter for the blaspheming foe, then I shall complete with a song of hymn the dedication of the altar."

They finished their meal of latkes. Mary Alice had prepared a dessert of doughnuts especially for the occasion. "Happy Hanukkah, dearest," she told him. "I love you. I have made you a little gift." She handed him a box wrapped with brown paper and tied with string.

"I know Hanukkah gifts are mostly for the young ones," he said, "but I still enjoy receiving them – especially from a pretty girl!"

"David, you flatter me so," she smiled. "Go ahead. Open it. I can hardly wait for you to see it!"

David untied the string and carefully opened the paper. "Oh, sweetheart," he exclaimed, holding up the contents of the box, "these are just the finest yarmulke and prayer shawl I have ever seen! I have a gift for you too but you can't see it until Christmas." He smiled as he thought about the sewing rocker that he had commissioned Jonas to make for her and which now sat safely packaged in a wooden crate hidden in the barn.

Though David was Jewish, Mary Alice was not. She was the daughter of a Lutheran blacksmith from Indiana. David's father and uncle, architects in Paris, had emigrated with their wives from Paris to New York shortly after the end of the Napoleonic Wars. David and his cousin had been born and raised there and had come to Minnesota soon after serving in the war with Mexico. They had first settled near Minneapolis but David moved to Thayer shortly before the Hancocks arrived.

"Tomorrow night I am going to fix you chicken and dumplings," Mary Alice announced.

"Then I guess I had better go to the chicken house now," he told her. "With the way it looks to snow, I may not be able to find my way out there by then." She opened her sewing basket as he reached for his hat and coat. His evening reading would have to wait but the anticipated meal would be well worth it.

"And challah for dessert," she called after him.

****

It was not the first Christmas Ball that Isaac had seen at Riverview Plantation but it appeared to him to be the strangest and the smallest. He also felt almost certain that it would be the last.

It wasn't that he had ever been close to the festivities. Only the house servants, decked out in livery, had gotten a close glimpse. But he and a number of other field hands had been given the 'privilege' of seeing to the guests' horses and carriages once their owners had gone into the house to eat, drink, and dance. Before, and in the early days of the war, there had been lavish decorations, elegant gowns, and handsome suits. There had been laughter and gaiety as friends greeted each other on the wide veranda. He had watched as young women flirted with each other's beaus even as they held tightly onto their own.

This year, it was different. There were few young men other than those who had come home missing an arm or an eye. The suits were worn and tattered. Many of the women, both young and old, were dressed in mourning and acted as if the ball were an obligation rather than a celebration. Even Mr. and Mrs. McManus appeared tired and sad as they welcomed their guests. He tried to muster up some sympathy for them but couldn't and soon gave it up as not worth the effort.

Isaac and his best friend, Joe, had put up the last of the horses for the evening and were relaxing on bales of straw bedding outside of the stables. There was nothing more to be done until the guests prepared to leave and needed the horses and carriages taken back to the house.

"I gonna run off tonight," Joe announced softly. "I cain't do this no mo. I don' wanna plant their cotton an' I don' wanna chop it or tote it. I jus' wanna go north an' be free. Jus' look at dem with their party."

"Don'." Isaac had to be careful. "Dey'll catch you and den dey'll bring you back an' dey'll hang you up like a hog an' den dey'll cut you down and hang you up again by da neck until you daid. And den dey'll likely whip da res' of us so we don' try to run off." His tutor would have cringed but he would have understood.

"Dey won' catch me. I gonna take one a dem horses."

"Don'," Isaac repeated. "We all gonna be free come summer."

"How we gonna be free? You think Mistah Angus gonna jus' up an let us go?"

"No, he's not gonna." Isaac looked around and spoke extra softly. "But Mistah Lincoln's army will an' dey comin'."

"How da ya know?" Joe looked at him. "I ain' see no army 'cept da Confederate army roun' here. Have you?"

"Nah, I ain't. But I know dey comin'. Jus' look aroun'. Des aren't da fancy horses dey used ta' ride. Des is their plow horses – not da ones what can run fast an' jump fences. An' mos' of des are old an' lame. Da army dun' took all da good ones. An look at dem," he continued, "Dey is whooped. Dey might not 'cept it yet but dey is whooped. Da white boy's don' come home on furlough much anymore an' dos what do look all beat up an' ragged. Remember what dey looked like when dey lef'? An' look at all da women dressed in black. Dey in mournin'. Da men ain' comin' back. Dey is whooped alright."

"You promise dey comin?" Joe asked.

"Jus' you wait and see. Dey comin'. You still wanna chance runnin' off an' gettin' caught?"

"Nah. I'll trus' you an' wait but dey better come."

"Dey will," Isaac promised him. "Dey will."

****

There were many more gathered for the meeting than the three chaplains had even dared hope. They were pleased at the turnout. At the same time, they realized that this might be the only or last service that many of the men would ever attend. In fact, many them would probably not see Christmas. It seemed out of place that most, if not all, of the soldiers had come carrying rifles or side arms but they knew that this was necessary were the Rebels to come charging down from the heights and attack.

Captain Martin opened the meeting with some welcoming remarks and a brief prayer. It had been decided ahead of time by the chaplains that each would deliver a brief sermon and that the preaching would be followed by a few familiar hymns and a closing prayer. Just as the captain finished, however, the air was filled with hundreds of voices singing 'Rock of Ages.' Joshua and the others soon realized that the voices were not coming from the throng gathered about them. They were coming from the heights. It took only seconds for their own flock to join the chorus. The chaplains wished that they could take this as a sign from above but knew, almost as a certainty, that within hours or days the men now joining in song would be desperately trying to kill each other.

"Our Heavenly Father," Joshua began as his turn arrived, "please bless these men who have gathered in Your presence and be with them in the trials which are sure to come."

He then began to address the men who had assembled. "Unless our leaders change their course, we shall all be soon engaged in a mighty struggle to preserve our beloved republic and to set free an oppressed people." Joshua knew that some among the 'congregation' did not share his belief that freeing an oppressed people was worth the sacrifices already made or would soon be called upon to make. He knew also that, for many others, it was either as or more important than saving the Union.

"There are many among us for whom this will be our final struggle. It is for God only, and not for us, to know which will perish and which will be spared. Knowing this, it is important for each of us to be ready to meet our Maker so that we stand before him with our souls cleansed and ready to enter into His Eternal Kingdom."

"For some among us, our final act in this life may be to take that of another. It is an awful thing to kill and something that no righteous or Christian man wants to do. We must therefore take comfort in knowing that God has brought us here to do His work. Our God is a gracious and loving God who, in his judgment, will take into account what is in our hearts. With that, it behooves us to do what we must do out of a desire to do His will and not out of rancor or malice."

"Some may ask, 'How has it come to this? How can we be called upon to do such an awful thing?' That is not for us to know. I believe that even our leaders in Washington, or those in Richmond, do not know or ever intended for so great a tragedy to befall our country. The Bible tells us, 'There is a time for war and a time for peace. There is a time to kill and a time to be killed. There is a time to sow and a time to reap.' We have been sent to reap what has been sown and can only pray to our Lord that this business will be soon finished and that the time for peace will return."

"'Yea though I walk through the shadow of the valley of death, I will fear no evil', the Psalmist says. 'Thy rod and thy staff, they comfort me. Thou preparest a table before me in the presence of mine enemies.'"

"Let us, therefore, go about doing God's work, trusting in his will and the righteousness of our cause. Let us pray for our enemies as well as for ourselves and be ready in mind and soul for whatever comes. Let us now pray together 'Our Father who art in Heaven ....'"

****

It was December 12. There was a harsh chill in the air and Darius felt the sting on his face. The sky was sparkling clear and a dusting of snow covered the ground. He shivered as he pulled his blanket around him. It provided some comfort as it was nearly new. Those possessed by many of the others on this hill were tattered and worn – much like the men whom they covered. He felt cold and a bit hungry but, at least, he had finally escaped the awful boredom of guarding captured Union soldiers at Libby Prison. For the first time since Manassas, he would finally get to see some action and he hoped it would come tomorrow. He would finally have some news to write to his father. He had decided, however, to omit the part about being stripped of his lieutenant's commission for assaulting a fellow officer who had rightly accused him of cheating at cards. Andrew might find out sooner or later but, hopefully, it would be much later. In the meantime, there was killing to be done.

Darius looked over the stone wall at the top of the ridge known as Marye's Heights. It was said that George Washington had once lived on this hill. Well, Washington had been a Southerner and a slaveholder, hadn't he? It would be appropriate to stop the invaders at this place. If they were to take the heights, Burnside would have an open road to march his army straight to Richmond. He knew that Lee and Jackson would never allow that to happen. He, *himself,* would make damned sure it didn't.

Below the ridge stood the town of Fredericksburg and just behind the town flowed the Rappahannock River. Darius stared at the hundreds of campfires before him. Somehow Burnside had managed to capture the town. In Darius' eyes, that was no more than a minor setback. Once the army had driven the Federals away from the ridge, it would be easy enough to re-take the town. No, there was no reason to worry. Let them come.

What *was* beginning to worry Darius was the attitude that Andrew had shown in some of his more recent letters. He had always felt that his father was too easy on the slaves. Now, recently, he seemed to sympathize more and

81

more with the Yankee soldiers whom Darius wanted only to kill. Andrew had even expressed sadness at the loss of life on *both sides* at the Battle of Antietam. Well, the old man just didn't seem to understand either war or slavery. He may not be able to change his father's mind about the first but, after the South won its independence, he meant to do something about the second.

In the meantime, there was that awful singing. He could hear it both from behind him and from the camp below. It was the same damned song and it was like they were singing it together! Behind him, chaplains, probably at the behest of Lee and Jackson, were holding an enormous prayer service with hymns and sermons. As the singing stopped, he could partly hear some of the prayers. 'Praying for the enemy?' What rubbish! He would pray to kill them all. 'Mercy?' Why show mercy? 'Forgiveness?' Forgiveness for what?! He pulled the cold half of the last cigar from his coat pocket and struck a match.

****

"December 12." Stark wondered that it had taken him so long to work out the plan and to make his choice. He looked across the table through the dim lamplight at the young man seated there. Toby looked to be about fourteen of fifteen years old – sixteen at the very most. Lean and muscular from working in the fields, he had been at Pine Hill only since the beginning of the cotton harvest. He seemed shy and had yet to make any close friends in whom he would confide. Andrew did not need more hands but took this one from an acquaintance in Milledgeville in settlement of a debt. There was no real attachment.

"You're not in any trouble – at least not with me." Stark lied. "You're a smart, young man and a hard worker."

The young man, still nervous about having been called in the night to the overseer's quarters, allowed himself a slight smile of relief.

"You deserve better than to be a slave here working cotton for the rest of your life," Stark continued. "I want to make sure that doesn't happen. But, you need to trust me. Do you understand?"

"Yessuh."

"Good. Now, first of all, you must tell no one that you've talked to me or what I have in mind for you – no one at all. If you do, I can't help you. Agreed?"

"Yessuh, Mistah Stark."

"Okay, now here's what's going to happen. I like you but Master Morgan is very displeased with you. He thinks you are a troublemaker. He only brought you here for the cotton harvest and plans to sell you to a broker who is buying slaves to send down the river to the rice plantations. You don't want to go down the river, do you?"

"Nosuh."

"And I don't want you to. So this is what I'm going to do. Tomorrow night, I am going to take you to a friend of mine who will take you to Charleston. Do you know where Charleston is?"

"No."

"It's on the seacoast. Another friend of mine is a ship's captain. He will take you on a ship to Canada. When you get there you will be free – no plantations, no slave hunters. You will be free to go wherever you want and do whatever you please."

"Won't Mistah Morgan think I run off and sen' the hounds after me?"

The question caught Stark off guard. He hadn't anticipated that the young man would think things through that far. "Don't worry about that. He depends on me to run everything and doesn't pay that much attention. I will cover for you and you'll be entirely safe. Just trust me. Tomorrow night, watch the lights at the house. When they are all out, come and meet me behind the cotton shed. I'll have horses and we will go. Now remember – not a word to anyone."

"Nosuh, Mistah Stark. Not a word."

Actually, Stark didn't mind if Toby told someone he was running off. It would make things better as long as he didn't bring anyone along.

"Good. Now get back to your cabin before anyone discovers you were here."

Stark rubbed his hands together in front of the stove.

****

Atlee and the others had left. Henry sat alone in the tent while most of the others in the company huddled around their campfires. It was a bone-chilling night – cold for Mississippi in December and cold even for a regiment from Minnesota. A lantern hanging in the center of the tent gave a sufficient glow for him to hunch over a lap-board and write in his journal.

Camp in Mississippi
December 12, 1862

Well, in less than two weeks it will be Christmas – the second one of this awful war. So many of us thought we would be

84

home with our families last Christmas and now there are so many more on both sides that will never see home again. It seems there is no end in sight to this terrible thing. I fear it will just go on and on and that the only way for a man to get out of it is to be crippled or killed. Now we can only hope and pray to our God that it will be done before next Christmas.

Most knew this war was coming but, somehow, those who should have been the ablest to prevent it seemed to be those who were either the least willing or able to do so. I'm sure that there were some men of good will on both sides who tried but, my God, it has all turned out so badly. Now, there are all of us out here in the field who really had so little say in the matter but must pay the price of their errors. If they could see us now, our forbearers would be sorely disappointed to see what has been done to this country for which they sacrificed so much to create.

There surely must be some good to come of this war. If we are indeed able to emerge victorious and resolve the issue of slavery forever, perhaps the Union will be stronger than before. Were it not for that evil, North and South have so much in common – our language, a great and bountiful land waiting to be filled, and our belief in the same merciful God. Yet none can predict what will accompany our victory. Either the land will be cleansed, much like the air after a mighty and terrible storm, or the bitter feelings caused by the war itself will be passed on to our children or grandchildren. We must all pray for healing and for the wisdom to prevent a scourge from ever being visited upon us again.

I once thought I should want to be a lawyer and possibly be engaged in politics in some form and hold an important office. I no longer wish for either. It seems that the lawyers and the politicians, for the most part, have created this thing that we are in and are mostly to blame for it. I wish now only to return home to my loved ones at the end of it and be able to farm and to raise my children in security and peace.

Presently, Sergeant Atlee returned with a cup of coffee and his pipe. He sat in the only chair in the tent. "What are you doing, Henry? Your journal again? I thought those were only for generals and such."

"Someday, the war will be over," Henry looked up at him. "Sometime, maybe not next year and maybe not during our lifetimes, someone will look back and try to figure out this madness. Perhaps they will be able to and perhaps not. For me, I have to make some sense of it now to help me get through it. And, who knows? After I'm long gone it may help my children and grandchildren to understand what happened and why we were here. I just don't know. Anyhow, I have to try."

CHAPTER V

For those who had been able to sleep at all, it had been a short night. For those who had not, it had been a long night filled with dread, reflection, and prayer. Joshua numbered himself among the latter.

The morning of December 13, 1862 began early at Fredericksburg, Virginia. A dense fog had rolled in overnight, blanketing the entire river valley in an ominous grey shroud. The chilly air was filled with an assortment of noises. There was the clanging of pots and pans and the clinking of tin cups and plates. There was the rattle of side arms and musketry as men prepared their weapons for the battle that everyone knew was coming. What was not there, and this drew Joshua's attention as he stood outside of his tent and buttoned his frock coat against the cold, was the chatter and lighthearted banter that usually accompanied the day's first meal. Few of the men spoke except those who were moving from campfire to campfire giving orders or checking on readiness. Each man seemed encompassed in his own small world, steeling himself in his own way for what he knew was shortly to come.

Those assembled were not strangers to battle. Only those replacements who had been brought in to refill the ranks after the terrible losses at Antietam had not seen it before. But this was different, and they knew it. McClellan was gone, replaced by General Ambrose Burnside, a man about whom many of them knew little. The army would be fighting an entrenched foe that would be firing from behind the stone wall that encircled the heights above. To even reach those heights, they would have to cross both a millrace and a vast expanse of barren ridge that provided no cover. Yes, this was going to be different, and it was going to be awful.

To Joshua's left, the sun began its slow rise, barely noticed behind the fog as if reluctant to see what the morning would bring. Soon the clanking of the pots and pans and the rattle of weapons being prepared gave way to the shouting of orders and the tramping of feet. Behind him, nearly invisible columns of soldiers began making their way southward through the town down Hanover Street and Plank Road toward the millrace.

The race was nothing more than a ditch. Having seen it the day before, Joshua guessed it to be perhaps twelve or fifteen feet wide and five feet or so deep. Perhaps two or three feet of water currently flowed through it. One could usually wade through the little man-made stream with water up to his hips or waist and easily climb the opposite bank. He would perhaps even find it a bit refreshing. Today, it would be different. Men would be weighed down with weapons and equipment. Those fortunate enough to make it across without being shot would find their boots and trousers thoroughly soaked with icy water and themselves facing even more menacing fire. There was no more cover between themselves and the stone wall at the top of the heights. Some would bring boards and other material foraged from the town in order to try building makeshift bridges. Others would decide to brave the water in order to take advantage of what little cover the far bank might provide. Although the fog might provide a bit of shelter, there was no advantage of surprise. They all knew that it provided no shield from the enemy bullets.

Joshua turned his attention once again in the direction of Marye's Heights, though the fog allowed him to see only the edge of the race perhaps fifty or a hundred yards ahead. He prayed one last time that Providence would see fit to intervene and stop the horrible bloodshed that he knew was about to occur. Almost as he finished, both his prayer and the uneasy peace were shattered by the crash of Burnside's

89

cannons firing through the fog. The hope was that the guns would either smash the stone wall or at least keep the Rebel sharpshooters pinned down and helpless behind it while their men marched up the ridge. Such hopes, it soon became apparent, would not be achieved. Most of Burnside's shells were falling well short of their mark. Lee's cannon, however, being fired from the heights, were not only showering the ridge but some were actually exploding among the Federal guns on Stafford Heights at the Federal rear. In addition, men were already falling prey to the rifles of the entrenched foe. "Stop it!" Joshua found himself yelling as if he were a parent trying to break up a fight between his children. "Stop it now!" He really didn't know if he was shouting at Burnside or Lee or, for that matter, anyone in particular. It really didn't matter as he failed to make himself heard above the shelling. If he had, no one of importance would have listened. "This is madness," he muttered to himself as he watched the infantry approach the half-built bridges and try to cross the only permanent bridge – a small one. "It's just madness!"

His eyes focused on the small foot bridge that spanned the race at a point near the mill. He didn't want to look. He closed his eyes and tried not to see but kept opening them. Every time he did this, it was worse than before. "Oh, God," he cried out, "make them stop!" But it didn't stop. One after another, the blue-clad young men tried to cross. Some actually succeeded only to be shot dead just as they stepped off the far end. Others fell on the bridge, blocking the way for those who came behind. Still others stumbled in mid-stride and fell from the bridge into the race. Joshua could only hope that those unfortunate souls were already dead when they fell and would not drown or bleed to death in the icy water.

He didn't remember how he had gotten there or how long he had been there, but Joshua found himself only feet away from the near end of the bridge. He wanted to be someplace else – any place else. But there was nowhere to go. Like being swept in a flash-flooding stream, he was being unwillingly moved forward by a current of blue-clad, nameless men. Most were bearded and many unwashed. Among the anonymous faces, Joshua noticed a variety of expressions. Some looked nearly void of feeling. Others showed a countenance of either fierce determination or almost paralyzing terror. Yet those in front all kept moving, clambering over the fallen that lay in their way and pushed by those crowding from behind. They seemed to think that the cramming and shoving would somehow make the bridge wider and allow them to move more quickly. But quickly toward what? Joshua wondered as he was pushed ahead. Don't they know what awaits them at the other end of the bridge?" Yet on they came, falling in front, crowding from behind.

Above the mix of voices and shooting, he heard a canister explode upstream where a company of engineers was attempting to construct a second bridge across the race. "Keep moving!" a voice called from behind. "Keep moving!" Joshua was near enough to the side of the bridge to see over as he was being carried along. In the race, a body floated face up, showing a large red stain on its chest – eyes wide open, staring at nothing. Closely behind it came a blue kepi missing its bill and behind that a canteen. Presently, the body disappeared from view as it continued its journey downstream and under the bridge. "Keep mo …" the voice came again but the order was never finished.

It seemed to Joshua that it took forever to cross the bridge but, again, what was the hurry? What he now saw happening before him was even worse than what he had just encountered. "My God! My God!"

****

Darius continued to stare over the stone wall into the fog. The camp behind him had been alive for some time. The sounds of men preparing their breakfast and having a last cup of coffee for the morning had given way to the clatter that accompanied the loading and preparation of weapons. Around the campfires, talk was mostly the bluster of men loudly and eagerly boasting of how they were going to best the Yankee invaders. "How dare they think they can just march into Virginia?! They'll never make it up the ridge! They're as good as whipped. By night, we'll be back in Fredericksburg. Today Fredericksburg, next week Washington!"

He felt the excitement course through his veins. How long had he waited for this moment while guarding the cowards at Libby Prison while others carried the fight? Well, now it was time for Darius Morgan to take the fight to the enemy and show them what he could really do. No more sitting around wishing he were somewhere else – anywhere else. No more sitting around writing letters home with nothing really to say. No more endless banter from other soldiers as bored as he but, he knew, far less skilled at fighting. Now, he would show both his officers and the Yankees what he was really made of. And, after that, he was certain to be made not only an officer again but a captain by the time the army reached Washington. But enough of such hopes. For now, it was just time to kill as many Yankees as he could in a single morning. Yes, for the moment, that was good enough!

It seemed like an eternity as he awaited the order to open fire. "What are they waiting for? Why don't they come?" The guns behind him remained silent. He was tempted to fire his rifle and begin the battle himself. It was already loaded and aimed at the near end of the little foot bridge. They would have to cross here. Generals Lee and

Jackson would never allow the Federals to lay more pontoon bridges across the river or makeshift bridges across the race. Yes, it was all going to happen right at the spot where his gun was trained. He briefly removed his finger from the trigger. His hand was beginning to cramp. He flexed the fingers on his right hand to relieve the cramping but did not lay down the gun. When the signal came, he was going to take the first shot and draw the first Yankee blood. Hell! What are they waiting for?!

Bright flashes appeared through the mist – visible before the thunder from Burnside's cannons reached the heights. At last! Still the order to fire did not come. Darius watched with fascination as shells exploded on the ridge, making craters but failing to reach the heights. A slight breeze from the north soon brought blue, acrid-smelling smoke. Presently, Lee's guns began returning the fire. Finally! But still, no order. At least, for the first time since Manassas, he was able to watch Yankees being shot at – and dying!

The fog began to lift, replaced with a smoky haze. Darius could now see the enemy marching through the town and beginning to form a line of battle on the far side of the millrace. All that was needed now was for the first of the bridges to be successfully laid. At the foot bridge, soldiers crowded and shoved each other trying to be the first across. Fools!

"Commence firing!" It had all come finally to this. The weeks and months of drilling, the endless boring hours of guarding prisoners at Libby with nothing to do in his off-hours, the marching followed by more drilling and more inspections. Darius focused his attention on the bridge. He peered down the barrel of the rifle into the ranks and squeezed the trigger. He would have preferred to look straight into the man's face as he shot and watched him fall. That would have to wait though. The distance was too great and so many were firing at once. For now, all he could do was fire into the ranks, hope he had killed a man, crouch behind the wall, reload, and fire again.

The engineers managed to lay a few small temporary bridges across the race. Soldiers swarmed across and tried to form ranks on the near side. Others ran headlong into the race and attempted to splash through it. As they tried to clamber out the other side, many were shot dead and fell back onto their comrades still trying to cross. One would fall, it seemed to Darius, and two more would take his place. There were far more than he could ever have imagined, but no mind. Once in a while, someone among them would manage to get off a clean shot and a soldier standing behind the wall would fall. Darius, however, was not concerned. After all, dying was for others. He was convinced that the Yankees would never reach the heights. The more of them that could be killed here, the better. Reload, fire! Reload, fire! "Keep coming, bastards! Keep coming!"

****

Jonas stood over the kitchen range warming his hands. He had just returned from doing morning chores at the barn and Em had to gently push him aside so that she could begin cooking their breakfast. "This one is going to be bad," he commented as he moved to the kitchen window and gazed outside. "I'd say there's a good two inches and it hasn't been snowing more than probably an hour or so. Combine that with the wind and it's going to be wicked. I ran a rope line to the barn so I can find my way back and forth if it comes to that.

Em walked to him and tapped his shoulder to get his attention. I worry about Ellie when she is out in weather like this," she sighed. "What if it snows heavily as she's heading home and she gets lost? Oh, dear! She could freeze

94

to death! I wish she hadn't gone this morning. How are you coming along with Henry's Christmas gift? Today is December 13 already. I need to send our package soon to get it to him."

"She'll be fine. Ellie's a smart lady. I'm sure she'll let the scholars out and come home before it gets worse. You mustn't worry yourself so, Em. It's not good for you. And yes, Henry's pipe is almost done. I'll have it finished today." He seated himself in the rocker, leaned forward, and resumed work on the pipe he was carving. He was careful that all of the shavings went into the firewood box after being teased earlier about getting some on Em's freshly swept floor. He had obtained some fine briar from one of the vendors who supplied special woods for the cabinet shop. The new pipe, along with some imported English tobacco, should make a splendid gift. "Have you and Ellie finished his vest and gloves?"

"Oh! I almost forgot to tell you," he continued before she had a chance to answer, "Will Britt came into the shop yesterday to check on the new kitchen table and chairs that he commissioned me to build for his mother. They're almost done too – just need a couple more coats of wax. She misses Thomas so much. Will thought that if they could have their Christmas dinner around a different table than the one they used to gather around, it might make it a little easier for them all. I hope it will.

"Will seems to be in pretty good spirits. He has asked me to make him a new leg and I need to start working on that soon. I want to make a really nice one."

The smell of fresh bacon filled the kitchen. Jonas missed the sizzle but knew exactly what it would sound like and nearly salivated in anticipation. "He has a lady friend."

"How nice for him. He's such a fine young man. Who is she?" Em turned away from tending the bacon and laid down her spatula in order to sign to Jonas."

"Mary Alice Weinberg's niece, Sarah. He's been courting her since October and seems quite smitten with her."

"Mary Alice hasn't told me about that. What does she think?"

"Maybe she didn't think it was her place." He continued carving. "Anyhow, she really likes Will and makes a big fuss over him when he comes to visit at their house. She is really proud of his war service and thinks he will make a fine husband for Sarah."

"Husband? Has he proposed?"

"Not yet, but I think he will," Jonas smiled. "By the way, I think you had better turn the bacon."

"I can't help worrying about her?"

"Sarah?"

"No. About Ellie. The snow could come quickly. It would be so dreadful if something happened to her. I get so afraid when she goes out alone – especially after dark or in bad weather. So many things could happen to her. Remember last winter when Elmer Thompson went out to check on his cattle and never came home and he froze to death and they didn't find his body until the snow melted? Henry would never forgive me for letting her go to school! Oh, dear!"

"She's not going to get lost, Em," Jonas tried to reassure her, wishing their conversation had stayed with Will and Sarah's budding romance. "If it gets too bad, she'll likely find somewhere to stay in town. And if something *were* to happen to her, no one, including Henry,

96

would blame *you*. You didn't let her go. She went on her own."

Jonas immediately regretted adding the last part. He had suddenly admitted to the possibility, however slight, that something *could* happen.

"Then I would blame *myself*," Em continued. "I would always blame *myself*."

Jonas was running out of assurances. He couldn't decide if he was angrier at Em for constantly coming up with new worries or with himself for not being able to reassure her. "You could always blame *me*. I didn't stop her either. Or, then again, just blame yourself that you didn't stop the *snow*. That would have been about as easy as stopping Ellie, maybe easier."

"Now you're making jokes about it, Jonas, and I don't think it's very funny. Poor Ellie could freeze out there and you're making *jokes*. Shame on you! She's your own sister and you're making jokes."

Again, Jonas regretted his comment, not because of what he had said – he felt that it was accurate – but because of the effect it had on Em. She was near tears. He knew that, whatever he or others might think about her fears, to *her*, they were as genuine as dawn and dusk. He got up from his chair and gave her a brotherly embrace. "She'll be fine, Em. God won't let anything happen to her. I promise."

"Promise?"

"With all my heart. I promise you."

Em and Jonas had finished their breakfast and were lingering over their coffee at the kitchen table when Ellie walked in. "I think I'm starting to despise winter," she announced.

"Oh, Ellie!" Em exclaimed. "I'm so glad you are home safe and sound. We were so worried about you! Weren't we worried, Jonas?" she signed as she spoke.

"*You* were worried," Jonas corrected her. "I told you she'd be fine."

Jonas and Ellie shared a knowing glance. "Ellie, I think you live in the wrong part of the world for seven months out of the year."

"Jonas Hancock, you are such a tease. Who taught you to talk to your sister like that?"

"My sister," he grinned. "And I don't mean Rose. Want some coffee? It's on the stove. Help yourself."

"Just for being so mean, I won't show you the letter from Henry that I picked up at the post before I came home. I'll just show to it Em and you can guess what's in it. That will teach you!"

"It'll take more than that," he muttered as he reached for his coffee. It'll take a heap more than that." For once, Jonas was actually looking forward to winter with its promise of snow instead of rain and thunderstorms. It might be cold, and there would be shoveling to do, but he had slept better these past couple of weeks than at any time since that awful day at Shiloh. Even the long hours of darkness didn't bother him since he enjoyed passing the evenings with Em and Ellie. If only Henry could be here too; it would be nearly perfect.

Camp in Mississippi
November 26, 1862

Dearest Em, Ellie, and Jonas,

I hope this letter finds you all well and getting along. Well, it's the beginning of

winter or, I am told, as close as we are likely to have for winter in Mississippi. Has it snowed yet at home? There seems not much to do here and each day is pretty much the same as the one before. Breakfast, morning roll call, drilling, our noon meal, some more drilling, policing and tidying up the camp, cleaning our weapons even if they haven't been used and most likely won't be until spring. Then we have evening roll call. I feel as many do here: that our time this fall could have been much more productively spent at home harvesting crops and laying in food and supplies for winter. Of course though, if the whole army was to do so, the Rebels would easily move in and take back all of the ground that we have fought for. So there is really no choice but to see this thing through and hopefully end it for good next summer or next fall.

In order to occupy our evenings and hopefully do some good, Sgt. Atlee and I have started a little school here in my tent. I was chosen to be the headmaster since I outrank him. There are several in the company who can neither read nor write and have depended on others to write letters home for them and to read to them the ones that they receive. We have determined to help them out by teaching them. We meet three or four nights a week for an hour or so after supper and on Sunday afternoons. They all seem quite earnest in their studies and more eager to learn than I was when I was a boy.

One student is a young black man who was a slave on a plantation near Shiloh and joined us shortly after that battle. He is not a soldier as he is much too young. I guess him to be about fourteen or so but even he does not know for sure how old he is. He has helped out the men in the company running errands and generally helping with chores. Though some of the company question my teaching him, most readily accept it, especially those in our little class. He is quite bright and gentlemanly. His given name is Amos but says he prefers to be called Theodore because it sounds more distinguished. He has taken the last name of Lincoln out of respect for our President. If I were to give marks, which I don't, he might well be at the top of the class. I think he will do quite well for himself once this whole thing is over and he is free to go wherever he wants.

Our Bibles are the only books that we have to teach from. We have only two slates and a small amount of chalk that, I am ashamed to say, was taken from a local schoolhouse by one of our foraging parties and brought to us. If you could somehow send a few more slates and perhaps some grammar books or spellers it would be really helpful. Have Em give you the money for them from our farm account or from what I have sent home.

That's all that I have for now. It's time for 'school.' Take care of each other.

As always, Henry.

****

Joshua stood transfixed, staring at the heights. Lee's guns continued to shower death upon ranks attempting to form up for the charge. The air was full of haze and reeked of the acrid smell of smoke and powder. His eyes began to itch and burn. It was getting harder to breathe. And the noise, the awful noise! Shouting, shrieking, crackling, popping, and the thunder!

The heights appeared to be on fire with the flash of hundreds of rifle muzzles. More makeshift bridges crossed the race. More men streamed across them and charged up the ridge into the fire. Charge, fire! Crouch down to reload. Charge, fire! Crouch down again. And on it went. The further the ranks advanced, the thinner they became, and the more were left behind for the next wave to trample over. Everywhere he looked were dropped rifles, dropped flags, men attempting to crawl, and those who would never move again. Some, but so few, appeared to have made it near the top but could go no further. Again, Joshua wanted to be somewhere else – anywhere else. But, for whatever reason, this was where God had put him. Time to do His work. He stepped forward and began to make his way toward the ridge.

The first man he reached was still moving but would never leave the field. Joshua kneeled over him and looked into the fading eyes. "Father, take my confession," came the raspy voice. "I have not confessed since …." The voice was labored and weak."

Joshua hesitated momentarily. He had never taken a Catholic confession but knew immediately what to do and say. First of all, God knew he wasn't a priest and would not care. The young man would never know the difference. And he knew the words. He had heard them over and over at the hospital. It was time. "Yes, my son … I forgive you." He made the sign of the cross, swept his hand gently over the unseeing eyes and, without getting to his feet, moved on. Yes, God would understand, and He would be pleased.

For the next man, it was too late. There was no final comfort to be provided. The best that he could do was to take a young hand into his own. "Bless you. Sleep in peace. May the Lord be with you always." He looked down at his own hand as he moved it away and noticed blood on his wrist, trickling from under his sleeve. Funny, he hadn't felt anything. He laid the young man's hand over his chest, got to his hands and knees, and moved on. It wasn't far. There was little ground now between them. Joshua felt that he could probably have crossed the entire width of the ridge without touching the ground.

He nearly lost hope of finding anyone whom he could really help. He seemed able to save neither lives nor souls. The dead had already gone to meet their maker. The wounded, it seemed, were about to make their final journey and his guidance would make no difference in how their last moments were spent. They had already made all of the choices they could in their lives. It was now up to a merciful God to decide where they would spend eternity. Hopefully, most had found Christ. Their souls, he hoped, would leave this Hell, which had defined the end of their time on earth, and ascend to Heaven. He had attended to probably ten men, maybe more. He had lost count and had nearly despaired of making a difference to any of them when a strong voice called to him from behind. "Help me," the voice pleaded. "I can't move my leg."

Joshua got down on his stomach and crawled across the chilled ground to where the corporal was lying. He was surprised. The man looked older than most here. His face was lined with years of living. His hair, along with his beard and mustache, had long since turned from the flaming red of his youth to the salt and pepper of middle age. Most men of such age, if they were here at all, were the generals standing behind the lines, giving orders for the younger men to carry out. "I'm here!" Joshua shouted as he crawled near. "Stay down."

"What is a man your age doing here?" Joshua asked gently. He regretted the question immediately, thinking it indelicate. Then again, there was nothing delicate here this morning.

"My wife died five years ago and my son died at Bull Run. I had to come."

"Well, I am going to get you out of here," Joshua told him, not really knowing how, or if, he could actually do it. "I am going to get you out and then you need to go home. He looked around for something – anything – to use for a splint. He could tell that the bone was splintered just below the knee. Unable to find anything useful, he soon gave up. "This is going to hurt. Put your arm around my neck and hold on. I need to get you over my shoulder." Slowly, and with effort, Joshua began to stand – wanting to get up only far enough to walk. No sense in being a better target than necessary. "Where are you from?" he asked the corporal, wanting to take his mind off of the wound.

"Boston," the man answered. "I was a dock worker. I came there from Ireland."

"God, please let me get him out of here," Joshua prayed silently as he nearly tripped over a corpse "Let me get him out of here. Let me save just one life today."

To Joshua's amazement, his legs grew stronger with each step. His spirits rose. The more he focused on the task at hand, the less he felt shaken by all that was going on around him. His steps became easier and quicker. There would be no getting the corporal back to safety beyond the race. The bridges still there were dangerous and jammed with men trying to cross and join the fight. After some searching, he found a downed log and laid the man behind it out of sight from the ridge. "I too am from Boston," he told him, remembering later that he had never asked the old man his name. "Go home. Perhaps we'll meet again someday." He patted the man on the shoulder and headed back toward the fight.

****

To Darius' best count, he had killed a dozen or so men and the morning was barely halfway through. Satisfying, but there was more yet to do. Up to now, he had focused his fire on those among the enemy who were the most threatening – those attempting to charge up the ridge with rifles and bayonets. For sport now, he aimed at a young man who had managed to get across the race and was running up the ridge carrying the flag of a New York regiment. He squeezed the trigger and watched with pleasure as both flag and soldier fell to the ground. The man tried briefly to get up but soon fell back and was still. He had also been watching, for a while and with some wonder, another man. This man also provided no threat as he moved among the dead and dying. He would kneel over a fallen soldier, talk briefly, perhaps provide some water or other comfort, and crawl on his hands and knees to another. Darius had even seen the man lift another man onto his shoulders, carry him back toward the race, and then head back to the ridge and again move among the dead and wounded. From his plain frock coat, devoid of any insignias, the man appeared to be a chaplain. "Time to meet your God." He squeezed the trigger but this time he did not take the time to see whether or not his shot had hit its mark. Instead, he ducked back behind the wall to reload.

****

Joshua felt a twinge in his shoulder but paid it little attention. It was little more than an annoyance – more painful than a bee sting yet not enough to distract him from the task at hand. He continued moving among the fallen, offering words of comfort to those whom he hoped could hear him, and saying a brief prayer over those whom he knew could not. Not really knowing why, other than because of simple curiosity, he pulled his watch from his vest pocket and opened it. 10:30. He replaced the watch and moved on.

Darius watched the young boy beside him drop his rifle and tumble awkwardly over the wall, screaming in pain as he went. The rifle clattered against the stone wall. The boy, however, began to roll down the hill and stopped silently after about two yards. His terror-filled eyes looked back toward the wall and the rifle. Darius watched a widening red stain appear on the boy's left shoulder.

The wound, Darius knew, was not, of itself, mortal. But the boy now had no cover. At any second another shot fired from the blue tide could spell the boy's end. "Stay down," he shouted, looking into the boy's face, "but crawl back!" There was no response. "Crawl!" he shouted again. "Now!" But still the boy did not move except to put his right hand over the damaged shoulder. Instead, he simply stayed where he was and gazed at the wall.

Darius again crouched behind the wall. He dropped another ball into the barrel of his Enfield, and placed a fresh percussion cap into the nipple. Again ready to fire, he cautiously raised himself above the wall and searched for a target. There were plenty. As quickly as men fell from the ranks, they were replaced by even more. The new surge simply stepped over them as so much carpet in a relentless attempt to reach the wall. Darius picked out a lieutenant who charged up the hill with his sword in one hand and a revolver in the other, shouting encouragement to the men behind him. "Goodbye, Yank," he muttered, and squeezed the trigger. Lieutenant, sword, and pistol pitched backward together as the ball found its mark.

This time, Darius did not crouch behind the wall to reload. The boy still lay where he had fallen, remarkably not yet struck by additional bullets. Darius shouted again but had decided by now that the boy was too paralyzed by fear to move on his own and would likely lie where he was until the next bullet killed him. He laid down his rifle, took a deep breath, and crawled over the wall toward the boy. "You selfish little son of a bitch. We're out here trying to kill Yanks and you're just going to lie there and let them kill *you*. Well, I'm not gonna let you do it. We need you and everyone else here shooting back at them.

Em had retired for the night. Ellie and Jonas sat alone in the kitchen, she at the table, Jonas in his rocker near the stove, smoking his pipe. Presently, Ellie crept quietly up the stairs and looked in on Em. Back downstairs, she moved her chair closer to Jonas' and said softly, "I think we need to let Henry know about Em's constant worrying. I don't want to upset him but he *is* her husband. I think he needs to know."

Jonas looked up. "Yes."

106

"I'll write him then."

"Yes."

Thayer, Minnesota
December 13, 1862

Dearest Brother,
I write you this letter in the strictest of
confidence. I have debated it in my
mind, for I wish not to upset you in any
way, but have decided that it is best
that you know. Of course I have not
read any of Em's letters to you before
she sends them but I imagine that she
attempts to put on a brave front for
you.

The truth is that Em worries
almost constantly to an extreme that I
fear may actually do harm to her
health. She frets daily for your safety
both for your sake and for her own
should something happen to you. She
speaks often of wondering how she will
able to care for you if you come home
crippled as so many have or of how she
will be able to carry on if you are
killed. She fears for Jonas when he is
out alone that he would not be able to
hear should he come into danger or
that he would not hear her if she were
to need to call him for help. She fears

that we should come on hard times if the animals were to die or the crops fail. She fears for the people of our town lest some plague or storm or fire may beset us all.

Jonas and I try our best to provide her comfort and to reassure her that all is well and is very likely to remain so but our efforts at times seem so futile. Our pastor seeks to calm her fears by letting her know that God is with us but she asks him why God allows terrible things to still happen to people who trust and believe in him. He seems to have no answer that will satisfy her. She seems well for a time after he counsels her but then shortly becomes agitated again.

I am hopeful that when you return home safely and well that her fears will pass but I wonder from time to time if such a state of mind will continue to afflict her for the rest of her life.

Again, it is not my intention to put upon you an extra burden in addition to what you already carry for being away from home and in harm's way but feel that what I have told you is something that you need to know. You must, I think, in your letters home, constantly reassure her and refrain from sharing those things that she may find upsetting. If you must share, you may send letters addressed only to Jonas and myself. If she picks up the mail in town, we will ask the postmaster to neither give her those letters nor to tell her that they arrived. In this way, we can read the letters first and then decide whether or not to share them with her. It may sound devious but I think it best. It is up to you to decide whether or not you agree.

Other than what I have just shared all is well here. We are healthy and comfortable. The weather has been nice and we are well-fixed for supplies with plenty of food on hand and plenty of wood for the stove.

David has been so good to help us with crops and chores. Jonas helps him some but he refuses to accept when we attempt to pay him for larger jobs that he does here at the farm. We are truly blessed to have him and Mary Alice for neighbors. We all send our love and prayers.

I will write again soon.

All of my sisterly love, Ellie

****

The stars were out again but shone only dimly through the smoke that still hung in the bitter air. Burnside had asked, and Lee had generously agreed, for a ceasefire to allow the Federals to come onto the ridge and retrieve their dead and wounded. The only condition was that no guns be brought. Armed Confederate soldiers still lined the stone wall lest an attempt be made to break the fragile truce and take the heights. Darius was just as happy to not be among them. What was the point of sitting out in the cold watching Yankees while not being allowed to shoot them? Instead, he sat in his tent with a blanket draped over his shoulders. He began writing a letter home.

Fredericksburg, Virginia

December 13, 1862

Dear Father,

Today our army achieved a most glorious victory over the Yankee invaders. The action began with our artillery throwing shell after shell into the enemy ranks as they tried vainly to assemble at the foot of Marye's Heights. Even before we were allowed to begin firing our rifles, our ears were treated to the shrieks and screams of the invaders as our cannons continued to cut them down. Once they began to advance on our position, they were greeted by our unceasing fire. Through the smoke, we were able to watch them walking and tripping over their own dead and wounded as they sought to move on us. Such fools they are that they think that they can just march into our country and destroy our homes and crops and unleash our slaves upon us! They should know that we will never allow such a thing to happen. I think George Washington would have been proud of the way we defended his boyhood home from being despoiled under the boots worn by boors and scum. I am pleased to say that I did my part and drew as much Yankee blood as any man here.

I sit and listen now to the moaning and groaning of the Yankee wounded that we have left scattered about the ridge. The only better sound that I can think of would be the silence that would come if they all should die.

We do not know if they will try to come again tomorrow or if they will turn and run back toward Washington. It is all the same to me. If they come, we will cut them down as we did today. If they run, we will pursue them and kill them as they attempt to flee.

That is all for now. I will write you again when I find the opportunity.

Darius.

****

Joshua sat on a cot in what had been a schoolhouse but was now a hospital on the north edge of town near the river. He had been offered laudanum for the pain but chose the hard decision not to take it. The pain he could handle. The dilemma was whether to remain lucid or to accept an induced fog that would provide a temporary respite from the awful images of the day. In the end, he had decided to remain lucid and began writing a letter home.

Fredericksburg, Virginia

December 13, 1862

Dear Father and Mother,

Today, I witnessed an event so horrible that, if I live to be an old man, I wish never to see or hear of it again. However, I fear that, before this awful war is over, it will be repeated again and again whether I shall be a part of it or not. I know in my heart that it is God's will that I should be here in order to provide comfort and guidance to those in the army. However, I only wish ...

****

Lt. Colonel W. Arnold Harkness, New York Volunteer Infantry sat in his tent and began to write an after-action report of the events of the day. It had to be done now. Though the images were painful, it was important that this be done while his memory was still accurate and before the passage of time began to blur the vital details. After recording to the best of his knowledge the troop movements, the orders given and received, and the casualties, he added a concluding paragraph:

"While watching the action and giving orders to the officers and men under my command, I witnessed the most heroic actions by one who is officially not an officer in the army but is assigned the rank of captain by virtue of his being a chaplain. His name, I have learned, is Joshua Gibbons. Without regard to his own life or personal safety, Chaplain Gibbons ministered to fallen soldiers while under direct fire from the enemy. His attempts to provide a last bit of comfort to dying men on the field were an inspiration to all of us who observed him. I personally observed Chaplain Gibbons kneeling over and praying with as many as forty men during the course of the morning and watched him carry on his own back at least three wounded soldiers from the field. Having visited the hospital and talking with the surgeon who treated him, I learned that Chaplain Gibbons suffered four separate, painful, but mercifully not lethal, gunshots to his right thigh, his left shoulder, his left forearm, and left upper arm. In light of these heroic actions, I wish to recommend that Chaplain Joshua Gibbons be awarded the Congressional Medal of Honor."

CHAPTER VI

The moon was nearly at its smallest. Greyish white clouds drifted lazily across the blue-black night sky, mostly eclipsing the stars. Stark shivered slightly. He wrapped his arms around himself as he stood near the corner of the cotton barn and waited for the lights to go out in the house. He had been much colder back in Indiana but this was still uncomfortable. He would have much preferred to spend the evening sitting by the stove in his quarters but this needed to be done. He had fortified himself with a fair amount of bourbon. He now wanted more but knew that he had to keep a clear head for the next few hours. There would be time to drink when the business was finished. He also wanted to smoke but didn't want the light of a cigar to give him away.

There were two horses – one saddled and one with only a bridle. The saddled horse was his own, the same one he would ride among the fields during cotton-growing season. The burlap bag that hung from the saddle horn held only a cotton knife. The other horse, a jet-black stallion, was Andrew Morgan's pride and joy. The horse had been a birthday gift from Annabelle – the last gift she had given him before she passed away. When pressured to sell the horse to the Confederate Army, Andrew had nearly agreed but, at the last minute, decided against it. Instead, he had called in some favors from friends in Milledgeville. In the end, he had been allowed to keep the horse after promising that the fine foals to be sired would be available as soon as they were old enough. It was no trouble to keep the horses quiet as they both knew him and were well-trained.

Stark grew nervous as he waited and simply wanted to have it done. Part of him hoped that Toby had told some others that he planned to run off. That would make the plan much more effective. At the same time, if others came along, there would be problems. He decided to watch from around the corner of the barn. If he saw that Toby was not alone, he would simply walk away and take the horses back to the stable. It would be as if the thing had never happened – unless Andrew somehow caught wind of it. He wanted a drink.

The light in the window of the library seemed to stay on forever. What was the man doing? It was nearly 10:30. Normally, he would have retired an hour ago. Had he learned of the plan? Was he keeping the lights on purposely? What if he wasn't in the house? What if he was at the stable checking on the prize stallion King William? What if he was watching from the shadows ready to catch both him and Toby? Stark's hands began to twitch and shake. It was cold but his palms were sweating. Eleven o'clock now – still the lights were on. No Toby. Fifteen more minutes – if nothing happened, it was off. But what then?

****

Toby did not have a bed of his own. The family to whom Andrew had sent him had five children and another on the way. Even if he had wanted to share a bunk with one of the boys, there were none available. His 'bed' was a ragged blanket on the dirt floor. At least it was near the fireplace. He kept mostly warm until the embers faded, as they now were beginning to do. Earlier, but after the family was asleep, he had remained wide awake – excited at the prospect of his upcoming escape and his resulting freedom. Now he was fighting sleep. He was becoming dismayed that he might doze off and miss this one chance. Trying to stay awake, he would periodically get up, quietly open the door, and step out into the cold. Each time, he would look toward the house to see if the lights were still on. Disappointed that they were, he would go back inside and sit by the hearth. He didn't have a watch and wouldn't have known how to tell time anyway but his internal clock told him that it was growing late. What if Master Morgan had somehow found out? If so, wouldn't someone have already come for him? Yet the thought lingered. What if they were waiting to see if he tried to leave? What if Stark had changed his mind about helping? What if this was all a trap or a cruel prank? What if it was a test of his 'loyalty?' He thought about calling it off but when he stepped out the next time, the house was dark. The decision had been made for him. There was no going back. He carefully closed the door behind him and headed for the cotton barn. God, it was cold!

****

Stark had given up. He prepared to return the horses to the stable but glanced once more toward the house. He was relieved to see the library window now dark. Soon, a light should appear upstairs in the bedroom and then go out. When that happened, it would be time. Would Toby come? Would he be alone?

****

Andrew sat in a chair near the fireplace. The house was as comfortable as could be expected considering how cold it was outside. Still, it was drafty and chilly. He shivered slightly, pulled his shawl around him and continued reading. He glanced at the calendar – December 13. In less than two weeks, it would be Christmas 'or such.' When Annabelle was alive, Christmas had always been special. The house was gaily decorated with a floor-to-ceiling tree in the front parlor. With an abundance of Austrian Pines from which to choose, he had always enjoyed his outing to pick the greenest, fullest, and shapeliest one he could find. Annabelle, with the help of the house staff, always decorated it with her special touch. She also added garlands and other greenery, candles, and glass balls about the house. Their home was truly festive. Friends called in informally and there was singing around the piano, tasty holiday treats, and fine liquor. There were dinner parties to host and attend. Now, with the war and with Annabelle gone, there was none of it. Christmas was become something to be endured rather than enjoyed.

He no longer hosted parties. Annabelle had always done the planning and overseen the preparations. He didn't know how to do it and cared little without her here to share it with him. He still received invitations to attend neighbors' parties but declined them all. The food, the cigars, and the brandy no longer tasted as good. The conversation always came back to the war. He now found such affairs boring and depressing. It was easier and more pleasant to simply stay home.

The one tradition that Andrew kept was one that he had always enjoyed but which never ceased to draw criticism from neighbors and Darius. Well, Darius wasn't here now and the neighbors could like it or not. He assumed that Stark would find it equally distasteful but that didn't concern him. Stark was a tool – a useful tool in keeping the plantation running but still, just a tool. A few days before Christmas each year, Andrew would 'host' an all-day party for the slaves. There was no liquor but he would provide a spread that included some of the best hams from the smokehouse, cakes bought from a baker in Milledgeville, sweet potatoes, and a small gift for each of the children. There was one more thing that he now did each year since Annabelle's death. It was this that drew the most ire of all from neighbors and his son. It was to grant freedom to one slave. Normally, the slave would end up staying at Pine Hill with his family and work for either a wage or a small share of the cotton crop. Life changed little for him except that he was guaranteed not to be sold, could come and go as he pleased with his freedman's papers, and was not required to take orders from the overseer. It was always hard to choose who was most deserving of this extraordinary gift. This, and there was little money for even a modest wage. Every spare penny was needed. Because of this, Andrew had chosen someone who had no attachments at the plantation. The newly freed slave would probably take his papers and leave. That someone was the newest addition to the plantation – the young slave called Toby.

Andrew looked up as the clock struck eleven. "God bless us, everyone." He closed the book and laid it on the lamp table. To his surprise, he had stayed up long past his usual bedtime. The fire was down to embers now. He took the poker and knocked down the last remnants of log. He replaced the screen to prevent sparks from igniting the carpet, picked up the lamp, and headed upstairs. As he reached the landing, he peered out through the small oval window into the darkness. He caught a faint glimpse of a figure near the cotton barn but paid it little attention. "Probably that damned Stark returning from one of his trips to the house in Milledgeville." He continued up the stairs to bed.

****

"Did you come alone?" Stark heard a rustling in some dry leaves around the corner of the barn.

"Yessuh."

"Did you tell anyone?"

"Nosuh."

Satisfied that the young man was telling the truth, Stark stepped from around the corner of the barn leading the two horses. "Good. We need to be on our way. We need to make as much distance as possible before daylight."

"Yessuh."

Stark helped him to mount King William. The horse jumped a little but was quickly calmed by Stark's voice and touch. He had handled and even exercised him when Andrew was either ill or not in the notion. "I need to tie your hands," he told the young man matter-of-factly. "If there are any slave hunters about, I will simply tell them that you have tried to run off and that I am taking you back. They will trust me. That will be the end of it and we will go on our way."

"Yessuh."

Stark tied the young man's hands, placed a rope loosely around his neck, and secured the other end to the horse's bridle. "That should do it. Best be on our way." With Stark in the lead and holding a rope tied to King William's bridle, they left the shelter of the cotton barn and headed across a small clearing and into the edge of the forest.

"How long?" Toby asked after a while.

"Not long," Stark answered. "Don't talk anymore. If anyone's about, we don't want them to hear us."

The forest was dense. There was no trail and Stark carefully avoided any roads. Pine needles continually scratched his face and brushed against his clothing. A branch knocked off his hat. He thought about dismounting to retrieve it but decided against it. Damn, it was cold!

About half a mile from the house, they emerged from the forest and came upon the small stream. The water was icy but was frozen only with a thin crust that was little more than frost. In many places, it was not frozen at all and continued to flow. Following the stream would allow him to avoid the annoying branches. Stark knew the stream. He was aware that the sand in the streambed would

119

sometimes shift, creating holes deep enough to swallow a man or even a horse. To avoid such a calamity, he had scouted the stream three days ago in broad daylight. "We'll follow the stream for a while," he said quietly. "If anyone sends dogs, they won't be able to follow the scent."

The mere mention of dogs sent Toby into a near panic but he tried his best not to let it show. He said nothing, wanting to let Stark know that he trusted him completely. As a child he had seen first-hand what dogs could do to a man. His uncle had tried to run off and had been brought back to the plantation across the back of a horse, mauled and barely breathing. The man had lasted only moments after being paraded in front of an assembled group of field hands and their wives and children

****

It had snowed all day. The wind-driven snow had made it impossible to see the barn from the house. Now it was long-since dark. Jonas could not see them but knew that there were drifts six to seven feet high against the house and other buildings. Had he been able to hear it, he would have noted both the rattling of the window panes and the haunting howl of a pack of gray wolves that had gathered in a copse of trees probably fifty or so yards away.

It was nearly ten o'clock. Em and Ellie had retired upstairs an hour earlier. He sat by the stove and put the finishing touches to Henry's pipe while he smoked his own. Ellie certainly would not have classes tomorrow. The snow was a hardship but he had enjoyed spending an entire day in the kitchen with his sister and his sister-in-law.

Presently, the stair door opened and Ellie emerged wearing a woolen nightgown and wrapped in a heavy blanket. "What keeps you awake at this time of night?" Jonas asked.

"Those letters my scholars wrote to President Lincoln," she lied. "I just can't put them out of my mind. When do you think that this terrible thing will be over?"

"I hope and pray that it will be soon," he answered, "but I'm afraid that it will likely go on for some time yet. From what I read, neither side seems to be gaining a real advantage. It just goes on and on with more lives lost every day. War is such a waste!"

"I agree. I just wish it could be done."

"We all do. And I suspect that most on the other side feel exactly the same way."

The stair door opened again and Em appeared. "You too?" Jonas asked her. What is really going on here?"

"Nothing," they signed simultaneously.

"I think I know." Jonas got up and opened the door to the cellar stairway. He emerged with a shotgun, loaded it, and placed it near the door. "Feel better now? Since we all appear to be awake anyhow, why don't you put on a pot of coffee and I'll read to us."

Friends and family always enjoyed Jonas' reading aloud. Whether he was delivering a sermon in the absence of the pastor or reading poetry, he always seemed to have a special touch that made everything come alive. His mellow reading tone was matched only by the wonderful tenor voice that made his singing a joy to hear. "Em, why don't you choose something?" He returned to his chair by the stove. Em disappeared and returned shortly with her selection. "Appropriate choice," he noted. "Marley was dead: to begin with. There is no doubt whatever about that. The register of his burial was signed by the clergyman, the clerk, the undertaker, and the chief mourner. Scrooge signed it: and Scrooge's name was good ...."

They rode upstream for about another half an hour. Stark then brought them up the opposite bank at a small ford. "That should be far enough," he announced. He preferred riding in the stream without the branches and needles but knew he had to get the horses out of the icy water. He valued his own horse but was more concerned that King William not come up lame.

They left the stream and continued through the woods until they reached a narrow, partly overgrown lane. It led only to a barn that had been abandoned when the house burned some years ago, so Stark knew that he was unlikely to encounter anyone. At night and with the cold, he felt particularly safe.

As they approached the barn, the little moonlight there was threw ghostly shadows against the reddish-grey, weathered boards. Stark dismounted and checked that the fence was solid before tying both horses to it. That done, he walked to one of the large doors through which had passed countless wagons full of hay and grain. The hinges were loose and rusted. That made it harder to open the door. The hinges emitted their first sound in years – a high-pitched screech. That was alright. There was no one to hear it except the two of them and the horses.

Stark stepped inside and looked around. The dim moonlight shone through numerous openings – cracks between the siding boards, holes in the roof where the shingles had long since blown away, and small doors that hung by only a single hinge. There was a musty smell. It was the kind of smell that accumulates through years of emptiness, not the pungent odor of an active barn housing horses or cattle. Hanging along one wall was an assortment of now useless harnesses and horse collars – the leather dusty, dry, and brittle. The small amount of hay and straw was long past usable for bedding. The few inhabitants of the barn were an owl, a couple of cats, and a few hapless rodents whose time would last only until the predators went in search of another meal. At least there weren't any skunks.

He went back outside and brought the horses into the barn. He led them to the edge of a feed bunk, returned to the door, and pulled it closed behind him. Next, he assisted Toby in dismounting from King William. The young man, who had rarely been on a horse, was more than eager to be off the beast. "Now we wait," Stark announced.

Toby had not spoken more than a few words during the entire journey. "My arms hurt. Kin you untie me now? I ain't gonna go anywhere."

"Soon," Stark answered. "Just something I need to do first." He turned, pulled the pistol from under his coat, and fired one shot through the young man's heart. Toby stumbled, fell backward, shuddered briefly, and was still. "Now," Stark muttered, as he reached to remove the ropes. He rolled the young man over with his boot to make sure that his shot had been fatal. Satisfied, he removed a flask from his saddlebag and allowed himself a much-wanted drink.

Sleep comes easily to a man without conscience or remorse. Stark figured that he had plenty of time to rest now. For the maximum effect on the slaves at Pine Hill, he did not wish to return with Toby's body until everyone was awake and well aware that both Toby and King William had gone missing during the night. He climbed a ladder to the loft, again opened the flask, and pulled his blanket around him to fight off the drafty chill.

CHAPTER VII

For the first time in days, Jonas awoke to bright sunshine. Normally, he would have awakened long before sunrise. Tonight, after staying up late reading to Em and Ellie, he had slept long and well. Though neither had said what they heard, he knew that it had to be wolves. With nothing to be done in the middle of the night, he had been able put it out of his mind. He had drifted off nearly as soon as he pulled the blankets over himself. It was true that he could have stepped out of the door and fired off the shotgun. But all that would have done was temporarily startle the wolves. They were hungry and would have soon returned. In the meantime, the livestock in the barns and sheds would have also become unnerved. The resulting commotion would have further drawn the predator's attention to them.

The sunlight poured in through the east window and shone directly in his face. After the snow ceased, the clouds had disappeared, replaced by a welcome, bright blue sky. Across the hall, both Em's and Ellie's doors were still closed. He suspected that, due to the shade on the west side of the house, they were both still sound asleep. He dressed and looked in the mirror. He supposed he should shave this morning – it had been three or four days – but decided to let it wait. There was more important business at hand. In the drawer of the night table was a revolver that he was now glad he had purchased before the war. Weapons were more difficult to come by now. He and Henry had always made a practice of carrying a holstered pistol when going to the fields, especially when venturing into the forest. This was still frontier, after all. Not all of the native creatures were friendly. If one they encountered happened to be rabid, it was prudent to have a gun. Satisfied that the pistol was properly loaded and ready, he buckled on the holster and headed down the stairs to the kitchen. He carried his boots in order not to wake the women

Once downstairs, he opened the firebox on the range and added wood to rekindle it for the day. There was still coffee from last night but, the fire having gone low overnight, it was not hot enough for his taste. He peered out of the kitchen window. The weight of the snow on the branches of the pine trees caused them to droop sadly but few, it appeared, had broken. The snow was drifted well up onto the window. The chicken house, he noticed, was nearly buried in a drift that he guessed had to be eight to ten feet high. There would be much shoveling to be done before he could open the doors to the shed that served as a horse barn and the other buildings where he had to do the morning chores. Still, first thing first.

The kitchen was beginning to warm some and the coffee was finally hot enough to drink. It felt good going down. He thought about fixing himself some ham and eggs but decided that, this too, would have to wait. He pulled on a woolen sweater over the one that he was already wearing. It would keep him warmer but the extra bulk made it harder to put on his coat. That accomplished, he added his hat and gloves. He could only open the outer door slightly against the snow but was able to get the shovel through just far enough to get a little of the snow out of the way. A little at a time, he worked away at the drift. He was able to get a little more on each shovelful until he finally freed the door barely enough to allow man and shotgun to squeeze through. God, it was cold!

Jonas' world, ever since the horrible day at Shiloh, had been totally silent. This morning, even had he been able to hear, the air was totally quiet. Not a thing stirred. Everything in his view was frozen in the moment. Struggling in nearly knee-deep snow, he trudged toward the shed to make sure that the wolves had not somehow gotten in.

It took him well over an hour. He had to examine the stables, the milking shed, the hog enclosure, the chicken house, the sheep shed, and the cattle shed. There were tracks everywhere; the pack had been busy and hungry. Fortunately, it appeared, they had also been frustrated. Though the shed doors, or what he could see of them above the snow drifts, were seriously scratched, it appeared that none had been breached. He could see tracks where the unsuccessful hunters had retreated toward a small copse of trees that stood isolated before the opening to the forest beyond. He looked back toward the house and thought about returning. He decided against it and began to follow the tracks.

****

Em stirred slightly and looked around her. Daylight now filled her room. She pulled the covers more tightly around her and suddenly realized that she should have been up hours ago. What time was it? How could she have slept so late? Then she remembered that it had been well after 2:00 a.m. when she and Ellie had returned to bed after sitting up listening to Jonas read *A Christmas Carol* in its entirety. She wondered if the other two were already up. She felt less guilty about oversleeping when she quietly peered into Ellie's room and noted that she was still sound asleep. It was at that moment that she heard the clock downstairs in the kitchen strike nine times. She crossed the hall to Jonas' room to see if he were still asleep also. Seeing that he wasn't, she presumed he was in the kitchen. "Good for him. The stove and the coffee will be hot and the kitchen will be warm." Jonas would be hungry but she could take her time. They normally did not eat breakfast until they were all together. Besides, Ellie needed her sleep.

She could take her time getting dressed although, with no heat in the bedrooms one didn't want to dawdle.

Once she was dressed, Em stood at the mirror and brushed her hair before putting it up. She was tall, nearly as tall as Henry. Her slim, youthful face – she was twenty-three, along with her soft auburn hair reaching nearly to her waist, made her look even taller than she actually was. Ellie, though they were about the same age, looked almost like a child when standing next to her.

She had nearly finished with her hair when she heard a loud knocking that seemed to come from the kitchen door. She assumed that Jonas would answer but then wondered why the knocking persisted. Ellie, who had been awakened by the knocking, appeared at her door still wearing her nightgown and wrapped in a blanket. The two looked at each other and asked, almost simultaneously, "Why isn't Jonas …? Of course," they remembered, "he doesn't hear it!"

"Em, Ellie!" they heard David shout. "Are you there?"

Em hurried down the stairs, followed closely by Ellie. She rushed to open the door noticing, only then, that Jonas was not in the kitchen. Quickly checking the parlor and the dining room, she returned to the kitchen. She glanced at the doorway where David was still standing and noticed that the shotgun was missing. "He's not here," she told them both.

"I guessed that," David told her. "I lost two sheep last night. There were wolves about. I came over to make sure that all of you were alright. On the way in, I noticed wolf paw prints around the buildings and then leading out into the forest. You two stay here and try not to worry. I don't know why he went but I'm going to go get him! He won't hear if there's danger."

David was an experienced cross-country skier and had used his skis to come to the house. He now debated whether to use them again or to use one of Jonas' or Henry's horses. He could make better time gliding across the top of the snow but the horse would be likely to sense danger before he did and alert him. Also, if Jonas were injured, he would need the horse to get him home. In the end, he chose the horse. He slung the rifle over his shoulder and headed to the stables with a snow shovel.

****

George and Harold were an unlikely pair. Half-brothers, they looked nothing alike. George was tall and slender with shaggy, dark brown hair but with tinges of gray. Weeks without shaving or being able to bathe made him look much older than his twenty-five years. Harold, five years older, was short and already balding. Weeks on the run with little to eat had caused him to lose much of his earlier bulk but he was still much the meatier of the two.

The two were sons of a small-time North Carolina tobacco grower from the eastern slopes of the Appalachian Mountains who supplemented his income by distilling homemade whiskey and by stealing hogs to be butchered and selling the meat to a cousin who owned a store in Raleigh. The little farm had only one slave. Neither Wilbur nor his sons had much interest in going to war to protect the fortunes of their more prosperous neighbors, the wealthy cotton planters in South Carolina or Georgia. Like many others, however, both George and Harold had found themselves caught up in the war fever that followed secession and the attack on Fort Sumter. They had willingly joined the army and marched off to meet the enemy at places they had never known existed – Manassas, Gaines Mill and Malvern Hill.

By Antietam, the war fever had broken. When the foray into Maryland ended in a retreat back into Virginia, the two took the opportunity to keep walking south. After stealing different shirts and trousers from the clothesline of an unsuspecting housewife, they discarded their uniforms and all other military gear with the exception of their weapons. Moving only at night and subsisting on what they could take from gardens, chicken yards, or smokehouses along the way, they continued to walk. The one thing that they resolutely refused to do was steal was a horse. If they were caught traveling on foot, someone would need to prove that they were deserters before meting out punishment. If they were caught stealing horses or riding stolen ones however, the consequences would be swift, certain, and final.

In the approximately three months since Antietam, George and Harold had made their way through Virginia, North Carolina, South Carolina, and deep into Georgia. Along the way, they carefully avoided any units of the Confederate Army moving north to join the fight. They had also kept to the less populated areas, avoiding cities like Richmond or Atlanta. They had no maps but only a general sense of where they were. Last night, they had seen a road sign pointing the way to Milledgeville, a few miles away. Moments later, they had stolen and cooked a chicken. Now they were hungry again – hungry, tired, and cold. They tramped along the banks of an icy stream, pushing their way through the pine branches that overhung the bank, scratching at their hands, faces, and clothing. Both would have liked to stop and rest but there was no place to lie down except on the half-frozen ground so they kept pushing through the branches, trying to avoid slipping and falling into the stream.

Finally, George, walking ahead, noticed an opening in the trees where a narrow lane led away from the stream's bank. They had been careful to avoid roads but the chance to move without having to constantly fight through the pine boughs was too good to pass up. Besides, the visibility wasn't bad and, if they sensed danger, it would be easy enough to duck back into the woods and disappear. Upon cursory examination, the lane appeared to be mostly abandoned and thus safer. What they failed to notice were two sets of hoof prints – fresh and from shod horses.

****

Stark stared blankly first at the empty horse stalls and then at the open barn door. The sun was shining. He had slept much longer than he had planned and immediately regretted having consumed the entire contents of his flask. What, only a few short hours ago, had been going exactly as he had planned, was now irretrievably ruined. He was certain that he had secured both the barn door and the horses. He had carefully chosen a spot in the loft that would be concealed from any intruders, human or otherwise, while providing him with an unimpeded view of anything that occurred below. He immediately ruled out bears or wolves. Even if he had left the door open, the horses' terror would have caused them to make a loud ruckus. That certainly would have awakened him. That, and the fact that Toby's body lay undisturbed right where he had fallen, left him with only two conclusions, neither of which he relished. The first was that both horses had worked their way loose and run off into the forest – possible for one, unlikely for both. The second was that the horses had been stolen. Hopeful that both had gotten loose and wandered only a short distance, he stepped out of the barn and did a quick but fruitless search. "Damn it all! Should of brought the dog!"

He returned to the barn and closed the door behind him. The first order of business was to dispose of the body. It was as useless to him now as it was to the unfortunate

Toby. His vision of parading his prize through the slave quarters at Pine Hill tied across King William's back was now no more than that – a vision. Hadn't that been the whole point after all – to demonstrate the futility and the expected consequences of trying to run off? Gone, too, was the expected reward for bringing the great Andalusian horse back to its owner. The only good part of this whole mess was that he would no longer have to slash his own arm with the cotton knife. It wouldn't be necessary to show that the escapee had tried to kill him before being shot in self-defense. It did not take long to find a shovel. It also took only a short time to dig a shallow hole in the dirt floor next to where Toby had fallen. This done, he removed the young man's shoes and rolled his body face down into the grave. Moments later, he finished re-filling the hole, covered it with dirty straw, and spat on it. The grave was not deep but if wolves or other scavengers came into the barn and dug it up, then so be it.

The body disposed of, the harder part was deciding what to do next. He thought about walking through the forest and heading westward toward the mountains but he had never been further west than where he was right now. He didn't know how far the forest extended or what might be in store for him in or beyond it. Should there be a chance encounter with a wolf or a bear, his only weapon was his pistol. The only load for the gun was what remained in the cylinder after shooting Toby. Since he had not taken care to unsaddle his horse when putting him away, all of the additional ammunition was long-gone in the absent saddle bags.

He could walk back to Pine Hill with neither his trophy nor Andrew's prized stallion. That would involve having to explain, not only how he had allowed Toby to escape, but also how he had allowed him to do so with the one indispensable horse on the entire plantation. Andrew was sure to question how the young man had been able to ride the spirited horse in the first place. An experienced liar, even Stark would be hard pressed to concoct a lie sufficient to allow him to avoid the man's extreme wrath.

Another possibility would be to go back the way he had come. Perhaps the horses had done the same and he might find them. Finding the horses, he quickly dismissed as extremely unlikely. He was certain they had been stolen. Even if he were to find them, he had no desire to engage whoever might have taken them. He thought about simply retracing his steps but then walking to Milledgeville instead of the plantation and departing north from there. The risk was in meeting someone who knew both him and Andrew who would tell Andrew about seeing him. The road from Milledgeville to Atlanta would certainly have units of the Confederate Army too. His Midwestern accent would likely arouse suspicion.

None of the options were pleasant. In the end, he decided to walk back the way he had come and return to Pine Hill. The walk would give him time to work out a lie. What he could not do, he realized, was to tell Andrew that slave catchers had taken both his prize and the horses. Firstly, it was not a certainty that Andrew would have hired slave catchers. Stark had heard him speculate about freeing the boy (Andrew considered any male, white or black under the age of sixteen, to be a *boy*.) In addition, if Andrew thought it likely that Toby had taken Stark's horse, which was easier to ride, and that Stark had used King William to go after him, then there was really no need for such help. Either Stark would return with Toby and *both* horses, or with King William only. Stark's horse was really of no consequence to Andrew. Any slave catcher intent on taking Toby and the horses would not have left him alive to identify them. He would be somewhere in the forest – as dead as Toby. No, the slave catcher story would not work.

Without really knowing why, he closed the barn door behind him then started walking back down the lane toward the stream.

****

Jonas, in spite of his several years of living in Minnesota, had never really mastered the technique of walking with snowshoes. He had tried a few times, but found them awkward and cumbersome. He had eventually given it up as not worth the effort. He wished now that he had given the task a little more consideration. The snow in the forest was deep and walking through it was difficult. Though he was wearing as many pairs of socks as the room in his boots would allow, his feet were still cold. At least here, in the forest, the snow was not as deep as it had been out in the open. Much of it had stuck to the branches of the pine trees, and what had reached the ground was sheltered and not drifted. The snow was no longer topping his boots and spilling inside but the earlier flakes were melting and making his woolen socks cold and damp. He thought about giving up the hunt but decided to keep going for a while. He should be approaching a small clearing soon. Possibly, he would find the pack there and get off enough shots to eliminate a number of them.

Just as he expected, the clearing appeared and, just beyond it, a small lake. "How odd that it took me so long to get here," he mused. When he, Henry and Ellie had first come to the farm, they had taken picnic lunches and eaten them at the lakeshore after church on Sundays. In the summer, it was an easy hike, but today his legs felt as though he had walked for a week. Sure enough, the wolves' footprints continued into the clearing but, other than the tracks, there was no sign of the wolves themselves. He decided to make his way across the clearing to see if, perhaps, they had crossed the frozen lake. If they had, he would give it up. He looked up at the sun and realized that

133

it was already noon. If he was to make it home by dark, there would be no time to continue the pursuit. The clearing was big enough that the wind had driven the snow into sizable drifts. He tried making way between or around the deepest ones.

Near a ledge that dropped ten feet or so down to the lake, he found a large downed log. Deciding to rest for a bit, he broke off a small pine branch from a nearby tree and used it as a brush to clear a suitable place to sit. He removed his gloves just long enough to take his pipe from his coat pocket and strike a match. The smoke from the pipe curled into the crisp air and mingled with the fog from his breath.

He looked over the ledge at the snow-ice, thinking how pristine the trackless expanse appeared. Suddenly it came to him that the snow was *too* pristine. The wolves had not crossed. They had doubled back into the forest and might now be between him and home. He abruptly discontinued his planned leisurely smoke and knocked out the ashes and unburned tobacco. To make sure the pipe was entirely cold, he stuck it briefly into the snow, then returned it to the pocket with his tobacco pouch and match tin. He wished he could feel his feet. He stood, stuck the revolver into the belt of his coat, and began to retrace his steps.

****

David was having doubts about his decision to ride Solomon rather than to use his cross-country skis as he followed Jonas' trail across the field and toward the forest. The horse was strong but they had not made the progress that he had hoped for through the deep snow. He could not reach his watch but judged by the sun that it was after noon. He had yet to make up for Jonas' head start. With the skis, he might have caught up with him by now and they would well be on their way home. In the dense forest though, the skis would have been hard to maneuver. There was no clear trail and he would have had to constantly work his way around the trees. He became much more concerned when he noticed something peculiar in the tracks. Beside the original set of tracks that Jonas had followed, there now appeared a second, fresher set. This told him that the wolves had doubled back and were now behind Jonas. The hunter had become the hunted. The wolves would travel silently through the snow anyhow but Jonas' deafness would give them an even more pronounced advantage. The going should have been easier in the forest where the snow had not drifted. Here, however, tree branches that were far enough above the ground that they didn't hinder a man on foot were proving to be an impediment to horse and rider.

David knew that he should soon be reaching the clearing. He looked down among the trees and saw that fresher tracks had diverged from the ones he had been following and trailed off to his left. A novice would have been relieved and assumed that the wolves had called off their pursuit in favor of something more interesting. David, however, knew it meant something entirely different. The wolves had sensed that they were closing in on their prey and had split to set their trap.

As they came closer to the clearing, David noticed Solomon becoming skittish and guessed that he had picked up the wolves' scent in the air. He had thought at the beginning to hang his holster over the saddle horn within easy reach rather than around his hips and under his coat. He now took the additional precaution of cradling the rifle in the crook of his arm.

Shortly after, horse and rider entered the expanse of the clearing. David gazed toward the lake and immediately spied Jonas trudging toward him. He guessed Jonas to be about fifty or so yards from the far end where the clearing dropped off into the lake. He waved wildly with his left hand but was unsuccessful in getting Jonas' attention. He could do only so much with his right hand without putting the rifle back in the scabbard. But he needed the long-gun handy in case of an emergency. So far there was no sign that the wolves had re-entered the clearing. He became cautiously optimistic that they had indeed decided to pursue different prey. He urged Solomon to quicken his pace and the horse responded as if he sensed the urgency.

David's optimism quickly vanished as he drew closer to where Jonas was walking. He looked past his friend and saw the first wolf emerge from the trees to gaze in Jonas' direction. Within moments, there were five. They were behind Jonas and to his left. David knew that he was unaware. He pulled the horse to a stop and waved again. Thankfully, Jonas saw him this time. David motioned for him to stand still and then pointed toward the wolves. Jonas saw them and slowly raised the shotgun. Before he could fire, he saw the one that he guessed to be the alpha male jump slightly and then fall into the snow. Knowing that David would need to reload, he fired the shotgun and took down another of the pack. He quickly discarded the weapon and drew the revolver. The startled wolves, now without their leader, retreated a little toward the forest but not back into it. David, not having reloaded, was rapidly approaching him with pistol drawn. Jonas fired his revolver toward the pack to hold them at bay. He bent down, retrieved the shotgun and leapt quickly on top of Solomon behind David. Keeping an eye behind them in case the remaining wolves decided to continue the pursuit, he was prepared to discard the empty shotgun and again use the revolver.

Once they safely distanced themselves from the wolf pack, David brought Solomon to a halt. He turned toward Jonas. He began to gesture wildly and, at the same time, shout. Jonas, of course, could not hear him but David felt a need to vent his displeasure and was certain that Jonas would get his message. "What were you thinking? How in hell," David was not given to vulgarity but today was sufficiently provoked, "did you think you could come out here all alone and just hunt down and kill an entire wolf pack by yourself?" He didn't mention Jonas' deafness. There was no need. "I always judged you to be an intelligent man, Jonas, but some days you just, by God, amaze me! Do you think *I* would have done something that crazy?"

Jonas thought about protesting but thought better of it. David was right of course, but there was no point in admitting *that* right now so he said nothing.

"Anyhow, just don't do it again. Let's take you to my house right now before your feet freeze. You can warm up there and I'll ride on over and let Em and Ellie now that you're alright – stupid and stubborn as hell but alright. You might want to begin thinking about what you're going to tell *them*."

CHAPTER VIII

George pulled his watch from his pocket and clicked it open. It was not really *his* watch but, like nearly everything else that he and his brother now possessed, he considered it to be the fair spoils of war. He had taken it from the body of a Federal corporal at Malvern Hill, deciding that it would no longer be of use to the man to whom the inscription read, 'To count the hours until you return to me – Elizabeth.' It concerned him little that Elizabeth, whomever she was, would never again see either the watch or her young husband.

It was just after noon, December 14 as closely as George could figure. It was the first time in weeks that the pair had traveled in daylight but today was special and they needed to move as quickly as possible from the scene of their good fortune a few hours earlier.

They had seen neither farms nor other people while moving up the stream. The lane had appeared to be deserted and the barn abandoned. They had noted the foundation of a house that looked to have burned long enough ago that saplings several feet tall had grown where once there had been rooms. They had been walking all night, in the later hours fighting the pine boughs along the stream. It had been either that or hug the stream bank so closely that they had constantly risked falling in. In places where the trees overhung the bank, they had found themselves hanging from the boughs and walking a part way down the bank's side. The barn had seemed a place to both hide and rest undisturbed until night when they would resume their trek.

As the first streaks of daylight had appeared, they had approached the barn and Harold had examined the latch. Pleased that it was only latched and not locked, George had opened the door enough to step inside. "Damn!" he had called out to Harold, more loudly than he meant to. "Look at this!"

Harold had stepped through the door behind him and seen the two horses – the chestnut gelding still saddled and, in the next stall, the Andalusian. They had walked around inside the barn checking feed rooms and box stalls to see if anyone was about. George had started to climb the ladder to the loft but had decided against it when he saw the barn owl staring at him from one of the beams just above. "Nothing up here," he had told Harold, who was standing with his back to him.

They had debated whether to simply stay in the barn for the day, as they had planned, or to take the horses and leave. Both had carefully examined the horses and Harold went through Stark's saddlebags. Money – quite a lot of money – some Confederate bills and a number of high-denomination Federal ones that Stark had obtained and saved before the war. To Stark's misfortune, he made a habit of carrying much of his money with him. Although he feared being robbed, he was more afraid of his money being stolen from his quarters when he was away from the plantation. This particular night, in his desire to get warm and have a drink, he had paid less attention to both his fortune and his spare ammunition.

Part of them said to take only the money and the other contents of the saddle bags. Part of them, though, told them taking the horses would help make better time in reaching Texas. Then again, there was the chance of getting caught and hanged as horse thieves. They had discussed it at length. George, the more adventurous of the two, thought that they should take the horses and run. If they could get far enough away before they were missed, he had argued, their odds of being caught would greatly diminish. They could then continue with the same horses or perhaps reach Alabama and sell them. George figured that the Andalusian

139

alone should be worth two or three 'regular' horses. Then, with fresh mounts, they should be free and clear all of the way to Mexico. With the money in the bags, they should be able to actually eat and drink at some of the saloons along the way and even, perhaps, sample some of the pleasures waiting upstairs.

Harold, more cautious, had advocated taking only the money and using it to buy horses at the earliest opportunity. This would give them less money to spend in the saloons but would also be less risky.

After a while, they had stepped back outside of the barn and continued their discussion. In the end, George had prevailed over Harold by agreeing not to dispute his claim to the Andalusian and convincing him that the horse would earn him great respect in Guadalajara. Once the issue was decided, they led the horses out of the barn and headed west.

****

While David sat Jonas down near the stove to remove his boots and wet socks, Mary Alice poured coffee for the both of them. Moments later, she sat next to Jonas and gently massaged his feet to bring back the feeling and circulation. David, meanwhile, went back outside and strapped on his skis. This done, he opened the kitchen door and called back inside. "I'll be back before dark. I can already taste the fried chicken!" Jonas waved to him and again wrapped his arms around himself, trying to get warm. With Mary Alice's touch and the warmth of the stove, he sensed the feeling beginning to return to his feet. As it began to reach the rest of his body, the shivering stopped. He pulled the blanket more closely around his shoulders and leaned back in the chair. Mary Alice brought more coffee but noticed that he had fallen asleep.

****

Stark was angry – angry at the world and everyone in it, including himself. He cursed those who had probably stolen both the horses and his money. He cursed Andrew, whose lack of discipline with the slaves had forced him to take measures into his own hands. He cursed himself for drinking the contents of the flask before the job was done and for leaving the saddle, along with the bags and their contents, unattended. When he had cursed just about everyone he could think of for ruining his life, he started over and cursed them all again. He reached the spot where he and Toby had begun to follow the stream a mere thirteen or fourteen hours ago. So much had gone sour. It didn't bother him that it had gone much worse for Toby. After all, that part had gone exactly according to the plan. His legs were tired and he sat beneath a tree to rest for a while. He contemplated staying in the forest overnight to let things back at Pine Hill settle a bit and then arrive tomorrow morning. That contemplation lasted only briefly, however, as he began to ponder being alone in the woods after dark. His mind began conjuring up visions of wolves, bears, and angry badgers. Perhaps, it would be best to go to the edge of the forest at Pine Hill and wait there for daybreak. He continued fabricating and practicing his story for Andrew.

The story, he considered, might mollify Andrew and avoid some of the man's wrath. Much worse, was something that even the most believable story would not fix. He was now totally without funds. A raise in salary was out of the question as the year's cotton crop still sat unsold in the barn and Andrew was unlikely to have money of his own. Stark was not only a little short, he was, due to one stroke of bad judgment, penniless. There would be no more diversions with the ladies at the Portman House in Milledgeville and the pleasures of Atlanta were now forever out of his reach. Nor would there be good liquor or an occasional fine steak. The only cigars would be the cheapest available – the ones that he had always held in disdain as tasting little better than rolled, dried out cotton leaves.

He knew that he had to leave the thick of the forest before dark but his legs felt nearly useless to him. Without the horses and without a need to hide a scent, he had avoided walking in the cold water. In places, it had become necessary to pull himself along by clinging to one branch, letting go only when he was able to grasp the next. Several times he had slipped and narrowly averted an icy bath in the stream.

He tried to shake off his depression over the turn in his fortunes by again rehearsing the story in his mind. "About eleven o'clock or so, I was lying awake and thought I heard noises coming from near the cotton and horse barns. I dressed quickly and went out to see what was going on. When I got to the horse barn I saw that my horse was gone. I immediately suspected your slave called Toby and went to his cabin to check on him. I knew that he normally slept on the floor by the fireplace. When I opened the door and didn't see him, I went back to the barn. I didn't want to wake you and thought I could quickly find him and bring him back. I didn't want to waste any time saddling a horse so I jumped on King William, rode him bareback – he *is* the fastest horse on the plantation, after all – and headed in the direction I thought Toby was most likely to take. I rode as far as the stream that heads up toward the old Watkins Plantation. I followed it for a while but then lost the trail. I had just turned around and was heading back when I encountered three armed men. One was riding alone and the other two were riding double. Before I could turn and get away, one of them had grabbed the reins and the other two were pointing pistols at my head. They took my gun and threatened to shoot me but said I could go if I gave them the horse. The one riding alone led King William away into the forest while the other two stayed for a while to make sure I wouldn't try to follow and then took off after him. As soon as they were gone I headed back here. I am *so* sorry. I was just trying to do my job. I think they were probably deserters from the army," he decided to add, hoping to divert any anger toward the fictional thieves and away from himself. This done, he allowed himself another round of cursing.

He looked for holes in the story that Andrew might find suspicious. Satisfied, he started to get up but found his legs still too tired. The longer he sat, the more he became consumed with what his life had become and what his future might hold. He could remain at Pine Hill and work for pauper's wages. He could leave but there was little chance of finding work elsewhere. Other planters' crops also remained unsold due to the difficulty of getting the crop through the Yankee blockade and on its way to the English mills. He might find work as a laborer but the thought sickened him. After all, that's what slaves were for. After considering all of the possibilities, he arrived at the only one that made any sense to him. Both terrified and confused, he pulled the revolver from its holster. Slowly, he raised it to his temple, and closed his eyes. "Hell, might as well get it over with."

****

Joshua lay on the cot and struggled to open his eyes. After writing the letter home last night, he had finally agreed to take some laudanum to ease his pain and help him, at least for a while, to escape the awful images of what he had witnessed yesterday. He slept again, briefly, and then made another unsuccessful attempt to wake up. His eyelids felt heavy and the laudanum kept drawing him back into the fog. He tried to sit up, thinking that the change in position would make him more alert, but found his body too weak and gave it up. Only after another hour did he begin to feel some semblance of consciousness. "What time is it?" he inquired of an orderly who happened to be passing by with an armful of red-stained bandages. "What is this place?"

"I think it's about two-thirty," the orderly responded. He did not see a clock in the room and would not have been able to reach his watch even if he had one. "This is a temporary hospital in Fredericksburg." He looked around at what, until recently, had been a school. There were black slate boards filling the entire wall at one end of the room. Rows of desks had been removed and stacked floor-to-ceiling in one corner. Had it been anything other than winter, they would probably have been thrown through the glass of the second story windows into the street below. "Probably won't be for long though," he continued without really meaning to. Shortly after, the young private moved on as if anxious to rid himself of the grisly load as quickly as possible.

A little more time passed and Joshua grew more alert. He began to realize what the orderly had meant by 'won't be for long though.' He wasn't a military strategist but he didn't have to be to figure out the rest. The army had suffered tremendously and he felt certain that General Burnside would lack the will to continue the fight. For that, he was grateful. There had been enough suffering and dying. He was less grateful for what he guessed would come next. The army would probably withdraw and allow the Rebels to re-take the town and the hospital with it. Those who could walk or who were fortunate enough to be carried away in the retreating wagons or ambulances would be taken along. The rest, he surmised, would face a far less desirable fate. They would be left behind. Those fortunate enough to see the end of the war would likely spend the remainder of the it in Confederate prison camps. Thank God that his wounds, though painful, would allow him to walk. He worried for those whom he had carried from the field, particularly the old Irishman. He found comfort now only in prayer. There was nothing else he could do for them. The laudanum had released its hold. He was determined to have no more of it on the chance that it might prevent him from being evacuated. He was tired though, and soon went back to sleep.

CHAPTER IX

It was Saturday so Ellie had another day away from school. She and Em sat together at the kitchen table. Ellie had gotten out her sewing basket as Em began writing a letter to Henry.

December 15, 1862

Dearest Husband,

We have just finished our breakfast and I need to go out soon to feed the chickens but have determined to write you a few lines beforehand. First of all, I hope that you and the men of the company are well. It is awful to be ill but so much worse when one is away from the tender care of loved ones. We have received your letter and think it is wonderful that you and Sergeant are putting your idle time to such a noble purpose as teaching the men to read and write. Ellie will be going back to school on Monday and thinks that she can secure some books and slates to send to you. We will put them in a package with the gifts that we have made for you. In all likelihood, you will not now receive them until after Christmas but please know how much we all love you and miss you. I will ask Ellie to post this letter separately on Monday and you should get it before you receive the package.

Your brother, without doubt, has to be one of the most stubborn men that our Lord has ever placed upon this earth! The only one possibly more stubborn would be my dear husband. The night before last, Ellie and I could not sleep as we kept hearing wolves howling I think near the orchard. Jonas, of course, did not hear them but sensed their presence and loaded the shotgun and placed it within reach. We sat up nearly all night as he read to us Charles Dickens' A Christmas Carol. He has such a nice reading voice. I closed my eyes and imagined that it was you who was reading to me instead. Ellie and I slept late yesterday and, when we came downstairs, both Jonas and the shotgun were missing. From his tracks, it appeared that he had checked the horse shed and other buildings and then walked off into the forest in search of the wolves. To our relief, David came by to check on us. He saddled up Solomon and went after Jonas. Needless to say, it was a most fretful day. Late in the day, David came by and told us that he had found Jonas. They had killed some wolves in the clearing over by the lake and then David had taken him to their house to spend the night getting warm. We expect him back soon now unless he is afraid of what Ellie and I will tell him and decides that it is safer to stay away!

That is all for now. We are all well
except for missing you. Always in love, Em.

****

Andrew stood with his hands clasped behind him and looked out the front window toward the lane leading to the river. He could see little of it since a dense fog had rolled in overnight shrouding everything in a cold, gray blanket. It had been little over twenty-four hours since he had awakened to find his prized horse, King William, the slave boy Toby, and his overseer Stark all missing.

He had debated calling slave hunters to find the boy. It was one thing to be allowed to leave but quite another to run off. Then there was the issue of the horse – not King William, but Stark's horse. He was quite certain that Toby would have been unable to take King William. Only two people at Pine Hill were able to even approach the great stallion on their own, those being himself and Stark. No, Toby must have taken Stark's horse while Stark pursued on King William. After much thought, he had decided to take no action. Stark's horse was of no consequence to him and, with money scarce, there was no use paying bounty for the return of a slave whom he had intended to set free in a couple of weeks anyhow. He assumed that Stark would soon return with King William and possibly Toby. Having seen Stark's displays of temper for which the overseer had been severely reprimanded, he found himself hoping that the boy made good his escape and would find freedom on his own.

For now, there was nothing to be done but simply to wait – to wait and try to figure out a way to keep the others from following Toby's lead. Except as a very last resort, violence was not to be used. He considered it largely ineffective – slaves who ran off usually did so because they were convinced that *they* would not be caught. Whipping

148

and other such punishments only increased resentment among them, making them less willing to work and more likely to abuse both the animals and the equipment upon which he depended for growing crops. Lastly, he considered himself to be a humane man and a Christian, not lightly given to inflicting suffering upon the less fortunate. No, it was best to wait and see what the day would bring. He looked out into the fog for a bit longer then wandered to the kitchen, stoked the fire in the range, and poured himself some coffee.

****

George and Harold still could hardly believe their good fortune. Since leaving the barn yesterday, they had travelled all day and night, stopping only briefly a few times to rest the horses and let them drink from a stream or creek. The longer they rode and the more miles they put between themselves and the barn, the more confident they became that all would be well and that their journey to Mexico would be an uneventful one. Harold had learned quickly that the high-spirited Andalusian was nearly impossible to handle alone but was quite gentle and manageable when close to his chestnut stable mate. Since that discovery, he had made it a practice that the pair was never more than a few feet apart. That, and the fact that Harold was far better in dealing with horses than he had ever been with people, made the journey somewhat relaxing. There would be plenty of time to break the horse's dependence on his companion when they reached their destination. Harold guessed that he was used to being ridden with a saddle and wondered that the only saddle in the barn worth using had been on the horse that George was now riding. A saddle would be more comfortable. He would make it a point to steal one at the first safe opportunity.

The same fog that enveloped Pine Hill Plantation extended to the west where George and Harold were now riding along a narrow lane flanked closely by forest on each side. This part of upland Georgia was less developed than the area they had left. It mattered little to them. They were only passing through. By the time this land became more populated, they would be long-since gone. They guessed between themselves, however, that, after the war, fine plantations would replace the forest as the cotton land to the east began to wear out. They soon left the subject and began talking excitedly between themselves about how grand their lives would be in Mexico. They would become wealthy ranchers with a great hacienda and servants to meet both their housekeeping and more primal needs and desires. Though neither had ever been to Mexico, they had heard stories from acquaintances who had fought in the Mexican War. The land, they had been informed, promised untold wealth to those who were ready and willing to seize it.

George was the first to hear the noise. They had not yet rounded the curve and the bridge was still hidden from their view by both the fog and the forest. But the sound was there. It was at once unexpected, unwelcome, and unmistakable. The clop of shod hooves on the cobblestone bridge, the voices, the slap of leather, and the jangle of sabers all spelled trouble.

"You two there; halt and dismount!" Captain Ambrose Bentley, before the war a Mayfield, Kentucky lawyer, was not in a good mood. For days, his procurement company had been scouring the countryside of eastern Alabama and western Georgia. They were searching for remounts to be shipped north to Jeb Stuart's cavalry in Virginia and the search was becoming more difficult each day. Bringing fresh horses from Texas had become much harder in recent months. Many of the best horses from the local plantations had either already been sold or had gone with their owners at the beginning of the war. Those that were left seemed generally unsuitable to be cavalry mounts. It was not his job to find plow horses to be employed for more menial tasks.

The two would not have attracted Bentley's attention except for the presence of the Andalusian and the condition of the horses. Both mounts appeared well-fed and well-groomed despite their 'adventure' of the last two days. George and Harold, by contrast, looked ragged, unkempt, and hungry. They had neither bathed nor trimmed their hair or beards in weeks. They had eaten only what they could either steal or manage to kill with their meager supply of ammunition. Bentley suspected that he had stumbled upon either army deserters, horse thieves, or both.

"Army weapons?" Bentley eyed the revolvers. "Where did you get them?" The two had not taken holsters from their own dead officers when leaving Antietam but had discreetly hidden the pistols under their coats along with what ammunition they could carry. Lately, they had taken to carrying the guns more openly.

"Found them," George lied, hoping that the simple answer would satisfy the officer without further explanation being needed.

"Where?"

"Milledgeville," Harold answered for him. "We found them near Milledgeville."

"Found them or stole them? Well, in any event, they're property of the Confederate States Army. We will be taking them now. Sergeant Henderson, search the saddle bags to see what else might be property of the army."

Harold looked nervously toward the bags behind the Chestnut's saddle and his glance caught Bentley's attention. "Maybe you two are property of the army also?"

"Invalided out," George blurted. "Just tryin' to get home."

Bentley was about to continue his inquiry when he was interrupted. "Holy Jesus!" Henderson had opened the first bag and had begun pulling out the contents. "Captain, look at this!"

George and Harold feared much more than the loss of the horses. That they were lost to them had been evident from the beginning of the encounter. Harold hoped that their two prizes would be separated and that the Andalusian would show his true temperament when some unfortunate trooper attempted to ride him. Even that though was a minor consideration. Of more concern was that each lie served only to create the need for a new one. Each new lie required them to carefully remember all of the ones before. The web was becoming increasingly tangled.

"What about the money? Did you find that with the guns?"

"Sold our tobacco farm."

"And carried it all with you in the army?"

"No wheres else to put it."

"The Federal money?"

"Took it from a dead Yank at Malvern Hill. He wasn't gonna need it."

"We southerners are soldiers, not grave robbers. Where did you get the horses?"

"There was more money. We used some to buy 'em."

152

"We haven't seen nice horses like that in a while. Where did you find them? We could use more like them."

"Outside Milledgeville."

"Who did you buy them from? Did they have more? You said you were invalided out. Why?"

"Don't recall their names. These here was the ones they had 'n I got sent home 'cuz I caught the consumption," George told him. He coughed to make it sound believable. He hoped the officer wouldn't ask to see a bill of sale. "Heard Texas was a good place to get over it."

"You said you were trying to get *home*. Lots of tobacco farms in Texas?"

Harold was having trouble breathing and could nearly feel a rope around his neck.

"And you?" Bentley looked at Harold. "You look healthy enough to still fight."

"Can't use my left arm." He took his left arm in his right hand and shook it around for effect.

"Care to show me your discharge papers?"

"Can't," George answered. "Got 'em stole off us by deserters."

"Deserters who stole your papers but left you the guns and the money and the fine horses?" Bentley asked coldly.

"The money and the guns was hid. Hid the horse too when we seen them comin' a way off."

Harold could feel the rope tightening and noticed that George had developed a twitch in his hands.

"I think you are a couple of thieving, gutless cowards," Bentley looked down at them. "I don't know whether to shoot you as deserters or hang you as horse thieves. My problem is I can't prove either and I'm short on time. I guess I'll just take the horses and the bags and let you go. If I see you again, I might be less generous. You best get out of my sight now before I change my mind."

George and Harold were more than willing to get out of sight. Bentley and his troops had barely started on down the road before the two disappeared into the forest and the fog. They wanted only to hide as completely and quickly as possible in case the captain did indeed change his mind. For the second time in little over twenty-four hours, they were both penniless and without horses, but now they were also unarmed except for George's penknife.

Bentley, at the same time, regretted his decision not to shoot or hang the pair. He had bigger things to do, however, and was in a hurry. He headed toward the railroad at Milledgeville with the two new prizes added to his collection. He would love to keep the Andalusian for himself but knew that wasn't for him to decide. He debated scouring other local farms and plantations for more horses but decided against it – best to get the horses he already had on a train headed north. Then he could rest his men and go searching for more.

****

Joshua sat atop a feed wagon, his back resting against sacks of oats and his legs on bags of ground corn. Beside him were a corporal with his left leg wrapped in bandages from knee to ankle and a private who had been one of the first wounded. The man's right foot had been amputated on the morning of the battle. Around them were ambulances and hundreds of other wagons. Some carried soldiers. Others carried whatever else the unfortunate, retreating army was able to bring back across the river in abandoning the town the night before. Among the wagons and ambulances were hundreds more men on horses or on foot, some healthy but many walking wounded, bandaged about the head or arms but more than happy to have escaped the carnage with their lives and their legs.

Looking back toward Fredericksburg, the young chaplain could see that the Rebels had wasted no time in re-occupying the streets and shelled-out structures. The schoolhouse, which only yesterday been a sanctuary for the wounded, was now a makeshift jail surrounded by armed guards. He knew that the occupants, as they became able to travel, were doomed to be moved south to languish in prison camps for the rest of the war – if they lived to see it. Many, he knew, would not.

Relief and guilt fought over Joshua's emotions. There was the genuine sense of relief that came with the realization that he was able to leave this awful place. He would, most likely, complete the remainder of his service as it had begun, ministering to those in hospitals back north. He would someday see the end of the war and go home to his thankful parents and sisters. The guilt came from wondering why he had been spared death on the field or the imprisonment that so many others were now facing. Had it been God's will that he was alive and free or had he been spared death in order to minister to those in prison? Had he somehow escaped that will and would he someday pay a larger price? As the sun rose higher in the sky and the town grew smaller and then finally disappeared from his sight, he continued to struggle with his anguish. There was little talk among the three on the wagon. Joshua could not tell if the others were silently fighting a mental battle like his own or if they were still enveloped in a fog of laudanum. Either way, it mattered little. They were safe as was he, and the war was over for them. The silence enabled him to try to sort things out. He envisioned himself getting out of the wagon and walking back toward the town but knew that he would not do it. The wagon rolled on and sleep overtook him.

****

Stark sat on his bed with the still-loaded revolver in his lap and looked out the window at the fog. At what would have been his last moment alive, the cowardice had overtaken him and he had been unable to pull the trigger. His mind had filled with awful visions of his lifeless body being ravaged by wolves or other undiscriminating creatures that would see it only as a convenient meal. He had seen his eyes being plucked from his head by crows or buzzards but, most of all, he had seen Toby standing by – watching it all and smiling. In the end, he had holstered the gun and begun walking through the forest to whatever awaited him at Pine Hill.

Now the fate was here. He hadn't lit a fire. There was no point in sending smoke up the chimney and signaling that he had returned. He didn't know if Andrew or anyone else had seen him come back. If they had, there would certainly soon be a knock at his door. If they hadn't, there was no rush in walking up to the house. He eyed the half-empty bottle of brandy sitting on the table. He badly wanted a drink but knew that, once it was gone, there would be no more. He might appeal to Andrew for a bottle but that would not be soon and he was uncertain that Andrew would oblige him. He calculated the time since he had mounted King William and led the doomed Toby into the woods – thirty-six hours, give or take a few. He eyed the revolver again but could not grasp the idea of just 'not being.' He got up, laid the gun on the table out of reach, sat back on the bed, and again began silently rehearsing his story.

****

David had warned Jonas of what awaited him at home. He considered going into Thayer instead. He could postpone receiving Ellie and Em's considerable wrath if he were to stop by the shop and put the rest of the wax on the Britts' new furniture. It would be only a temporary reprieve, he realized however, and the intensity of their ire would only grow with every moment that he delayed facing it. He thanked David and Mary Alice for their care and then asked to speak privately with David outside. "There's no charge for Mary Alice's Christmas chair," he told David when they had stepped outside. "Come by the house or the shop when you can and I'll give your money back." David argued briefly but unsuccessfully. Jonas headed to the barn and began to saddle Solomon. It would not be an enjoyable morning but he took some small comfort in the thought that each angry word would be said with love.

Had Jonas been able to hear it, it would have been considered a tongue-lashing. He dared not avoid it by looking away. Ellie started first. As his sister, she considered it her prerogative but Jonas knew that, when she finished, Em's turn would come. Ellie began by setting her tiny frame directly in front of him. He knew that, if he were in her schoolroom, he would be sitting on a stool in front of the entire class while wearing a pointed hat. She stood before him, hands on her hips. Her stare was every bit as cold as the snow he had trudged through when hunting for the wolves. Within moments, she pointed a finger and waved it directly in his face. She knew that he could mostly read her lips so she began with her well-practiced teacher voice. He grew certain that the worst was yet to come when she used his middle name. "Jonas Christian Hancock, you are the most foolish, boneheaded ..." To make sure that Jonas caught the entire brunt of the lecture, she soon pulled back her finger and began to sign as she spoke. Her countenance, which had been merely cold when she started, had turned to ice. "How on God's green earth could you ever think …?" She did not mention his deafness directly. She didn't need to. "That was the most irresponsible…"

Jonas looked expectantly to Em for her support. Seeing that she only seemed to be waiting for her turn, he lifted his hands and covered his ears. Ellie reached up and pulled them away. "Don't you dare mock me, young man!" She was in full teacher manner. There was nothing he could do except to let her go on until she was satisfied. That, he surmised, would be a while.

After what seemed forever to him, Ellie stopped speaking and gesturing. She reached up to throw her arms around him. He leaned down and let her kiss him on his cheek. Squeezing his hand, she stepped back and smiled.

Em began where Ellie had left off. Taller than Ellie, she did not need him to lean over for a hug and a peck on the cheek. For a moment, Jonas thought he had been reprieved but his relief was short-lived. Finishing the brief show of affection, she stepped back and began much as Ellie had begun. "Jonas Hancock!"

Good. She had not used his middle name.

"You are the most inconsiderate, irresponsible …!"

He wanted to close his eyes but had learned his lesson when he had covered his ears.

"I don't for the life of me know what you were thinking, How could you …? Whatever got into you? Are you and your brother both cursed with that same infernal Hancock Pride? Don't you remember what your Bible says about pride?"

Ellie, a Hancock herself, wanted to speak but didn't.

Jonas wished David were here but decided that both he and Mary Alice, if she were here also, would probably side with Ellie and Em. Better that they were at home after all.

"What if something happened to you? How would we run the farm until Henry came home? How could two defenseless women …?

"You scared us of our wits! Speaking of wits, what happened to yours! You certainly didn't take them with you! There," she sighed, "we won't speak of it again." She knew she would still send the letter to Henry and hoped that he would set his brother straight in his next letter home. But Jonas knew that she *would* speak of it again, and often. She had chastised him in the past for doing things that she found worrisome and expected no different going forward.

He thought about standing up for himself but considered his odds. One man – two loving, but right now very angry, women – might as well be back facing the enemy guns at Shiloh! And, in the end, it would change nothing. He delivered his rebuttal but only in his mind – safer that way.

*"Well, **I'm** going to speak of it even if you two don't hear me. I may be deaf but I am certainly not irresponsible or inconsiderate. Alright, I should have gone and gotten David. I will grant you that. But the wolves would have gotten a bigger head start and I needed to kill them, not just chase them away. Besides, I promised Henry that I would look after you two and this place and I intend to do just that whether you like it or not! I can't always be dependent on David or other folks for everything. Do you think I couldn't see how worried you both were last evening? I didn't need my hearing to know there were wolves or a bear out there last night. Your faces showed it*

just as plain as day. Do you really think I wouldn't do something about it? And especially you, Em, the way you worry about the livestock and how we might not eat if something should happen to them. I could never hold my head up again in this community or this family if I didn't protect you two and the stock. I do have my pride, you know!"

"May God help you if you ever do such a thing again!" Em hugged him. "Did Mary Alice fix you breakfast?"

****

Milledgeville, Georgia

December 18, 1862

Received of Capt. Ambrose Bentley, CSA

16 horses of various breeds suitable for use by cavalry regiments of the Army of the Confederate States of America:

    4 Stallions

    5 Mares

    2 Fillies

    5 Geldings

Conditions from fair to very good.

Most aged 4 to 7 years.

Note: Also brought in:

    1 Andalusian stallion, excellent condition, 5-6 years old;

        Temperament unsuitable for cavalry service.

1 mixed-breed chestnut gelding, good condition, 5-6 years old;

Companion horse to Andalusian – required for Andalusian to be usable.

Captain Bentley requests permission to purchase the Andalusian and the chestnut gelding for personal use and to remove them from service.

Testified: Lester Harris, Quartermaster Corps, Confederate States Army.

CHAPTER X

Celia sat on the bed in Stark's quarters sobbing. She had drawn her knees up under her chin and was clutching the sheet that she had pulled around her. "Please, Mistah Stark. Not again," she begged, but it was plain to her that he would pay no mind to her plea. "Please, no mo'," she implored him, hoping that her next utterance would change his mind. "I is with child."

The revelation did her no good. Without looking at her, he leaned over the edge of the bed and removed his second boot. "Really?"

She could tell from his tone that he was neither surprised nor concerned. He grabbed the sheet and pulled it away from her. After what seemed an eternity to her, he again sat at the foot of the bed and began to dress. He tossed her the rumpled sheet and she wrapped it around herself. "So, whose is it?" he asked, again appearing not to care.

"My baby is Toby's," she answered haltingly.

"I doubt it." He did not look up. "He's barely …"

"He's says he seventeen or eighteen – not sure. He said he gotta' leave but he's a comin' back fo' me. He said our baby gonna be born free. He said you was gonna help him go."

Stark turned suddenly and stared at her. Her bronze skin was nearly flawless, unlike that of the girls who had worked alongside their parents in the cotton fields. In the warm glow of the lamplight, he had to admit to himself that she was actually quite pretty. Too bad, he told himself silently. "What else did he tell you?"

"Nothin'," she answered quietly. "Jus' you wuz gonna help him."

162

"Who else did he tell?"

"He din' tell no none. Said it was jus' our secret. Tol' me not tell a soul."

"Did you?" he asked.

"No. Jus' like he said. I din' tell no one."

Stark feigned sympathy. He buttoned his shirt and pulled on his boots. "I see. Well he can't come back. It's too dangerous for him. He'd get caught for sure and I couldn't help again."

She looked at him pleadingly. "Please. I want him. I need him. Please, Mistah Stark, take me to him. I do anythin'."

He got up, walked to the window and stared outside. "Very well," he turned to her. "Go back to your cabin. When everyone's asleep get some of your things and when the lights are out in the mansion meet me out behind the cotton barn."

"Oh thank you, Mistah Stark. She smiled for the first time all evening. "Oh thank you! God gonna' bless you fo' sure!"

"I'm sure," he muttered. "I'm sure."

****

Theodore could hardly catch his breath. It seemed he had been running forever though it had barely been an hour since he had first heard the voices and the ominous baying of the dogs. His heart was beating faster than ever before in his life and his lungs felt as if they were on fire. Though his legs seemed to be getting heavier with every step, he dared not stop. To do so would mean, at worst, being torn apart by the dogs or, at best, being hauled back to the plantation in irons to be tied up and whipped. The night was cool but he was sweating. The salty moisture was causing his eyes to sting. There was no stealth to be had as the dry leaves cracked and crumbled under his worn-out shoes. He wished he could stop for even a moment but knew that to do so would be to give up.

Ahead, he could hear water running over rocks. They gave give him a second wind. A stream – if he could only make it to the stream, perhaps there was a chance. If he could run in the water, the dogs might lose the scent allowing him to escape. His legs grew a little lighter and he felt himself running a bit faster. Yet the sound from the dogs seemed to grow louder and draw closer. Suddenly, he stumbled over a fallen log. Picking himself up, he realized that any chance of reaching the stream before the dogs descended upon him was gone. Terrified, he climbed the nearest tree to await the arrival of the slave hunters. Just out of reach of the dogs, he felt a hand grab his shoulder. Suddenly, he awoke.

"Whoa, son! Easy! You need to get dressed though. Lieutenant Hancock needs to see you in his tent." Atlee had never called a soldier 'son' before but had developed a special affection for the young man. At 41 years old, he was easily old enough to be the boy's father. "He says he needs to talk to you about something urgent."

Theodore sat upright, rubbed his eyes, and looked about the still-dark tent. "It's the middle of the night. What does he want? What time is it?"

"A little before eleven-thirty. As to what he wants, he wouldn't tell me. Only that he needs to see you now and that it's important." Though it was against his nature, Atlee lied. He decided, though, that, in this instance, it was harmless enough. He waited as Theodore dressed and pulled on his boots. Together they left the tent and headed down what passed for a street through the camp. There was a light but cold mist falling. The sergeant was annoyed that the wind kept blowing droplets onto his glasses, making it hard to see where they were going. The camp was mostly asleep except for the sentries who took their turn in the wet chill so that their comrades could safely doze. Here and there a few hardy souls huddled around campfires. A few tents displayed a soft, yellowish glow. Inside, the occupants sat together drinking coffee, smoking their pipes, and telling each other stories. The ground was damp and cold but it wasn't muddy and was far from frozen as the two made their way along. Theodore continued to inquire as to why he had been called out in the middle of the night. Atlee steadfastly pled ignorance hoping that an impish smile would not give him away.

When they reached Lieutenant Hancock's tent, Theodore could see several figures shadowed behind the light of the canvas. "What's happening?" he again inquired.

Atlee's only response was, "You first." He opened the tent flap and stepped aside, placing his hand on the young man's back.

The men in the tent came to attention as Theodore entered. As he looked around, Theodore noted that, in addition to Lieutenant Hancock, there was the company captain, the second lieutenant, and his classmates. "Come in," Henry invited him. "And, no, you are *not* in any trouble." He reached out to take the young man's hand.

"Why am I here?" Theodore asked, still unsure.

Henry reached into his pocket, pulled out a watch, and clicked it open. "Remember this moment," he began. "Remember it well, for it will come only once in your life time. It is ten minutes before midnight," he said, looking both at the watch and at Theodore. "Ten minutes before midnight on the 31st day of December in the year of our Lord, one thousand eight hundred and sixty-two."

Theodore suddenly realized the significance of the date and time though he had forgotten about it before going to sleep.

"In ten minutes' time," Henry continued, "according to the Proclamation of Emancipation issued by President Lincoln, you will no longer be considered contraband of war but a free man – free to come and go as you please, just as any other man."

Theodore's heart again began to race, this time with excitement. "But …"

Henry held out the watch and carefully placed it in Theodore's hand. "Theodore's eyes began to tear as he looked down at the watch. But I don't …"

"A free man should have a watch," Henry told him, "so we are making sure you have one. Read the inscription."

"Theodore Lincoln – a free man. January 1, 1863."

"And a free man who can read should also have a Bible," Henry went on. "We have all signed it to commemorate the occasion." Each stepped forward to shake Theodore's hand. Just as they finished, Theodore looked down at the watch and noted as the second-hand ticked midnight. He barely heard Henry ask him, "Do you have any thoughts of where you would like to go?"

****

Doctor Sean Gibbons stepped out of the front door of the hospital onto the sidewalk. When he arrived for work that morning, it had been cold but bright and sunny. Now the sleet slapped his face and he was sure it would turn to snow overnight. The last surgery of the day had been difficult but, he felt, successful. The young lady should make a full recovery after falling from her horse. There might be a slight limp but it would be barely noticed. He mused that it might be safer for ladies to ride astride of their horses rather than side-saddle. But this was Boston after all, not some little town out in the states and territories beyond the Mississippi. No, a lady just didn't do that here.

He thought about walking home. He needed the exercise and normally found the stroll a good way to clear his head and begin to relax for the evening. The clip-clop sound of a horse pulling a cab soon changed his mind. He stepped onto the street and hailed the driver. He could relax away from the sleet. Besides, his legs were tired from being on his feet more than usual today. He climbed into the cab and soon found himself anticipating the promised dinner of fried chicken and mashed potatoes.

Always in the back of Gibbons' mind lately was Joshua. At least the doctor's work at the hospital provided a distraction for him. He often wondered how his wife was able to bear the uncertainty day after day at home. He was sure that her show of optimism was feigned for his own benefit. He appreciated her attempts to keep up his spirits but, knowing how she must worry, felt sorry for her trying to maintain the façade. Each night on the way home, he found himself hoping that there would be a letter from Joshua. At the same time, he always felt uneasy that there might, instead, be a letter or telegram from the war department.

His anxiety had worsened some time ago with the news that a great battle had occurred at Fredericksburg, Virginia. The available news was that the battle had gone horribly for General Burnside's army and had ended in a retreat that left behind thousands of Union soldiers dead, wounded, missing, or captured. Joshua, being a chaplain and technically a non-combatant, should have been out of harm's way. But Gibbons knew enough of war to understand that no one was truly safe. He also knew that his son was not the kind to stay away from danger if he felt that duty called him to do differently. For now, there was nothing to be done but to wait, to hope, and to pray. Those things, he and Mrs. Gibbons would do fervently.

Presently, the cab came to a stop in front of the Gibbons' home. The three-story row house was more than adequate for the two of them and the maid but had been of a comfortable size when Joshua, his sisters, and Katherine's late mother had all lived there together. Though Sean's practice was successful and the family could have afforded a mansion on Beacon Hill, they had found this neighborhood quite pleasant and more to their liking. Sean emerged from the cab and paid his fare. "A most happy and pleasant new year to you," the driver remarked.

"Thank you and the same to you."

With the distraction of work and thoughts of Joshua, Sean had forgotten that tomorrow would be January 1, 1863. New Year's Day had never been particularly noteworthy at the Gibbons household and tomorrow would be just another day at the hospital like any other. But tonight would be different in Boston. In spite of the impending foul weather, there would shortly begin rallies and torchlight parades. There would be speeches and celebrations. The prominent orator and publisher, William Lloyd Garrison, was scheduled to address the Abolitionist Society. At the stroke of midnight, church bells all over the city would ring to celebrate the official end of slavery in the rebellious South. No, this was not going to be an ordinary New Year's Day.

Sean found Katherine on the settee in the family parlor, with Lydia the maid leaning over her. Katherine appeared to be crying and Sean saw that she was tightly clutching an envelope to her breast. His heart sank. Tears welled up in his eyes as he reached out his arm to comfort her. Katherine looked up as he approached. He suddenly realized that her tears were not ones of sorrow. "It's *from* our boy!" She handed him the envelope. He sank his head into her lap and joined her in the blessed sense of relief.

Fredericksburg, Virginia
December 13, 1862
Dear Father and Mother,

Today, I witnessed an event so horrible that, if I live to be an old man, I wish never to see or hear of such a thing again. However, I fear that, before this awful war is over, it will be repeated again and again whether I shall be a part of it or not. I know in my heart that it is God's will that I should be here in order to provide comfort and guidance to those in the army. However, I wish only that this horrid thing could be done and that all from both sides could return safely and in peace to their homes and families. I do not wish to write all of the details just now, or perhaps ever. I am sure that you will understand and will have read enough of it by now or soon in the newspapers. Please know for now that I am well. I must honestly tell you that I have received some wounds but they are minor compared to those that afflict so many others of our army. I expect to fully recover. I am presently in the hospital but expect that our army soon will evacuate the town. If so, I will retreat with them. I fear that many here will not be able to be moved and will spend the remainder of the war as prisoners of the Rebels and will receive little compassion or care.

I do not know where I will be sent next, whether I will remain with the army in the field or be assigned to a hospital as before. I suppose that it is possible that I will be invalided out though I do not believe that my wounds are serious enough that such will be the case. If I am sent to work in a hospital, I am in hopes that it will perhaps be in New York, Philadelphia or even Boston though I will be content to be wherever God and the army need me.

I need to sleep now but will write more later.

Always in love,

Joshua.

****

Andrew stood at the window of the library and looked out into the darkness. Behind his back, he clutched a letter from Darius.

Fredericksburg, Virginia

December 13, 1862

Dear Father,

This morning our army achieved a glorious victory over the Yankee invaders. Our army accounted for itself proudly and, by noon, the field was littered with more Federal dead than any of us can count. None of those invaders will again threaten our country and our freedom to own our slaves and grow our cotton. We expect that they will soon evacuate the town of Fredericksburg and never again come into Virginia. I am pleased and proud to say that I did my part. I can accurately count that I personally killed at least twelve, perhaps more. One or two came so close that I could actually see their faces as they took my shot. What pleasure! I hope I can continue to do more as we pursue the cowards back out of Virginia. I am confident that my contribution has been noticed by those above me and that I may soon be promoted. I ...

Andrew walked back to his desk, laid down the letter, and allowed himself a small glass of brandy from one of the few bottles left in the house. The room was dark except for the light from the fireplace and a dim lamp on the chair-side table. It was becoming harder to get oil for lamps. Besides, even a brightly lit room would do little to raise his spirits this evening. He swallowed the last few sips of the brandy, sat at the desk, and leaned forward with his head in his hands. "Annabelle, my dear Annabelle, what have we done?"

After a while, he got up and stood for several moments staring silently into the fireplace. He took one last look at the letter and touched a corner close enough to ignite it. "Good-bye, Darius." He watched the corner begin to blacken and disappear. He then tossed the rest into the fire and watched as the entire thing was quickly consumed. When it was gone, he picked up the lamp, set it on the desk and turned it up a bit. His hand shook as he drew several sheets of paper from the top drawer and began to write. At least this one decision that had weighed so heavily on him was now made. "I, Andrew David Morgan, being of sound body and mind, do declare this to be my last will and testament …" When he had finished, he wrote a second, exact copy. All that was left now was to have his signature witnessed on both his next time in Milledgeville and to deliver one of them.

*****

Isaac again carefully scouted the stable to make sure that no one else was about. He was certain that no one would be but one couldn't be too careful. It was late into the evening and the plantation was quiet, dark, and cold. The entire McManus family, along with the drivers needed to take them there and wait for them, had gone to a New Year's celebration at a neighbor's home. From what Isaac had read, there should not be much to celebrate. With New Orleans and most of the lower Mississippi River now under Union control, there would be no more selling of cotton. There would be no money to buy the luxuries that the white folks had long seen as necessities. And even if there were money, such items would be nearly impossible to obtain. Silks, liquor, and cigars were becoming increasingly precious. More importantly to Isaac, the weapons and ammunition that the Confederate Army depended on were also becoming increasingly scarce. With that, Grant's army should be able to advance more quickly through Arkansas and Mississippi bringing with it what Isaac anticipated more than anything else – freedom!

Satisfying himself that no prying eyes or ears were about, Isaac sat on a bale of straw and waited for Joe. He knew he was taking a chance confiding in Joe but had finally decided that his friend was trustworthy and that his secret would be safe. Besides, what he was about to tell was welling up inside of him and he felt he could no longer contain himself. He had to tell someone and it had to be tonight. Presently, he heard a rustling of footsteps in some loose straw. "Joe?"

"That me," the voice answered softly and hesitantly. "What you doin'?"

"Need to tell you something," Isaac answered him, "but I can't tell you here. Let's walk out to the other side of the cow pens. I can't tell you here and you've got to promise not to tell a soul.

****

Stark waited until the lights were out in the house. He stood behind the corner of the cotton barn where he had met Toby. There were no suitable horses available to take Celia to the place where he had left Toby's body but it wouldn't matter. Besides, he had no desire to spend either the time or the energy to make another trip to the old barn. The moon came out briefly through an opening in the clouds and there was just enough light to make out the dial on his watch. "11:45" Why did the old man wait so late to go to bed? "Oh, well." He finally had and now it was time. He had little doubt that Celia would come. If she had told anyone that she was going to run off to look for Toby that was fine. In fact, it was good as long as she didn't reveal also that he was going to help. That part worried him a little but he didn't think it likely and he soon dismissed it.

"Mistah Stark, are you here?" he heard her whisper from the shadows. "I don' like dark. Mama alus' said there was bad things 'n evil in the dark."

"Don't say my name," Star rebuked her quietly but with authority. "And don't talk."

"Is it far?" Celia asked.

"I told you not to talk," he answered, "but no. We need to go before anyone sees us. Now, follow me and don't lag behind." He was glad that she had chosen the deep blue or green dress and the dark bandana for a head covering. They would stay well into the woods and avoid the lane. Even so, there would be less chance of being seen. It hadn't occurred to him that the girl only had one other dress, a lighter-colored one that she wore to help ward off the hot summer sun. She carried that one in the makeshift knapsack made from an old pillowcase discarded years ago from the house.

He led her in the same direction he had taken Toby but soon doubled back. Instead of heading toward the stream, he opted to follow the lane that led to the river. He was careful to keep them on a parallel course a number of yards into the woods. The going was a little harder. They tramped through the remains of wet, slushy snow that had fallen a week ago but it hadn't completely melted due to the shade from the trees. His boots and her shoes, which he considered barely worth the name, left some tracks but it didn't worry him. The temperature was above freezing. Their trail should soon disappear. Even if it didn't, he would explain that his own boot prints were ones that he had left in trying to find the girl to bring her back.

They made their way along, Stark leading and the girl a few feet behind. As they neared the riverbank, he heard her softly begin to sing. He was tempted to tell her to quit but decided that it wasn't loud enough for anyone to hear so let her continue. Besides, she would be quiet soon enough. He had never heard her sing and noted, without telling her, that she had a nice voice. "Pity."

They arrived near the landing. Stark looked out over the river and could dimly make out the lights of Milledgeville on the other side, upstream. "I dasn't know how to swim," she told him.

"You won't need to," he assured her. "There's a cove downstream with a boat."

They began walking downstream. This time, instead of going through the woods as they had along the lane, they worked their way along the edge of the steep bank. Stark knew that he was taking a chance walking so close to the drop-off in the darkness but he was looking for something. It was a necessary risk. He was careful to hold onto tree branches to avoid slipping off the edge and instructed Celia to do the same. The singing had stopped as she needed all of her breath and strength to navigate the treacherous footing. "Is it much farther?" she asked him again.

"No, you won't have to go much farther." He continued to watch over the edge to where the river met the bank. The dark ground and the equally dark water made it difficult to see what he was looking for. Still, he decided, it was better than having bright moonlight and the chance of someone in a passing boat see him as he finished his 'task.' He estimated they were, perhaps, a quarter of a mile from the landing. He felt his left foot slip over the edge and lost his balance, nearly sliding down the bank. At the last moment, he grabbed a small branch and recovered. Pulling himself up, he looked down at the cave-off that had caused his fall. Again, the moon had come out from behind the dense clouds. He could see where a large tree that had grown along the bank for years had fallen into the river. The top was invisible in the water but the trunk, lower branches, and roots reached the bank and appeared firmly attached.

Celia clung to the branches and walked up to him. He stepped behind her and reached over her shoulder, cupping his hand around her breast. "No," she protested. "Don' do dat no mo'."

"As you wish." Without hesitating, he moved his hand and grasped her shoulder. With his other hand, he grabbed her jaw. He was the only one who heard the sharp crack as he broke her neck.

Stark worked his way down the bank along the tree trunk. He carefully checked both his footing and his grip as he dragged the girl's lifeless body. "You can still be of some use," he muttered into her unhearing ears. "When I find you tomorrow, your friends will see that the forest and the river are dangerous places for someone who tries to run off." He continued pulling her body toward the water's edge. It was laborious work and took him the better part of twenty minutes. His arms and legs ached from the contortions needed to avoid slipping and falling. Above all, he dared not lose his grip on the body and let it fall uselessly into the river. At the water, he wedged the girl tightly into the branches of the fallen tree. Minutes later, he satisfied himself that all was secure and climbed carefully back up the bank. At the top, he retraced his steps to the warmth of his quarters.

He glanced at his watch: 2:15. The whole thing had taken about two and a half hours. He allowed himself three drinks of his precious whiskey, pulled off his muddy boots, and lay down on the bed to sleep.

It began as a low rumble to the west, accompanied by intermittent flashes of light – barely perceptible to anyone who might have been awake at that hour. Certainly, it was not enough to arouse Stark. He had risen briefly about half an hour after going to bed and helped himself to the remainder of the whiskey. Dawn, a few hours later, was nearly meaningless and the sky remained nearly as dark as if the sun had not bothered to rise.

When he awoke shortly before noon, Stark's mind was still in a fog from the whiskey, the fatigue from the night's work, and a fitful sleep. He dragged himself from the bed and stumbled across the threadbare carpet to the window. The lightning and thunder, which had intensified during the night, had now mostly subsided. The wind, though, had picked up to nearly gale force speeds. It drove the rain against the window in unremitting sheets. His window normally afforded him a view down the lane and all of the way to the landing. This morning, however, the rain allowed him to see only a short distance beyond the stoop.

When an occasional flash of lightning managed to briefly illuminate the lane, it showed him only a muddy mixture of water and the red Georgian clay. There were no real puddles, only a sea with an archipelago of little islands in spots where the ground was a bit higher. The sea was fed by not only the rain that fell directly into it but also by numerous tributaries caused by wagon ruts that wandered among the various outbuildings. Today, there would be no going out to 'find' Celia. In fact, it was unlikely that anyone other than her father and Dahlia would even realize that she was gone. It was even more doubtful that they would mention it to anyone. He lit a fire in the stove and slumped into the old armchair. There was nothing to be done. Perhaps the storm would become a fortunate occurrence. It would seem even more likely that the young girl had tried to take advantage of it to run off and join Toby –that she had lost her way in the forest, fallen into the river, and drowned as the fallen tree snared her. Yes, it might work even better than he had planned.

The first day of 1863 ended much as it had begun. The sun still made no speakable appearance and the rain continued unabated. The clay had long since absorbed all of the water it could and a red, clay-filled tide flowed relentlessly from the roads and cotton fields into the river. Even those who had lived in Milledgeville all of their lives would say later that they had never seen anything like it.

There was no one to see it. The tree that had lain only partially in the water barely twenty-four hours ago was now much less visible. Increasingly, the river's current tugged at branches just above and below the surface. All the while, the river sought to swallow the dirt bank that held it. Large chunks of dirt that had been part of the land now turned to loose morsels of mud, slid into the water, and were quickly digested. The entire tree began to slide into the river's grip. The soil that had held and nourished it was no match for the rushing water. The slide began slowly but accelerated quickly. Within the span of a few hours, the bank collapsed and the tree, still holding the precious young cargo in its grasp, slipped into the torrent and began its journey to the sea.

CHAPTER XI

Ellie set the table for supper while Em stood at the stove frying fresh trout. Jonas and David had been back to the lake numerous times since the encounter with the wolves two months ago. David had taught Jonas to be more comfortable using snowshoes and it had become nearly second nature to him. They now only ventured there together, well-armed against any dangers they might encounter. Using blocks of snow and ice, they had built themselves quite a comfortable fishing hut some distance from the shore and augured a good-sized hole through which to drop their lines. Today's catch was particularly bountiful. David had plenty to take home to Mary Alice and Jonas had brought home enough for a nice-sized meal for the three of them. There was plenty left over to hang in the smokehouse near the hog that Jonas had recently butchered.

Jonas slid his chair away from the table to allow Ellie to finish her work and was engrossed in his newspaper. All three were startled when the door to the outside opened suddenly without the usual warning knock. "Henry, my darling!" Em shrieked excitedly as she dropped her spatula and dashed toward him. "How did you ...? What are ...?"

"You didn't get my letter, did you?" he smiled as he picked her up. He gave each of the others a warm hug and then stepped back as Jonas looked at him. Henry nodded toward the door. "Oh – I'm sorry. Theodore, I'd like you to meet Emma, Ellie, and Jonas."

"This is Theodore Lincoln."

Ellie signed the words to Jonas who stepped forward to shake the young man's hand.

"I forgot. You didn't get my letter. I hope ...."

"Of course it's alright," they responded almost as one.

"I hope you can all do what I promised him," Henry continued. "Ellie, I told him you would tutor him in his reading and writing and get him started with his mathematics." Ellie smiled and then signed to Jonas, "I told him you would teach him to farm and how to make furniture." Jonas nodded his agreement.

Em gave her a husband a smiling but questioning look.

"And I told him you would always make sure he would have a warm, clean place to sleep and meat and apple pie in his belly!"

She gave him a teasing pat on the arm. "Of course."

"All I have asked of Theodore," Henry continued, "is that he will apply himself."

"And you?" Ellie asked. "What are you going to do for him?"

"I have to go back." He hadn't planned on talking about that yet but decided he may as well address it. "This thing isn't over. There's so much more yet to do."

Ellie silently relayed the message to Jonas.

Em tugged at his arm. "Henry, don't say such things – at least let's not talk about it tonight."

"Not for a few weeks," he assured her. "And I won't be going back into battle. That part of the war is over for me."

Ellie continued apprising Jonas of the conversation.

Em noticed the patch over Henry's left eye and reached out to touch it. "Henry, what happ-"

"I was going to tell you," he interrupted. "It's why I've been furloughed home. I had a little accident. My eye is there but I won't see out of it again."

"And they would not invalid you out?" Jonas asked.

"It was offered but I declined."

Em's jaw dropped. "You what?!"

"As I said," he went on, "it will be just for a while and I won't be going back into battle. I have volunteered to spend some time in the provost service in Memphis. I will be interviewing and assisting freed and escaped slaves who want to join the army. Memphis is firmly in Union hands now. There's very little danger and I may even be home for good before the war ends."

"Well, I suppose …" Ellie seemed, if not happy, at least satisfied. "I didn't mean to … I just love you so much. I don't want anything to …"

"Nothing will happen to me, Em. We'll have our whole lives to spend together. I promise."

Theodore tugged at Henry's arm. "May I ask you something?" he asked quietly.

"Certainly, Theodore."

"Have I died?"

"What? Why would think that?" Henry spoke softly so that only Theodore could hear him.

"Because this is what I always thought Heaven would be like when I got there."

"Trust me, young man," Henry answered him. "You are very much alive."

Jonas eased past them and headed out the door. "Excuse me", he called behind him, "need to bring in more trout."

"Oh no! The trout!" Em shouted, looking back at the skillet that had started to smoke. "Henry, go after Jonas. He'll need to bring more than he thinks!"

The next night, Henry and Jonas sat alone at the kitchen table. It was the first time since Henry had left before Jonas to join the army. The others had all gone to bed – Ellie and Em to their rooms and Theodore on a cot in Jonas' room. Jonas had already offered to work with him at the furniture shop to make him a proper bed at the earliest opportunity. Theodore was thrilled at the idea of having an honest-to-goodness bed that would be his very own. He was even more excited that someone would take the interest to teach him a real trade.

Henry poured them each a coffee and turned up the lamp. Jonas spoke first. "So what really happened to your eye?" Henry gave him a quizzical look. "What really happened to your eye?" Jonas repeated. "Wasn't an accident, was it?"

"What makes you ask?" Henry wrote on a sheet of paper and handed it across the table.

"We've been brothers for a while," Jonas answered quietly. "I've always been able to tell when you were hiding something. Remember when you were sweet on Amanda Ainsworth and wouldn't fess up? Well, I knew. So, what really happened?

"I was twelve. Amanda was eleven. Alright, here it is. But you need to take a blood oath not to ever tell anyone. Swear?"

"Swear. Now, out with it."

Henry reached again for the sheet of paper. "We were in a skirmish with a Rebel patrol that we ran into while foraging. We were outnumbered badly and got ambushed. Looking back at it now, I think we were very fortunate not to have been captured."

Jonas took a sip of coffee and filled his pipe while Henry continued to write.

"It was our worst fight since Shiloh. Anyhow, as I said, we were out foraging. We had just about finished at a local farm. I felt bad about it but we had our orders. It was just a small farm – much less than what we have here – probably never had more than one slave if even that. There wasn't much left to take but we had orders to take whatever there was that we could use. We were just leaving when we were attacked by Rebel cavalry. It went on for quite some time. We lost four men and several more were wounded. Near the end of it, several of us had taken cover behind a stone wall. I had just reloaded and come back up over the wall to fire when a reb ball hit near my head and caused some small stone fragments to go flying. One caught me in the eye and tore the cornea. Moments later, our own cavalry arrived and chased the rebs off. They had been sent to look for us when we were late getting back to camp. Anyhow, I don't want Em to know how close I came to getting killed. You know how she worries. After all, you and Ellie are the ones who told *me*.

They poured more coffee and talked far into the night about many things – Jonas talking and Henry filling pages of paper and handing them across the table.

"After we received word that Albert had been killed at Fredericksburg," Jonas mentioned, "I told Lucille that we want to keep renting this farm as long as she is willing. She hasn't said what she wants to do. She is talking about moving back to Indiana to be near her sister."

"We should see if she will sell to us," Henry answered. "If we could arrange something before I have to go back, we could farm the place together when I come home for good and you could still run your shop. I'm sure Theodore would want to help us both. Too bad about Albert. He was a fine man and a good friend. Gonna' miss him. This war is such a waste, Jonas. So much death and suffering! And for what? It's just organized slaughter. It's madness!

"I agree. We should see her. It's been two months. Em, Ellie and I have already made our condolence calls and have had her here for dinner a few times. I don't think it's too soon to mention it."

Henry stood and gathered all of the pages from their conversation. Opening the door to the stove, he tossed them in and knocked down the ashes with a poker. He put in enough wood to hold the fire until morning and closed the door. Jonas leading the way, they crept silently upstairs to bed.

****

Captain Gibbons sat nervously in the ante-room while his parents shared a settee nearby. Beside the door, a uniformed guard stood at parade rest, rifle at his side. Probably loaded, Joshua surmised. In a stand to the guard's left stood a flag which Joshua knew bore stars, even for the eleven rebellious states that had left the Union. Across the doorway, was a stand that held another flag. The emblem on the flag was hidden from view by the furls but Joshua knew what it was.

He looked up briefly as he heard the outer door of the ante-room open, studying the man who stood in the doorway. The man was stocky but of average height and wore a graying beard that extended to the middle of his silk vest. There was still snow on the top and brim of his black hat. It appeared that he had brushed it from his woolen topcoat but some remained. Joshua noticed damp areas where some had melted as the wearer walked from the building's entrance into the ante-room. His spectacles also had water droplets where there had been snowflakes. In his hand he held what appeared to be telegrams.

The man walked briskly and purposefully past the small family and knocked on the office door. A young man, whom Joshua judged to be only slightly older than himself, opened the door. "Good morning, John," the older gentleman told him.

"Good morning, Mr. Secretary," the younger man replied. "Come on in. He has been expecting you."

"Secretary of War Stanton," Sean leaned over and told his wife quietly.

"I know," she answered.

After what seemed an eternity to Joshua, the door to the inner office slowly opened. Joshua expected to see the same young man who had escorted Secretary Stanton. The opening instead revealed a tall but stooped man dressed in a dark gray suit and wearing black boots. The suit was clean and well-tailored but the man himself appeared worn and haggard, much older than a man should look who had just seen his fifty-fourth birthday. He smiled slightly but, it appeared, with an effort that seemed to come with not having done it often for some time.

Joshua quickly jumped to attention and saluted.

The man briefly returned Joshua's salute and quickly stepped forward to take his hand in a firm grasp. "From what I understand," he said, "it is *I* who should be saluting *you*."

"This is an honor, Mr. President," Joshua told him quietly. Odd, it seemed, that he should be more nervous now than he remembered being under enemy fire at Fredericksburg.

"Would you please introduce me?" the president asked. Dr. and Mrs. Gibbons had risen and were now standing behind Joshua near the door. "I would be pleased to meet the parents who would raise such a fine and brave young man."

Joshua could feel himself blushing and hoped that Mr. Lincoln would not notice.

Stepping behind them and holding the door, the President ushered them into the office. "Captain Gibbons, Dr. and Mrs. Gibbons, please meet my secretaries Mr. Nicolay and Mr. Hay and, of course, Secretary Stanton."

Mr. Stanton stepped forward to shake Joshua's hand. "I am proud to make your acquaintance, Captain Gibbons. I shall no longer call you 'Captain' as I have recommended to the president that you be immediately promoted to the rank of Major."

"Thank you, Mr. Secretary." Joshua was barely able to get the words out. "But I don't think that ..."

"Major," the secretary smiled, "you surely would not question a decision made by the Secretary of War, would you?"

"No, Sir, I didn't mean to ..." Joshua felt the president's hand rest on his shoulder and heard him actually chuckle."

"Of course you didn't," the president said. "I sometimes find it hard to question him myself. "By the way, I apologize that you and your parents had to wait so long this morning. They tell me I still have a war to run. Anyway, we have other business to tend to."

Joshua had not noticed the two boxes sitting on the edge of the president's desk. Mr. Stanton picked up the first and opened it. "Major Gibbons, in recognition of wounds received in battle in the service of your country, I am honored to pin upon your chest this medal representing the Order of the Purple Heart."

The president picked up the second box. "I do not wish to upstage the secretary," he smiled, "but I, too, have an award to present."

Secretary Stanton held the box as the president opened it. Joshua hoped that no one noticed his wide-eyed expression as he gazed at the star-shaped medallion attached to a blue ribbon adorned with a field of white stars. "Mr. President," he stuttered, "I have heard of these but I never expected to ..."

"Major, remember what Mr. Stanton told you about questioning the decisions of your superiors. On behalf of the Congress of the United States," the president stepped behind Joshua and carefully placed the ribbon around his neck, "I am proud to present you with the Medal of Honor for extreme valor and meritorious service in the face of the enemy at the Battle of Fredericksburg. Congratulations, young man."

****

The air was brisk yet not uncomfortably cold and Isaac felt the bright sun on his back. It actually seemed a bit warm, especially for mid-February. He crouched, carefully hidden behind a row of bushes, and relished the welcome and long-awaited scene that unfolded before him. Moving southward along the road, which ran parallel to the river that gave the plantation its name, was a long column of gray-clad soldiers. Those who could walk plodded slowly along, too weary to move more quickly, even from the battle that was still taking place only a short distance up the river. Those who could not walk were either carried on stretchers or rode on wagons filled with whatever precious supplies could be salvaged and brought away from the field. The scant quantity of ordinance and other material would be used if the discouraged army should halt and try to make another stand. The mules and horses appeared worn and gaunt – even more so than the tired men who walked among them. Isaac tried to muster some sympathy for those parading in misery before him but could find none. Instead, the sound of cannon and small-arms fire coming increasingly closer only served to buoy his spirits. He watched for over an hour as the procession trudged along. Only when he was sure that he would be able to keep the scene forever vivid in his memory, did he leave the hedgerow and head back toward the plantation buildings.

What Isaac witnessed near the mansion house made him even more exuberant. On the drive where so many had dismounted from their horses and carriages to dance, drink, eat, and party, there now stood a small patrol of Confederate cavalrymen. The soldiers watched grimly as Angus McManus and his family loaded what few possessions they could carry onto three small wagons hitched to mules. He noted, with satisfaction, that these were the same mules that he and the others had used to plow the cotton fields. It angered him that the house slaves appeared to be helping. He decided, though, that they probably had been told either that the advancing army was something to be greatly feared or that they would be beaten if they did not help. Either way, he was confident that the family, by mid-day, would have joined their friends and neighbors fleeing south. Yes, he decided, this was a day to be enjoyed.

Looking for his young friend Joe, Isaac walked back toward the barns and wandered about for an hour or so. Unable to find him, Isaac decided that the boy must have left already and that he might catch up with him on the road. He strolled back toward the house in time to see the small caravan heading down the drive with four of the house servants trailing behind. Though he felt for the slaves who must have been cowed into going along, he had no sympathy to waste on the family. All that remained for him now was to avoid the area where he guessed the fighting was taking place and find a Federal camp. He took one last look at the mansion, turned, smiled, and began walking north.

****

THAYER GAZETTE

FEBRUARY 18, 1863

THE LION RETURNS

Captain Henry Hancock, known by his men and the community as the *Lion of Shiloh* for his courage and leadership in that great battle, has returned to Thayer. He is presently on furlough as he recovers from a wound to his eye that he suffered while in camp. While eligible to be invalided out from the army, Hancock has decided to remain in the service of the Republic. He will be posted in Memphis, Tennessee where he will assist with the handling of new volunteers. Captain Hancock is residing at the family's home outside of town and would welcome visits from friends and acquaintances while he is there. We also expect to soon see him walking around the streets of Thayer. Henry has mentioned that he looks forward to helping his brother, Jonas, get the ground ready for spring planting before he returns to duty.

****

Stark sat with his head in his hands and pondered the scribbled note that lay on the table before him. He had made coffee but hadn't bothered to cook breakfast. He wasn't hungry. It had been nearly three hours since he had wakened and found the paper that had been slipped under his door during the night. Whoever had left it there had been able to do so without disturbing the dog. That worried him. If someone could approach the house unnoticed by the beast, what else could they do? Come inside perhaps? Not likely, but possible – and the possibility made him nervous.

The note contained only two words. But those two words carried two possible and very different implications. Perhaps whoever had written the note thought he had helped Toby and Celia to escape and was expressing gratitude. If so, they would seek no revenge and he could feel safe. This first possible explanation, the more comforting one, brought him a short-lived sense of relief but seemed unlikely. He quickly discarded it.

The likely explanation, the one upon which he dwelled, particularly unnerved him. It was that someone knew what he had done to Toby, Celia, and the unborn child. He must, more now than ever, look over his shoulder. It would be too dangerous now to walk about the plantation after dark. And what about Andrew? Would he find out? What if one of the slaves should be bold enough to approach him and tell what he had seen? How many of the slaves now knew? Some? Perhaps all? Was it now too dangerous to even remain at Pine Hill? Should he stay or go? If he were to leave, where would he go? Presently, he gulped down the last swallows of his coffee, which had gone cold, and began to sob – not out of remorse but out of fear.

"We know," the note said – nothing more. It bothered him that any of the Pine Hill slaves could write. He tried to figure out which one could have learned and who might

190

have taught him. It was, of course, illegal for a slave to learn to read and write but few among them would have cared for the legalities. They could, after all, be punished equally for such an offense at the master's discretion. It mattered not whether it was legal. There was greater legal danger to life, limb, and freedom for a white person or a free black man who dared to *provide* such instruction. Most knowledge that the slaves had of the Bible came from word of mouth. The story of Moses was the one they seemed to enjoy most. That bothered him. There ought to be severe penalties, he had told himself, for even mentioning Moses' name.

It could be any of a number of the slaves, he finally decided. There was no way to really know. He considered searching the cabins and belongings but ruled it out. Whoever had a pencil and paper, or perhaps even a book, would certainly keep them well hidden. A search would be hard to conduct without Andrew finding out and asking questions.

****

"It's not too late, is it?" Theodore asked.

Drops spattered on the window but last night's rain that continued into the late-April morning had been a gentle one, not a thunderstorm. Henry, Jonas, and Theodore sat at a table overlooking the dock at Minneapolis where the riverboat, *Alpaca,* sat waiting for the remaining supplies to be loaded. The vessel was already lying low in the water, laden with sacks of flour from nearby mills as well as a multitude of other supplies headed downriver to Grant's army. At Rock Island, the remaining deck space would be filled with arms and ammunition from the arsenal.

Henry could not yet answer as Theodore's question had come during a mouthful of scrambled eggs. Jonas, who knew both the question and answer, replied for him. "Even if he could, he wouldn't change his mind, you know."

"I know, I just thought I'd give it a last try," the young man half grinned. "I've heard the ladies talk about how stubborn *both* of you are."

"And you think you aren't?" Henry teased. "I heard Rose say just the other day that you're the worst of the lot!"

"Well, I'd say I have a way to go yet." They all laughed and Theodore took another sip of his coffee.

The jovial mood turned serious as both Henry and Theodore noticed Jonas begin to stare sullenly at the riverboat. None of them spoke for a while. Finally, Henry tapped him on the shoulder to get his attention. "Same boat, isn't it?"

"Same boat as what?" Theodore asked.

Jonas turned to him. "Same boat I came home on. Weather was a lot like today – wet and chilly. We'd been on it for days, those of us who could no longer fight, and the coffins were below decks with the bodies that were being shipped home to be buried. There was Will on his crutches and Thomas …"

"I'm sorry," Theodore said. "I didn't mean to bring up something painful."

"It's alright, Theodore. It was already there as soon as I saw the boat docked there yesterday. My God, how we all reeked from not bathing!"

Henry tried to lighten the mood. "Something like when we've all been working outside and Em doesn't want us in her kitchen!"

"Yeah, kind of like that," Jonas smiled. "Kind of like that."

"How long do you need to be gone?" Theodore asked. "Can't I go with you? I could help out just like I did in the camp. I could do all sorts of things for you."

"I would like that. I would like it very much, but no. You were a boy then but you're a young man now. There will be people there to run errands. I need a strong, faithful young man to stay with Jonas and work the farm and keep him out of trouble." He placed his hand gently on Theodore's shoulder. "Besides, he continued, "and you are not to tell the women, if the rebs come back and there's more fighting, I don't want you anywhere near it! I shouldn't be gone that long." He noticed a tear begin to well up in Theodore's eye and wished he hadn't said the last part.

Blasts from the boat's whistle signaled the beginning of boarding. Henry stood, picked up his bag, and shook hands with both of them. "Now, finish your breakfast. Take your time but don't miss the stage back to Albert Lea. You know how Em worries."

CHAPTER XII

Memphis, Tennessee

April 30, 1863

Dear Em and All,

Well I am here. I arrived by steamer about mid-morning on the 28th and have since been quite busy settling in. This is the first opportunity I have had to sit and write a few lines. The weather is quite pleasant – sunny and balmy. We ran into a storm on the river above St. Louis but the boat's pilot was quite skillful and we never felt to be in danger.

My quarters are comfortable by army standards and I should be very pleased to spend some time here if it were not for being separated from my friends and loved ones. I am sharing a room with an officer from the quartermaster corps in a hotel that has been commandeered for our purposes. It is directly across the street from the City Hall. We have taken over that building to use as offices for the provost, the quartermaster, and as a recruiting station for the many freed slaves wanting to come into the army.

If it were not for our presence in the city and the many soldiers bustling about, you would not see that there is a war going on. I am told by those who have been here for a time that the city's residents are, for the most part, resigned to our being here. They are not particularly friendly but neither do they appear openly hostile. I think that most want simply to be left alone as much as possible to go about their lives and business. As the army serves as the police department, there are the occasional instances of burglary and drunken mischief to be dealt with but I believe that these would occur anyhow and are not especially related to the city's occupation by our troops. It is said that there have been only a few incidents involving disrespect of the soldiers and that only one of those resulted in some physical harm. In all, I feel safe in going about my duties. I feel a little guilty that my injury has caused me to be removed from the fighting when so many remain in the field but take comfort that such was not of my doing and that I can still serve in some capacity.

I must stop now as it is time for dinner but will try to write more later. Take care and know that you are all loved.

Love,

Henry.

P.S.

I have just returned from dinner and heard some news, not yet confirmed, that it appears that General Grant may be within a few days of

*marching on Vicksburg. If true and if he is
successful, perhaps it will be a great help in
shortening the war.*

Henry sat at his desk and looked toward the window.
The warm sunshine of the previous day had given way
overnight to a cold rain that the wind drove violently
against the glass panes. The dark sky had forced the
building's occupants to use candles to go about their work
even though it was nearly noon. It was weather like this
that made him particularly homesick. On such a day back
home, he would be working in the horse shed repairing a
harness, or in the tool shed sharpening hoes and spades. Or
perhaps, after having done the morning chores, he would sit
by the kitchen range reading while savoring the aroma of
bread baking in the oven inches away. A game of chess
with Jonas would make such a day particularly pleasurable.
Then again, the office was warm. His uniform and boots
were clean and dry and he could look forward to a hot
lunch. All in all, he was much better fixed than he had been
last April in the weeks after the awful days at Shiloh.

Though the office door was nearly always open, the
young corporal always made it his practice to knock before
entering. Henry looked back toward the door and laid his
pipe in an ashtray near his ink well. "Yes, Harlan. What is
it?"

"There is someone who insists on seeing you," the
corporal told him. "He would not be turned away. He says
that he was told to ask for you personally and he showed
me this." He reached out with the envelope. "Shall I bring
him in?" Normally, Henry did not personally interview
each of the young freed men coming to the army. That was
the job of his subordinates. His own job was to administer
the process of bringing them into the army, to solve

196

problems and adjudicate disputes that might arise, and to co-ordinate with the quartermaster to make sure that the training camp was properly equipped and supplied.

Henry remained seated as he sized up the young man who stood silently before him, nearly at attention. The man was bigger than Theodore – older, taller, and more muscled. He was dressed in gray overalls with a threadbare, but clean, cotton shirt and nearly worn-out shoes. At some point someone had given him a ragged but serviceable army overcoat from which the insignias had been removed. The coat was too small as evidenced by the too-short sleeves but provided him some protection against the rain and cold. The man had said nothing since being ushered into the office, waiting instead for Henry to speak. His face was nearly devoid of expression. He appeared tired.

Henry had read the letter before having the man brought in and now had it spread before him on the desk. "You have read this?" he asked.

"No, Sir," the man replied. "It was addressed to you. It was sealed. I didn't feel it was my place."

"I see. That was very gentlemanly. I'm sure you were curious."

"Yes, Sir."

Henry began to read aloud. ***"Dear Captain Hancock, I would like to introduce to you a young man who arrived at our camp in late-February, having walked away from a local plantation that had been abandoned as the army approached. I believe that you will find this man worthy of your special attention. He is very literate, which I believe speaks to his character given the risk that he undertook by learning to*** *read and write. His given name is Isaac and he has taken the last name of Douglass out of admiration for Frederick Douglass. At my request, he has been allowed to travel with the army. I have not sent him north sooner as I did not wish him to arrive in Memphis until I knew you would be on duty there and could personally assist him in joining the army. Isaac is a hard and willing worker who takes instruction quickly and well. I think he has the makings of a fine soldier. It is my hope that, rather than being given rudimentary training and sent to the line, he might be sent to Fort Snelling, Minnesota for additional instruction. In my opinion, with military training, this man could be an excellent liaison between our white officers and the colored troops who will serve under them.*

I will be most interested to learn of your decision.

Sincerely,
Lt. Leland H. Atlee,
Minnesota Volunteer Infantry.

"Well, Mr. Douglass?" Henry looked up at him and waited.

"Mr. Atlee is a good man."

"Yes – a good man and a good judge of people. If Lt. Atlee tells me you will be a fine soldier, then you will be a fine soldier. I am inclined to follow his recommendation. It will take longer for you to get to the line but I fear that this

198

war is going to last for some time yet. There is no hurry and I think it will make you a better soldier. I will leave the decision to you whether to stay in camp here or to go to Minnesota."

"Minnesota, Sir. I would like to go to Minnesota."

"Very well, then it's settled. I will swear you into the army here. Corporal Harlan will take you to the quartermaster to get you a proper uniform and make arrangements for travel. There is a steamer leaving for St. Louis tomorrow for supplies.

****

Harold and George took turns riding on the aging mule and walking alongside. The animal had been deemed unsuitable by the troops combing the area looking for replacements to pull wagons and artillery. Even with mules being hard to come by and the standards now being lower, the poor beast had been rejected as not worth the bother. He had seemed hardly able to move himself along, let alone able to haul anything of value. He had only come into the pair's possession days earlier when they had done some work for a local farmer who was unable to pay them. He was more than eager to save the hay that the creature would consume.

It had been a long trek, taking over seven months to get from Maryland to western Mississippi. All that remained was to cross the river into Louisiana, then into Texas and head for Mexico. They were now so far removed from Antietam that they ceased to see themselves as either soldiers or deserters. Like many others in the Deep South, they now saw themselves simply as displaced persons trying to make their way the best they could. They had not found a chicken to steal for quite some time. It now was hard to find even a rabbit to snare and roast. Harold, having once been pleasantly plump, had lost more weight than

199

George. The muscled arms and legs of the past had given way to folds of sagging skin and his once-fat cheeks now appeared hollow and wanting.

The day was warm and humid – more like mid-June than the end of April. It had rained for a time the night before and the mud stuck to what now passed for shoes. For some time, they had walked the well-traveled roads instead of trails or paths through timbers and fields. They were far from the fighting and had decided that the risk of running into soldiers was low enough to be outweighed by the convenience that the roads offered. Still, they mostly avoided towns. They knew, though, that if they hoped to cross the river on the ferry at Vicksburg there would be no avoiding the army that would be there.

Harold longed for a cup of hot coffee while George had long-since smoked the stump of a cigar that he had found. They were not arguing but neither was in a particularly good mood as they trudged along. For long stretches, they hadn't said a word. During their journey they had pretty much discussed every topic that was of interest to either of them and their occasional discussions with the local farmers had produced little news.

They had only a vague idea of where they were. They had no maps and the road signs pointing the way to the numerous small towns of the area meant little to them. They knew only that they had continually walked west and figured that sometime soon they must reach the river and find a way to cross. George pulled the soiled handkerchief from his hip pocket and wiped his face as they rounded the bend in the road. "Dammit!"

It was all reminiscent of their encounter with the Confederate patrol in Georgia. "You there! Halt!"

George managed a grim joke. "At least I don't think they'll want the mule." He stayed on the animal's back as the sergeant unholstered his revolver and walked toward them.

"Dismount and identify yourselves."

George slid from the mule and both he and Harold produced empty hands to prove they were unarmed. They had agreed ever since Georgia that, if approached, they would use the same story. In fact, they had used it numerous times in their visits with farmers for whom they had done odd jobs. With time and use, the story had become much easier to tell believably and the two were confident that it would again serve them well.

It was nearly noon and the patrol had stopped for a brief respite and meal. George and Harold recounted to the sergeant their story about being invalided out. Their increasingly emaciated condition made the story even more believable and it was accepted without question. They enjoyed their first taste of what they considered real food in days. Harold had his coffee and one of the troopers presented George with a whole fresh cigar to smoke. As the pair expected, the troopers expressed no interest in the sad mule.

The small interlude had actually turned out to be enjoyable. George and Harold were able to find out they were only a few short miles from Vicksburg. They learned, though, that Grant's large and growing army was in the vicinity and was soon expected to make an assault on the city. The ferry, they were told, was no longer operating.

The soldiers offered to allow the duo the choice of either going on their way or accompanying them back to the city. Fearful of running into one of Grant's less understanding patrols, they decided to leave on their own and try to make their way south to New Orleans. Harold had just taken his turn aboard the mule when they heard the first shots.

****

Thayer, Minnesota

April 30, 1863

Dearest Husband,

I am missing you so sorely today. Even though it has been a short time since you were here, it seems as an eternity. I cherish the time that we had together but, in some ways, it has made me more lonesome for you. I look forward so to the time that this war is over and we can have our life together. All the same, I feel a little selfish knowing that there are so many whose husbands will not be coming home or will never be able to work or to enjoy their lives in good health. I grieve for all the little ones who will never know their fathers.

Enough of sadness. I have other news to share with you. I have suspected, and Dr. Hanson agrees, that I am with child. I am hopeful that you can be home by the time our first little one is born next winter. I think that, if we should have a son, we should name him David or, if a daughter, Mary Alice. I hope you will agree but, of course, we do not need to decide just yet. They have both been so good to us!

Ellie is at school today and Jonas and Theodore are in the timber cutting wood to

202

make fence posts. I made them a lunch to take with them.

I have just finished washing clothes and have hung them out to dry. I propose to make some bread this afternoon and wish you could be here to share as I know you enjoy it so.

I will add more to this letter a little later and hope to send it with Ellie to post when she goes to town for school tomorrow. Please stay in good spirits and know that you are loved and missed by all here.

As always in love,

Em.

Well, I have made up dough and set it to rise. Jonas had that awful dream again last night. A storm came up suddenly during the night and, even though he couldn't hear the thunder, he must have somehow sensed it. I had hoped that with not having the storms during the winter it would have gone away for him but he seems to fear it will be with him always. We had forgotten to warn Theodore about it and he didn't know what to think when Jonas began to scream in his sleep. We woke him up and got him comfortable but I do not think he slept the rest of the night for fear of dreaming again.

I don't know much about what he dreams. He has never told me. I'm sure it has to be terrible if it frightens him so. Has he told you? He doesn't seem to want to talk about it so I don't ask though I sometimes wonder if it might do him some good to talk about it.

****

Stark couldn't tell if he was awake or dreaming. It was the chance that he was awake that disturbed him. It was dark and raining and hard to tell the difference between night and day. He was sitting up in bed and what he *did* know was that he was warm, shaking, and sweating. He wasn't feeling well and had been running a fever for a few days now. He hoped it was simply the fever causing him to hallucinate but they seemed so *real*! He lay back down and covered his head with a pillow but it did no good. Moments passed and he moved the pillow away but they were still standing at the foot of the bed, silently staring at him.

Toby was wearing the same overalls that he had worn that night in the barn. His unmoving eyes looked straight and piercingly into Stark's. Stark had no desire to get out of the bed and look more closely to see if the young man was wearing shoes. The girl, Celia, stood next to Toby. Like Toby, she was staring at him. But, unlike Toby's, her head appeared to loll awkwardly to one side. Her once-pretty, smooth, bronze skin was bleached out to a dirty brown and both she and her clothes were soaked in muddy, red water. Celia held an infant to her breast but the child appeared lifeless with its head draped loosely and helplessly over her arm. Behind them there stood another, shadowy figure that Stark could not identify. The figure spoke in a low, soft, yet menacing voice. "We know. We all know what you did."

"Leave. Leave now and don't come back," he ordered. But they didn't leave. They continued to stare at him. "Leave, I said. Leave now," he told them again. He felt himself barking an order but, at the same time, he sensed his lips quivering. "Go away. Leave me alone!"

"We know," came the voice again.

Stark again covered his head with his pillow, pulled his knees up under his chin, and waited. Later, when he dared to look, the sun shone through the window and the figures were gone. There was not much to do today and what there was would have to wait. He tucked the pistol into his belt underneath his coat, summoned what little courage he had, and headed out toward the stream, the lane, and the barn. He had to know.

****

It lasted only moments. But when it was over, six of the soldiers were dead including the ones who had provided the cigar and the coffee. Harold had jumped from the mule. Both he and George had hidden in the bushes at the first sound. They peered out from the brush at the scene unfolding before them. Blue-clad troopers were moving among the bodies, checking each and removing weapons or any other items deemed useful. Across the road stood the survivors of the ambush – hands in the air – being disarmed. More Federal soldiers stood aside holding newly acquired horses.

Still crouched in the bushes, George turned away from the road and began to make a break for the heavier thicket some distance behind. Harold tried to grab him but it was too late. At that moment, he saw a trooper stare at the bushes and begin to approach them, pistol drawn. "You there! Drop your weapons. Come out with your hands where we can see them! Do it now or you're dead!"

CHAPTER XIII

Theodore stopped briefly and leaned on his hoe – the first break he had taken in over an hour. He stood shirtless while the only concession Jonas had made to the heat was to roll up his sleeves to just past his elbows. The work was hard but, to Theodore in particular, it was rewarding. For the first time in his young life, he was toiling not only for mere subsistence but for real pay – money to do with as he wished. Em's food was good and it was plentiful. She always made sure that he had clean and well-mended clothes. The bed that he and Jonas had built had a thick goose down mattress and a feather pillow. He had no desire at all to leave the farm and his new friends. At the same time though he relished the sense that, if he wished to leave, he was free to do so without being hunted down and punished. The best part of his new life, however, was that for the first time ever, he was being treated as a man and not as a work animal or a piece of equipment.

They had worked all morning, weeding the corn field. It appeared that there would be a real crop. The rains had come at the right time and in the right amount. The temperatures had been nearly perfect and the cornstalks were upright, lush, and deep green.

Theodore looked to the sky and noted that the sun was directly overhead. He expected that, at any moment, either Em or Ellie would ring the dinner bell and it would be time to head to the house for lunch and a few moments of welcome rest. As he heard the bell, he tapped Jonas on the shoulder. Pulling the prized watch from his pocket, he opened it to show Jonas that it was noon. Hoes over their shoulders, they whistled as they walked toward the house. Theodore looked back over his shoulder and noticed the storm clouds beginning to build and roil on the horizon. Jonas did not.

Em greeted them as soon as they finished cleaning up at the washstand on the back porch. Always the gentleman, Theodore had put his shirt back on before entering the house. The smell of fresh-baked bread and fried chicken wafted throughout the kitchen and neither he nor Jonas had realized how hungry they really were until that moment. "Ellie went to town this morning for some coffee, sugar, flour, and cloth for a new dress," Em announced, signing as she spoke. "We have a letter from Henry."

"After we eat." Jonas was already pulling a chair from the kitchen table. "Those horses out in the barn are lucky we have something much tastier to eat."

Theodore looked at him quizzically. "I'll explain later," Em told him. "Theodore, would you like to give thanks?"

"I'm always thankful these days, Mrs. Hancock." Despite being at the farm since February and feeling more like a member of the family with each passing day, he still only addressed Em and Ellie as Mrs. and Miss Hancock respectively. "Our Father who watches over us and provides for us …"

Memphis, Tennessee
June 28, 1863

Dear Em and All,

I hope this letter finds you all well and content. I think often of you and of our little one who is to come. I so look forward to holding our child in my arms. It is hot here today and I think that the moisture from the river makes it feel more uncomfortable than it otherwise would.

As we have no word otherwise, I assume that General Grant has continued his siege at Vicksburg but not captured the city. Though I have no sympathy for their cause, I cannot help but feel some sorrow for the innocents caught up in this thing – especially for the children. No food or other supplies are allowed in and I assume that much of what is already there is consumed by the army. There surely must be much hunger and privation. I hope that General Pemberton will soon see fit to surrender the city peacefully. That will help to alleviate the suffering of the residents and spare the armies on both sides from numbers of needless casualties. In addition, having the city will allow our boats to move freely up and down the river all the way from St. Louis to New Orleans. It will cut off the Deep South from getting any help from Texas or other Rebel areas to the west.

Our own army, on the other hand, is well supplied with everything needed as well as being able to easily move more troops down the river. It seems that every day we continue to send more soldiers, supplies, and ammunition. With all of that, I do not see that the war here in the west can last much longer. I think that, once Little Rock is taken and Arkansas is securely in Union hands, most of the fighting will be in Virginia, the Carolinas, Georgia, and eastern Tennessee. If so, it is possible that my work here can be concluded. I do not wish to unfairly raise your expectations but, if that is to be the case, perhaps my part in the war will be finished and I will be able to come home before the winter sets in.

I have a letter from the young man, Isaac, whom I wrote you about. He has arrived at Fort Snelling and is proceeding with his training and seems quite happy about it. Though I am placed where I am needed, I somewhat envy him his posting. If I were stationed there, I might be able to come home to visit occasionally. He expects soon to go into the field and to probably be attached to one of the colored regiments serving under General Sherman.

I am glad to hear that Theodore seems to be adapting well to our family and seems happy to be spending his time with us. I hope he is able to keep up with his lessons as I think he will do pretty well for himself.

We are hearing that General Thomas Jackson has died. If not for the loss that this causes for the South's efforts, I should be saddened by his passing. From what I have heard, he appears to have been a devout and righteous man.

Has Lucille Anderson moved back to Indiana yet and have you managed to settle with her for the farm?

I will try to write more to you later.

Love to all of you,

Henry.

****

Joshua sat in his small office on the first floor of the army hospital in Baltimore. The heat was oppressive even with the window open and a slight breeze blowing from the harbor. It was nearly time to lead the evening prayer service for those of the staff who wished to attend. His day, as with nearly all days lately, had been spent making rounds ministering to the spiritual needs of the patients in all of the various wards. He was Chief of the Chaplains at the hospital. Though he had others to assist him, more and more patients kept coming. With wounded arriving now from the Battle of Chancellorsville, the tide seemed endless. It depressed him that as many seemed to be going to cemeteries as were going home. He had begun to wonder more often lately how long he could continue witnessing the enormous suffering without losing his mind. "Dear, merciful God," he prayed, cupping his hands before him and bowing over his desk, "I am your faithful servant and I know that you answer our prayers in your own way and in your own good time but I beg you, if it be your will, please stop this madness. Have these men not suffered enough? How much more must there be before it is done?"

Somewhere in Virginia.

June 28, 1863.

Dear Father,

I have not heard from you for quite some time though I continue to write to you. I assume that you are receiving my letters but suppose that even the mail is uncertain in these times. I wish to know if you are well and if the plantation is in order as much as possible. I am hopeful that the slaves are present and working on the cotton crop and have not begun to run off thinking that Lincoln has actually set them free.

I am certain you have heard by now of our great victory at Chancellorsville and that we have nearly driven the Yankee cowards from Virginia. We were all saddened to learn of the death of our great leader General Jackson. General Lee will certainly miss him as we prepare to march to Washington and force the enemy to sue for peace and grant us our well-deserved independence. I look forward to that glorious day when our army marches down Pennsylvania Avenue past the tyrant's palace while all that the residents of the city can do is stand by and watch us. If Lincoln can be captured before he is able to flee, I would even like to watch him hang. From what I know of General Lee, however, I am not supposing he would allow that to happen.

My duties call and I must stop for now but please write me and let me know that you are well.

Your faithful son,

Darius.

****

The heat was stifling and the moist Pennsylvanian air made it an effort to breathe. Darius had undone most of the buttons on his woolen tunic and was tempted to discard it but hadn't. By nightfall, it would become uncomfortably cool. He would want both it and the blanket that he carried rolled up and tied across his back. He removed the cap from his canteen and swallowed the last of the tepid but precious water. Up and down the line, others were doing the same as they stood and waited for the regiment to be called up. Some stood silently watching what was unfolding before them. Some prayed and read from the small Testaments that they carried in their pockets. Others re-checked their weapons for the second or third time and chatted among themselves both to pass the time and to calm their nerves.

Darius was one of the silent ones. His ears filled with the constant roar of the great guns exchanging volleys in the distance and the closer crackle of small-arms fire. The rebel yell sounded from those already charging through the woods up the hill called Little Round Top.

For the first time since joining the army, Darius was genuinely afraid. It was easy to be brave when guarding prisoners in Richmond. Forgetting the boredom and the desire for action, he now longed to be back where the enemy was helpless and unarmed. Bravery had come almost as easily at Fredericksburg where he had crouched behind a stone wall to load his weapon. One had only to look over the wall, fire into the ranks of soldiers trying to advance across the open field, and crouch again behind the wall to safety. Today, it was different. It was the Yankees who held the high ground. The only cover for the advancing army was timber and, in some places, a dense and almost impenetrable thicket.

Throughout the morning, wave after wave charged into the woods only to be repulsed and come running back to the line. With each futile charge, fewer were coming back. Those who made it back seemed changed. The physical wounds were obvious. There were bloody scalps, torn faces, and arms that seemed held in place by nothing more than torn sleeves. Some made it back with their bodies intact but terrified expressions frozen on their faces. Others cried while a few dropped their weapons, curled up on the ground, and covered their ears. Up and down the line, officers and sergeants exhorted the able-bodied to get up off the ground and re-join the fight. A few reluctantly obeyed while others seemed to not hear. Darius tried not to imagine what they had seen that could bring eager and confident men to such a state. Whatever it was, he hoped it was over before he, himself, had to see it.

He gazed up and down the line. All around him stood rows of shining bayonets. They were nearly the only thing uniform about this army. There were men with full beards beginning to show gray. Some faces were clean-shaven or showing a few days of stubbly growth. Others appeared too young to have ever shaved at all. There were slouch hats and a variety of other head coverings, some actually army-issued kepis. There were homespun shirts, some plain and others with stripes or faded plaids. Some were clean and others had been worn for days in the July heat without washing – stained from sweat and dirt. There were standard uniform trousers. There were ordinary pants so often and crudely mended that they were more patch than pant. Some were held by belts weighted down with holsters and cartridge boxes. Others were kept in place by an assortment of suspenders of many colors and types. The boots and shoes were as haphazard as everything else. Many were army issue – others not. Most of the better boots had been removed from the bodies of dead Federals left on the field at Chancellorsville.

Darius could nearly tell the exact moment when each charge reached its height and began to fall back. At that moment, he could no longer hear the Rebel yell above the fire. It all seemed suddenly wrong to him – not the killing and the dying – that was to be expected. But it was supposed to be him and his friends doing the killing and the Yanks doing the dying. He was not at all eager when the order came and the line began to move forward into the trees.

Yards into the forest, the line ceased to be a line at all. It took on more the appearance of a mob with no defined ranks. What had, shortly before, at least somewhat resembled an army now looked to be more a mass of individuals moving erratically around trees, bushes, rocks, and each other. Some moved quickly, some hardly at all. The pace seemed to pick up as they neared the scene of the actual fighting. There was some attempt to form back into a line but the only result was organized chaos. The ragtag group yelled and charged up the wooded slope.

It was a decision that each had to make as the mass tore through the trees – to fire toward the defenders at the top of the hill, hoping to hit one, or to hold on to the one precious load in the barrel of his gun. Once fired, there would be little chance to stop and reload. The empty rifle would become only a club or a large handle for a bayonet. Darius had decided ahead of time. He would hold his fire for as long as possible.

He had gone only a short distance when he saw what had brought such terror to those who had gone before. No longer were there only trees and rocks to step around or roots to step over. Bodies littered the floor of the forest, lying in a variety of grotesque positions. Finding it impossible to step around each, the army was advancing over them as if they were stones – both the dead and those still living but unable to move. Looking ahead, Darius could see men who had, moments before, stood in the line with him, now added to the litter. He wished he could be anywhere else. But he wasn't anywhere else. He was here, and the mass of humanity behind him kept pushing him forward. He could now see the top of the slope, the stone wall, and the muzzle flashes. He could still hear the yell but it was strained and hoarse. There were fewer men left to provide its voice. The crackle of small-arms fire was now a constant din with no discernible break between one shot and the next. Soon, the only battle cry that he could hear came not from the men around him but from the defenders at the top of the hill: "Remember Fredericksburg!"

He was one of the few to nearly reach the wall but feared what would happen if he were to make it into the breach. There would be no sudden victory or even much chance of survival. He remembered the thrill of killing men at short range at Fredericksburg. Now the thrill would most likely belong to some Yank rabble. It might be a gunshot or a well-placed stab with a bayonet or a sword. Whichever it was to be, he hoped it would be quick and painless. He decided to fire his shot. Might as well take one more of them with him.

It was not to be. Nearing the wall, he aimed and pulled the trigger. It was too noisy. He couldn't tell if his gun had fired or not. What he *did* manage to hear was a voice calling from behind to fall back. As he turned to retreat, he took a glance behind him. At that moment, the entire Federal line clambered over the wall with bayonets fixed and began charging down the hill.

He had no idea how far he had run before he tripped on a protruding tree root and dived headlong onto a fallen log. When he awoke, the first thing he noticed was that all of the shooting and yelling had stopped. In the eerie quiet, Federal soldiers moved through the timber checking the fallen to see which were dead and which might receive medical attention. Most would not. Darius sat with his throbbing head in his hands and waited for the inevitable capture. This part of the war was certainly over for him. He began to envision the prison at Richmond. But this, he knew and dreaded, would be different. He could only hope that his captors would never learn of his past as a guard. Presently, he felt the slight touch of a bayonet point between his shoulder blades. "You, stand up and raise your hands!"

Only a short time later, Darius found himself among rows of others – seated with hands clasped behind their heads. A corporal and a private moved along the line and stopped at each prisoner. "Your name?" the corporal would ask. The private would write it down and they would move on to the next. "Your name?" It was his turn.

"Moran," he answered. "Sergeant Davis Moran." It sounded strangely natural as he said it.

****

Henry had time on his hands – too much of it, he had decided. Each day of his work required less than three or four hours. Since he had been assigned no other duties, there was more free time than he could recall having since before he had been old enough to begin helping out with chores as a child back in Ohio. He had no desire to spend his days wandering about Memphis. For the first time since coming to the army, he had time to think.

At first, the thoughts had been mostly of home – wondering daily what was going on with the farm and his family, musing on what his life would hold after the war. He thought about the young men he was recruiting into the army. How would they account themselves in battle? How many would see the end of the war? How many would be too badly maimed to enjoy their newly found freedom?

Most disturbing of all was that awful recurring vision. Unlike the nightmares from which the family had often heard Jonas awaken, the vision could come to him at any time and at any place. It did not happen only at night. Nor was it triggered by lightning and rain. Once the vision began, it was all-consuming and must play out to the end. It could not be stopped by a friendly voice, a gentle shaking or a compassionate hand.

It always began with a fine gray mist, seen but unfelt except for the unsettling chill that accompanied it. Gradually, the mist would coalesce into a face, blurry at first but by each moment coming into focus. The face was that of a man Henry guessed to be younger than himself, but made old before its time by the strain of battle. The face sported a full but somewhat well-trimmed beard that was already beginning to show traces of gray. The countenance was one of fierce determination tempered with a sense of dread. Sweaty with the heat of battle and a warm April day, the entire face showed streaks of spent black powder that ran from forehead to neck. Atop the man's head was a gray kepi, pulled nearly over the eyes and bearing the insignia 'CSA.'

There was no sound but, as Henry watched, a bullet entered his sight and moved slowly, almost imperceptibly toward the face. He gazed, transfixed by both bullet and face. After what seemed like several minutes, the bullet disappeared from view. The look on the face morphed from one of determination to one of wide-eyed shock and a stream of blood slowly flowed from beneath the kepi and down the bridge of the nose. Slowly, the face moved backward and out of sight. The silence was replaced by the mournful wailing of a woman and the voices of children calling out for their father. It seemed that the wailing and shouting would never stop.

It was Sunday morning. There was no work to be done today but Henry had risen early. He had been unable to sleep except for perhaps a few moments. Saturday night had been hot and sickeningly humid. He had tried opening the window to his quarters but there was no cooling breeze to be had and he had only succeeded in allowing what seemed to be an entire hoard of mosquitos to enter the room. Both man and bed linens were sticky with sweat. The day ahead promised to be no more comfortable.

Henry stood over the basin of hot water and looked into the mirror. He prepared to lather up to shave. Shortly after, the image in the mirror began to be obscured by the familiar gray mist. Even though the room was still hot and humid, he began to feel a clammy chill come over his body. Sensing what was coming, he sat his shaving mug and brush on the washstand next to the bowl and moved away from the mirror.

There was one thing only that he had come to count upon to prevent or stop the hallucination. The stopping of it had, of late, become his greater demon. Reaching into his footlocker, he felt around for two bottles, one large and one the size of an apothecary vial. He sat both on the table near his bed and poured a generous amount of whiskey into a glass. Next, he poured in a small but sufficient amount of laudanum. Careful to first place both bottles back into their hiding place, he sat on the edge of the bed and quickly consumed the entire contents of the glass. Lying back on the bed, he soon found himself enveloped in a comforting fog.

****

Vicksburg, Mississippi
July 14, 1863

Captain Henry Hancock
Office of Colored Troop Recruitment
Memphis, Tennessee.

Dear Henry,

On Sunday last, the regiment entered the city of Vicksburg to begin our part in the Federal occupation and to maintain martial law.

For all intents and purposes, there has ceased to be a city. Some estimates say that our batteries fired as many as twenty-five thousand shells into the town in the twelve months prior to our laying siege. Some say that, since the siege began in early May, we have fired as many as twenty-four hundred per day. There is little of value that remains standing and it appears that large numbers of the residents have taken to living in caves dug into the ground in order to avoid the bombardment. Everywhere one looks, there are piles of rubble where buildings once stood and blackened chimneys where there were once houses.

There is scarcely a cow, hog, horse, or mule that has not been taken to feed General Pemberton's army. It is said that the Rebels had begun to slaughter and eat the horses and mules both to survive and to keep us from capturing them. One sees few dogs or cats and we are assuming that the population turned to them for food to avoid starvation.

It is said that we have taken more than thirty thousand prisoners along with hundreds of large guns and great stockpiles of ammunition. I see a formidable task before us in feeding and sheltering the prisoners and in transporting them to camps. I anticipate that most of them will not fare well but I have little sympathy for them. The best that can be said for most of them is that they will now away from battle.

I have always prided myself on being a good Christian and a compassionate man but I also have trouble feeling sympathy for the adult civilian residents of the city. I only feel for the children who had no say in bringing about the national calamity but am certain that even they, as they grew to adulthood, would have done little differently than their parents.

I have saved most of my compassion for the freed slaves who wander about the city. While in bondage, they have suffered the privations even worse than their masters. They have now been left largely to fend for themselves as the army is, as yet, unable to do much to assist them.

As we move around town, we see numerous signs advertising slave auctions. Where we find them, we attempt as best to either deface or otherwise destroy them. This morning, we came across the site of one of the actual auctions. There were still chains and other accoutrements lying about, some still attached to the posts where the slaves had been tied up to be shown off to prospective buyers. We found the sight so sickening and reprehensible that, with the captain's permission, we set fire to it and burned it to the ground.

I must close now as there is much work to be done. I hope this letter finds you in good health. Please address correspondence to my attention at the Office of the Provost.

Best Respects,

Lt. Leland Atlee
Minnesota Volunteer Infantry,
United States Army.

****

 The room was dark except for the faint yellow and orange fingers that kaleidoscoped among the shadows on the ceiling. Henry sat on the edge of his bunk, holding his head in his hands. They were the first tears that he had shed since his father died. The war had been going on for some two and a half years. He had seen death and come to grudgingly accept it as an unfortunate but natural consequence. Even Edward Kaler's death, though not battle-related, he had come to see as a part of war. But this … this was different.

Lawrence, Kansas.

August 26th, 1863

Captain Henry Hancock
Office of Colored Troop Recruitment
Memphis, Tennessee.

Dear Cousin,

   You will undoubtedly have heard of this before you receive my letter but I am compelled to write anyhow.

   This past Saturday, I had business in Lecompton. Had my business been instead

222

in Lawrence I would probably now be dead. I had risen very early and arrived in Lecompton about the time I normally would have been finishing my breakfast. Instead of cooking anything, I had thrown some cold biscuits in my knapsack and did not take time to make coffee.

After finishing the business, I immediately left to go back to my farm. As I was nearing there, I could see an enormous cloud of smoke just over the hills to the east. Mustang was already tired from our journey but I spurred him on after just a brief rest and some water. I didn't want to tarry as I knew that something must be terribly wrong and wanted to be of some help if I could. As I continued to ride, I began to develop a terrible dread that something happened that was much worse than just a fire at the sawmill or the livery stable. As I got closer, I could hear shouting and what sounded like gunfire.

What I saw next is too painful to describe to you. You will likely read of it in newspaper accounts and that will need to suffice. Just as I was arriving, the horde of border ruffians, whom I have learned were led by William Quantrill, was riding off to the east away from the scene of their crime. They were continuing to whoop and holler and still shooting their weapons back toward the town.

Henry, I am a grown man and, like you, have seen battle, but I still weep when I think of what happened here. I grieve not only for the lost souls and their widows and orphans but for our land. What has happened to us that a people can perpetrate such wanton cruelty on each other? I know that it is not only Rebels. I have heard accounts of atrocities committed by Jayhawkers and Unionists upon innocent populations in Missouri. From our reading of history, we both know that wars have been around since the earliest days of man. I remember reading Plato's quote that 'Only the dead have seen the end of war.' It seems though, that in most wars in this century, particularly those in Europe, the civilian populations have been left largely alone to go about their business. Armies would gather in the field and shoot it out among themselves. As horrible as it was, the greatest effect on the majority of the citizens was that boundaries on maps changed and different rulers took charge. I never recall reading that Napoleon or Wellington went out of their way to massacre innocents.

Henry, I really believed that, after I spent my time at the hospital in Fort Scott and was invalided out, I had seen the end of this war. I must now conclude that Old Plato must have been right. I understand, from accounts that I have read, that the Rebels are still very active in Missouri, especially in the southern part of the state and the Ozark Hills. I fear that there will be more incursions into the northern part of the state and into Kansas. Those incursions will undoubtedly be met with harsh reprisals, more retaliatory attacks, and much before what you have called 'the nasty business' is finally settled. I am glad that most of our friends and loved ones live back in Ohio and Minnesota far out of harm's way.

I must close now. If you write to me, send to the post office in Lecompton in care of my friend, George Sanders. I know that he will hold letters for me. The post office in Lawrence is destroyed and it is uncertain when mail service will resume.

Pray for peace.

Shelby H.

****

Camp near Little Rock Ark
October 12, 1863

Captain Henry Hancock
Office of Colored Troop Recruitment
Memphis, Tennessee.

Dear Henry,

I have a little leisure time this afternoon that affords me the opportunity to write you a few lines to keep you informed as to how we are getting along. We are well, that is Baker, Akers, Miller and myself. There is not much sickness in the Company or Regiment. The weather has been splendid but just now it is raining and I have to huddle under our little shelter and write on my knees. It does not seem to rain much. The weather has been cool but this day it is warm. There has been some difficulty about supplies. For several days we were on less than half rations but I think we will get plenty now the supply train has come in. The cars are running regularly from here to Devall's Bluffs but there is only one engine and very few freight and no passenger cars. The Rebels burned what few they had. I have no news to write concerning our movements. We are here in camp and that is all I know about the matter. I am thinking that this whole army will not winter here of course and that we are likely to leave as any others. Some will be left here however as an occupation garrison to maintain order and make sure that the Rebel elements in the city do not cause too much trouble or disrupt the flow of supplies in and out of the city. We have not been told whether the regiment will be assigned that duty or moved elsewhere. It is afternoon. I concluded to write a little bit more. It did not rain enough to lay the dust. Our mail has been badly mixed up. Well, it has commenced to rain again and I am again obliged to seek shelter. We are not yet as well fixed as we were at our encampment at Vicksburg. I never knew that I set so much store by victuals until I came into the army. I can get along tolerably well for all but bread. You know that the army hard bread is a nuisance and we have to live on it most of the time. I would rather have any old crusts that I once would have thrown to the dog. I would rather have corn bread made of water meal and salt after it had been baked for a week. The boys do not all dislike it as bad as I do but none like it. We have no way of baking if we had flour but we can make a kind of fritters cooked in our frying pans that are pretty good while hot but it takes a pound of grease and no little work. We get occasionally a nice mess of sweet potatoes. If we had some good butter to put on them and sweet milk to drink with them they would be splendid. We get some nice sweet pumpkins but have no way of cooking them to make them fit to eat. Under all privations I console myself by thinking it won't last much longer and when it is over I will be better capable of appreciating home comforts back in Crestville.

There is an Iowa regiment in the camp next to ours. They are the 29th Volunteers. They have already been assigned and providing provost duty before our arrival. Whether or not both regiments stay will depend on how much trouble the Rebels intend to make. That regiment is from Union County in southern Iowa. I have made the acquaintance of a Lieutenant named Ira who is a farmer like us and came to Iowa from Pennsylvania before the war. He has also been a schoolmaster and country sheriff. We have gotten on quite well and hope to visit again if both regiments are kept here. He lives near a town called Afton. He tells me that there is a little village nearby named Thayer that sounds to me to be much like Thayer, Minnesota.

Union County is only about thirty miles from the Missouri border. Ira said that it always seemed odd to live so close to a state that still allows slavery. He noted, though, that slavery is less common in northern Missouri where the climate and land are much like Iowa. Most of the farms are too small to support a slave and many have only one or none at all. Some of the farmers have even joined Iowa regiments. He says that is much different than Missouri's border with Kansas where there has been such trouble with both sides raiding each other's towns and farms.

I would like to hear from you and whether you have any news from home that I may not have heard during our excursion from Vicksburg to here. Should you write me, direct to the regiment via Helena Ark.

Lt. Leland Atlee
Minnesota Volunteer Infantry.

United States Army.

Chapter XIV

A cold fog had rolled in from the sea overnight and now enveloped the harbor in a thick, misty shroud. On a clear day, Joshua could easily see Fort McHenry from his office window. This morning, he could barely see the sidewalk that ran in front of the hospital. From where he sat, he could hear disembodied voices coming from the street and the clip-clop of horses' hooves as taxis carried the city's residents to their daily chores.

The workload of ministering to the needs of hundreds of wounded from the Battle of Chancellorsville had barely begun to subside when it was replaced by the even more overwhelming task that followed Gettysburg. That tide had ebbed with time and most of the wounded from that battle had now, in one way or another, left the hospital. Some had been able to return to duty with the army. Others had been sent home to either continue their recuperation or to begin learning how to live without various limbs or faculties. The less fortunate had gone home to be buried in family plots or one of the many military cemeteries that the war was rapidly filling.

Joshua had continued to pray for an end to the violence but became increasingly discouraged as his fervent prayers, for reasons known only to God, seemed to go unanswered. There was a lull in the fighting in Virginia following Gettysburg but the war was far from settled. Few of the casualties from September's Battle of Chickamauga in Georgia had been brought to Baltimore, but that did nothing to comfort him. It was only geography. The killing, the maiming, the grief, and the suffering seemed to just go on and on. He could no more see the end of it than he could see the fort in the harbor. Like the fort, he knew it was there but he could not feel or touch it.

He sat alone in the office in a chair near the window and picked up the letter he had earlier placed on the chair-side table. While he felt honored to accept the invitation that it contained, the thought of the occasion only deepened his sense of melancholy.

The Executive Mansion
Washington, D.C.
November 6, 1863

Major Joshua Gibbons,
Chief of Chaplains
United States Military Hospital
Baltimore, Maryland

Dear Major Gibbons,

In recognition of your valorous actions at the Battle of Fredericksburg and your excellence and compassion in ministering to the spiritual needs of our wounded soldiers, the President of the United States requests that you accompany his party to the dedication of the cemetery at Gettysburg. If it should be your wish to accept this invitation, please reply by telegram as soon as possible that we may provide you with details with respect to travel arrangements and accommodations.

Respectfully,

John Hay, Secretary to the President.

He carefully re-folded the letter and placed it in his desk before leaving to lead the morning service and make his rounds.

****

Seven hundred and fifty miles to the west, Major Robert Herschel MacDonald, Chief of Surgeons also stood looking out the window of another hospital. Actually, it was not a hospital at all but a few rooms sectioned off at the end of a barracks where Robert and the two other physicians had carved out some rudimentary offices. Like Joshua's, his view was also limited by the weather but here it was not fog. The wind was driving snow nearly horizontally across the Mississippi River that had already begun to freeze for the winter. Though the Illinois shore was less than a mile distant, he could not see it. His wife, Rose, had begged him not to report for work but he had come anyhow. Even though the camp was not yet occupied and its 'hospital' had yet to see any patients, there was much to be done. Within weeks, he and his staff would be working day and night treating the sick and wounded prisoners who would be coming to the Federal Prison Camp at Rock Island.

Though he had to measure his words in expressing his feelings to his superiors, the Major was far less than satisfied with the conditions they would meet upon arriving at the camp. From accounts received of prisoners who had been exchanged earlier in the war, it was common knowledge that conditions at the Confederate prison camp at Andersonville, Georgia were far worse than inhuman and deplorable. He knew that the naval blockade had nearly destroyed the South's ability to take care of its own soldiers and civilians and that some of the privation could be attributed to this. He knew also that the North, with its nearly unlimited resources, would treat its prisoners little better. He had toured the barracks where the prisoners

232

would be housed as well as the exercise yard and the mess hall. The provisions that had been laid in appeared far too meager for the number of men expected to come and the hastily built barracks seemed designed to provide little protection from the brutal wind that would blow across the snow-covered river. The sanitary facilities also appeared grossly inadequate and he feared having to treat outbreaks of typhus, dysentery, or even the dreaded smallpox. He feared even more the prospect of the contagion spreading to the guards and civilians who would also work or live on the island and the community around. He had even considered moving Rose and their soon-to-be-born baby to the port city of Muscatine, Iowa about thirty miles down the river. Special care would need to be taken to prevent any contagious or ill persons from crossing either the only bridge that connected the island to the shore or the ice beneath it. "Difficult at best; impossible at worst," he mused. "I just wish this damnable thing was over." The snow was blowing harder now and he considered that he might have to stay overnight – thus being one of the first 'prisoners' to occupy the facility.

In their little apartment a few miles south and up the hill from the island, Rose Catherine MacDonald sat at the kitchen table and began writing a letter to her brother and sister.

Rock Island, Illinois
November 9, 1863

Dear Ellie, Jonas, and All,

I hope this letter finds you all well. I have just put two loaves of bread in the oven to bake and thought I would take a few moments to write and let you know that we are doing well. We have just moved to a different apartment. I think I told you that we were going to. We have the upstairs of a home up on the hills a few miles south of Robert's work. Our place is small and will probably feel smaller once the baby arrives but it is adequate and we both prefer it to the boardinghouse where we had been living. We have three rooms and even have our own kitchen! We could have lived in officers' quarters on what is called Arsenal Island but Robert did not want me there and I did not want to live in another city down the river. I did not want to be away from him when the baby comes so we have compromised. It makes me feel selfish when so many wives are alone but I think it is best for us. I so hope that Henry can come home before Em has her baby.

Robert does not say much about his work but I think he is discouraged about the conditions at the prison camp. Even though they are the enemy, he feels compassion for the men who will come there and feels badly for them. We all pray that this war will be over soon and that all on both sides can return to their loved ones and live in peace. I have joined a group that sews bandages for the wounded of our army. We were getting together once a week but I have not been there for some time. One of my friends comes

*by once in a while to pick up what I have
finished and to bring new material.*

*How is your friend Theodore doing? I
am glad that you have taken him in and are
teaching him to farm and do cabinetmaking.
It is nice that you have extra help while
Henry is gone.*

*It is snowing this morning and I feel it
will be a long, hard winter before we again
see the flowers and the grass. Once I am busy
taking care of our little one, though, I think
the time will pass quickly. That is all of the
news I have for now. I will try to write more
soon.*

Love to all of you,

Rose.

****

Andrew stood with his back to the north wind and
watched the Early-November sky. Canada geese had made
only a brief stopover for rest and food at the area's ponds
and cornfields and were winging their way on southward.
The fall had brought more than the usual amount of rain.
Normally, he would have welcomed the rain as it provided
much-needed moisture for next year's cotton crop. But that
was the problem – too much cotton. He pondered whether
or not he should even bother. Last year's crop still sat in the
sheds. No brokers would be buying cotton they couldn't
sell. And to whom could they sell it? Certainly not the mills
in Vermont or Massachusetts. Certainly not to the ones in
Leeds or Manchester England with every port in the South
blockaded by the Union gunboats. The government was

buying some to make canvas for army tents. But the Confederacy was short on cash and was making many of its purchases with bonds to be redeemed after the war.

All of the output from the few mills in the South was being gobbled up by the army. There was no canvas to be had to cover the cotton bales stacked outside on the ground. Only a couple of months after the harvest, many of the bales were already beginning to rot. Before long, the entire year's crop would be ruined beyond salvage. Andrew had so far managed to stretch his savings far enough to pay Stark just enough salary to keep him around. He yearned for his considerable funds sitting in banks in Manchester, England and Chicago but had access to none of them. He considered letting Stark go. The man had been acting strangely lately – secretive, nervous, and even more sullen. His queries had been shrugged off but he could not help feeling that the overseer was hiding something deeply disturbing.

With little for them to do if he could not acquire seed for next spring's cotton planting, he had considered allowing his slaves to leave. This certainly would draw the ire of his friends and neighbors. But there was little they could do to him that Sherman's army would not do a dozen times worse if they reached the area. His greater concern was for his slaves. Where would they go? How would they fend for themselves? At least with them here, he could continue to watch over them and try to meet their basic needs. Also, if the South were to win the war, there would again crops to be planted, cultivated, and harvested. Perhaps the gesture would buy some loyalty and keep future peace on the plantation.

Then, there was Darius. Though he had stopped answering the boy's letters, he had continued to receive them on a somewhat regular basis until mid-July. Neighbors had received mail from sons and brothers who had been taken prisoner but, since he had not, he had to assume that Darius had either been killed or had perhaps quit writing to him. The last letter was dated shortly before the disastrous defeat at Gettysburg.

He stared at length at the pile of rotting cotton and felt raindrops beginning to pelt his hat and coat. He stood for a bit longer, then turned, and headed toward the house.

****

Darius gazed disgustedly at the empty tin plate before him. The food, if one could call it that, at Camp Douglas was meager and tasteless. The only sense to be derived from it at all was the bitter aftertaste of meat that had gone rancid. Yet his angry belly was begging him for more. He looked to either side up and down the long wooden table in the prisoners' mess – rows of other tables, more empty plates, more indignant looks and a low din of grumbling throughout the room.

"Fat Bastards! Look at them," he muttered to George and Harold seated directly across from him. He gestured toward the guards stationed at intervals about the hall. "If the Yankees in our prisons down south don't eat, it's because there's no food. Damn Yanks have all the food in the world and won't share it. I think the cowards are starving us just to keep us weak so we can't take 'em. And look at the coloreds with guns. Who'd think you'd ever see that?! When this thing is over, they're all gonna pay! Every damned one of them, colored or white, they're by God gonna pay! Count on it." He felt himself starting to raise his voice and lowered it so as not to draw attention from the targets of his ire.

"Amen to that," George added. Though Darius was mostly unconcerned about their condition, he and Harold were more emaciated than most in the camp. Any real strength had long since left them. Most being held in the

237

prison had eaten regularly, if not well, up until the time they had been captured. The unfortunate pair had not had a real meal in well over a year.

None of them spoke further as they sipped down the last swallows of cold, bitter coffee. Darius had no real friends in the camp and talked little with his fellow prisoners. If one had secrets to keep, it was dangerous to speak freely in a place like this. It was especially so among men who had previously been strangers and could be turned into informers with so little as some hot coffee or freshly baked pie. He had seen in Richmond how effective such a technique could be. He could only envision what the rest of his short life would be like if it were discovered that he had been a guard there.

George and Harold also had no friends. They spoke little except to each other. Even then, they were careful not to be overheard. Privacy was hard to come by in this place. At least they had little to fear from the guards as long as they behaved themselves. After all, how threatening could a starving man be at barely ninety-three pounds? Their greater fear was that other prisoners would learn that they were deserters.

And it was cold. Darius speculated that the barracks and the mess hall had been built, not only without care, but were intended to be as uncomfortable as possible. There were few windows and the heat in August and September had been stifling. The odor from that many sweating bodies cramped in close quarters along with the dearth of sanitary facilities had caused him to vomit on more than one occasion. October had provided a brief respite. Now the same wind and snow that was buffeting Rock Island had crossed the northern Illinois prairie and found its way in to the crude structures near Chicago.

There had been talk about the barracks of some prisoners being perhaps exchanged or paroled. Such paroles, it was known, would be conditional upon the parolees agreeing to go home and not take up arms against the Union. George and Harold, having lost the will to fight all the way back at Antietam, would readily agree and happily go on their way. Darius, on the other hand, would be content to lie and to resume the killing as soon as possible. Only the dire consequences that would result from being captured again would deter him. So far, no such offers had been made to any of them so he guessed it really didn't matter. There was also talk of numbers of prisoners being perhaps transferred to a new prison further west at someplace called Rock Island. That was also a matter of indifference. The place could not possibly be any worse than here at Camp Douglas. His only real pleasure here had been watching guards execute three ex-slaves who had been captured fighting for the South.

****

Joshua had returned from his rounds and sat again at his desk. During the intervening hours, the fog had burned away. He now had a clear view of the harbor and the fort. He opened the desk drawer and again studied the invitation. Moments later, he handed an orderly a note to take to the telegraph office down the street.

To: Mr. John Hay, Secretary to the President.
From: Major Joshua Gibbons, Chief of Chaplains

United States Military Hospital
Baltimore, Maryland.

Please extend sincere thanks and regrets to the President. Too many memories of Fredericksburg to visit another battlefield. Hope for understanding.

Best wishes.

Next he set about composing another letter.

*United States Military Hospital
Baltimore, Maryland*

*The Honorable Edwin Stanton, Secretary
Department of War
Washington, D.C.*

Dear Mr. Secretary,

After much consideration and fervent prayer, I am writing to you to request that I be separated from the Service of the United States as soon as possible. I can highly recommend a replacement who has served under me at the hospital. He is most understanding and compassionate and will be an excellent servant of our Lord and our soldiers.

I feel that it is God's will that I have seen enough of this awful war. Prayer after prayer for an end to the killing and suffering have seemed to go unanswered though I know that He has His reasons for all that is happening. I have felt my faith wane with each passing day. I have been offered a position as pastor with a small Methodist congregation far from the fighting. I am now convinced that it is His will that I begin this new phase of my ministry.

Please let me know as soon as possible by telegraph or letter your wishes regarding this matter.

Your faithful servant.

Major Joshua Gibbons
Chief of Chaplains.

Addressing the envelope and laying the letter aside, he immediately began another.

Baltimore, Maryland
November 9, 1863

To the Bishop
Methodist Conference of Eastern Minnesota
Minneapolis, Minnesota.

I am writing in response to your generous offer. I have requested of the Secretary of War that I be separated from

the service at the earliest possible date.
Conditional upon a favorable disposition, I
am pleased to accept.

Sincerely,
Major Joshua Gibbons,
Corps of Chaplains
United States Army.

****

The bright orange, red, and yellow leaves that had decorated the hills around Memphis in October had long-since fallen. Now, in late November, there was only a stark, gray landscape. Henry would have otherwise found that depressing. But he sat at his desk and lit a celebratory cigar. Corporal Harlan had just handed him the envelope he had been eagerly awaiting. He kept handling the paper and re-reading it to convince himself that it was, in fact, genuine. He called the corporal into the office to give him the news.

"I guess you'll be needing to go to the mercantile to buy a new suit," the young man told him. "We'll all miss you here, Sir. May I say that it has been a privilege to serve with you."

"Thank you, Corporal. But I reckon it's time to go home."

CHAPTER XV

The last Thursday of November was sunny and balmy but the citizens of Milledgeville hardly noticed. Cold and rainy weather would have much better fit the city's mood. The South had won only one significant battle since Chancellorsville in May and that had cost Lee his best commander in Thomas 'Stonewall' Jackson. It seemed particularly ominous that the battle had been fought on Georgian soil at a place called Chickamauga – far closer to home than the grassy fields and deep woods of northern Virginia. Since Gettysburg, the town had been in deep mourning. Many of its most prominent citizens, as well as lesser-known residents, had lost sons and brothers. Some of those lost had been brought home to be buried in the town cemetery or in family plots on local plantations. Most families, though, could not afford to bring their loved ones home and settled for simple markers at empty graves. Still others had received no word at all. Among them was Andrew Morgan.

This was the day that President Lincoln had proclaimed to be the first official day of national Thanksgiving. The inhabitants of the city were singularly uninterested. There was little to be thankful for. That Lincoln, whom most now saw as the sole cause of their sorrows, had made the proclamation caused particular disdain. "Perhaps the Yankees are thankful with their victories and their full bellies. Let them have their little holiday. Wait and see how thankful they are next year!"

Andrew sat on a bench under a tree on the courthouse lawn and puffed intermittently on a cigar. There were fewer and fewer pleasures to be had. Most of the finery had gone away. Women who were not in mourning, and there were few, dressed more simply these days. Most of the horses pulling wagons or being ridden were ones that the army couldn't use. Coffee wasn't plentiful but, unlike many other things the South had once taken for granted, it could still be had. There seemed to be plenty of tobacco to go around. One enjoyed what one could still get.

Next to him on the bench sat a young corporal. Andrew tried his best not to stare at the empty sleeve. He found it difficult, though it had become a common sight. The sleeve had not been cut off but was neatly folded and sewn just below the shoulder. Perhaps the boy's mother had not accepted that the arm was gone and had kept the sleeve. Was she hoping that the arm would somehow grow back? After all, why ruin a good shirt? Here was something she *could* be thankful for. The boy had come home alive.

Andrew engaged him in some trivial conversation. "Warm today. Maybe it will be a mild winter. Saw some geese flying south yesterday." He was careful to mention nothing about the war. Even the mundane talk brought little response except for an occasional "Humph" or a "Yes, Sir" or "No, Sir."

In spite of himself, he found his gaze turning back to the sleeve. Apparently the young man noticed and Andrew quickly changed his focus to the mercantile across the street. "Gettysburg," the corporal told him without looking up. "Place they said was called Little Round Top. Didn't seem so little. We never got hold of it."

The shade seemed to deepen as a small skiff of clouds drifted across the sun. Andrew had never met him before. Most of the young men who had come around the plantation or had attended Annabelle's parties had gone into the local regiments as officers. Had Andrew seen him as a boy, odds were that he had been clerking in a store or renting out horses at one of the liveries. Anyhow, he didn't recall. He was tempted to ask if the corporal knew Darius.

The young man spoke again without prompting. "Andrew Morgan, right?"

"Yes, but how did you …?"

"Church. My ma and I saw you in church a lot. My name's Adam Kendrick."

Andrew still had no recollection but didn't say so. For the first time in his life, he genuinely felt regret that he and Annabelle had never paid much attention to the so-called 'common people.' It occurred to him that the young man seated next to him was a better man than Darius.

"There were so many of 'em," the young man continued. "So damned many. We never had a chance. We never had a goddamn chance … I'm sorry. I didn't mean to say that. I didn't mean to curse. I'm so sorry. Ma and Pa taught me never to curse. It's just that … I'm so sorry. Pa got 'isself killed at Malvern Hill."

Andrew, for the first time, looked the young man straight in the face. He noticed tears beginning to well up. "You said you know me." He still debated whether or not to ask. "Did you know my son, Darius?" Now, it was out there. He waited.

"I knew him," Adam said after what seemed an eternity. He did not look up. "I'm sorry, Sir, I can't say I liked him."

"A lot of people didn't," Andrew admitted. "You needn't be sorry. It's just the truth."

"He was a bully."

"He was. I'm genuinely sorry if he treated you badly."

"Not me, just some others," Adam went on. "I lit into 'im once. Beat 'im up kinda bad when he accused me of cheating at cards. I never cheated no one."

"I'm sure you didn't, son." Andrew told him. "I'm sure you didn't. Do you know what became of him?" The young man seemed drawn back to Gettysburg and he immediately regretted asking the question. His curiosity, he realized, wasn't worth causing the young man to recall what he had seen. "I'm sorry. I didn't mean to …."

"It's alright. I saw him that day. We had charged up through the woods. Like I said, we never had a chance. It was like running into Hell. We got part way up. Some got up there but mostly they're the ones who didn't get back. Fire and yelling everywhere. Somebody gave the order to retreat and we did. I almost made it too – before I got shot. Guess I was lucky though. If I hadn't got shot, probably woulda' sent me back up. I don't think anyone shoulda' gone back up there. They just kept sending more and more until there was no one left to send. I saw Darius in the last group. Never saw 'im again. Yanks came runnin' outa the woods like a horde of mad hornets with bayonets. We were lucky to get away. That's all I got to say. I don't wanna talk about it anymore."

"You don't need to, son. You don't need to." Andrew reached over and gently placed his arm around the young man's good shoulder. "Thank you." The clouds drifted on by and took the shade with them.

****

Henry stepped onto the porch of the hotel in Mayfield, Kentucky and gazed across Main Street toward the town square. He was glad that both his uniform and his discharge papers were in his bags back in his room. He would collect them after he had strolled about town for a bit and eaten some breakfast. He had debated going out into

246

the streets but had decided that, with nothing to identify him with the army, the danger was minimal.

Mayfield, he had heard, was a more hostile place toward the Union these days than Memphis. The residents of Memphis had demonstrated themselves to be at least passively accepting of the army. Mayfield and the surrounding counties, however, had been less so. When Tennessee had first left the Union, several of the counties had actually passed articles of secession and informed the state legislature of their intention to become part of Tennessee. In the end, that secession had proved meaningless and things had remained as before. But the hostility remained even as both the Union Army and the state militia had demonstrated that they were firmly in control. Slavery was still legal in Kentucky since the state was not technically in rebellion. Most knew it would not last but much of the white population seemed determined to hold onto the 'peculiar institution' for as long as possible. They appeared genuinely afraid of what might follow.

Henry's wanderings eventually brought him to the stockyards. There was a wide variety of cattle and hogs waiting to be shipped north by rail to the packing houses in St. Louis and Chicago. It still amazed him that, in spite of having an immense army to feed and equip, the North seemed to have greater prosperity and bounty than at any time in his memory.

Near the cattle pens was a corral of horses. Unlike the hogs and cattle, the horses were not here for shipping. Standing by the corral was a gentleman whom Henry guessed to be in his late thirties or early forties. He was obviously a man of some means. The brown riding boots were highly polished. He wore light brown trousers and a darker brown, well-tailored suit coat and complementary wide-brimmed hat. He was clean-shaven and trimmed except for a small, discreet mustache and goatee. He was

247

engaged in what appeared to be a lively but cordial conversation with an older but less well-dressed man. As the sign on the corral said 'Horses for Sale' Henry guessed them to be negotiating a transaction. He hesitated for a time and then approached them. He had been thinking of purchasing a Kentucky horse to bring home to Jonas. It would also provide a means to get home to Thayer after getting off the boat in Minneapolis.

The men appeared to have completed their business. Shortly after the buyer haltered his three new acquisitions and led them away.

"Henry Hancock." He reached out his hand.

"Adrian Bentley."

"Fine lot of horses."

"Thanks. They belonged to my brother."

"Belonged?" Henry inquired. Immediately, he considered the question too impertinent and wished he could call it back.

"My brother, Ambrose. He was a lawyer here in Mayfield before the war. I have a farm just outside of town. I kept them for him."

"And?" Again Henry wished he had not asked.

"He was killed at Chickamauga," the man answered, appearing not to mind the question.

"Which side?" Henry asked, unable to control his curiosity.

"Does it matter?"

"No, it doesn't. Not anymore." He vowed to himself to pry no further. "I shouldn't have asked." It was then that he noted the chestnut and the Andalusian together in a separate pen already haltered and tied to the fence. He nodded toward them. "What about those two?"

"Those were his too," the man answered. "Kind of a curious pair – damnedest thing. The Andalusian is as gentle as rain when he's with the chestnut but he's the devil's own when they're apart. I've tried working with him but never got far. Maybe breed him to a gentle mare and you might get something worth having. Hard to say. Are you interested?"

Henry pondered for a bit and nodded back toward the other corral. "I've been looking at the bay mare. Throw her in at a fair price and I'll buy all three." Satisfied, he headed back to the hotel for breakfast.

****

"So, this is Thayer." Joshua sat beside Will Britt on the seat of Will's wagon as they completed their journey from Albert Lea. "Seems the further we go, the smaller the towns become."

Will grinned. "I guess so. I'll admit it's not exactly Boston."

After leaving the army at Baltimore, Joshua had returned briefly to Boston to visit his parents before heading west. The train had taken him first from Boston to Chicago and from there to Rock Island. From Rock Island, he had traveled north on a riverboat to Minneapolis. At Minneapolis, he had boarded a stagecoach to Albert Lea. Will had met him in Albert Lea and the two had continued on to Thayer with a brief stopover in Crestville.

"Not that I'm complaining, mind you."

"It will take some getting used to," Will cautioned him. For one thing, the town wakes up early and goes to bed early. There will be days when you can get knee-deep in mud just crossing the street and days you can hardly see the other side though the blowing dust."

Joshua surveyed his new surroundings. The town had one real 'street' that was lined by nearly all of the businesses. Access to the houses behind was mostly by wide paths, most of which were as yet unnamed. There was Britt's Mercantile, the only general store in town, that served also as the post office and the only restaurant. There were a barber shop, two blacksmith shops, and various other small concerns. "That's Jonas Hancock's cabinet shop." Will pointed to a small, non-descript building about halfway between the two ends of Main Street.

"Jonas Hancock?"

"Henry's older brother." Joshua remembered the name 'Henry Hancock' as one of the board members who had signed the letter inviting him to come to Thayer to serve the town's Methodist congregation. "He lives at the farm where you will be staying until you get settled in a place of your own. "No rush, Jonas tells me. You're welcome to stay as long as you wish. You may find it a bit crowded though. The house isn't big. Henry is away at the war, in Memphis, but his wife Em is there and expecting their first child soon. Of course, there is Jonas. There is also Theodore. Theodore ran away from a plantation in Mississippi and wandered into Henry's camp. When Henry came home last winter on recuperation leave he brought him along. He's a hire and helps work the farm. Henry's sister, Ellie, lives there too and teaches school here in town.

"Is her husband away at war too?"

"Ellie's not married." Will thought the question mere curiosity but added, "and she's pretty." He thought he saw Joshua blush a bit and changed the subject. "We need to stop here in town to water the horses and then I'll take you to the farm."

"There's one other thing you should know about Jonas. He's stone deaf from the war. They tell me that he sometimes wakes up screaming from nightmares."

****

She was beginning to prepare lunch while Em sat at the kitchen table and watched. Jonas and Theodore were outside doing chores. "What do you think he will be like?" Ellie asked.

"I don't know, Em told her. "All I know is what I've heard from Henry, which isn't a lot. I know that he's young and has served in the war. Henry hears that he's *very* handsome and isn't married.

"Well, I don't *care* if he's handsome of if he's married or not" Ellie answered back.

"I'm sure you don't," Em laughed. "I'm sure you don't."

"Well, I *don't*."

Ellie had her back to her but Em guessed that she was blushing. Her suspicion was confirmed as she saw Ellie move to the window to peer at the wagon coming the lane.

CHAPTER XVI

Jonas had come inside and now stood at the kitchen window. He gazed absently at the lane leading up to the house. Ellie was at the stove fixing lunch while Em now rested in the rocking chair nearby. Joshua and Theodore sat at the kitchen table. Joshua was working on Sunday's sermon. Theodore, who had come in shortly after Jonas did, was poring over a mathematics lesson that Ellie had given him.

As a figure appeared at the end of the lane, Jonas commented, "I wonder if he's selling horses." The figure was bundled head to foot against the early December cold and rode one of the horses as he led two others. "The chestnut looks good and sturdy. The bay looks solid too. I think Henry would like them both. I sure do admire the black Andalusian. I wouldn't mind having *him*. I doubt that one's for sale – probably couldn't afford him anyway."

Theodore left the table to have a look. "He's a beauty alright." Suddenly, he bolted toward the door. "It's Henry!"

Ellie left the stove and quickly followed with Jonas close behind. Em tried to get out of the rocker to tend the stove but, being so close to her delivery, was having difficulty doing it. "Goodness! Really? Praise the Lord!"

"Stay sitting," Joshua told her gently. "I'll tend the stove."

Theodore and Ellie were running at full pace and shouting with joy. Jonas, who was just as excited but more reticent to show it, moved more slowly and merely waved. Henry returned the wave and continued up the snow-covered lane. Joshua, meanwhile, continued stirring the potato stew. "Hope Miss Ellie fixed enough," he commented to Em. "I have a feeling your husband is going to be really hungry."

That night, under layers of quilts, Henry fondly cradled Em and laid his hand gently over her belly. "I think we're having a boy," she remarked.

"How do you know?" Henry asked. He was talking to her but stared hopefully through the darkness toward the ceiling.

"He's big and strong like his father," she answered. "And *quite* handsome," she added.

"Anything else?" he asked, relishing the compliments that were coming his way.

"Stubborn," she laughed. "He's *very* stubborn."

****

Stark sat on his bed with three lamps on in the room. Two days ago, he had walked to Milledgeville and returned with two bottles of whiskey. It was not the good liquor from days past. In fact, it was the cheapest he had been able to find. By purchasing the cheaper liquor, he could buy more. Since he no longer drank for the taste, the quality didn't matter. The lamp oil and even the cheap whiskey were splurges on his meager salary that he had recently learned would soon be suspended altogether, but he needed both to get him through the night.

He had spent considerable time lately searching futilely about the house for the 'We know' note that had mysteriously appeared months ago. He thought he remembered where he had last placed it but it was not there. Nor had it been in any of the numerous drawers or cupboards. He had looked in the same places repeatedly, always with the same result. He had begun to wonder whether or not the note had ever even existed but could not put it out of his mind.

Still, there had to be something. His trip to the barn the day after the apparition's first visit had left him temporarily satisfied that Toby's body was still where he had buried it. But there had been three more of the unnerving occurrences since that night, with each seeming more real than the one before. Tonight, he was certain, would be another. He cared little about Christmas but tonight was Christmas Eve. He had always believed Charles Dickens' little book to be a fairy tale – but still, he determined not to sleep.

It was cold but not snowing. The wind rattled the panes in the windows and an unpleasant, chilly draft blew through the room. It was an eerie noise that sounded like multiple voices. "We know," it said, over and over. Branches scratching against the windows and clapboards became boney fingers. Stark poured another drink from the already half-empty bottle on the night table. The wind blew harder and the voice and the scratching became louder – another drink. More waiting for them to appear. He looked up at the clock and noticed that it was eleven o'clock. He observed, too, that the pendulum had stopped but had no idea when he had last heard the ticking. The gun lay on the night table just within reach. It seemed that an invisible hand was over his own and pulling it toward the weapon. Helpless to resist, he felt his fingers clutch the revolver's grip and draw it toward him – slowly, but toward him nevertheless. A strong gust rattled the window harder than before. Stark closed his eyes, raised the revolver to his temple, and pulled back the hammer.

****

Inside the mansion, shadows from the fireplace in Andrew's study danced randomly about the ceiling and walls. It was the only light in the room. The windows in the house were sealed more tightly against the winter than those in Stark's quarters. The same wind that disturbed

Stark caused only occasional updrafts in the fireplace. Otherwise, it seemed to be only a gentle hush that Andrew found to be rather soothing.

Across the hearth from Andrew, a figure sat shadowed against the fire. The two had been sharing some of the last of Andrew's rapidly diminishing supply of Indian tea – acquired before the naval blockade had shut off nearly everything from coming into Southern ports from Queen Victoria's empire. Tea and other goods could still be had from the more fortunate blockade runners who were able to reach Confederate shores with their cargoes. But such success was becoming increasingly rare and the goods ever more expensive. Andrew had been able to create a semblance of tea from some herbs he had grown in his garden but considered that it would be a poor substitute once the real tea was gone.

They had not talked for a while – each lost in his own thoughts, but eventually Andrew spoke. "I have taught you to read and to write and to cypher," he told the young man. "I did so at great risk to both of us but I have no regrets. Now, there is only one more thing that I can do for you. Then you must make it in the world on your own." He reached out with an envelope that the other man hesitatingly grasped and then opened. "You are now a free man," Andrew continued. "Free to come and go as you wish. You may stay here through the winter but, come spring, I think it best that you go. When Sherman comes with his army, which I am now certain he will, Georgia is going to become a very dangerous and unpleasant place for white and dark folk alike. I hope you can be spared that. When you choose to leave, come to me. I will give you one hundred dollars in Yankee money. That should get you as far as Ohio or Indiana with money left over to keep you until you find work. In the meantime, carefully keep our secret – for both of our sakes."

"There is something you should know," the young man told him after thanking him profusely. "Something you should know about Mr. Stark. He helped Toby and Celia to run off."

Andrew said nothing but patted him gently on the shoulder.

****

The two trains left Chicago within hours of each other. One headed east into the darkness, the other west. Both carried ragged soldiers – thin and many with empty sleeves or trouser legs, some partially blind. Others appeared physically unharmed except for starvation, but they carried blank expressions as if unaware of their surroundings. Some were much too old to be here – others too young.

The eastbound train, carrying prisoners to be exchanged, headed south around the southern shore of Lake Michigan into Indiana and toward Virginia. Soldiers only slightly less weak than Harold and George, and unaware of the pair's past, offered up their seats. Each man on the train had been given a bag containing an apple, a sandwich made with fresh meat, a cookie, and two Yankee dollars that they could use to purchase additional food with on the journey. It was Christmas Eve. Though they were formally still prisoners and not yet parolees, most on the train felt already free. Some would disregard the parole agreements they had signed, rejoin the army, and continue the fight. Most would be unable in either in body or spirit. George and Harold, who had gained parole by confiding that they had not fought since Antietam and had no desire to do so again, simply wanted to be left alone. George had the window seat. For a while, he stared out at the blowing snow and then slept.

The westbound train had a much shorter, but far less comfortable, journey. The night had become even darker as the doors on the wooden boxcar were rolled shut and locked. If a man was fortunate, he was able to be near an outside wall where the gaps between the boards provided at least a small amount of fresh air. Darius was not fortunate. The cold air outside had been quickly replaced by a damp, reeking heat from so many bodies crammed into the car. There was no room to sit and many of the weaker passengers remained standing only because there was no space in which to either lie or fall down. No sanitary facilities had been provided. By the time the train stopped for coal and water, most had wet or messed themselves. Even then, the cars remained closed. Darius, who had considered Camp Douglas to be the lowest circle of Dante's Hell, was on his way to an even lower circle. That awaited him at Rock Island.

****

The wolves howled from behind the trees, protesting the cold, the snow, the wind, and the lack of food. Inside the house, their discontent was nearly inaudible to the occupants who had just finished their Christmas Eve dinner. Ellie and Mary Alice had cleared the table and, with Jonas' help, washed and put away the dishes. There had been a brief prayer service and Jonas had sung a hymn while Ellie accompanied him on Lucille Anderson's piano.

They were still gathered in the dining room. Ellie, Mary Alice, and Em sat at the table working on their embroidery. In one corner Jonas was instructing Theodore in chess. The new minister, to whom Theodore had given up his bed until he could find housing, sat in a rocking chair and held the baby Patrick David Hancock. Gently rocking, Joshua sang his favorite childhood lullaby and tenderly stroked the child's face.

Henry, alone, was not in the room. He had retired to spend a few moments in the formal parlor that Jonas and Theodore had turned into a library for him. He sat at his new desk, opened his journal, and began to write.

I am truly one of the most blessed souls whom God has ever allowed to walk his earth. Though the terrible war goes on, I pray that it shall soon end and the healing can begin. I have arrived back in the company of loved ones and friends, sound of body – able to work and to provide. Though there is a great task for others yet to finish, I take comfort and solemn pride that I have done my part and given all that could have been asked. December 24, 1863.

PART II

CHAPTER XVII

Just as before, Hamilton Stark was unable to pull the trigger. In what would have been the last moments of his thirty-one years, the overseer at Pine Hill Plantation began to imagine himself as dead. It wasn't the thought of no longer being alive that disturbed him. Nor was it a fear of going to Hell. He had long since discounted the idea of either Heaven or Hell and believed that everything simply stopped at death. To him, the reality of eternal damnation as the wage of 'sin' was as foreign as that of salvation and grace for those who lived lives of mercy and compassion.

What brought him to pull away the revolver and carefully release the hammer was something of much greater consequence but far less philosophical. He had always seen himself as strikingly good-looking. It was this that made the sight of the little family standing at the foot of his bed even more dreadful. He saw himself, like them, as grossly disfigured. He looked into a mirror at flesh that was torn and bloody. As he watched, the image before him changed to one of a man who had been dead for days and whose body was decomposing.

He laid the revolver on the night table and gave it an extra shove to move it out of reach. "Go away!" he shouted at them. "Go away and don't come back! You're dead. I killed you! I had to! You don't belong here. Go now! Leave me alone!" As he had done when they appeared before, he closed his eyes and covered his head with his pillow. Pulling his knees up to his chest, he wrapped his arms around himself and waited for the unwelcome visitors to disappear.

****

Sergeant Isaac Douglass could not sleep. He pulled the blankets more tightly around him for warmth but the chilly air in the tent was not the problem. He had walked away from a Mississippi cotton plantation as his former owner and family fled south to avoid Grant's advancing army. Later, he had joined the army and been sent to Minnesota for training. Now his job was to make soldiers from freed slaves who were coming into the army. It was not going well and it was this that caused him to toss and turn as much as the narrow cot would allow.

There were many skeptics in the army who claimed that colored troops were a bad idea. "They can't learn and they can't fight," some were saying. "They shouldn't have guns. When the shooting starts, they will turn and run. They should all be sent back to Africa." To Isaac's disappointment, many of his recruits seemed determined to prove the statements correct. Intentional or not, it was happening. Somehow, he had to prove them wrong. But how?

They constantly bickered among themselves. Those who had been house slaves felt themselves more important than those who had been stable hands or craftsmen. Those who had been stable hands or craftsmen felt superior to those who had been foremen. Those who had been foremen now looked down upon those who had been field hands. And all of them seemed to view their white officers as nothing more than new masters or overseers. Desertions were becoming rampant but few among the officers seemed concerned as long as weapons and equipment were left behind.

Isaac felt trapped in the middle. How could one *not* feel that he had simply traded one master for another? There were orders to be followed and consequences if they weren't. Those who flagrantly and repeatedly disobeyed could find themselves chained or in a cell. Officers who had shared neither the humiliation of slavery nor the anticipation of freedom seemed blind to the disillusionment. Those whom he was charged with turning into soldiers appeared unable to understand that discipline and order were necessary both for winning battles and for staying alive. Somehow, he had to bring them together. General Sherman needed soldiers. Isaac's soldiers needed to both give and receive respect. He had to find a way! At least tomorrow would be Christmas. There would be no drilling which would bring him some temporary peace. Finally, he slept.

****

The desk that Jonas and Theodore had made for him did not have a flat top. Instead, there were two parts. The top was a glass-door case made to protect Henry Hancock's most treasured books – ones that he already possessed and the ones he hoped to acquire in the future. Below was a section containing a writing surface that could be pulled out when needed and pushed back in when not. A folding panel then concealed both the green baize writing surface and a row of pigeonholes. It was in the center pigeonhole that Henry kept his journal. Below, was a two-door section for keeping personal papers – those that he might need close at hand but would not use every day. A nearby wall sconce held an oil lamp.

Other than the journal, there were few reminders of the war in the little library. Both Henry and Jonas' uniforms had been neatly folded and placed in a trunk at the end of the upstairs hall and awaited a final journey up to the attic. A holstered revolver hung on a peg behind the door to the cellar stairway near the rest of the small arsenal needed to protect the farm from vermin and predators. The most visible reminder lay on a table facing the bay window of the library. This reminder, that shared its space with a stack of Harper's Magazines, an atlas, and whatever book Henry was reading at the time, was a map of the United States. On this map, he would trace an ever-shrinking

Confederacy. One day, he would roll up the map and store it away in the trunk with the uniforms.

Henry and his older brother had both left the war before its end and come home to Minnesota. At Shiloh, Jonas had been left permanently and totally deaf from the explosion of a canister near the artillery caisson he was tending. The explosion had killed all of the other members of his gun crew and had left him with a recurring nightmare that was triggered by thunderstorms. Henry had lost the use of his left eye during a skirmish that occurred during a foraging expedition in Mississippi. The eye had remained but the torn cornea made it useless. Though the damage was not obvious to others, he continued to wear a patch since the eye would not automatically blink to protect it from dust or other foreign objects. It pleased him that his wife, Emma, found the patch made him look dashing and a bit mysterious. He supposed he would have to give it up when his good eye began to require eyeglasses.

Henry had brought home with him a young man who had run away from a Mississippi plantation as the army had approached. The boy, too young to join the army, had performed various chores around the camp. He had learned to read when Henry and a friend started a small class during their spare time to teach other soldiers who had never learned. The boy, whose given name was Amos, had changed it to Theodore and was now employed as a farmhand by the Hancock brothers. Ellie, Henry's sister and a school teacher, continued to tutor him while Jonas, as a cabinetmaker, was teaching him to build furniture.

From the library, Henry could hear the soothing sound of a lullaby being sung to his son who was now almost three weeks old. The voice belonged to Reverend Joshua Gibbons, who had recently moved to the area and was staying with the family until he was able to find a residence of his own. The new minister, originally from

Boston, had been a chaplain in the army and had been awarded the Medal of Honor for his actions in saving wounded soldiers while under fire at Fredericksburg.

Another voice that filtered into the room came from David Weinberg, a devout Jewish neighbor, who had accompanied his Lutheran wife to the little Christmas Eve gathering. David, a veteran of the Mexican War, had helped with the farm while Henry and Jonas were away. He had also once saved Jonas from a threatening pack of gray wolves. David was assisting Jonas in teaching Theodore to play chess.

Henry extinguished the lamp and rejoined the group in the dining room. "Merry Christmas, Captain," Jonas looked up from the chess table and smiled.

Jonas considered it a bit of a joke and Henry was mildly irritated at being called 'Captain' by his own brother. What did *not* irritate him was when friends addressed him in the same way. In fact, the new nickname rather pleased him in somewhat the same way as Em's comments about his eye patch. After all, he had earned it. "Why not?" he asked himself. "Why not?"

****

Rock Island, Illinois
December 24, 1863

Dear Brothers, Ellie, and Em,

It is Christmas Eve. We have great news to share. You have a new niece. She was born three days ago and is such a beautiful baby! We have named her Rachel. It seems so fitting because her little blue eyes look so like

Mama's. With your new little Patrick, it seems as if we now have Mama and Papa with us again. I like to think they would be pleased.

I felt so pleased and comforted that Robert was able to be here to deliver our baby. Mrs. Adams, our landlady, was so kind to be here to assist. She has been here quite a lot since to help take care of Rachel so that I can get some rest. She makes such a fuss over her. She never had grandchildren of her own and seems so anxious to share in our joy. She says she gets really lonely downstairs. This is her first Christmas being a widow and I feel so sorry for her.

Robert is at work this evening and said he will probably be there all night. He has been so busy ever since the first prisoners arrived at the camp. Most all seem malnourished and in need of some sort of medical attention. He doesn't share much with me as he says it's very unpleasant. He says he doesn't want to bother me with it but I think he also doesn't want to think about it when he is at home. It disturbs him so. He tells me, but please don't tell anyone else, that he thinks that the doctors at Camp Douglas didn't take very good care of the men and some would have been pleased to just let them die. There is a new group coming in by train tonight and he fears that they have fared no better than those already at the camp.

Our apartment has been warm. We have used a little more coal in the stove but Robert says it's not healthy for Rachel to be cold. I must admit that I don't like to be cold either. I can't imagine living in Minnesota. We don't have a thermometer in our apartment and don't need one but there is an outdoor one at the camp. Robert says it was thirty degrees below zero when the first prisoners were brought in three weeks ago. I feel so sorry for them. We are told that we are supposed to consider them as the enemy but Robert and I both have trouble doing that. I think that most are people just like us and want nothing more than to go home.

I am getting tired and need to rest so will close now. Our love to you all. Kiss and hug little Patrick for us.

As always, pray for peace,

Rose.

****

Prisoner Darius Morgan had once guarded Federal Prisoners of war at the Confederate prison in Richmond, Virginia. Known to his captors as Davis Moran, he had been captured at Gettysburg and sent to Camp Douglas near Chicago. Now he found himself on his way to the newly established Federal camp at Rock Island. He peered through a crack in the siding of the boxcar into the cold Illinois night. There was little to see. The heavy, wind-blown snow limited visibility to no more than a few feet. It was cold near the outside of the car but he much preferred that to where he had been an hour or so earlier. It had taken him nearly that long to shove and push his way from the middle of the car. At least now, the small crack provided a small bit of fresh air.

That little bit of fresh air, however, provided scant relief from the overwhelming scents that filled the car. The mass of humanity crowded into the space gave rise to numerous odors, the least unpleasant of which was sweat. Others, unused to the motion of the car, had started losing the small amount of stale food that they had been given prior to starting the trip. The thin layer of straw strewn about the floor of the car at Camp Douglas had already absorbed as much waste and odor as it could. It was now useless.

Darius' legs felt weak. The prisoners had been forced to stand in line in the cold for two hours waiting to board the train as guards checked and rechecked their manifest, taking turns with each other to go back inside and get warm. Another hour of standing unable to stretch or change position had caused his legs to ache. Working his way to the outside wall of the car had drained him even further. Now, even if he could sit, the fouled bedding made that option repugnant to him. Without a watch, and no light to see the dial if he had one, he could only guess how long it had been. He had no idea how far they had come or how much longer it would be before they reached Rock Island. Thirst overtook him and he began to drift in and out of consciousness. He could no longer will his legs to support him and his knees began to buckle. He remembered nothing more until the door was pulled open and a tidal wave of bone-chilling air rolled into the boxcar. "Everyone out! Form a line on the platform! No dawdling!"

****

Doctor MacDonald stood near the tracks that terminated well inside the camp gate. Wrapped in a heavy overcoat and wearing a cap and gloves, he could still feel the stinging, yet numbing, cold. With an assistant beside him, he watched those who were able to walk emerge from the car. "My God," he muttered. "My Dear God."

CHAPTER XVIII

Henry watched a light rain spatter on the window of his library and leaned over to make notations on the map that lay on the table before him. There had not been a thunderstorm but, instead, only a slight shower. The rain had done little more than settle the dust. Jonas had been spared his awful dream that often haunted him when he sensed that a storm was happening. Already, the sun had begun to come out. The day promised to be quite balmy for early April in Minnesota. Done for the time being with the map, Henry returned to his desk and opened the journal.

It is not my intent to write every day or to record everything that occurs here at the farm. My life now is, for the most part, mundane. The lot of my activities, I believe, would be of little interest to those who would come after me. I prefer, rather, to live my life with my family as it unfolds. I mean to savor every moment that I am given on this earth without needing to preserve each one for posterity. Some events or occasions, however, are so momentous that I must comment."

We have learned that General Grant has been promoted to General-in-Chief of all of the U.S. Armies. I hope that his skill and tenacity will bring about the conclusion of the war in a short time. Events, though, indicate that such may not be the case and that the war may yet go on for some time. Our armies have advanced to within two or three miles from Richmond yet seem forever unable to capture the city. Meanwhile,

269

Nathan Bedford Forrest has been conducting raids in Western Kentucky and Tennessee. My belief was that, with our government now in control of the entire Mississippi River, such events would no longer have occurred there.

Today is the second anniversary of the second day at Shiloh. I am sure that it is as much on Jonas' mind as well as those of the Britt family and others who lost their loved ones. I shall not speak of it to any of them and only make note of it here. I so wish that the entire nasty business was over long ago by now.

We have two foals and some calves – the first since we have owned the farm. Perhaps that is a sign from God that he plans for life to go on.

April 7, 1864.

The once-pristine boots had become worn and shabby. Even if he had the money, which he did not, there was no replacing them. The last pair of new boots had long-since disappeared from the sparsely stocked store shelves in Milledgeville. That most others were no better off than his provided little comfort. After all, *he* was Hamilton Stark. *They* were *not*.

He leaned on the handle of the pitchfork and looked disgustedly down at them. There would be no point in having new ones anyhow, he decided. The ones he wore were stained yellowish green and reeked of stable muck. In only a short time any new ones would be in the same condition. Since being let go as overseer at Pine Hill Plantation, the only work he had been able to find was at

Greene's Livery and Hay Yard in Milledgeville. He had, at first, resisted but hunger had won out. It was now forcing him to do what, only weeks ago, had been unthinkable.

His employer, Andrew Morgan, had decided to plant no cotton this spring. With the barns full of unsold and rotting product from last year, there was no point in trying to grow a new crop. Besides, the seed was expensive and hard to obtain. He had, instead, ordered his slaves to plant the fields to carrots, corn, sweet potatoes, cabbage, and turnips. After there was enough for his personal use, they could keep and store as much as they desired for themselves. Any remaining, he would try to sell in Milledgeville. With the slaves growing food for themselves, there was little need for an overseer. Stark's tenure was over.

Stark's only good fortune was that Andrew had allowed him to continue to live free of charge in his quarters at the plantation. The quarters were not spacious or well-furnished. At best, he would have considered them adequate but he could afford to live nowhere else.

He hoped it was near quitting time but had no way to tell for sure. Last week, he had traded away his pocket watch for a bottle of whiskey. The whiskey, which he would have once thought barely suitable for 'white trash', he had quickly consumed. Rather than sip for the taste, he now gulped it quickly for the brief respite that it provided from his troubles. Today, he had neither the whiskey nor the watch and little prospect of acquiring replacements for either. He would simply have to wait for Sam Greene to come out and tell him it was time to go. To his relief, that happened quickly. He placed the fork inside the stable, washed his face in the disgusting water in the horse trough, and headed toward the bridge and home.

He did not walk quickly. His feet and legs were tired from the long day of removing and replacing the bedding in the stables. He was not inclined to rush. It did not occur to him, nor would he have cared, that those whom he had once watched labor in the fields had endured this same fatigue for nearly every day since growing old enough to walk.

After crossing the wooden bridge across the river, he sat on a large boulder to rest. He did not want to touch the muck-covered boots, but did so anyway – removing them so he could rub his feet. The same anger that had filled his thoughts during the day welled up even more. He directed none of it toward himself. It was all other people's fault, he had long ago decided, that it had come to this. Most of all, it was the Yankees who were to blame. They had started the war. It was Lincoln who had tried to free and arm the slaves. It was the Yankees who were bottling up the harbors and making it impossible for Morgan to sell his cotton and continue to pay him. It was they who had ruined everything! Their time would come, he vowed, and he would do all in his power to make it happen.

At length, he pulled his boots back on and resumed his southward trek. To his relief, the evening air was beginning to settle in and a slight breeze came up. He was sweating less now that he had taken a brief rest but it did little to improve his mood.

As Stark approached the turn that would take him up the lane to the house and barns, the sun had set and darkness was approaching. He paused momentarily, made the turn, and continued up the hill. There was still no hurry as nothing inviting awaited him. Dinner would be scant and the same thing that he eaten last night and the night before that. His first pay had been rapidly depleted. Decent food was becoming scarcer in Milledgeville, and more expensive. What he was able to buy with his meager salary, he would not have bought at all in better times. Tonight's fare would consist of some salt pork that was little better than rancid, and bread already stale days ago when he had bought it. It would be nearly a week before he would receive his next pay.

He made it a point not to continue past his quarters toward the cabins and the fields. It wasn't just that he was tired. There was no longer a reason to visit the fields and he had no desire to interact in any way with those working there. What he could *not* avoid from his quarters was the *view* of the fields. There was barely any daylight left in the former cotton field. In days past, quitting time had been strictly observed and the slaves had been more than eager to vacate the fields at first call. Now, shadowed in the waning daylight, they continued to work. Tonight, the moon would be nearly full. It would not surprise him if they continued to work well into the night.

Once in his quarters, he would no longer have the view. Semi-darkness would soon cloak the field. The night, however, would do nothing to quell the noise coming from the field and it was the noise that disturbed him the most. Closing the windows was not an option. Though the night was cool outside, a damp and stifling heat had built up in the house during the day. Some noises would not have bothered him. When the fields were quiet on spring nights, he had rather enjoyed the sounds of crickets chirping and frogs croaking from the small pond nearby. He had found it relaxing and it often helped him sleep.

The sound that now annoyed him was that of talking and laughter. He had never allowed such prattle when supervising the slaves working in the cotton fields. It disturbed him that they were now doing it, and that he could do nothing about it. It disturbed him even more that they were working on their own gardens and were happy.

And there was the singing – that gawd-awful singing. There were hymns and spirituals. There were songs about Moses and sweet chariots. There was a song about following the drinking gourd. Though unfamiliar with it, Stark had heard that it had something to do with escaping and going north. Worst of all, Andrew Morgan was allowing it all. He wondered if the man wasn't losing his mind. Deciding that he was more tired than hungry, he ignored the unappetizing food that he had set out on the table. He sat in a chair near the cold stove, pulled off his boots, smoked the end half of his last cigar, and fell asleep.

****

The ice on the river surrounding the island was nearly gone. Only intermittent floes now floated lazily by. This morning, however, the entire river valley was shrouded in a dense fog as warm air hovered over the still-cold water. The balmy days of early April provided a welcome respite between the bitter cold of the winter just passed and the hot, humid, and mosquito-ridden summer to come. Darius could not see the part of Arsenal Island that lay beyond the camp fences. Had he been able to see it, the lifting of the fog would have shown him a scene not greatly different from those back home. There were large stands of pine that had mostly regained their shape once they were relieved of the heavy snow. The lilac bushes and redbud trees that surrounded the officer's quarters would soon reach full bloom, as would the tulips and daffodils. There were still numerous large patches of snow in areas shaded from the noonday and afternoon sun but there were also patches where the grass was turning green.

None of the scenery, however, would have done anything to lift his spirits. While pretty to behold, it was all beyond his reach and only served to make him homesick for Georgia. The camp itself was intentionally kept drab and dismal. Not only was the Government unwilling to spend the money necessary to make the camp a hospitable place for its occupants, those in charge were singularly uninterested in doing so. Darius had lost track of what day it was and had long-since decided that it made little difference. One day in this miserable place was not at all different from the day before and the day that would come next.

****

The day dawned bright and clear without yesterday's morning showers. It was also unusually warm for early April, which disappointed Joshua not at all after the brutal winter. The chill of the morning had quickly morphed into a warm, soothing breeze. The partly open window facing the street allowed him to savor it to the fullest.

From his small room above Mr. Hamman's barber shop, he could hear the voices of Thayer's merchants and tradesmen as they prepared to open for the day's business. There was casual banter as they greeted each other while sweeping the sidewalks. Not much of it, as there was work to be done, but what he heard, he found comforting. There was nothing like it in Boston. The merchants there, he recalled, had rarely spoken to each other as they performed the morning chores. They had seemed too preoccupied with the task at hand to share more than a brief "good morning." Often they had not appeared at all but had sent clerks and apprentices outside to do the tidying up. The employees had been mostly careful not to appear to be loitering lest they receive either a scolding or a dock in their pay.

What Joshua did *not* hear, and he missed it, was the clip-clop of the hooves of shod horses making their way up and down brick streets. Though the county seat town of Crestville, a few miles distant, had managed to place cobblestone in a few blocks of its downtown, Thayer had yet to do so and the streets remained nothing more than packed earth. It pleased him that the residents took care that the streets were kept smooth and mostly free of horse droppings though. Rarely was there trash or litter to be seen as the merchants had joined together to hire two men and a wagon to routinely remove it.

He tried, with difficulty, to focus on the task at hand. Today was Good Friday and he had yet to finish working on the sermon for his first Easter in Thayer. It was not the war that was bothering him. Though there were occasional reminders, he had managed to put much of it out of his mind. He refused to read newspaper accounts of the army's progress, preferring to limit his involvement to nightly prayers that it would end. There had been no reports for some time of casualties among the area's soldiers still involved in the fighting. Perhaps, he continued to hope, the little town had sacrificed enough and the remainder of the sorrowful burden would fall elsewhere.

What interrupted his focus was something far less important to the country but increasingly important to him personally. The clang of the bell at the school where Ellie Hancock was teaching mere blocks away only served to make concentrating more difficult. They had quickly become fast friends when he moved in with the Hancocks upon arriving in Thayer in December. He had enjoyed talking and laughing with her while he accompanied her to town on days when she was teaching school and he had business at the Church. While riding their horses, they had discovered numerous common interests and found no trouble conversing on a wide range of topics. Since moving to town in mid-March, he had seen little of her except at Church services and on an occasional Sunday when he had been invited to dinner at the farm. He especially missed her smile and her laugh. He frequently imagined himself sitting next to her on the front porch of the Hancock house and holding her hand. He could stand at his window and see the schoolyard through an alley between two buildings across the street. More and more frequently, when the students were taking recess, he would catch a glimpse of her watching over them.

The school bell stopped ringing and Joshua assumed that all of the students were now inside beginning their lessons. He had started keeping track of when recess began. He figured that he had about an hour and a half until that time to give his full attention to the sermon. Still, the words would not come. Deciding to give up the effort for a while, he got up from the table and went downstairs for a shave.

****

Henry and Theodore had finished the morning chores and were hitching up mules before heading to the fields to plow. Henry preferred doing the plowing in the fall as soon as the corn was picked. That allowed the ground to, in his words, 'ripen.' The corn stubble had more time to decompose in order to provide nutrients for the new crop. Also, with plowing done, there was more time to do the additional work necessary for preparing the seedbed. That meant planting could be started as soon as the danger of frost had passed. This past winter, much of the plowing had been left undone. Henry had not arrived home from the war in time to help. Jonas and Theodore, even with some help from David, had been unable to complete the task before an early freeze had hardened the ground and made further work impossible.

Theodore, not to Henry's surprise, was a hard and diligent worker. He remembered how hard the young man had worked in the army camp running errands and doing chores. Though not yet full-grown, he could handle a mule and plow as well as any man whom Henry had met and was always eager to do more than his fair share. Though careful not to sound patronizing, Henry took every possible opportunity to sincerely praise the young man's work. At times, he had to nearly force him to slow down or take a much-needed break. "Good job," and "Well done," were common. "Hurry up," was never uttered.

Jonas had taken the day off from the fields to run some errands in town. In the barn, he threw a saddle over the back of the great Andalusian that Henry had brought home. Henry had given him the horse as a Christmas present and also in recognition of the hard work that he had done while Henry was still away at the war. In the next stall stood the chestnut gelding that Henry had brought home and presented to Theodore. Jonas had named his horse Napoleon. Theodore had named his Ned, in honor of a friend who had been beaten for running away and then sold south at the age of ten or eleven.

When the pair of horses had first arrived at the farm, the high-spirited Andalusian had been impossible to handle when not in the immediate company of the gelding. Jonas and Theodore had found that, by riding together and gradually increasing the separation between them, they could decrease Napoleon's dependence. Within a few short weeks, it had become possible for anyone on the farm to ride the great beast alone with ease and comfort. The saddling completed, Jonas placed his foot in the stirrup and swung himself aboard.

Jonas enjoyed singing as he rode. He could not hear himself, but knew he had a pleasant voice and decided that there was no harm in it. He had done it while working to tame the Andalusian and felt that it might still have a calming influence on the horse. As he approached the bridge over Crescent Creek, he was singing 'Amazing Grace.'

Joshua could hear Jonas' voice even before he rode around the curve and saw him approaching the bridge.

After his shave, he had still been unable to concentrate on the sermon and, for the time being, had given up. He had learned the basics of sign language in his three months of living with the Hancocks but this morning had written a letter and was on his way to hand-deliver it to Jonas at the farm. Some things, he had decided, were too important to run the risk of being misunderstood. They met at the end of the bridge.

Jonas spoke first. "Morning, Joshua." From the beginning, they had referred to one another neither as 'Reverend' nor 'Mr. Hancock.' The mutual respect did not require them to use titles and, as they had now become fast friends, it seemed a silly formality. What are you doing way out here on a Friday morning?"

Joshua took his time. He had not anticipated meeting Jonas until he reached the farm and had not rehearsed an opening for his intended business. "Just seemed like a good time to go out for a ride. And you?"

"No really important reason. Decided the horse needed exercise and Em said she needed some things from town to prepare Easter dinner. You're still coming aren't you?"

"Wouldn't miss it." Joshua decided to forgo trying to do a lead in to what he wanted. He reached into his pocket, retrieved the envelope, and handed it as casually as possible to Jonas. "Open it. It's important." There was nothing to do now but to wait.

They both stayed on their horses, only inches apart. Jonas was pleased that Napoleon was on his best behavior and did not seem at all disturbed by the presence of the other animal. He held the envelope in his left hand and used his free hand to pull his eyeglasses from his coat pocket. Joshua watched him eagerly for some sign of his thoughts but the stone-faced Jonas gave no clues. Finally, he folded the letter, placed it in the envelope, and handed it back to Joshua. He placed the glasses back in his pocket, and finally spoke. Though only a moment had passed, it had seemed like an eternity to the minister.

"I'm sorry," Jonas told him. "What you are asking is something that I cannot give."

Joshua hesitated, taken aback by the answer. He had been almost certain he would not receive such a response from one of his closest friends. "I see," he responded weakly. "But I don't ... I mean I thought ... Is there a reason that ...?"

"The reason," Jonas smiled, "is that what you are asking is not mine to give. It is not mine to give because Ellie is her own woman. She is strong and independent with a will of her own. While she is my sister and I appreciate the gesture; if you want permission to call on her you are going to have to ask her yourself!"

Joshua, while relieved, now had a new problem. He had hoped that Jonas, if he approved, would broach the subject with Ellie and report back to him whether or not Ellie was interested in having him visit. Clearly now, that was not going to happen. Though Jonas would not stand in the way, he would now have to approach her himself. The hero of Fredericksburg was very much afraid.

They rode back to town talking little.

****

Ellie was returning from class and had stopped at the post office. As she arrived home, Theodore was the first to greet her and extended his hand to help her down from the buggy.

"Theodore! Why thank you. You're just the person I wanted to see. I have something for you." She shuffled through the mail and handed him a small brown envelope.

"For me?" he exclaimed. "Someone wrote a letter just to me?"

"It would appear so, young man," she smiled.

"Wow, no one ever wrote to just *me* before. People write to all of us but no one ever wrote just to me!" He turned and ran toward the house. "Henry! Em! Jonas! Guess what!"

Ellie caught up as they all gathered in the kitchen. "So, Theodore," Henry inquired, "who is it from?"

"I forgot to look," Theodore answered breathlessly. "I was so excited to get a letter just to me. It says it's from the Abolitionist Society of North Central Iowa. It's all the way from a town in Iowa! I wonder what they want!"

"Open it!" Ellie chimed in. "Don't keep us all in suspense."

Theodore stared at the envelope itself and fondled it in disbelief.

"Well," Henry asked, "how long are you going to make us wait?"

Theodore turned over the envelope and began cautiously working at the flap trying not to tear it as he went. Jonas opened his penknife and handed it to him. "If you go any slower, you'll need a lamp to read it!"

Theodore reached laughingly and eagerly for the knife and was soon unfolding the envelope's contents. "They want me to come and give a speech!" he exclaimed. "Me! They want me to come all the way to Iowa and give a speech!"

"Well, I'll be!" Em spoke up for the first time. "It looks like we have someone famous in the family."

Theodore was now beaming. Not only had he received a letter and an invitation to give a speech, Em had just called him family. They all had treated him as a member of family since his arrival at the farm, but no one had used the word until now. He continued reading to himself and the wide smile suddenly vanished. "I don't want to go," he announced abruptly as he handed the letter to Jonas.

Everyone turned their attention away from Theodore, who had suddenly left the room, and focused on the astonished Jonas who now stood holding the letter. He read aloud. "In our years of meeting, we have never had the opportunity to hear from a real live slave. We would like you to come and talk to our group about the evils of slavery and how badly you and the rest of the colored people have been so brutally abused by your master. We especially want to hear about …"

"I think that pretty much says it," Jonas added. "No wonder he's upset."

Henry followed Theodore to the dining room. "Let's talk a little later," he told him. "I have an idea."

After dinner, Henry, Jonas, and Theodore gathered in Henry's library. Jonas had ridden to town and asked Joshua to join them. "We understand why you don't want to give the speech," Henry began. "No one here will blame you if you decide not to go, but please hear us out. We'll all stand behind you whatever you decide to do. Firstly, you're not a *slave*. You haven't been one for years and you never will be again. You're an intelligent and accomplished young man. So let's start there."

"But they want to hear from a *slave*," Theodore interrupted him. "That's why they invited me. They want to hear about ..."

"Then here's what you need to do," Joshua explained. "You need to go to the meeting. But don't give them what they are expecting to hear. Instead, give them something much better. Instead of telling about your life as a slave, tell them about your life as a *free man*. Let them know what a young colored man can achieve with his freedom. They may not know it yet, but that's what they really *need* to hear."

****

Isaac had finished breakfast and stepped back into his tent before going to call the roll and prepare H Company for morning inspection. Moments later, he emerged to the sound of angry shouts and cursing. Running toward the source of the commotion, he soon found what he had feared. To his great dismay, but not surprise, he found his own recruits were causing the ruckus. He had managed to turn his first company of men into respectable soldiers. From accounts he had heard, they were now as disciplined and effective as any in the colored regiment to which they had been assigned. He had asked to be allowed to continue leading them as they prepared to accompany General Sherman's army into battle. His request had been denied, however, on the grounds that he was too useful in his present role to be risked at the front. So, here he was, still behind the lines, with a *new* company of recruits who had been in the army for less than two weeks.

Just as in his previous company, he found rampant resentment and mistrust directed toward both himself and the regiment's white officers. The same old internal jealousies had also appeared among these new recruits. He had learned much in the weeks since December. Still, he resented being the target of the same slurs that these men had used in talking privately about their overseers in the cotton fields. His explanations that, he too, had worked in the fields seemed useless to stop the grumbling over being 'ordered about.' He found, however, that other sergeants training other companies were confronting the same problems. This helped to ease his discomfort. Also, his eventual success with his first company had earned him significant respect from the officers. He found it best to keep that respect hidden from those whom he was charged to train lest it might fuel even more resentment from them. He had been told that his dedication might someday bring an officer's commission. This, he especially needed to keep secret.

Though the sun was shining this morning, there had been showers during the night. What had once been a plantation owner's groomed and manicured front lawn was now a muddy quagmire. Isaac was not pleased at having to work in such conditions. He was still trying to make his men proud of their newly issued uniforms. But there was nowhere else to train. Everyone had to deal with the same reddish clay mud.

What others were not dealing with was a band of ruffians rolling in the mud, shoving each other, and swinging wildly at each other's heads. Fortunately, they had been neither issued real weapons nor taught how to load them. Had that been the case, Isaac feared that a real shooting war might have developed right there in the camp. Fists were bad enough. Mini balls or bayonets could spell disaster.

Company H's young second lieutenant stood nearby. He was clearly angry. It appeared to Isaac that the man was helpless to quell what was quickly becoming a full-blown riot. There was only a momentary pause in the scuffle when the lieutenant drew his revolver and fired a single shot into the air. That gesture was greeted with a flying ball of mud that nearly knocked the gun out of his hand. Others, who had heard the shouting and then the pistol shot, came running from various directions to see what was happening. Some seemed content to merely watch. A few others jumped in and took sides without knowing what the argument was about.

"Sergeant," the lieutenant shouted at Isaac, barely able to make himself heard above all of the other noise, "you need to ..."

Neither man could have anticipated what happened next. Had Isaac closed his eyes, he could have nearly heard Moses come down from Mount Sinai and smash the tablets containing the Ten Commandments. The voice did not come from the middle of the fight. It came from the circle of spectators surrounding it. Isaac recognized the man as one from his own company who had chosen earlier to not become involved.

Isaac would not have guessed the voice to be that of Private Jesse Stoker. He had known the young recruit only briefly and was surprised that he had joined the army at all. He was small in stature –under five and a half feet tall, and weighing, Isaac guessed, less than one hundred and twenty pounds. In addition, he had seemed particularly timid. He had spoken only when spoken to and Isaac suspected that he had been bullied by others in the company.

"Stand up!" Jesse ordered those in the mud. "The rest of you, fall into line – now!"

To the amazement of all watching, the brawlers immediately obeyed. As order was restored and the company formed into ranks, the private began pacing back and forth, ankle deep in the mud. Once in a while, he would stop and look upward into the sullen faces of those standing before him. "Are we soldiers or a mob?" he asked them.

Now that they had become quiet, he no longer needed to shout. With an air of authority and calm self-assurance, he continued. Isaac was pleased that he was using the pronoun 'we' instead of 'you.'

"We here to become soldiers," Jesse went on. "We here to be an army an' march into Georgia an' attack da ones dat made us pick der cotton. We cain' do it usselves – we don' know how. Da' army can whoop dem and make dem pay for what dey done to us. Mistah Lincoln's army done come south to help us. Lots of dem died try'n to get here an' we got to help dem finish it. We got to let 'em teach us how to march an' shoot an' tell us who to kill."

"Look at us. We fight'n each other when we got to fight da mastahs. We ain' no good – our new uniforms all muddy. We's jus' free field hands – nothin' more. We's got to be soldiers and we's got to be proud. If we go to fight without knowin' how, we all gonna be daid an' da mastahs is gonna win an' our little uns gonna be slaves agin. Dat's all I got to say." He walked to the end of the line, still in front of the recruits and facing them. For a brief time, he said nothing. Finally, he turned to Isaac and the lieutenant. "Dey yours. I done said my piece." He stepped back into the ranks and waited.

****

To Theodore, it seemed as if he were sitting on a throne but the chair seemed uncomfortable and somehow out of place. It and several others like it had, for the evening, replaced the hard benches that normally occupied the choir loft in the church. All of them had high, ornate backs as tall as a man's head and arms that felt awkward. The oversized chair made him feel small, and feeling small made him feel vulnerable. He would have much preferred one of the plain and familiar chairs from Henry and Em's kitchen. He hoped no one would notice him fidgeting as he sat and waited his turn to speak, going over the speech one last time in his head.

He gazed out over the assembled crowd, wishing to see even one person of color. Seeing none, he felt very much alone even though the entire Hancock family was seated prominently in the front row. If only his mother could be here, though he was not sure he would recognize her or that she would recognize *him*. He tried to remember her face but it had been so long and the memory had blended over time into the faces of so many other women who had worked the fields at the plantation. They had all seemed tired and worn beyond their years. He guessed his mother's face had been much the same, though he had been only a small child the last time he saw her. He remembered, only slightly less vaguely, the face of the woman who had taken him in the day that his mother was led away. What he *did* remember was the love and kindness that she had always shown him in their brief time together.

Again, he scanned the faces of the members of the North Central Iowa Abolitionist Society. Still, oil lamps in the sconces that lined the church's walls showed only white men. How many, he wondered, had ever seen a colored man before and how many had come to the meeting only out of curiosity.

Presently, the woman at the piano began to play and the crowd joined in singing the familiar hymns. The hymns provided him some comfort and he tried to imagine himself at home in Thayer on a normal Sunday morning. Even so, he wished that he had not agreed to speak at the meeting and longed to be nearly anywhere else at this particular moment. He wished the evening were over but it had barely begun. He looked at the program on his lap and noted that there were three others to speak before him and wondered how long they would talk. They would certainly be more eloquent than he and that worried him. The entire family, along with Joshua, had helped him put his thoughts into words and had patiently listened to him practice the delivery. But it was now he and not they who would have to stand at the pulpit and deliver the speech to a hall full of strangers.

The local minister was first to speak. "Friends and neighbors, we are gathered this evening ..." Theodore reached into his pocket and felt the precious watch that had been given to him on the first night of his official freedom. He worked it nervously between his fingers, hoping that no one would notice. He wished he could open it and check the time but to do so would be rude so he continued to discreetly fondle it. He welcomed Henry's confident smile from the crowd and acknowledged it with one of his own.

Each of the speakers going before him seemed to be more interested in hearing the sound of his own voice than in presenting a sincere message. "Pompous asses," he found himself thinking as each seemed to out-bluster the one before. Each ended his long-winded speech by finally raising what Theodore considered to be the only reason for the Society's continued existence – that in issuing the Emancipation Proclamation, Lincoln had freed only the slaves held in the rebellious states. Slavery still continued undisturbed in the border states such as Missouri and Maryland and in the very capital of the country, Washington, D.C.

Theodore found himself hoping that the crowd would tire of the speeches and disperse before his turn came up. But finally the last of the three vacated his 'soapbox' and the minister arose to introduce Theodore. Each of the previous introductions had seemed to run nearly as long as the speeches themselves. The minister rambled on about everything each speaker had ever accomplished. Theodore's introduction was brief and curt. It did nothing to assuage his feeling that he had been invited here chiefly as a curiosity. The minister noted only that Theodore had escaped from a plantation somewhere down south, wandered into a Union Army camp, and now lived with the Hancock family working as a field hand. There was no mention that he could read and write better than many white men serving in the army, that he was working as an apprentice cabinet maker, and that he was becoming quite accomplished at chess. As the introduction ended, he received only silent stares rather than the wild applause that had followed each of the other introductions. He tried the best he could to gather his thoughts as he took the pulpit and began to speak.

He had considered long and hard how to address the crowd. "Friends and neighbors," did not seem suitable, as most in attendance were neither. "My fellow citizens," failed because he was not yet a citizen of either Iowa, Minnesota, or the United States. Finally, he had settled on a simple "Ladies and gentlemen," though he was now having some doubts that this greeting was any more appropriate than those he had rejected.

"Ladies and gentlemen, I am honored to be asked to address this meeting of the North Central Iowa Abolitionist Society." It occurred to him that, only one sentence into his speech, he had already lied. He vowed that what he had just said would be his only untruth, no matter how uncomfortable it made him feel.

"My name is Theodore. I was invited here to talk about life as a slave. So I will. I was born a slave. I never knew my mother.

"Now that I have talked about being a slave, I will say what I really came to say."

Henry gave him a knowing smile and a slight nod. "Go on," he mouthed.

"I am not here to talk to you about *ending* slavery. Slavery needs to end for good. But that it is not enough. That is only the start."

Upon hearing this, the minister rose from his chair and headed toward the pulpit and Theodore. As he moved, he made eye contact with Henry and became immediately aware of a menacing stare. Halting in mid-stride, he quickly retreated to his seat. Whether or not Theodore had noticed the minister's action, Henry didn't know. He hoped that he hadn't. Either way, the young man now seemed steady and calm. "This is good."

"I am not educated – not yet. But I will be," Theodore confessed. "It is less than two years ago that I began learning to read and write."

Looking into the crowd, he could see expressions of disbelief. Was the surprise, he wondered, that he had only begun to learn or that a man of color could ever learn? At this point, did it matter? He had come to say what he had to say – so be it.

"I'm sure everyone here can read and write better," he said. "I make many mistakes. My grammar is still sometimes poor. My spelling is sometimes bad. Arithmetic is hard for me. There are many words I try to read but don't know what they mean. But here is something I have learned."

"Freedom is more than not having a master or an overseer. It is more than not having to work without pay." He could feel his confidence starting to grow. Henry, Jonas, and the rest in the front row could sense it too. He began to feel relaxed and began to release his grip on the edges of the pulpit.

Soon though, he began to hear a murmur in the crowd. Was it the sound of approval or disapproval? Hard to say but there were few smiles. Men and women whispered in each other's ears. A mother covered her child's ears. No matter. He would go on.

"There are things that I can do as good as any white man." He could see Ellie, who had done most of his teaching, cringe at the grammar lapse. "I mean as *well* as any." She smiled and he continued. He thought about telling how he could plow a perfectly straight furrow but didn't. They might think a black man was expected to do that and could do little else. Again, a plantation skill. "I am learning to make cabinets. I could have my own shop someday and compete with any man in town." Jonas smiled in agreement.

It was getting dangerous now. Probably no one here, even in favor of freeing slaves, wanted to admit that a colored man could be so skillful and savvy as to compete with his own business. So be it. Go on.

"When I get better at doing my sums, I can work in store selling things and handing out change. Maybe I can teach others how to do them so they can work too."

Henry noticed the minister again beginning to rise. Once again, he stared him down.

"What I mean to say is that freedom isn't just being able to come and go as I please or work for pay." Henry had warned him that what he planned to say next would be unsettling but he was determined to say it. "Freedom is the chance to be anything I want to be or learn any job I want to learn. Freedom is what I have learned from the men

I met in the army and what I have learned from my family in Minnesota." He nodded toward the front pew. Family? he could imagine the crowd thinking. Family?

"Freedom is being treated with respect. Freedom is being treated like normal folk. Freedom is being treated like a *man*.

"That's what I came here to say. Thank you." He nodded and headed toward his seat.

The speech, after all of the crafting, rehearsal, and other preparation, lasted a scant ten minutes – by far the shortest speech of the evening. As had occurred after his introduction, there was no applause except from his friends and family. Disappointed but unsurprised, he returned to his seat as the minister returned to the pulpit to bring the program to a close. No "Well done", no "Thank you, young man." No, there was nothing to acknowledge that he had even been present.

Theodore and the Hancocks awaited the benedictory prayer, thankful that most of the proceedings were concluded. None expected what followed. "And Dear Lord, we ask your Divine intervention that *all* of those held in bondage in our country may soon be *free* from that bondage and that they will soon be on ships back to Africa, the land of their ancestors, where they truly belong."

Theodore looked questioningly at Henry and Jonas and signed, "Will I have to go?" Both returned his glance and shook their heads in an emphatic "No!"

"They didn't hear a word I had to say," he told them later. "They didn't *want* to hear."

"On the contrary," Henry answered him. "They may not have *wanted* to hear it but, believe me, they heard every word. They heard every eloquent word.

"What does *eloquent* mean?"

"It means you got their attention, Theodore. What you said will make them *think*."

Three nights later, Henry sat at his desk in the library, joined by Jonas and Theodore. The brother's had agreed that a letter to the abolitionist society over the group's treatment of Theodore was warranted. Theodore had abstained, saying that he would just as soon forget the entire matter. Nevertheless, he agreed to join them, hoping to temper their anger and perhaps persuade them to moderate the letter's tone. There was no purpose, he pointed out, if the group lost support in its effort to have slavery abolished in the remaining states. Jonas suggested that they also send a copy of the letter to numerous northern Iowa and southern Minnesota newspapers so that all could see it.

"To the president," Henry began to write. *"North Central Iowa Abolitionist Society. Sir,"* he continued, purposely omitting the traditional greeting 'Dear.' *"What our family witnessed in the treatment of our good friend, Theodore Lincoln, at your meeting on Wednesday last, was an abomination second only to that of slavery itself. For this young man to be treated in such a fashion after coming to the meeting*

at your own invitation represents the most heinous form of exploitation imaginable.

"That the courtesy you gave to your other speakers in your introductory remarks was not given in like fashion to Theodore represents a grievous insult to a fine young man. Theodore has proven himself to be a most conscientious worker as well as a bright student in mathematics and English. When the black people are made citizens, which I hope they will be, we think that Theodore will be as fine and productive a citizen as any white man.

"We find your comment that all persons presently or previously held in bondage be sent to Africa, a place where none now living are in any way familiar, to be particularly contemptible. We hope that any such plan for compulsory resettlement will be soundly rejected both by those in authority in our nation and by the Almighty.

Yours truly,
Henry Hancock
Jonas Hancock

CHAPTER XIX

Robert hadn't realized that he had uttered his prayer aloud while standing on the train platform at Rock Island. Neither had he realized that it had been overheard. "My God. My Dear God, please have mercy upon these men and please forgive us for what we are doing to them. What manner of beasts have we become that we can treat them so?!" He remembered later ordering the sergeant to move them inside and get them blankets. The order was quickly countermanded by the man's immediate superior and the prisoners had remained on the platform for another hour and a half. As a result, Robert had performed numerous surgeries in the succeeding few days to remove fingers and toes too badly frozen to be saved.

Within a week, the major was not only relieved of his position as Chief of Surgeons at the prison but was demoted to the rank of captain. He was not imprisoned or released from the army because of the need for his skills. His superiors, however, had made it clear that they suspected him of harboring sympathy for the enemy. One had even used the word treason. His protest that, once in prison, the men under his care should no longer be considered the enemy went unheeded. He continued to work but found himself shunned by most around him for fear that, they too, would be considered sympathizers. In March, he found himself assigned as a field surgeon and on the way to Tennessee. By July, he was in Georgia. "You need to learn how barbaric our enemy is," they had told him. "The best way to learn that is at the front!"

It was now summer. What had started as pleasant spring weather in Tennessee had wilted into a blistering, humid heat from which there seemed to be no escape. Robert had rolled up the sides of his tent to let what little breeze was available to pass through. It provided little comfort so he sat outside on a makeshift bench and placed a scrap of lumber across his lap for a desk.

Kennesaw, Georgia
July 1, 1864

My Dearest Rose,

I have a few moments before I must make my rounds at the hospital tent so I have determined to write you a few lines. First of all, please know that I am well and am as well fixed here as one can expect to be given our circumstances. The weather has been hot and there is humidity but I guess not much more than at Rock Island with the river so near.

I do not know how much longer we will be at this location as it is possible that the hospital will be moved as the army advances further toward Atlanta. In such case, I imagine that the wounded that are here now will be evacuated to other hospitals away from the front. I expect that we will continue to receive our mail as we have, so continue to address your letters to me in the same fashion. I am always happy to get your letters. I know that you are busy with little Rachel but please continue to write as often as you can. I appreciate your sending her little lock of hair and I carry it always in my pocket. It makes me feel as if I am closer to you both. If you could arrange to get a photograph of her for me that would be wonderful but have them make it not too large.

I am pleased to hear that Jonas and Henry and Em and Ellie have invited you to move in with them until the war is over and we can get a place of our own. Even if the house is crowded, I think you should feel quite comfortable and Rachel and Patrick can get to know each other. When I come, I think I should like to live in Wisconsin or perhaps in Iowa but not in Davenport. I would not want to awaken each day and see that horrible island. Even if the prison camp is torn down after the war, which I hope it will be, I do not wish to be reminded of all of the misery that is taking place there. In fact, I would not be disappointed to never see the place again.

I must close now. Please remember how much I miss you and long for the day when our little family can again be together. Kiss Rachel and tell her Papa loves her. Continue to pray for the war to be over.

Always in love,

Robert.

P.S. If you decide to move, I think you should ask Mrs. Adams if she should wish to buy our furniture. That way she can rent the space already furnished to the next tenants. If she does not so wish, try to sell it for a reasonable price to someone else and we will buy new furniture when I come home.

Kennesaw, Georgia
July 1, 1864

Dear Henry,

I have just completed my rounds here at the field hospital and feel a need to write to you. After you read my letter, please burn it. I never wish to speak of it again.

The conditions here are abominable. I know that the War Department and Sanitary Commission do what they can for the wounded but I confess that it seems to me to be woefully inadequate. Never have I seen such misery. The tents are hot and humid and there are flies and mosquitoes everywhere. The army cannot prevent those things. But the food that is brought here for the wounded is hard for them to chew and is sometimes rancid by the time it arrives. A man who has been wounded in the head or face cannot be expected to chew hard-tack or half-cooked beef. It irritates me all the more because I feel that this is an

*administrative problem and not a result of
any real shortage. I think there are
profiteers who sell inferior goods to the
army and get kickbacks in return. I suspect,
too, that there are some in the quartermaster
corps who steal the best supplies and sell
them to supplement their pay. When I was at
Rock Island, I saw boatloads of supplies
heading down the river every day but I
wonder now where it all went!*

*The surgery that we must perform here
is little short of butchery. There are so many
grievously wounded that we can never spend
the time that is needed. A limb that might be
saved if a little more time were available is
simply cut off in a matter of moments in
order to make the operating table available
for the next man. Men who might otherwise
go home to lead productive lives are turned
into cripples and invalided out. Two days
ago, I had to amputate the arm of a young
musician who before the war was
apprenticed to a violin-maker. Just before he
was given the morphine, he had begged me
to save his arm. An ambulance driver broke
down in tears as he told me of shooting a
man who been belly wounded. 'The man,'
he said, 'was crying out in pain as the
ambulance pulled away to pick up others
who could still be saved.' He told me that he
closed his eyes and put a bullet in the poor*

man's forehead in order to hasten his end and put a stop to his misery."

And then there is our surgery. Henry, I have seen more cleanliness in a pigsty. The operating tables are nothing more than boards set across pairs of saw horses. The men are moved from stretchers to the tables and sometimes laid right on blood from the men before. If the orderlies try to rinse the tables with buckets of water between surgeries, the ground soon becomes so muddy that it is difficult to stand or move about. Amputated limbs are merely tossed aside into a great pile like so much cordwood. The piles draw flies and mosquitoes that often find their way to the tables themselves. It is not uncommon for orderlies to have to shoo away flies from an open wound while we are working.

I could tell you more but it sickens me to have to report such things. I have written what I did because I thought it might ease my mind to tell someone. Again, please burn this letter as soon as you have read it. Do not share it with anyone and please do not ask me to ever speak of it.

I hear that George McClellan is running against President Lincoln in the upcoming election. I suspect that he will get much support from the army if he pledges to sue for peace and end the war. I might be tempted to vote for him myself if it weren't for the tremendous sacrifice that has already been made to preserve the Union and end the horrid practice of slavery. I think that we have now come so far that there is no choice but to see the thing through.

Sincerely yours,

Robert.

****

Darius stood as close as allowed to the stockade fence and tried to rub the sweat from his face. With nothing but his already sweaty hand to use, the effort was largely futile and the salt continued to sting his eyes. He wished he could have a shave and a haircut but his meager pay at the camp did not allow him the luxury. While some others occasionally received a little money mailed from home, he did not. What little money he had, he quickly spent to buy a piece of fresh fruit or meat that was soon gone.

There was only a small gap in the stockade fence, barely large enough for a squirrel or a rabbit to go through – not nearly enough for a man. But it was large enough for Darius to catch a glimpse of the docks at Davenport, Iowa. In looking the short distance across the water to the north, he now realized that the South's effort had been doomed from the start. Before his capture, he had seen shortages of nearly everything that the South had needed to fight the war. Once the ports were blockaded by Lincoln's navy, nothing was available unless it could be either made in the South or captured from the Yankees. Cotton, sugar, tobacco, and corn were still available though not abundant. Guns and ammunition were not. Even so, he had continued to believe that southern courage and heart would carry the day over Yankee cowardice and lack of will. That was until now. There they were – the *Star of Minnesota* lined up behind the *City of Dubuque* and the *Illinois Queen*. All of them were riding low in the water – their holds, he assumed, laden with Iowa beef, Minnesota flour, and Illinois corn – all headed to supply the largest army on the continent. Stacked on the decks were cannons, ammunition, and boxes of rifles all produced at the arsenal less than a mile away on the other end of the island. It was now only a matter of time. For him, that time could not come soon enough. Only after this damnable war was over could he leave this place and find a way to exact his revenge.

For now, however, Darius had a more immediate concern. So far, he had been able to hide his past as a prison guard at Richmond from his captors. He was well aware that, if the guards here had such knowledge, it would almost certainly prevent his ever leaving the camp alive. Among the latest group of prisoners to arrive at the camp, he had noticed the face of one of his fellow former guards. The man had been a private whom Darius recalled bullying. Darius, of course, had no remorse and would not have considered it bullying. What he had done, he had done only to amuse himself. The man's feelings were of little consequence. What bothered him now was that the man might recognize him and seek to benefit by telling what he knew. He had watched the new arrival for several days. As yet, there was nothing to indicate that he had been recognized. Still, it was a chance he could not take. It would have to be dealt with – better sooner than later.

"You there!" Darius heard a voice call from the corner tower near where he stood. "Back away from the fence or you're dead where you stand."

In his musings, he had not realized that he had walked so closely to the fence. He looked toward the source of the voice and could see the muzzle of a rifle pointed directly at him. He knew that the guard would not ask again and quickly backed away to the permitted area. He had seen the same guard before at less distance. The guards on duty now were part of a detachment of colored troops whose uniform badges identified them as part of a regiment from Minnesota. He seethed at the idea of them carrying weapons. That such beings were now in control of *his* life where as once he had once been able to order *them* about only caused the hatred to grow – toward both them and Minnesota. "Your time will come," he vowed silently.

****

The heat was sweltering but Isaac paid it little attention as he walked back and forth in front of Company H. Every few steps, he would stop and stare into the eyes of one of the men. A perfectly cleaned rifle would be presented for his scrutiny, examined closely, and handed back. Polished brass buttons adorned spotless uniforms and black leather cap bills gleamed in the sun.

There had been no more scuffles and very little grumbling since Jesse's stern lecture early in the training. The men had quickly learned how to efficiently fire and reload their weapons and how to move from a line of battle into a marching column. They had become superior marksmen whom many considered to be the best in the regiment. Some who were better shots had even been removed from the company and placed in a special group to receive additional training as sharpshooters. What pleased Isaac as much as the company's performance was the respect that his men now felt for themselves and the respect they had earned from the regiment's white officers. It pleased him even more that he had been allowed to remain with the company. When the time came, he would lead them into battle.

He knew that the weapons would not remain freshly cleaned. The uniforms would become dirty, torn, and tattered. Many, perhaps his own, would be soaked with blood. But, the dirt and the blood would not come from fighting each other as when the men had first arrived in camp. The company was now well disciplined. The men had become brothers. Any new dirt, rips, and blood would come from confronting the enemy.

The company had not been yet called into action here at Kennesaw Mountain but few doubted that their time was near. All one had to do was to look around and sniff. Along with a blue haze, the acrid, sulfuric smell of cannon and rifle smoke still hung in the air. One could not take a breath without inhaling the residue of used gunpowder. And there were the visual reminders. Only a short distance from the encampment was a road that carried two streams of ambulances – one headed for the field hospital and another going empty back toward the field to gather more wounded. The traffic had not ceased since the worst of the encounter ended two days ago. It showed no signs of slowing down.

Not far away was another reminder. Men who had been able to make their way back sat around in groups waiting for whatever might come next. Many were walking wounded – not severely – enough injured to remain in the hospital but also not well enough right now to continue the fight. There were bandages on heads, arms, legs, hands, and feet – some reasonably clean but most stained with brown, dried blood. Faces were covered with a grimy mix of sweat, dirt, and smoke. Beards and hair had gone untrimmed. There was little talking and few smiles. Most bore a countenance of dazed disbelief in what they had seen. Other expressions seemed to indicate only feelings of grim determination.

The army had taken a beating. The only consolation, and that consolation was mostly confined to the officers, was that the action had taken an enormous toll on General Johnston's Confederate Army. That army, much less able to stand the losses, would certainly have to abandon the disputed land soon and withdraw back toward Atlanta. To most of the regular soldiers, getting back to the camp meant only that they had lived long enough to get a bit of rest. Soon they would be ordered to go back into another battle from which they might not return. Though Isaac wanted to be here with his men, he tried not to think about that part. He completed the inspection. Satisfied that all was in order, he presented the company to the lieutenant and stepped back into the ranks.

****

Henry took off his hat and wiped his face with the handkerchief that he carried in his back pocket. The wheat was nearly all cut. He and Jonas and Theodore had been working for days to get it all threshed out and ready to be hauled to the mill. And the weeds needed to be hoed out of the corn field. The garden was another matter but Ellie and Em were in charge of that. They took turns watching Patrick while the other weeded the sweet corn, green beans, and tomatoes. Soon it would be time to start putting up garden crops to be eaten next winter.

The three had finished their fried chicken, mashed potatoes and pie and were preparing to head back to the field but stopped near Albert's old semblance of a barn. "Another project," Henry commented to Theodore but facing Jonas so that he could read his lips. The barn was hardly worth the name. Albert Anderson had hastily erected it as a shelter for his horses soon after acquiring the farm and before turning his attention to building the house for his new bride, Lucille. Within a few years, they had decided to build a house in Thayer where Albert had joined his brother in a law practice. Henry and Jonas had rented the farm and moved into the house but the large barn Albert had planned remained unbuilt. Now that Jonas and Henry owned the farm, they had decided it was time to build a proper one. The oak trees felled in the timber last spring were curing nicely. After the wheat was finished and before the corn was ready for harvest, they would work on turning the logs into beams and planks.

Even with work to be done, they had decided to quit early this afternoon. Today was the Fourth of July and the entire family planned to attend the celebration in town. It was the eighty-eighth anniversary of the Republic and the first since the victories at Vicksburg and Gettysburg. The party had originally been planned for daytime but the planning committee had decided to wait until evening since the weather would be a bit cooler. The farmers could get in nearly a full day in the fields. There would be a picnic, a torchlight parade, music, and speeches. The 'Captain' had been asked to recite President Lincoln's speech from last November's dedication of the cemetery at Gettysburg. He had been memorizing and rehearsing for several days in his effort to present it with just the right tone and emphasis. Jonas had been asked to sing 'The Battle Hymn of the Republic.' Ellie's students were to perform a medley of other patriotic songs. For the first time, there seemed to be real hope that this would be the last *Fourth of July* of the war.

They stood for a while, staring at the spot that they had chosen for the barn. Henry pointed and talked while Jonas made comments of his own about what the new building should contain and how it should be designed. Theodore, not feeling that it was his place to express an opinion, stood quietly by and listened. He was especially pleased and proud when Henry turned to him. "Theodore, what do you think?"

"I think we should cut some more wheat," he grinned. "But I also think the oat bin should be bigger and could I maybe have a stall for Ned?"

****

Joshua gazed over the crowd from the steps of the church. The log structure had been put together in a matter of days when the first settlers of the community had decided that a church building was an immediate need. The congregation that had built it and used it first was the Lutherans. As their numbers multiplied, they had soon outgrown the little building and generously donated it to the Methodists who were beginning to arrive. Today was Saturday, the ninth of July. With the weather so hot, it had been decided to hold the ceremony outside. All of the benches had been moved to the front lawn. Some had brought kitchen chairs from home while yet others had decided to simply stand by in the shade and watch. With some help from neighbors, Henry and Jonas had loaded their piano onto a wagon and hauled it to the church. Ellie would accompany Jonas' vocal hymn though he would not hear her. What was important was that Will Britt, his bride, and their guests would.

"Dearly beloved," Joshua began, "we are gathered here in the sight of God and in the presence of these witnesses to join this man and this woman in holy matrimony, which is an honorable estate, instituted by God and signifying unto us the mystical union which exists between Christ and His Church. It is there not to be entered into unadvisedly, but reverently, discreetly, and in the fear of God. Into this holy estate these two persons come now to be joined." He had his hymnal open to the proper page but had studied hard to memorize the entire ceremony and had rehearsed it numerous times in the privacy of his lodgings. It was his first wedding as Methodist Minister here in Thayer. It was, in fact, the first in his ministry. There was no chance, he had decided early on, that he could make a mistake. It was a wedding that he could not have imagined. Both the bride and the groom were Methodists and members of his congregation. Since both of Sarah's parents had passed on, she had asked David and Mary Alice to take on those roles for the day. Mary Alice, Sarah's aunt, was Lutheran. David, her Jewish uncle by marriage, was to give her away. He had asked to wear his yarmulke but had agreed, since it was a Christian ceremony, not to wear his prayer shawl. Since Mary Alice was 'the mother of the bride,' it had been agreed that the Lutheran Minister should participate by delivering the opening prayer. David was to walk Sarah down the aisle and give her away. Since no Rabbi was available, Will and Sarah had asked him to present a Jewish blessing.

Will, Jonas observed, looked especially well dressed in his Sunday best. He was particularly pleased that Will's limp was hardly noticeable. Most present knew that Will had lost his left knee and leg at the Battle of Shiloh some two years ago. Those who did not, would have guessed that he had nothing but a mildly sprained ankle. The artificial leg that Jonas had created for him seemed to work to perfection.

Sarah's best friend, Ellie, had made her wedding dress – working on it evenings after helping with chores on the farm all day. Sarah had nervously wondered if it could possibly be finished on time in spite of Ellie's almost daily assurances. Finally, on the morning after the Fourth of July celebration, Ellie had invited her out to the farm for the final fitting and all was well.

Joshua stood on the third step of the church, while Will and Sarah stood on the second so that they could be seen by members of the crowd near the back of the lawn. "William Edward Britt, wilt thou have this woman to be thy wedded wife, to live together in the holy estate of matrimony? Wilt thou love her, comfort her, honor and keep her, in sickness and in health; and forsaking all others, keep thee only unto her as long as you both shall live?"

The young minister hardly heard Will's very audible, "I will." As hard as he had rehearsed and as hard as he tried to remain focused, his thoughts suddenly shifted. As he watched the couple before him, those nearby noticed that he seemed to hesitate. Looking at Will and Sarah, Joshua imagined himself standing beside Ellie while another pastor asked him the same question. He found himself briefly glancing toward where she was seated next to Henry and Em. He thought he caught her eye. She smiled, and he jerked his head slightly as he tried to drive the thought from his mind and return to the task at hand. "Sarah Grace Hanson, wilt thou have this man to be thy wedded husband …?"

Joshua completed the ceremony without further pause but wondered whether anyone had noticed his lapse. "Forasmuch as William and Sarah have consented … Those whom God hath joined together, let no man put asunder. Amen."

Joshua again looked in Ellie's direction, this time nodding a cue for her to move to the piano. Jonas left his seat and joined her. As usual, when Jonas prepared to sing, a hush fell over the entire gathering in anticipation of the treat that they were about to receive. The only sound was the gentle rustle of leaves as a slight breeze began to move through. Though he knew the words and music by heart, he looked down at the hymnal before he began. Unable to hear the piano, he watched his sister's fingers begin to move across the keys. Remembering what each key sounded like, he was able to follow her accompaniment. His baritone voice echoed through the trees and could easily be heard even by those standing at the back. "Oh love divine and golden, mysterious depth and height, To Thee the world beholden, looks up for life and light ..."

To the disappointment of the congregation, the hymn seemed to end nearly as soon as it had begun. Joshua again spoke. "On behalf of Will and Sarah, I would like to thank the ladies of the church for the wonderful feast they have prepared for all of us to enjoy as we celebrate this joyous occasion." Most eyes had already turned to the gingham-covered tables laden with chicken, barbecued beef, various salads, and numerous cakes and pies. "I know that there are Lutherans and others gathered with us today who would like to dance. You will recall that the *Methodist Discipline* prohibits dancing. That said, the Bible also tells us to make a joyful noise unto the Lord. I see that Carl Erickson has brought along his fiddle, which I assume has only one real purpose. Given that, I will join you as we partake in this wonderful meal. I shall then excuse myself and take a long, leisurely, afternoon stroll in the forest. After that, I may find myself a little pond and do some fishing."

CHAPTER XX

The September air was pleasantly cool. A slight breeze rustled through the forest canopy. The leaves had begun to turn color but were still days away from their annual orange, red, and yellow brilliance. They had begun to dry but few had fallen. Henry and Theodore easily noticed the difference in sound from mid-summer when the leaves were lush and green.

The two had finished the lunch that Em had prepared and sent with them to the timber. They were aware that they had a short time to work there before the corn would be ready to husk. When Henry and Jonas decided that the crop was ready, almost all other work would cease until the crop was safely put away for winter. For now, however, Henry had determined that they should take a short nap before returning to work. They lay on their backs and looked through the treetops at the bright azure sky.

They had spent the entire morning chopping and sawing branches from the oak trees that they and Jonas had felled in late-February. The process was necessary in order for the horses to drag the logs from the forest. Once there was a clear path to the road, a crew from the sawmill could load them onto giant wagons and haul them to the mill. After continuing to cure through the winter, they would be ready to be cut to the proper size and formed into a ridgepole, floor joists, posts, and beams.

Jonas had not joined them since he had a chore of his own. Today, he was finishing the roof on an additional room to the house. Rose and little Rachel had arrived in Thayer in August. Ellie had more than willingly shared her bedroom with her sister and niece but Henry had decided that the house needed to be bigger anyhow. Em had needed little convincing, anticipating that Patrick would not be an only child.

Theodore was tired but not sleepy. His arms ached a little from the sawing and chopping but he had grown quite muscular in his year and a half or so at the farm. The fatigue would soon pass. For now, he had something more momentous on his mind. "In a few months I will turn seventeen," he commented, turning his head toward Henry.

"You will," Henry answered him lazily.

"And I'm a free man; free to come and go as I please," he continued.

"You are," Henry replied, starting to become curious about what had prompted this discussion. "For going on two years now. I seem to recall that you have a watch that says so. He remembered fondly the New Year's Eve that the officers and men of the Company had celebrated Theodore's emancipation by giving him the engraved watch.

"That means I'm old enough, right?" Theodore asked.

"Old enough for what?" Henry was no longer on his back but was up leaning on one elbow, facing the young man.

"To join the army, of course."

Henry bolted upright. "Why on earth ...? I'm sorry." He quickly caught himself. "I shouldn't have said that. You're a man now. I *know* why you want to go. You want to do your part. If I'm right, you feel you have a debt."

"I *do* have one," Theodore answered him. "I have a very *large* debt to you and to Jonas and to Lt. Atlee and to Em and to Ellie. I owe you all everything. I've been thinking about it a lot lately. You know I wouldn't leave you for anything else."

"I know you wouldn't," Henry assured him, still struggling to overcome his surprise. "I should have expected no less. It's just that ..."

"That what?"

"Well," Henry measured his words carefully, "it's that, when I brought you here, I felt like I was taking you away from all that had gone bad in your life – that I was giving you a fresh start; a chance to get an education, to learn a trade, and to live out your entire life as you see fit. I didn't envision ..."

"You *did,*" Theodore interrupted him. "You gave me all of that. It's what I want too. But now I need to *earn* it."

"But," Henry continued, "what if you don't come back? What then?"

"Come back from the war or come back to the farm?"

"The war," Henry replied. "I meant the *war*. Whether you would come back to the farm would be your own choice, though I would hope you'd do it.

"I will come back. I know it. But if I don't, I will have been a part of it. I would have no regrets about it. When you went, or when Jonas went, did you know if you'd come back?"

"No. No one knew."

"You went anyhow, didn't you? You knew there was a chance you wouldn't come home and yet you went anyhow."

"We did."

"I have to," Theodore insisted. "I've made up my mind. So many men died so I could make my own choice. If I don't do it, it's not right for *them*."

Henry knew that there would be no dissuading him. "What are you going to tell Em?"

"The same thing I just told you."

Henry gave up. "So, I guess there's really nothing more to say. Do this one thing for me."

"What's that?"

"Wait until you actually turn seventeen. Do you know when your birthday is?"

"I don't guess I really know. I never really thought about it much. Someone told me once it was in the spring."

"Em's birthday is April 11," Henry told him. "I think she'd be honored to have you share it. So let's say it's April 11. You'll turn seventeen on April 11, 1865. We can leave that day and I will personally go with you to St. Paul. I think they will let an old captain swear you into the army there. Do we have a deal?"

Theodore smiled and leaned over to shake his hand. "Nap time's over. We best get to it."

Henry handed him an axe. "No need to tell Em or any of the others. They'd just spend the entire winter worrying about you." He didn't tell Theodore the rest. *I know I will. I'll just have to pray this whole thing is over by then.*

*****

Darius had not seen the man since July. Perhaps he had only imagined him. After all, it had been a long time. Or maybe they had placed him in another barracks. There were dozens of them. He wasn't sure how many but he guessed that there were at least seventy or eighty, perhaps as many as one hundred. If all were like his own, each held at least one hundred men.

There was a good chance that he wouldn't be recognized anyhow. He had lost weight. With his beard and long hair, he hardly looked as he had when he had guarded the Yankee officers at Libby Prison. He had decided some time ago not to give it another thought. What *did* concern him was that it was already September. The mild weather represented a welcome relief from the stifling heat of July and August and the first freeze would put an end to irritating mosquitoes and other pests. But that was little comfort. October might be nice and perhaps part of November also. But he remembered December. The memory was not a pleasant one.

Deciding that there was nothing more to be seen anyhow and not relishing another confrontation, Darius began to wander half-heartedly back toward the barracks. He had only walked a few steps and kicked up a modicum of dust when he was approached by two of the yard guards. They were unarmed. Weapons were not allowed in the yard unless there was a disturbance to be put down. But neither did one wish to provoke them for fear of harsh, swift, and certain reprisals. His better judgment told him to simply stand still when they told him to halt and then wait to see what they wanted.

He had seen the pair before as they patrolled the area. By standards of the camp, they did not seem overly hostile toward the captives. Their primary duty seemed to be to break up fights, which occasionally broke out in the streets between the barracks. Even in doing that, they seemed to be mostly interested in settling things peacefully and making sure that the men did not subject themselves to the harsh punishment meted out to brawlers. At times, he had even seen them smile slightly at the participants after a disagreement had been resolved. It surprised him that these and some other members of the Minnesota colored regiment assigned here were actually less cruel than those from the white contingent. Still, they were freedmen and former slaves. That alone was sufficient cause for disdain and a silent vow of revenge.

The two guards seemed in earnest and to have singled him out from others in the vicinity. This puzzled him. True, he wandered closer to the fence than was allowed but he had peacefully obeyed the command from the tower to move away. He had gone to particular lengths to obey the camp's rules and not draw attention to himself. Only in this way, he had come to realize, could he expect to leave this place alive when the war finally ended.

"You," the first guard called out, pointing toward him and quickening his step. "Stay where you are." In moments, the pair were standing on either side of him and holding his arms. To his alarm, they quickly cuffed his hands behind him and began to march him toward the camp headquarters. He was tempted to ask them the reason for his arrest but decided against it. There was no point in drawing their ire. Besides, he told himself, they probably didn't know and were only following orders to detain him.

Darius didn't have long to wait. He soon stood before a door where a sign read 'Hosea Billings, Captain of the Guard.' Once inside, the two who had brought him there were quickly dismissed. He stood alone, still handcuffed, in front of the desk. Behind him the guards on either side of the door were armed with rifles that were undoubtedly loaded.

The office was sparsely furnished. The entire collection of furniture consisted only of the captain's desk and chair, two straight chairs without arms, and a small table on top of which sat a cabinet with a dozen or so pigeon holes stuffed with assorted envelopes and papers. Captain Billings sat behind the desk. A Minnesota regimental flag hung on the wall behind him. Darius guessed Billings to be about six feet tall when standing. He appeared to have once been much stouter. Darius guessed he had lost significant weight recently due to disease or some other cause. Deep wrinkles lined his face and his ashen skin appeared to hang in folds under his jawline. Large dark circles under his eyes caused him to look much older than he probably was and his thinning hair had turned mostly to a brownish-gray. After a time, he spoke without looking up from the book that lay open on the desk. "You don't know who I am, do you?"

"No," Darius answered feebly. The question seemed odd since he did not recall having ever met the man. He felt the point of a bayonet jab him in the back. "No, *Sir*," he spoke more loudly. It was a reluctant 'sir' and he didn't remember ever having uttered the word to a Yankee officer.

"Well, that's the difference here, isn't it?" the captain scoffed, looking back at the book. "It seems the tables have turned. Your name may or may not be Davis Moran, as it's listed in the camp manifest, but it doesn't matter. Believe me, I know who you are."

Darius felt his knees grow weak as he slowly recognized the captain. He hoped that the realization would not show on his face.

"Yes, indeed," the captain spoke again, this time staring directly at him. "I definitely know who *you* are." He brushed his hair backward and revealed the large scar on his forehead above his left eye. "Now do you know me?"

Darius stood silently until another jab in the back prompted him to speak. He remembered personally delivering the blow that had created the scar. There was no point in lying. "Yes."

Another jab. "Yes, *Sir*."

"It isn't a fond memory, is it?"

317

"No, Sir," Darius answered without prompting.

"That's good," Billings replied. "In fact, I have no fond memories at all of my time at Libby Prison. I plan to make it my calling from now on to make sure that your remaining days here at Rock Island are equally as miserable as mine were there. I believe that I know just where to start."

A long silence followed as Darius waited anxiously to see what sort of retribution Billings had in mind.

"First of all, you look awfully ragged. I believe that a haircut and a shave would be in order. We have a barber here in camp. He was captured at First Manassas and spent quite some time as a prisoner at Belle Isle before he was exchanged. I believe you will find him very accommodating but, alas, not very careful. A clean-shaven head and face should be quite handsome. Don't you agree?" He waited and continued to stare. "Well?"

"Yes, Sir," Darius muttered, looking down to avoid the captain's gaze and knowing it was the only answer he could give.

Captain Billings had one of the guards summon the pair who had brought Darius in. "The prisoner here tells me that he is in need of a haircut and shave," he addressed them. "Escort him to the barber. Be sure to tell him that our friend here was a guard at Libby Prison and so he need not take particular care with his razor. Then, bring him back here and take him downstairs. I think it's time that our guest learns some prison etiquette. I know a couple of men in the regiment who would be more than happy to instruct him.

****

Britt's Mercantile was one of the first businesses to be established when Thayer was settled. Charles Britt had moved here from Illinois with his wife and twin sons, Thomas and Will, shortly before the Hancocks arrived from Ohio. The store was not large but was well-stocked for one in a town this size and Charles seemed able to carry nearly everything that the local residents needed. He had done well for himself, having the only general store in town. He had easily resisted the temptation to take advantage of his monopoly by raising prices. His customers were, after all, his friends, and deserved to be treated as such. He was also aware that they had the option to do their shopping in Crestville, even though that would involve traveling some distance. He had no illusions that his store would always be the only one in town and was aware of the importance of a loyal clientele.

The building that housed the mercantile was a frame structure with clapboard sidings that Charles had again whitewashed this past summer. Jonas had arrived in time to help finish the interior work and had built most of the shelving and the sales counters on-site before opening his cabinet shop down the street.

The store's interior consisted of only two rooms – a large one in the front for all of the sales and a smaller one in the back that served as a storeroom. Behind the building was a separate structure that served as a smokehouse and, during the winter, a freezer. Just inside the front door were two sales counters that faced each other from opposite sides of the room. As one walked in and turned to the left, there was the counter for selecting kitchen utensils, farm tools, other assorted hardware, and a selection of pipes, tobacco, and cigars. Across from it was the counter featuring yard goods, groceries, coffee, assorted small notions, and a few small jars of hard candy. Guns and ammunition were sold from a third counter toward the back of the store. Another small counter close by served as the town's post office and allowed Charles to supplement his income with a small stipend received for serving as postmaster. One thing that Charles refused to sell in his store was liquor. For that, one had to visit the harness shop and livery stable.

Thayer had yet to boast a restaurant. In its absence, Margaret Britt had sectioned off a small area near the stairs that led up to the family's apartment. She had outfitted the space with three small tables that she always kept covered with fresh, red gingham cloths. From there she offered a limited menu of homemade pies and daily servings ranging from beef stew to fried chicken or cornbread and beans. While most of the people working in town lived there or nearby and went home for lunch, she managed to do a thriving little trade feeding farmers who came to town on business and the town's numerous bachelors eager for a home-cooked meal. Jonas and Theodore were regular customers, frequenting the tables when in town working at the shop.

Henry and Jonas had just finished their lunch at Britt's and lingered over their coffee. It was a Thursday in early September. The hay was all put up for the winter. It was too early yet to harvest the corn. Em, Rose, and Ellie were busily canning the last vegetables from the garden and making preserves. It was raining so there would be no work today on the barn beams. Yes, it was a good time to leave the farm for a while and run errands in Thayer.

There was little talk in the store and the small restaurant that didn't center on the upcoming elections. The town was nearly evenly divided among those supporting the re-election of President Lincoln and those supporting his Democratic opponent, the erstwhile general, George 'Little Mac' McClellan. Henry and Jonas both counted themselves among the former. Now, with William Sherman's army running almost unopposed through the South and on the verge of capturing Atlanta, victory seemed within reach. It seemed totally irrational to sue for peace as McClellan advocated and threw away everything that had been gained at such a terrible cost.

McClellan's supporters maintained that the war was no closer to being won than it had been after McClellan's own army failed to pursue Lee's forces following the Battle of Antietam. They pointed to the carnage still taking place in northern Virginia as Grant seemed unable to break through the Confederate defenses surrounding Richmond. It was time, they said, to cut the losses and to avoid more bloodshed on both sides – to allow the South to leave the Union. It had been folly, many of them also maintained, for Lincoln to issue the Emancipation Proclamation and give the South further motivation to continue the fight. There had, as yet, been no serious injuries but several fistfights had erupted in Thayer over the issue in recent weeks. There promised to be more in the remaining time leading up to the November election.

As strongly as Henry and Jonas agreed on the need to re-elect Lincoln, they disagreed just as strongly over who should represent their district in the upcoming Congress. In the interest of keeping harmony in the family, they had mostly agreed to differ on the point. That was until Jonas, without consulting his brother, had written an editorial published in the Crestville Tribune shortly prior to the Republican Party caucus. In his editorial, Jonas had thrown his support behind the inflammatory radical candidate who had sought to unseat the more moderate incumbent. To Henry's great disappointment and Jonas' equally great satisfaction, Ezra Watson had already been chosen by the caucus and was now officially the party's nominee.

The two had nearly finished their coffee when the short, rotund and balding Watson walked in the front door. "Gentlemen, good day!" he loudly greeted the store's patrons. By either choice or oversight, he failed to acknowledge the ladies also present. After all, they could not vote and so were of little concern to him. "Ah, and I see here we have my good friend Jonas Hancock," he shouted as he glanced toward the back of the room. "Hello, Jonas. It's good to see you! And I see you have also brought Henry. Or is it 'Captain' Henry?" He nodded toward Henry with a smile that seemed more a sneer than a genuine greeting. "Henry Hancock, the great lion of Shiloh, so we meet again."

Henry rose to leave. "Indeed, we do meet again, Ezra. The pleasure is entirely yours," he said loudly enough for all in the room to hear.

"What was that about?" Jonas tugged at his sleeve.

"It's personal, Jonas. From the regiment. Let's go. And, by the way, I'll be voting Democrat for Congress. All Watson wants is revenge. If enough like him are elected, it will take generations for the wounds of the war to heal. Think about it. Think about it long and hard. Is that what you really want?" He made his way to the front door, resisting the temptation to confront the candidate but taking care to avoid him instead.

They met later for the ride home. The rain had stopped and the sky had cleared a little but they still threw a canvas over the supplies to keep them dry in case the rain should return before they reached the farm. "You really believe it, don't you?" Henry asked Jonas after they had seated themselves on the wagon."

"Believe what?"

"You know what I mean – that punishing the South by taxing them to death, shutting off their commerce, and starving them is fitting. What do you think all of that will accomplish?"

"I believe as Watson does," Jonas answered. "What you call revenge, we call justice. They must be made to pay for all of it – slavery, the cost of the war, the lives lost like Thomas Britt and Albert Anderson and all of the others. Think about it – my hearing, Will's leg, your eye, all of the men they maimed who can never do another day's work. Yes, I believe it. If it takes generations for them to pay the debt, then so be it."

"And how do you expect them to pay it back if you starve them out? And then what? Will any of it heal the wounded or bring back the dead? They suffered too, remember. There's nearly nothing left south of Maryland or Kentucky that's usable."

"It's not my problem how they pay for it," Jonas retorted. "They brought it on themselves and on the country. It was their war. They started it. Whatever is left, the government should take. Use it to take care of the wounded and their families and the orphans. If there's anything still left after that, let them fight over it themselves."

They had talked without looking at each other. Henry turned to face Jonas. "It's madness!"

"It's justice. I wonder what's for dinner."

"I wouldn't expect much. Remember, they've been doing preserves all day."

"I hope it's chicken."
                              ****

Albert and Lucille Anderson had never gotten around to setting out a fruit orchard while they lived at the farm. Jonas and Theodore had begun planting apple seedlings the first spring that they were both at the farm together and the entire family had pitched together to put in more this past spring. Even the yearling trees, however, were not yet sufficiently mature to bear fruit. Since David and Mary Alice had a fine number of adult trees, they had invited the Hancocks to pick as many apples as they wanted for the coming winter. It was Saturday morning and school was not in session, so Ellie and Rose had eagerly hitched up a wagon and headed out to accept the invitation. Em had stayed behind to bake bread and tend the babies.

Rose, the eldest of the Hancock siblings, had met Robert while he was visiting his cousin in Thayer shortly after the family arrived from Ohio. They had immediately become attracted to each other and married even before Robert returned to St. Paul for his last semester of medical school. He had barely begun his practice in Minneapolis when he had enlisted in the army and was posted to the arsenal at Rock Island. Though Rose and Ellie had tried to keep in touch with letters, they eagerly looked forward to spending more time together catching up after their time apart.

While Ellie drove the team toward the Weinberg farm, the two laughed and joked as they had when they were children. They now considered themselves to be adults but, on this particular day, did not feel a need to act their age. Though they loved and respected their brothers, the two men remained easy targets for their jokes. That Jonas and Henry could laugh at themselves made the teasing seem harmless enough. Thus it seemed to be a quite appropriate way to pass the time as the wagon jostled them along the road.

Mary Alice smiled and waved at the pair from her front porch as they pulled into the drive. Since David had gone to Thayer on business, she had decided to join them in the apple picking. They loaded Mary Alice's empty baskets into the wagon with their own. She climbed aboard the seat and together the three had headed off to the orchard.

"I'm worried about Joshua." Ellie pulled an apple from a tree and carefully placed it in her basket. It was the first serious word she had spoken all morning and it caught Rose off guard. Mary Alice was some distance off.

"Is he ill?" Rose queried. "He has looked like the picture of health to me every time I have seen him lately."

"No, he's not ill," Ellie responded. "I thank God for that. He just seems somehow different than when he first came calling. He doesn't talk or laugh like he did when he was staying at the farm. He always seems nervous about something."

"Is he remembering the war too much? Henry says that he saw a lot of horrible things."

"They all did. But no, I don't think that's it. I wouldn't blame him but I think it's something else. I've asked him but he just gets more nervous and more standoffish so I haven't pried further. I just wish he would tell me."

"Is it something at the church?" Rose asked. "Maybe there's something there that bothers him."

"No, I don't think that's it. He seems happiest when he's talking about that. He really loves the congregation and singing and working on his sermons. He positively glowed when he baptized little Patrick. It's something different."

"What else could there be?"

"I don't know. He keeps acting like there's something he wants to say but always stops short – as if he becomes afraid to say it."

"Why didn't you say that to begin with? Rose smiled. "Silly girl!"

"Say what?!" Ellie looked at her. "And how dare you call me a silly girl? I'm not a *girl* any longer. I'm old enough to make my own decisions and to teach school."

"I know you are," Rose laughed. "Are you also old enough to see when a man is in love with you and is trying to get up enough nerve to tell you so and ask you to marry him?"

Ellie gasped. "No. Truly? Do you really think so?"

"What else could it be?"

****

The evening chores were done. Henry and Jonas had retreated to Henry's library with their pipes. Since nearly coming to blows a week ago, they had agreed to discuss the Congressional election no more. They would each vote their own conscience and not allow either their votes or the election's outcome to get between them. Theodore sat in a chair in the dining room studying his latest mathematics lesson while Em, Ellie, and Rose busied themselves with dinner preparations and setting the table. While more work had to be accomplished before dark, the family, in general, enjoyed the shortening daylight and longer nights. The day's tasks were normally finished a bit earlier. There was a little more time to visit, read, play music or chess, and to watch and listen to the babies.

As the family was about to gather at the dining room table, the ladies heard a knock at the kitchen door. Rose answered it to find David standing with a rolled-up newspaper under his arm. He strode in without waiting to be invited. "Em, Rose, Ellie." He barely greeted them as he made his way to the library. "I need to see Henry and Jonas!" He stayed only moments. "Got to go," he told them on the way out. "Mary Alice is waiting with dinner!"

Dinner consisted of Em's special combination of beef and lamb stew with vegetables and fresh dumplings. There would, of course, be fresh apple pie for dessert. The ladies were eager to learn what had prompted David's short and unexpected visit but refrained from asking. It had been long understood that there would be no over-dinner conversation until after Grace had been said and then only briefly while the serving dishes were passed. Talk would be suspended while the family ate the main course and then again be permitted over dessert and coffee.

"… and in Jesus' name, Amen." Jonas, whose turn it was, finished the blessing and then all chimed in, "Amen." The ladies waited more eagerly for the news than for the stew while Theodore seemed equally anxious for both.

"So, Henry …" Em was the first to speak. She rose and began to ladle the stew into each person's waiting bowl from the large serving bowl that sat in the center of the table.

Henry held up his bowl as the next to be filled. "Sherman has captured Atlanta! There is talk that, with the South divided, they might not be able to continue much longer. The war might be over by spring!"

Henry and Theodore exchanged furtive, knowing glances. Ellie saw them. She shot Henry a quizzical glance but said nothing. Henry thought Theodore looked disappointed.

CHAPTER XXI

NEW YORK TRIBUNE

NEW YORK, WEDNESDAY

NOVEMBER 9, 1864.

LINCOLN RE-ELECTED

He has nearly all the states
All New England voted for him
New York close but pretty sure
New Jersey for McClellan
Delaware and Maryland Union
Pennsylvania Union
COPPERHEADS NOWHERE

****

It had always been in Jonas' nature not to pry into other people's business – especially that of friends and family. It had also been in his nature to be curious. On this day, the two sides of his nature engaged in a mortal conflict and the curious side ultimately prevailed.

It was Sunday morning, November 13. The rest of the family had left about half an hour ago for Church. Jonas, who rarely missed a Sunday service, had been nursing a bad cold for several days and had stayed home. He had just poured himself another cup of coffee and now found himself standing at Henry's desk. The night before, Henry had written in his journal. Em had called him to the kitchen and he had later gone to bed without closing the book and placing it back in its usual spot. Now it lay open and Jonas could not resist looking.

November 12, 1864

Thankfully, Lincoln has been re-elected. Though I thought such would be the case, I am much relieved that it has now occurred. For McClellan to have won would not only have given the Rebels new hope, but would also have represented a great disservice to those who have given so much to ensure that the Union is preserved.

Though it may have given the Rebels courage, I am not certain however that McClellan's victory, should it have occurred, would have affected the outcome of the war. With General Sherman now in control of Atlanta, I think that the South is sufficiently crippled that they will not be able to sustain the war for a great length of time. It must now only be a matter of weeks or months until they must accept the inevitable and give up the fight. I think it is even possible that victory might be achieved before McClellan would have taken office. Such a day of rejoicing it will be when the business is finally settled and those in the army can come home to resume their lives with friends and family!

To Jonas' relief, Henry had not noted, even in his journal, his pleasure that Ezra Watson had been defeated in the Congressional contest. He was about to place the journal back on the desk when he sneezed. The book slipped from his grasp and fell to the floor. As he reached to pick it up, he noticed that an envelope had fallen out. Curiously, the envelope from Robert MacDonald was addressed only to Henry and not to Rose or to the rest of the family. He placed the journal back on the desk just as he had found it but was unable to resist opening the envelope.

Kennesaw, Georgia
July 1, 1864

Dear Henry,

I have just completed my rounds here at the field hospital and feel a need to write to you. After you read my letter, please burn it. I never wish to speak of it again.

The conditions here are abominable. I know that the War Department and Sanitary Commission do what they can for the wounded but I confess that it seems to me to be woefully inadequate. Never have I seen such misery. The tents are hot and humid and there are flies and mosquitoes everywhere. The army cannot prevent those things. But the food that is brought here ...

When Jonas had finished reading the letter he refolded it, being careful to do so just as he had found it, and placed it back in the journal. He issued an unheard apology to both Robert and Henry and headed back to the kitchen for more coffee.

****

Stark stood in the hay yard for what he knew would be the last time. He had hoped only to collect the pay that was due to him and quickly return to Pine Hill. Any chance of receiving the pay had now disappeared. Sam Greene had left the yard and gone home as soon as word arrived that Sherman's army had burned Atlanta and was again on the move. The yard and livery had already been emptied of every horse, carriage, or wagon. There would be no more work. Where he would go, Stark did not know. He knew only that he would not remain in Milledgeville.

The city had descended into a full-fledged panic nearly from the moment that word was received. People scrambled to round up friends and loved ones. Houses were being emptied of as much of the contents as could be carried in whatever forms of conveyance were available. The railroad depot had been overrun by desperate crowds seeking to board trains to Savanna while the tracks still existed. Store owners were hastily boarding up doors and windows, both to protect their wares from looters and in the vain hope that locks and boards would somehow protect their inventories from Sherman's army.

Rumors abounded and were spreading as quickly and wildly as the flames that were consuming Atlanta.

Sherman had incited a slave rebellion prior to burning Atlanta. Slaves were running about the city plundering and looting stores and homes and turning on their masters.

All male residents were being rounded up and imprisoned in camps outside of the city.

Slaves and Union soldiers were raping defenseless women and girls on a mass scale.

Every building in the city had been burned to the ground including ones being used as hospitals for Confederate wounded.

Stark had never been a patient man. Despairing of receiving his pay, he walked away from the yard and headed back to Pine Hill. What would sometimes have been a pleasant and not over-taxing stroll soon became an ordeal. It took him nearly an hour to shove his way through the crowd that clogged the street between the hay yard and the bridge over the river – ordinarily a five-minute walk. He drew the ire of more than one of the fleeing residents as he attempted to shove them out of his way. He loudly cursed a small boy after tripping over him and falling headlong onto the brick street.

The bridge itself was like the narrows of an hourglass. The closer he came to the approach, the denser the throng grew and the harder it became to make any progress. A few mounted officers from the town's police tried to direct traffic and restore order but their efforts were quickly proving futile. Some had even tried to join the flight by attempting to swim their horses across the river.

Caught in the flow, Stark felt himself being shoved from behind and carried along with the crowd. He could move neither more quickly nor more slowly than he desired. Once on the bridge, he tried to content himself with simply riding the exodus, but only grew more anxious and agitated with each passing moment. Multiple catastrophes began to play themselves out in his head. What if he should fall and be trampled to death by hundreds of panicked feet? What if the bridge should collapse under all of the extra weight and trap him, drowning, underneath it? What if one of the horses on the bridge should rear up and strike him with a downward hoof? What if …?

After what seemed like hours, the massive throng that engulfed him reached the far bank of the river. He hoped to find more room to walk and breathe but the congestion did not subside. The road was little wider than the bridge. On one side, the dense pine forest and thicket made passage nearly impossible. On the other, underbrush and a steep drop off to the river made it equally difficult for the crowd to fan out. As a result, the narrow column continued as before. Finally, choosing what he considered to be the lesser evil, he shoved his way to the edge of the road and exited into the forest.

What Stark found as he reached Pine Hill disturbed him more than anything he had seen all day. In fact, it bothered him more than anything he had seen in his lifetime. Shortly before dusk, Andrew had let it be known that every slave on the plantation should assemble on the lawn in front of the mansion. With only half an hour or so left of daylight, he now stood on the steps ready to address the ragtag assemblage. Stark watched nervously from a distance as Andrew stood on the steps, his hands behind his back, and began to speak.

"You have been loyal servants to me and to my beloved Annabelle. You have toiled long and hard in my fields and in my house. In return, I have tried to treat you well and to care for you the best that I have known how. I have provided you shelter and food and medicine. When those among you could no longer work, I have allowed you to remain under my care. I have tried never to separate you from your loved ones. You have my gratitude. As the Bible says, I will now say to you, 'well done, good and faithful servants.'

Now, the time has come that we must say goodbye. Soon, Mr. Lincoln's army will arrive here. Mr. Lincoln has already proclaimed you free. I believe that he means well but I do not know how his *army* will treat you or how they will treat any of us. I have heard that they are burning slave cabins along with mansion houses and cotton barns. I have heard that they are stealing from slave and master alike in order to feed themselves.

The time has now come for all of you to leave. I am no longer your master. You are no longer my slaves but free men. You should all return now to your cabins and quickly gather all that you can, especially your food and clothing. Take them and go far into the woods.

When the army has passed, any of you who wish are welcome to return. I will again care for you as best I can. I will provide each man a plot of land that is his own. If your cabins are burned, I will try to help you re-build them and will try to give you equipment to raise your crops. For each man who is willing, I will pay him to help me again raise cotton.

But now you must go. I pray that God may grant you safe passage."

Within the span of five minutes, the entire world in which Stark had immersed himself since coming to Georgia had crumbled before his eyes. He was not pleased, but neither was he startled. He was surprised only that Andrew had not waited a little longer to see if perhaps the army could somehow regroup and stop Sherman's advance.

There were a multitude of reactions among the eighty or so persons who had gathered. There were cheers from some who now saw an opportunity that they had not expected to come in their lifetimes. Children too small to understand cheered simply because their parents did. Some of the elderly slaves whom Andrew had either allowed to retire or had assigned tasks equal to their declining abilities were bewildered, uncertain as to what would become of them. Some simply wept, while others prayed either loudly or to themselves. Someone in the crowd began to slowly sing a spiritual about crossing the River Jordan. Soon, nearly all had joined in as a chorus began to waft toward the darkening woods.

Like Moses' band of Hebrews in their favorite Bible story, the slaves began their exodus. They packed the meager belongings from their cabins into any sort of carrier they could manage. Some used bed sheets slung over their backs to form makeshift packs. Others used feedbags taken from the stables. Still others carried the bags that they had once hauled into the fields for picking cotton. Most of the food grown on the plantation through the summer was also gathered and transported into the woods. What was not carried away was Andrew's personal cache. Everything that had not either been granted to the slaves or sold in Milledgeville was stashed safely away in a locked, underground cellar near the garden behind the mansion. Within two hours of Andrew's speech, the once bustling Pine Hill was empty of occupants except for Andrew and Stark – Andrew in the mansion and Stark, at least for now, in his quarters.

Stark realized now that his options were even fewer than he had first thought. Going was out of the question. Neither, did he have a desire to go back to the road and re-join the throng of newly displaced people fleeing southward. He was not familiar with other routes to the south or which ones might have already been cut off by Sherman's troops seeking to halt the retreating Confederate Army. The idea of staying at Pine Hill where now-free slaves whom he had once supervised in the fields might sometime return was equally distasteful. And then there was the 'We know' note that had mysteriously appeared in his quarters and then just as mysteriously disappeared last Christmas Eve. Who was it that *knew* and what did they know? Even more disturbing, what did whomever had written the note intend to do now that he was free? Anxious and very much afraid, he walked slowly back to his quarters, lit a lamp, and locked the door.

****

335

Darius lay on his bunk and listened. It was long past lights out and the snoring of other prisoners in the bunks around him made him jealous. A brisk breeze found its way through the cracks in the walls of the hastily and shabbily built barrack. Thankfully, it was not the bone-chilling wind that was sure to come later and the thin blanket kept him comfortably warm.

He longed for the restful sleep that had eluded him since September. Tonight though, as he had on many recent nights, he fought sleep and tried to keep himself awake. Sleep, when it did come, was anything but a pleasant slumber. More times than not, his sleep was fitful and filled with a recurring dream of his experience in the basement of the guard captain's office.

Darius had not seen a mirror. Such objects were considered contraband in the barracks. The glass could be broken and turned into a weapon. That he did not have a mirror did not disappoint him. He had no desire for one but had repeatedly imagined what it would show. Running his hand across the left side of his face, he could feel where his beard how grown back in two months. He could also feel the scar over which the beard would never return. The scar began just below his ear and ran along his jaw line ending at his chin. He took some comfort that the whiskers surrounding the scar, when brushed over it, made it nearly invisible.

His knee would never completely heal from the beating. The pain was with him most of his waking hours and some swelling remained. The surgeon's incision had scarred over but the man, either by intention or incompetence, had made sure that he would be left with a permanent limp.

After a time, he lost his battle to stay awake. He soon found himself again standing outside the door at the bottom of the basement stairs. The door slowly opened and showed a small room lit only by a small lamp on a wall sconce. Silhouetted between him and the lamp were two shadowy figures that appeared to be wearing masks. The only furniture in the room was a single oak chair with leather straps attached to the arms and front legs. He felt his legs beginning to weaken as the two figures emerged from the shadows and half-carried him to the chair. He heard one of them dismiss the pair who had brought him down the stairs. Now there was only silence as they strapped his arms and legs to the chair. He was surprised when one of the men turned out the light and the room went pitch dark. There was a brief light as they opened the door and closed it behind them. He heard steps and assumed that, for whatever reason, they had gone back upstairs. He was somewhat encouraged that this was, perhaps, the extent of his punishment – to be left sitting alone in the dark.

Darius lost track of the time. His legs ached from not being able to move or stretch. The fresh cut on his face had clotted some but was still bleeding. He wanted to wipe away the blood but, of course, couldn't. And it was cold. Even though it was September, he found himself beginning to chill while sweating. His mind began to wander, purposely, as he tried to think of anything at all that would change his focus from his discomfort. The effort failed him. The only vision that seemed able to occupy his consciousness was the final charge at Little Round Top. He could see only the angry blue wave as it clambered over the wall with fixed bayonets and came angrily down the hill toward him.

A creaking of the basement door jarred him out of the vision. One of the men held the door open to allow enough light for the other to re-light the wall sconce. That done, the door closed and the two stood before him, one of them holding a length of heavy chain. The last words he recalled were, "This is what Minnesota thinks of secessionist traitors!" He relived the pain in his knee that had come with the first of the violent blows from the chain. Waking with a start – sweating and chilling, he vowed to remain awake for the rest of the night.

The next morning Darius, for the first time as a prisoner, asked for paper and a pencil to write a letter home.

Federal Prison Camp
Rock Island, Illinois

Dear Father,

I must ask you to cease and desist of having any kind thoughts or respect for any in the Union Army. You wrote me once that there are trials and sorrow on both sides. I can tell you that the Federals, especially the ones that I know to be from Minnesota, are the most cowardly beings ever to inhabit the earth. They are crude and heartless barbarians that deserve the most painful death possible. They deserve to then spend eternity, if there is one, in the lowest reaches of Hell. I intend to make it my life's work, if I ever get out of this place, to make things right. I wish to make as many of their lives as possible as miserable as can be. I intend to start by ...

Sincerely,

Darius.

The letter was the last he would ever write using his right hand. He never knew that his letter was burned and never left the camp.

****

Darius had spoken sparingly with other prisoners in the camp and had come to trust only one. The closest he had to a friend was the young private who slept in the bunk above him. The boy's name was Wallace. "Wallace who?" Darius had asked him once.

"Wallace Nobody," the boy had told him. "Just Wallace." That had been the end of it. He had never inquired again. He had learned, though, that the boy was from Alabama. After receiving word that his older brother had been killed, he had begged his parents to let him join the army. They had denied his repeated requests and ultimately he had run away from home. Less than two weeks after arriving in Mississippi, he had been captured and sent to Rock Island.

On this particular night, Darius lay awake staring at the bottom of Wallace's bunk. He assumed that the boy was sound asleep as were most of the other prisoners. A sideward glance toward the door told him that the guard was also asleep. "Are you awake?" came the soft, tentative voice from the upper bunk.

"Yeah, can't sleep," Darius answered cautiously.

"You hungry?"

"Reckon so. We're always hungry here. Aren't you?"

Wallace didn't answer but slipped his hand down over the edge of the bunk. "Here. Take this."

"What is it?"

"Just take it," Wallace told him.

Darius reached up and found that the boy had handed him a dinner roll – no longer warm but soft and fresh. "Thanks. Where did you get it?"

Wallace leaned up on an elbow and scanned the barracks in order to satisfy himself that no one was listening. "I work in the camp bakery." He leaned over the bunk to be closer to Darius and whispered, "I took it. I was tired of making 'em for all of the Yankee officers and us just gettin' the dry crusts and the old moldy stuff that they won't eat so they serve it to us."

"They'll catch you," Darius whispered to him. "Just as sure as damn hell, they'll catch you. You can't do it again." The next night, there was another roll. A week later, his admonition to Wallace came true.

Dawn was just breaking and a small amount of daylight appeared through the wall cracks and what passed for windows. The familiar voice of one of the guards echoed from the open door of the barracks. "Alright, all of you secessionist bastards and yellow-bellied scum, out of your bunks now! Fall in in front of the barracks now!"

Up and down the rows that lined each side of the building, there was scrambling and cursing. Some had slept in the rags that had once been proud gray and butternut uniforms. Others had chosen to strip them off and sleep in their soiled and reeking undergarments and were quickly pulling on trousers. "Damn, what's all the fuss about? What are the damn-to-hell Yanks up to now? Hey, guard, you're worse than scum! Hey, maybe the war's over and they're turning us loose! No chance in hell of that. They'd just as soon shoot us all before they'd do that!"

"Hurry up you Rebel sons-a-bitches!"

Darius noticed that Wallace was not climbing from his bunk. Not only was the boy not there, but it appeared that he had not been there all night.

The scrambling and cursing continued as prisoners began filing through the door and taking their places in rows in front of the barracks. "Silence!" barked the familiar voice. The command became unnecessary once the assembled prisoners saw what was taking place before them. The voices turned to whispers as they speculated among themselves as to what was to happen next.

Three men were lined up behind a table facing the formation. In the middle stood Private Wallace. He was flanked on both sides by guards standing at attention with rifles and bayonets. Captain Billings was busily tying the boy's right hand to a block of wood on the table. Satisfied that his knot was tight, he stepped back and began to loudly address his 'audience.' "This thief has stolen food intended for the sustenance of the fine officers who run this facility and provide for all of your needs. We do not tolerate stealing in this camp, especially by those entrusted to work here. We do not tolerate it now and, by damn, we will not tolerate it in the future. In order to set an example and to prevent it from happening again, we are going to demonstrate what happens to thieves here. Any of you who are tempted to take what rightfully belongs to the only lawful government in these United States, pay special attention!"

From his place in the ranks, Darius could see that Wallace was barely able to stand. He was trying his hardest to appear brave and not to cry in front of his fellow prisoners. Despite his best efforts, the boy's chin and lips were quivering. Tears ran from underneath the blindfold and down his colorless cheeks. Billings approached one of the guards and borrowed his rifle. "This will do nicely." Without apparent emotion except for a slight, menacing

341

smile, he raised the butt of the weapon above the diminutive hand that had provided the dinner roll.

Darius could not help himself. "Wait!" he heard himself shout.

Giving Wallace a temporary reprieve, Billings handed the rifle back to the guard. "Who said that?!"

Darius stepped forward from his place in the line. "I did."

Billings grinned in anticipation of even greater satisfaction than he had earlier imagined. "Ah, you! And to what I owe this interruption?"

"He didn't do it."

"Of course he did it! Just as sure as you're a low life, slave-holding, worthless Johnny Reb, he by God did it! Two guards watching the bakery saw him do it. Now he's going to pay." He again borrowed the rifle and raised it above the boy's hand.

"I made him do it. He didn't want to but I made him."

"And just how did you do that?" The rifle did not move from its position.

Darius was used to lying. It had always come easily and naturally to him. This was the first time he recalled ever doing it for any reason except his own self-interest.

"I knew he worked in the bakery. I told him that, unless he brought me fresh food, I would find his family after the war and kill his mother." Wallace's countenance had turned from paralyzing fear to one of confusion.

"You told him that, did you now?" Billings asked. "And he believed you?"

"He's young. They believe anything."

"Well now, that changes everything. Maybe I should just punish you both!"

Darius suddenly realized that his attempt at gallantry may have been entirely in vain.

"Maybe I should do what I planned for Wallace here and shoot you. How about that? I think that would be fair. Don't you agree?"

Darius felt his face flush and his palms begin to sweat.

"Bring him here," Billings continued. The guards flanking Wallace stepped toward Darius who haltingly moved forward to meet them. Only now did he realize that they were the pair who had assaulted him in the 'crypt' and ruined his knee.

Within moments, Darius stood next to Wallace behind the table. "Untie him." Billings spoke to the guards and nodded at Wallace. "Tie *him*." He pointed at Darius and again raised the rifle.

****

Henry was pleased that autumn had been mild. September had brought a welcome relief from the summer's heat. October and early November had been pleasantly cool with brief periods of sharp cold. There had been enough rain to give the ground some much needed moisture going into winter but not sufficient to hinder harvesting the corn crop. Henry, Jonas, and Theodore had plowed the fields as soon as the last of the corn was shoveled into the crib. They had been able to finish the job without a land-locking freeze bringing their progress to a halt. Enough wood had been cut and brought up from the timber to fuel Em's kitchen range for the entire winter.

November was entering its fourth week. The trio had now focused on a new task – one that could be accomplished even in cold weather. It could be done as long as snow or ice didn't interfere or the cold was not so extreme as to cause the wood to splinter when cut. All of the limestone blocks from the quarry outside of Crestville had been delivered and lined up in rows near the spot where the new barn would stand. So too, the oak logs that had been sawed into beams sat stacked nearby – each cut to exact lengths according to Henry's plan. All available daylight, and there was getting less and less of it, was being spent moving blocks to the precise spots needed for the foundation and cutting tenons and mortises that would join the beams together to create the building's frame.

Theodore had not spoken again of joining the army. Henry had had not brought up the subject and was pleased that the young man hadn't either. He hoped that Theodore had lost interest. Rather, he suspected that with each passing day, Theodore had become increasingly resigned that the war might end before the date of his agreed-upon enlistment. That prospect, to Henry, was one of great relief – not only for Theodore's sake but for the sake of all whose lives and health might be saved by an imminent end to the conflict. That what he had called 'the nasty business' was about to be finished filled him with a profound sense of pleasure. The only thing that pleased him more at this moment was the secret that Em had shared with him last week – that she was again with child. She had thought about telling the rest of the family but they had decided to wait and announce it at Thanksgiving dinner as their special reason to give thanks.

On Monday night they all sat around the dining room table. Jonas, who had mostly recovered from his cold, had been able to work all day. As had become their weekly custom, Joshua was invited to join them and was seated next to Ellie. Em, Ellie, and Rose had prepared a beef roast and mashed potatoes along with corn that had been put up last summer and stored in the cellar with the rest of the winter's supplies. Joshua, whenever joining them, was asked to offer the blessing. "Dear Father, we ask Thy blessing on those of us gathered around this table and for the bounty which Thou hast provided for our sustenance." He continued, knowing that only one at the table would disagree with the rest of his prayer. "We ask that Thou also be with the innocents of the city of Atlanta during the tribulation that the war has now brought upon them. We ask that Thou protect them from harm and bestow Thy grace upon them." He stopped far short of asking God to provide strength to the Confederate army.

According to the custom in the household, there was no visiting during the meal itself. What conversation there was consisted of requests to please pass the potatoes and a protest from Patrick who didn't wish to eat his corn. His outburst prompted a similar disturbance from Rachel who readily ate her corn but obstinately refused to touch her peas. Both rebellions were quickly quelled and the meal went on without further incident. Once the main course was finished, Em and Rose cleared away the dishes. Ellie remained seated next to Joshua and they discreetly held hands. Em and Rose soon returned with coffee but all agreed that it seemed best to let their meat and potatoes rest for a bit before adding peach pie. Conversation resumed over the coffee but any talk of the war was studiously avoided. Talk, instead, centered on the upcoming Thanksgiving celebration and the community feast that was being jointly planned by the ladies of the Lutheran and Methodist Churches.

While the others were visiting, Jonas kept finding himself glancing at Joshua and Ellie. He hoped that they were too pre-occupied with each other to notice his watching. At one point, Joshua leaned over and appeared to whisper something in her ear. She responded with a slight, shy smile and seemed to blush a bit. Aside from the pair, only Jonas knew what was about to take place. Presently, Joshua arose and began to nervously address the little assemblage. "Ever since coming to Thayer nearly a year ago, I have developed a deep and abiding respect for the Hancock family. From the moment when I first arrived here, you welcomed me into your home, provided me with shelter, and made me feel like one of your own. That respect and admiration has only grown as I have gotten to know each of you better."

Rose, Em, and Henry smiled at each other as they began to recognize what was about to happen. Rose raised her hands to her mouth as she resisted the urge to giggle. Joshua continued, now realizing that any surprise in the announcement he was about to make had disappeared. "I have grown especially fond of one particular member of the Hancock family." He looked down at Ellie who was now in full blush. "Nothing would now give me more pleasure than to actually be a member of the family. I have asked Ellie to be my wife."

Joshua had no more than finished when Henry stood. In a fashion not often seen at the dinner table, he began to loudly clap his hands. The gesture was soon joined by all except the babies and there was a feast of congratulatory hugs and handshakes. Lost in the moment, Em glanced at Henry and appeared to be about to announce that Joshua would not be the only new member of the family. He gave her a return look that told her, 'Not now. Don't take away from Ellie's moment.' Quickly receiving his message, she moved to give Ellie a sisterly hug.

As the ladies were washing dishes in the kitchen, Theodore sat reading in the dining room. Henry retired briefly to his library. Spread on his map table was the latest copy of Harper's Weekly that had arrived in today's mail and which Joshua had brought with him from town. Jonas and Joshua, for the time being, were nowhere to be seen.

ATLANTA ON FIRE

Night came solemn down upon the city and as the flames spread from the public buildings and the depot that had been fired, the whole heavens became illuminated by the lurid glare, while the unexploded shells in the dwellings and warehouses became heated, and as they exploded in rapid succession, one almost imagined that the scenes of August last, when one hundred thousand heroes confronted the Rebel stronghold, were being re-enacted.

Standing upon an eminence overlooking the doomed city, I had an excellent view of the conflagration, and never had I beheld so grand a sight. As night waned, the gentle breeze carried the destroying element from house to house, and block to block, until one half of the Rebel city was in flames, the glare of which was so bright that soldiers a mile distant read their last letters from home by the light.

The next morning, I rode over the city among the ruins, where nothing remained to tell the tale but teetering walls and blackened chimneys that, like gravestones, stood there as monuments to departed glory.

Henry stood over the dimly lit table. Dipping his pen into the inkwell, he gazed briefly at the circle that he had placed in September around the surrendered city on his map. Making a large 'X' over the circle, he drew another line toward the southeast and Milledgeville.

.

CHAPTER XXII

Taylor Adams had lived in Milledgeville since his childhood and had, for many years, been pastor of Elm Street Presbyterian Church. He was short with a ruddy complexion and was slightly round while not plump His hairline had long-since receded to a few thin strands of comb-over that appeared to be a quite futile attempt to recover his lost youth. His most attractive facial feature was a neatly trimmed salt and pepper beard. There was nothing especially noteworthy about his voice. It was neither nasal nor particularly high or deep. Its most distinctive feature was a peculiar accent that seemed to be a combination of Dutch and a Southern drawl. His father had been born Joseph VanOdoms in the port city of Rotterdam sometime around the beginning of the American Revolution. Taylor was not sure exactly in what year. VanOdoms had emigrated from Holland sometime in the first few years of the century and changed his name to Joseph Adams. The elder Adams had ever explained to any of his friends or children the reason for either the emigration or the name change but Taylor had a theory. He had always suspected that his father had been somehow, as a young man, involved in the slave trade.

For virtually the entire span of his ministry, the reverend had been a close personal friend of Andrew Morgan. He had married Andrew and Annabelle and also buried Andrew's parents. He had baptized Darius as an infant. When the baby raised a ruckus during the service, Taylor had made light of it and joked to Andrew and Annabelle that the boy was bound to spell trouble. Andrew often reflected on the comment made in jest and was disappointed that it had turned out to be a prophecy rather than a passing, light-hearted comment. Years later, the Reverend Adams had presided over Annabelle's funeral service. For a long period after her premature passing, he had visited Pine Hill Plantation almost weekly. He and Andrew had spent many evenings playing chess or simply visiting.

It was late afternoon. That meant, at this time of year, it would be dark within an hour. Actually, it hadn't been light all day. Ever since dawn, a deep overcast had hung like a pall over the city. It was a cold shroud that carried with it intermittent showers of small, stinging ice pellets that peppered any exposed skin like a thousand pricking needles. The ice had stopped for the moment and the reverend looked up. The wind was throwing the clouds about and, with them, herds of leaves – leaves that had either just been torn from now-barren trees or been scooped up from the streets and hundreds of unraked lawns. It was not like the citizens of the tidy little city to leave their lawns unkempt. But now it mattered little. Some of the lawns belonged to those who had already fled. Others lay untended because either the owners no longer cared to tend them or the slaves who would have done the work had simply walked away. Oblivious to it all, a 'V' of geese winged southward overhead in search of warmer climes in which to spend the upcoming winter.

The blustery weather was the least of Reverend Adams' concerns though it added to his discomfort. He stood in the street in front of the church and watched a company of blue-clad soldiers empty the church sanctuary of its contents. The pews that families of his congregation had used for generations to observe services, weddings, and funerals were now stacked like so much cordwood near the church's front steps. The pulpit that he had used for his entire tenure and the previous pastor had used for nearly forty years before that lay smashed on the sidewalk, having been carelessly tossed from the front door. "At least they could have carried it out," he told himself. "At least they could have shown a little respect." He was thankful that the pew Bibles had been carried out carefully and placed in a wagon underneath a canvas top. They, at least, would not be burned or left to mold on the damp brick street.

"We need the space," he had been told. "The Army," by which he knew that they meant the *Union* Army, "now owns everything in this secessionist city," the town's remaining residents had been told. "We intend to use all of it. When we leave, you can have what's left." Most knew what had happened in Atlanta and anticipated that little of use to them would be left behind. The reverend had asked to be allowed back into the Church office but his request had been brusquely denied by the sergeant who appeared to be in charge of the 'sacking.' "That's army property now," he had been told. "You best be on your way." He had received the same answer when he asked if he could remove some personal papers from his study in the parsonage.

There was one item in particular which the Reverend wished to retrieve from the church in addition to the pulpit Bible that a young corporal named Jesse had brought out and handed to him. Nearly two years ago, Andrew Morgan had brought him a sealed envelope. He had not revealed the contents. He had said only that the document inside was important. In addition, Andrew had instructed him to only open the envelope upon his death or instructions. The reverend consoled himself that Andrew had probably kept a copy or would prepare him a new one if the original should disappear. He would make it a point to visit Andrew at the earliest opportunity and ask him if he would do just that. In the meantime, he would make one more attempt.

The sleet had started again. The reverend attempted, as best he could, to hold the Bible underneath his coat in order to keep it dry. Nervously, he approached a young lieutenant. Outranking the sergeant, perhaps he would be more reasonable in acceding to what the Reverend deemed to be a modest request. Even with his personal view that slavery should be benevolent, the reverend still held strongly to his belief that the colored race belonged, by predestination, in a subservient role. It bothered him to see someone who probably had very recently been a slave to be wearing the uniform of an army officer and armed with a revolver and sword. He knew, though, that any chance of success would require him to be respectful and civil.

"My name is Reverend Taylor Adams," he introduced himself quietly and calmly.

"Sir."

Taylor had expected more than a curt, abbreviated reply.

"This is my church," he continued.

"Now it belongs to the army," the lieutenant replied. "Perhaps when we are done with it, you will get it back."

The Reverend knew better than to ask if the lieutenant's comment represented a promise. He was familiar enough with war to know that promises were rarely made and rarely kept. He was certain that more than one church such as his had perished when Sherman's army had burned Atlanta. "I understand," was the most he could muster. He had avoided looking the lieutenant directly in the eye but did it now in an attempt to bolster his case. "I have only a small request, Lieutenant ...?" He phrased the lieutenant's name as a question, hoping that if he could address him personally it might help.

"Lieutenant Douglass," the young man replied. "My name is Lieutenant Isaac Douglass."

"As I said, Lieutenant Douglass, I have only a small request. There are some personal papers in my office that I ..."

Isaac did not allow him to finish. "I'm sorry, Reverend. I am truly sorry for that we must take your church and I am truly sorry that I cannot abide by your request. As I said, this is now property of the United States Army and I have my orders that no civilians are allowed."

"But I ..."

"But what? Is here something I said that you didn't understand?"

"I was just going to say that ..." The reverend hesitated and decided not to continue. He had thought about trying to explain 'benevolent slavery' but reflected that any such explanation would be fruitless. "Never mind," he finished, turned, and walked away hoping to spend the night at the home of someone from the congregation. Before leaving, however, he decided to try one more time to ingratiate himself with the lieutenant. He looked back over his shoulder. "I hope our sanctuary will be a comfortable billet for your men." Within a moment, he wished he had kept silent.

"Thank you," Isaac answered him, "but it's not for them. They will be somewhere else. Our company was told to clear the building out to make room to stable cavalry horses!"

The Reverend continued to walk away. He had tried his best but it was now obvious to him that there was nothing else to be done. Tightly clutching the pulpit Bible under his coat to keep it from harm, he resumed his search for a place to spend the night.

He had gone only a few steps when he felt the touch of a hand on the back of his shoulder. At first, he hoped that Lieutenant Douglass had changed his mind and had come after him. He had not. "Reverend Adams, my mother is here. She saw that they wouldn't let you into the parsonage."

The reverend turned and looked, puzzled, at the young man who had just spoken. "Adam Kendrick," he introduced himself. "You probably don't know me."

"I ..."

"It's alright," Adam assured him. It's a large congregation. Ma and I always sit way in the back. The rich folks sit closer but we understand. We figger they're the ones that pay for the church."

The reverend was unsure what to say. He was embarrassed that he actually did not recognize the young man. "You might be surprised," he answered. "Some of them are pretty tight with their money. Sometimes I think they come to church just to make sure their neighbors will see them there."

"Anyhows," Adam continued, "Pa never went with us. He read his Bible every night though and always said Grace before our meals. Said he was pretty sure Saint Peter would understand. I hope he was right."

"Your Pa's dead then?" the reverend inquired. He immediately regretted asking such an obvious question.

"Got killed at Malvern Hill. I guess he's buried somewhere there. At least I hope so. We never really got no word about it. We did put a marker though. You came out and said a few words over him. Ma really appreciated that. She said you done real nice."

The reverend was even more embarrassed now at not recalling either Adam or his mother. "I'm so sorry for your loss. I'm sure he was a good man. And, yes, I think Saint Peter understands about his not coming to services. There are times I'd rather not be there myself."

Adam smiled slightly at the last comment. "Anyway, if you got nowhere else to go, Ma and me would be real proud if you'd stay with us. You can have my room. I kin' sleep in the parlor."

"I'd be really obliged," the Reverend quickly answered. "Don't you think people might talk though?"

"Na," Adam told him. "We're practically family – my first name bein' Adam and your last name bein' Adams. Besides, who's left to talk? Almost the whole town headed south."

"I see your point and, yes, I'd like to take you up on your offer." It was now that the reverend, for the first time, noticed Adam's missing arm and the sleeve that had been carefully folded up and sewn.

Adam noticed his glance. "Gettysburg," he said simply.

"Ma's still here somewhere. Let's go find her. By the way, Pa was about your size. You look like you could use some dry clothes."

****

The gunfire could be heard all of the way to the plantation as the embattled Confederates struggled vainly to keep the invaders out of the city. Once the gunfire ceased, the defeated army's remnants moved down the road past the plantation while their commanders sought an appropriate place to make another stand.

Joining the disillusioned and retreating army and, in the process, impeding its passage were throngs of civilians. The intrepid residents of the city had remained in their homes after the earlier wave of refugees left. Now despaired of living out their lives in the town they had always called home, they traveled on foot or with carts or carriages. Some carried only what they had managed to cram into a suitcase. Others attempted to haul away everything they owned.

Andrew knew he would stay. Pine Hill Plantation was home. He had lived nowhere else. His parents and his beloved Annabelle lay buried in the family plot near what remained of Annabelle's flower garden. He often spent time sitting on a bench in the shade of a large oak tree near her grave talking or reading to her. It provided him comfort though he knew she could not hear him. He had never talked about the war or his disappointment with Darius. He had always assumed that, when his time came, he would lie here beside her. Nothing different had ever crossed his mind.

Stark's reason to stay was more practical. He had no attachment to this place and loathed many things about it. There was simply nowhere to run. Milledgeville itself, now an occupied city, was out of the question. He recalled his panic when caught up in the crowd fleeing the city. That recollection made it impossible to join the new train of civilians trekking southward. In addition, he envisioned that the same road would be used by Sherman's troops as they pursued the desperate remains of the Confederate army. When those remains turned to make a stand, as he calculated they would, he had no desire to be anywhere near the conflict. He was afraid to hide in the forest. Former Pine Hill slaves, if they had remained in the area at all, could be anywhere in the woods. He could not allow himself to be at their mercy. His only real chance, he had decided, was to remain at the plantation and hope that Sherman's troops would move down the road and leave the place unmolested.

****

To say that the home Adam Kendrick shared with his mother was modest would be an understatement. The downstairs contained only a kitchen not much larger than the space most homes allotted for a pantry and a sparsely and shabbily furnished parlor that doubled as the family's dining room. A steep, narrow staircase led to two small bedrooms and a tiny hall closet. Even so, the little home a few blocks from the main business district was not theirs. It was rented from Nathaniel Kendrick's cousin Artis who lived in Atlanta.

Before the war, 'Nate', as his friends called him, had worked as the manager at Sam Greene's Livery and Hay Yard and supplemented his meager salary doing odd jobs for various merchants around town. Susan Kendrick, Adam's mother, had taken in sewing and laundry from some of the town's more well-to-do residents who did not own a house-slave but had no desire to do the work themselves. The family had always managed to 'get by' but little more.

After Sumter, Nate had gotten caught up in the war fever that had quickly swept across the South. He joined an infantry regiment, 'not to save slavery,' he had assured the family, 'but to protect our home.' His army pay, he had told Susan, would help to pay off some debts and even, perhaps, allow them to put a small sum aside. Besides, he would only be gone for a few months. It would only take that long for Lincoln's troops to quit the fight. Then everyone would come home and get on with their lives.

When Nate was killed at Malvern Hill, the pay stopped. Fortunately for Susan and Adam, Artis had allowed them to continue to live in the home rent-free. Adam worked at the hay yard. As the war took its increasing toll on Milledgeville's income, many of Susan's clients had decided to 'lower' themselves to doing their own sewing and laundry. As a result, her income had declined but she and Adam had still managed to get along on their remaining income and their vegetable garden. Adam had decided though to join the fight and pick up where his father had left off. He had enlisted to serve with Nate's same regiment but did not share his father's delusion that victory would be either quick or easy. The war had ended for him at Gettysburg where a Yankee mini-ball had shattered the bone in his upper arm, bringing both an amputation and his discharge. No longer able to pitch hay and muck at the yard, he had found work clerking at a local general store.

It had been a little over a week since Adam and Susan had brought the Reverend Taylor to share their house. True to his word, Adam had given up his bedroom and now slept in the dining room/parlor. As Adam had predicted, there were few remaining in Milledgeville who were aware of the new living arrangement and even fewer who cared. The reverend's congregation had mostly fled the city. Those still there were too pre-occupied with their plight to concern themselves with where the middle-aged pastor was spending his nights.

The little trio had just seated themselves around the dining room table for their evening meal. Days before, one of Susan's remaining clients had paid her bill with a chicken. The best of the unfortunate bird had been consumed by now but Susan had used what remained to make a chicken-flavored broth with some small pieces of breast meat to give it a bit of substance. The reverend had just finished blessing the last of the chicken. They were ready to begin their short meal when Adam spoke. "I never did think it was right, you know," he addressed the reverend.

Susan Kendrick looked in horror at her son, knowing what was coming but also knowing that she probably could not stop it. "No," she protested. "Adam, not now. Don't …"

"I have to say it, Ma," Adam interrupted. "I have to tell him so that he understands."

The reverend was, by now, completely confused about what Adam wanted to say that his mother was attempting to silence. He took another sip of the thin soup and laid his spoon carefully on the saucer underneath his bowl. He gave them both a puzzled look and then focused his attention on Adam. "What wasn't right?" he inquired. "The war?"

"Not the war," Adam looked him in the eye. "The war had to be. What isn't right is *slavery*. Slavery is never right! 'Benevolent' or not, it's still *slavery*. There, I've said it."

The reverend appeared to choke slightly as he sought to comprehend what he had just heard. He had never, in his entire ministry, been challenged on the subject. He had been challenged numerous times about his philosophy of 'benevolent slavery' as he admonished his parishioners to treat their slaves more humanely. He had even engaged in heated arguments with some after preaching the doctrine from the pulpit on Sunday morning. Several had even gone so far as to demand that the Elders dismiss him. But he had never been called upon to defend slavery itself and he found himself patently unready to deal with the subject. "Young man," he began to try. "I have never …"

A knock at the door brought both the conversation and the meal to an abrupt halt. Not waiting for his knock to be answered, their next-door neighbor rushed in. Breathlessly, he announced, "They're setting the town on fire!" Through the open door they could all hear the shouting and general commotion coming from the street. "The Yankees are burning us out!"

The neighbor had barely cleared the doorway before the reverend charged through it. Had the unfortunate man been even a slightly bit slower or had the minister been younger and just a little quicker, they would have both ended up in a pile on the front stoop. There were no apologies or excuses for the hasty exit. Adam and his mother both knew where the reverend was headed. Adam had a strong sense as to what he would find. Had there been a little more time, he would have tried to calm him in order to prevent him from witnessing a nearly inevitable catastrophe. Such an attempt, he considered, would have been futile given his small stature and his missing arm. He consoled himself that, perhaps, it would be best if he reverend *were* to witness it. The sight might, after all, validate what he had just said.

The panicked minister ran as quickly as his nearly fifty-five year old legs could carry him in the direction of the Elm Street Presbyterian Church. He paused only momentarily after about five blocks to bend over, grasp his knees, and attempt to catch his breath. He moved more slowly afterward, arriving just in time to see something for which his worst nightmares had not prepared him. Standing on the brick sidewalk across the street, he heard the last clang of the church bell as it came loose from its hanger in the steeple, descended through the vestibule, and came to rest in the basement. The bell was closely followed by the steeple itself. Moments later, the roof collapsed, leaving only a brick shell from which the stained glass windows were already broken out. Flames now jumped skyward from the entire structure including the empty window frames. Shortly after, the back wall began to crumble and the 'temple of benevolent slavery' passed into history.

Across the way, the parsonage was also engulfed in flames. The minister, who had always prided himself on his ability to remain calm in the face of adversity, could no longer contain himself. He started across the street to register his protest, knowing full well that the damage was already done. In the middle of the street, he stopped. His legs suddenly felt weak and he was again having trouble catching his breath. This time, however, there was no relief as he paused. Instead, he felt a sudden, ominous pain in the middle of his chest. He attempted to shout out to a group of soldiers who stood on the sidewalk ahead with their backs to him watching the inferno. He thought he called out but the words would not come. Still trying to move toward them, he clutched his chest and was dead before his body crumpled on the pavement.

Adam, meanwhile, had taken off in a different direction. Cautioning his mother to remain in the house where he felt she would be safe, he made his way the few blocks toward the city's main business district. Even from their house, he had seen the bright orange flames leaping skyward. The light they created gave the illusion of midday and smoke billowed across illuminated sky. He had hoped with all of his heart that this day would never come. What he saw before him now was the very scene that both he and his father had joined the army to prevent. Neither would have gone to war to save slavery. Home, however, was worth dying for.

He had seen this night coming ever since Gettysburg. He had always tried to push it to the back of his mind. Now, it was here. Gathered along one side of the street was a throng of angry, disheartened merchants and shop owners. A few, he knew. Many others, he did not. He recognized his former employer, Sam Greene, whose livery stable stood near one end of the street and appeared fully engulfed. In the middle of the street stood a line of Federal soldiers with fixed bayonets whose job was to keep the angry residents at bay. Behind the soldiers, other soldiers moved systematically from business to business, setting fire to each as they went. The town had already been looted of everything that Sherman's horde could use. The only purpose now seemed to be to destroy everything else that might be of value to the hapless residents of the doomed city. Included in that destruction was the Portman House, whose pleasures the Federal soldiers had happily sampled during their stay in the city. Both the madam and the girls stood by, glumly watching, as their livelihood was torched by men who, only hours before, had been their customers.

With nothing more to see or do, Adam headed home to check on his mother and do whatever he could to ensure her safety. He felt certain that the reverend would find the church and, perhaps, the parsonage also destroyed. Part of him wondered if God himself might have ordered it in retribution for generations of suffering. Though he liked Reverend Adams personally, he had never accepted the doctrine. He had believed since a young age that slavery, by its nature, could never be *benevolent*. Much better that it was gone.

What Adam had much more trouble accepting was the destruction he had just witnessed. War, he knew, just like a flood or a tornado, did not discriminate between the guilty and the innocent. But what he had just seen was not an act of war. It was one of senseless cruelty. Among the townspeople whom he had recognized and whose property was now burning, he knew few who had owned slaves. They were normal, God-fearing people who went to work each morning hoping to make a fair and decent living for their families. While it was true that much of the money that had passed through the shops over the years had been made from growing cotton, much also had been honestly earned by people like himself and his parents. Despaired of being able to understand why it had all happened, he quickened his gait and went on his way.

****

Jonas' night had not been good. Thunderstorms were unusual for the area around Thayer this time of year but they did occasionally occur. This one was particularly violent and, though Jonas heard none of it, he was well aware of its presence. It started mid-afternoon and continued as the family turned in for the night. Jonas fought sleep, knowing that any benefit from sleep, he would pay for by the vivid and terrible nightmare that the storms often triggered. After the rest of the family retired, he sat in a chair beside the kitchen range swilling strong, black coffee. But he was fatigued. Until the beginning of the storm, he had worked with Henry and Theodore on shaping and fitting beams for the new barn. Ultimately, the coffee was no longer sufficient to keep him awake and he drifted off to sleep.

It was not the great clap of thunder or the flash of lightning that startled Henry from his sleep. He had long since become accustomed to such storms and normally slept peacefully through them. He had even most times begun to sleep through Jonas' screams that accompanied the nightmares. Jonas no longer expected the family to gather around him when they happened. Over time he had taught himself to become fully awake and aware that they were only dreams. After a long period of anxiety, he was normally able to return to sleep. The dream had never occurred more than once in a night. Tonight was different. The screams this time were *especially* loud and shrill. The same shrieks that had awakened Henry also aroused the babies who themselves began to wail as loudly as their little lungs would allow. Within moments, all of the inhabitants of the house had gathered in the kitchen very much awake.

The rain had abruptly stopped and Henry stepped outside. His attention was immediately drawn to an ominous orange glow over the horizon in the direction of Thayer. He stepped back inside and summoned Jonas and

Theodore. Within moments, the trio had mounted their unsaddled horses and were racing toward town to see what was happening and if their assistance might be required. Little was said but all were equally anxious about what they might find. Jonas aboard Napoleon, who was easily the fastest of the three horses, quickly outpaced the others. He spurred the horse on, fearing that the cabinet shop might be the source of the flames. As he neared town and saw that his fear was misplaced, he reined the horse in and allowed the others to catch up.

To his relief, the fire was some distance from the stores and shops.

Shortly afterward, the three stopped their horses and dismounted. A large throng was gathered around the fire that was quickly consuming the little log Methodist Church. No one in the crowd was moving. There was nothing to be done as the flames finished their work. There was not a source of water close enough to form more than a token bucket brigade. By the time the fire had first been noticed, even an effective brigade would not have been enough. The tinder-dry logs that formed the walls and the shake-shingle roof were no match for the fast-spreading flames. Within half an hour of its start, the fire had consumed the entire structure, leaving only an unrecognizable pile of ash and charred timbers.

Henry found Joshua standing, stunned, at the base of a tree near a sign that identified the church. "Lightning," he announced. "Most likely, it was lightning."

"Not much doubt," someone else spoke up. "Looked to me when I first got here that the roof was the first to go."

Joshua stared sullenly at the pile of ash, appearing not to comprehend what had just happened. "Why?" he muttered to no one in particular. "Why would God …?"

At precisely that moment, the Lutheran minister arrived on the scene, placed his hand around Joshua's shoulder, and provided an answer that seemed to bring immediate comfort to everyone. "I believe that God just decided tonight that He wanted a larger and finer house," he told the little assemblage. "And I have no doubt that we can have one finished by Easter. In the meantime, I think He would be pleased if we all were to worship in the same one."

****

Had either Andrew or Stark looked north and a little to the west over the pine forest of the plantation, they would have seen the orange glow lighting the sky over Milledgeville. As it was, both were asleep in their respective quarters. Neither had slept particularly well lately. In the last week, they had barely spoken to each other.

Both men awoke nearly at the same moment. The silence of the night gave way to the snorting of horses and the slap of harness. Mules brayed, wagon wheels creaked, and the air filled with the shouting of orders. Neither man lit a lamp but both looked out their windows at the long column coming up the lane. Dressing quickly, Andrew grabbed the shotgun from beside his bed and made his way to the front porch. Stark had lately made a habit of sleeping in a shirt and trousers. It remained only to pull on his boots. Reaching to the night table, he grasped the revolver with its remaining precious two rounds in the cylinder. He wasted no time in racing out his back door toward the heavy thicket behind the cotton barn.

Chapter XXIII

Darius awoke and looked around – not that there was anything to see. The room was completely dark. He remembered that he was not in the barrack but was, again, confined to what he had come to call the 'crypt.' It seemed to take only a small infraction to bring him here. On one occasion, he had been given no reason at all. He decided that it was merely a result of Hosea Billings' pledge to make his time at Rock Island as miserable as possible. Even his best efforts to obey the camp rules would change nothing.

He had no idea if it was night or day or even how long he had been here. He knew only that it was not pleasant. What could hardly be described as a bed lacked the pretense of a mattress. It consisted only of some rough-sawn boards thrown over a couple of empty wooden crates. The only sanitary facility was a bucket in one corner of the room. He had to find it by memory and by feeling his way in the dark. Occasionally, but to no particular schedule, the door would open briefly and someone would throw in a canteen of water and some stale bread.

And it was cold. He had one blanket but it was thin and provided him little protection against the chill. Even before this most recent confinement, the welcome and unusual warmth of early November had given way to a brutal cold. He expected that to last for the rest of the winter. The shakes and shivers were almost constant now but had become so commonplace that he had nearly taught his mind to ignore them. What he was *not* able to ignore was the effect that the damp chill had on his damaged knee and hand. The throbbing seemed to be with him nearly every waking moment. At times, it woke him from sleep. The knee, he figured, had healed about as much as it would. The hand, though, remained badly swollen and hurt him constantly   whether it was cold or warm. He could not move his fingers at all and could rarely bring himself to look at their grotesque misalignment. He doubted that he could ever use them again.

Still, he was not sorry. The boy deserved none of this. He probably would not see him again as the guards had assigned him to a different barrack after the 'incident' He wondered what had happened to him after he, himself, had been carried away. Knowing Billings, the boy may have still received his intended punishment. His own sacrifice may have been wasted. He closed his eyes and tried to banish the thought from his mind.

He knew that there were pain remedies that would provide relief. His requests for them had proved no more successful than those for warmer clothing and additional blankets.

His face felt frosted and nearly numb. When his hair and beard had begun to grow back they had provided a degree of protection from the chill. But before being brought to the 'crypt' he had again been sent to the barber and had both his head and his beard shaved clean. Mercifully, the barber had shaved him cleanly this time and had not cut him again. Still, the head and beard shaves were humiliating. They only strengthened his resolve to someday exact revenge upon those who had wronged him. That resolve grew stronger with each passing day whether in the barracks or the 'crypt.' While he had once wished to be dead in order to be free of this place, he now had a new purpose. He was more determined than ever to walk out of this place at the end of the war.

****

"Company H, Halt!"

From his hiding place in the thicket, Stark could see neither the house nor the spot where the lane turned into the drive along the veranda. He was not inclined to risk being discovered just to get a better view and was content to watch the rear of the column and listen. In his haste, he had not brought with him a coat, a blanket, or gloves. He wished now that he had at least one of those things. What was earlier a cold mist had turned to sleet. The skin on his hands and face began to burn with the cold. The sleet pellets felt like a thousand needles pricking his face. A hat or scarf would provide a bit of relief but he had grabbed neither. He stuck his hands in the pockets of his trousers seeking what little warmth might be available. He kept his face toward the ground to let the back of his head take the brunt of the icy assault. He wanted to rub his ears but that would mean taking his hands out of his pockets. Besides, they felt so brittle that he feared rubbing them would cause them to break off. His clothes were still a bit warm but that only caused the sleet to melt. It turned quickly to cold water that soon began to soak through to his skin. He wanted to curse but had to do it in only in his mind.

The entire raid lasted little more than two hours. Andrew Morgan lived only long enough to see the first moments. Stark heard the calm and measured voice of the Company H's captain. He sensed that the speech had been rehearsed and used numerous times in the preceding weeks. "By order of the Department of War, this plantation and everything on it are declared contraband of war and, as such, property of the Federal Government. I am authorized to seize that property and I intend to do it."

"By God, you'll seize nothing!" Stark heard Andrew shout. "This is *not* Federal property and it never *will* be! You are trespassing. I'll thank you to leave."

Stark could not see whether Andrew raised the shotgun but guessed that he had brought one from the house. There was only a pistol shot and no further exchange of words. He surmised that Andrew was now dead. "No great loss," he told himself. The sole priority now was his personal survival. His nose ran and he found himself fighting the urge to sneeze.

Though he still wanted to protect his face from the sleet, Stark looked up briefly. The soldiers, wagons, and mules had fanned out from the column and were dispersing across the plantation grounds. "Take everything the army can use," he had heard the captain order. "Burn the rest!" The measured, practiced tone had given way to one of anger. "Don't leave anything the secessionist bastards can use!"

He could hear doors on buildings being ripped open or battered in as the search for anything useful continued in earnest. The few useful mules left at Pine Hill were lead from the stables toward the assorted gathering that had been the column. Shots told him that the old, sick, or weak ones were being dispatched rather than left behind. "The loft is clear full of hay," he heard someone shout.

"Clean it out before you burn the barn. The horses won't care if it's Rebel hay! Get a wagon over there to clean out the oat bin. Be sure to pour coal oil in the well."

Stark lay on the ground, now curled up into as tight a ball as possible to protect himself from the sleet. He could no longer fight the urge to sneeze. He hoped his position would muffle the sound.

"That's it!" he heard someone shout. "Done here," another voice echoed. "Nothing more," came a third. "Got all the cattle and hogs. Pretty skinny but should have a little meat on 'em."

"Then let's be on our way," the captain ordered. "Lieutenant Marley, burn the house. Lieutenant Douglass, take some men and fire the cotton barn. Sergeant Warren, take the stables. Sergeant Smith, burn the cabins." Stark found himself peeking over his arm at Isaac Douglass' boots sonly inches away

****

"Forgive me, Father, for I have sinned." It was the second time in his life that Henry had been inside of a Catholic Church. The first had been many years ago back in Ohio. His parents had taken him to the funeral mass for a boyhood friend. The boy had tragically drowned while swimming in Sumner's Creek. Henry had never envisioned himself sitting in the confessional booth, yet found it strangely comforting and welcoming. Now that he had said the words, he waited anxiously. Would Father Patrick Lewis accept him or would he ask   whether or not he was Catholic. Would he reject him if he wasn't? He remembered his late friend and subordinate, Private Edward Kaler, speaking of the peace that he had always felt after receiving the Father's forgiveness. He hoped that he could, perhaps, feel a little of the same.

Henry had left the farm well before dawn. He had left Em a note on the kitchen table saying only that he had business that needed tending to in Crestville. He would be home in plenty of time for the evening chores.

"You are not a member of my flock here at St. Elizabeth's, are you, son?" asked the gentle but gravelly voice from behind the panel. Henry's heart sank at the thought that his entire journey might turn out to be fruitless as well as awkward and embarrassing.

He decided to confess the smaller infraction first. "No, I am not a member of your parish. Nor am I even Catholic. I was baptized Methodist." He waited.

"I surmise by your voice that you are a *young* man." Henry had not felt young since before Shiloh. He sometimes felt himself to have grown old there in a single day.

"Yes, somewhat so."

"You must have very heavy burden to be a Methodist and yet feel a need to come to me. Normally, I should wish to take confessions only from those of the Faith. But I can tell that you are very troubled and in need of comfort. Yes, I will hear your confession. What have you done that torments you so?"

Henry stumbled as he tried to get the words out. He was relieved at the Father's compassionate attitude but still felt hesitant about having come to him. "I have killed a man," he began. "In fact I have killed many. I have left children as orphans and women as widows." He began to sob. He wondered if the Father could hear the sobbing as well as the words.

Father Patrick could feel in Henry's words torment, grief, and genuine contrition. He sensed that he was not hearing a confession of murder. "And did you take pleasure in killing these men?" he asked as a formality, already knowing the answer.

"I did not," came the expected reply. "I took no pleasure in any of the whole business."

"You were in the war, weren't you?" – another formality question that required no answer. "Tell me that what you did, you did to rid the nation of the abomination of slavery."

"I cannot say so," Henry answered haltingly. He feared that the sought after forgiveness may not come.

Though not Catholic, he feared that dire consequences might befall him if he lied in the confessional.

Father Patrick was taken aback at what occurred to him. Perhaps the killings that were being confessed had not taken place in the war. Perhaps the man speaking to him had actually committed murder but was only now feeling remorse. He did not believe the voice to be that of a Southerner. He wondered though if, perhaps, the man had been a Confederate soldier or, at least, a Southern sympathizer. He began to ponder whether to send the young man away but recalled that he had already promised to hear the confession, regardless of where it might lead.

"I prayed and wished for the end of slavery. I hoped that the war might bring it."

Patrick hoped that whoever was on the other side of the panel did not hear his sigh of relief.

"But that is not why I went to the war," Henry continued. "I had always hoped that our Union could be saved in another way."

"Things do not always work out as we hope they will. That is not God's way. With so many people asking Him for opposite things, I should think that He would find such a thing to be impossible, even for Him."

"I went only with the hope of saving the Union," Henry continued, still sobbing slightly. "I felt badly for the plight of the slaves. I cannot say for certain that I would have gone if the Union could have been preserved while slavery continued. For that, I am now ashamed. I knew men who fought only to free the slaves even had the Union not been in peril."

"And are they better men than you for that?"

"I don't know. I just don't know."

"Nor I. But that is not for me to judge. Only our Heavenly Father can judge what lies in men's hearts. But my own heart tells me that they are not."

"Thank you, Father."

"Do you wish to tell me more?"

"I need to tell you all. I need to tell you everything."

"Then do, son. Empty your soul to me."

Henry began, afraid though that the vision might occur as he was speaking.

"I have already confessed to killing many. Most, I can't remember. For that, I am truly repentant. There is one in particular that, as hard as I try, I cannot forget."

"Tell me."

He told all, except for the vision and the drinking. As he left the church, he gazed at the crucifix above and behind the altar. But it was not the figure of the crucified Christ that most drew his attention. It was the nearby statue of the Virgin Mary. The eyes of the Virgin appeared to be looking directly into his own. He had expected to see a countenance of sadness but the eyes seemed to express more a feeling of disapproval. It was the look that he recalled seeing in his mother's face when he had misbehaved as a child. Pausing briefly, he turned and left the church.

Later, a few miles from Crestville, Henry decided that Solomon needed a drink and led him to a small pond a few yards from the road. As the horse was drinking, Henry found himself gazing into the water. At first, he could see his own reflection in the clear pool. He looked tired and ragged, older than his years. Soon the reflection began to disappear into a murky fog. Shortly after, the face that had haunted him so often began to appear. He pulled away as Solomon continued to drink and reached into his saddlebag.

****

Finally, determining that he was alone, Stark cautiously emerged from his hiding place in the thicket and looked around. What had been Pine Hill Plantation was now fully involved in fire. Some of the smaller structures such as the smokehouse, the blacksmith shop, and the corncrib were already reduced to piles of glowing ashes. Fingers of flame reached skyward from the doors and windows of both the house and his own quarters. He turned with a start toward a crashing sound as the roof of the stable fell and the walls caved in around it. His nose picked up the stench of the burning mule carcasses that had been left behind. Some distance behind the stables, the slave cabins had nearly vanished.

Andrew's body lay face-up in the driveway. As he approached, Stark could see a small round hole just above Andrew's still-open right eye. Reaching down, he pulled Andrew's arms from the sleeves of his coat and removed it. He spread it over the iron hitching rail near the porch where it could dry from the heat of the burning house. At least the old man had left him something he could use. Next, he removed the boots and set them aside to dry along with his trousers.

The heat from the burning house provided some respite from the chill. The sleet had mostly stopped now and Stark sat on a stone step leading to the porch, hoping that his own clothes would begin to dry. He knew that the warmth of the fire would be only temporary. No shelter would be available. Then, he remembered the food cave near the garden. After some time, both his and Andrew's clothes had mostly dried. He left the warmth of the steps, slipped on the coat, and went in search of the cave.

He found the cave securely locked and assessed his chances of ever finding the key as remote at best. He checked the pockets of the coat. Not finding it, he returned to where he had hung the trousers. Still not finding the key, he came back to the cave. Picking up a large rock from the edge of the garden, he repeatedly struck at the lock and hasp. Neither the steel hasp nor the thick oak door and frame gave signs of yielding. Again returning to Andrew's body, he picked up the shotgun. Surprised that it had been left behind, he satisfied himself that it had not been fired. He debated for some time about attempting to use the single load to shoot his way into the cave. The cave, he knew, would provide two things he desperately needed – food and shelter. But the gun, once fired, would be useless against predators or human scavengers. In the end, he fired the gun's single round and crawled into the cave.

He awoke not knowing how long he had slept or whether it was day or night. The temperature had plummeted and it was nearly as cold in the cave as it was outside. At least there was no wind and both his and Andrew's clothes had mostly dried. He pulled the coat tightly around him for a blanket and tried to go back to sleep but couldn't. He wished he could light a fire to get warm but the cave had no outlet for a chimney. Finally, he got up and pushed open the cave door.

Light streamed in. Though Stark had known of the cave, he had never been inside. Even with the sunlight from the open doorway, the cave remained mostly in shadows. He was able to look around, though, and see what the storage contained. He was pleased that there seemed to be a large supply of food, everything from cabbages, potatoes, and other vegetables, along with a bin of apples and even a rack holding several smoked hams. To his surprise, there was also a shelf containing several bottles of bourbon and a few boxes of cigars. He remembered seeing Andrew smoke only occasionally but recalled that the fine cigars had always been available for visitors. He did not recall ever being offered one himself. To his dismay, there appeared to be no guns, ammunition, or blankets.

Encouraged by what had been left in the cave, he climbed the stairs and peered outside. The clouds had disappeared but haze and smoke still hung in the air. The fires that had lit the night sky were now piles of ash and still-glowing embers. Only foundations and blackened chimneys remained of the plantation's buildings. He emerged from the cave and walked around, surveying his new and unfamiliar surroundings. He found that Andrew's partially clad body was already frozen nearly solid.

****

At the Hancock farm, the balmy weather that had defined early November had turned suddenly and brutally frigid. Work on the beams for the barn had stopped. Henry had always maintained that cutting wood warmed a person twice – once when doing the cutting and then again when it was burned in the stove. Working on the beams, though, was different. The wood itself was now frozen, making it more difficult to work with the required precision.

It was Tuesday. Breakfast was over and the morning chores were finished. Since there was nothing more to be accomplished outside, Henry decided to ride to Thayer for the mail and some supplies that Em had requested. Jonas and Theodore joined him and the three rode off, joking to themselves about having a much-needed break from the women and the babies. It had snowed overnight but the morning was bright and clear. Within a mile of leaving home, they dismounted and walked in order to keep themselves warm. The hot coffee they had consumed just prior to leaving had quickly lost its warming effect. They eagerly anticipated having more when they reached their destination. Henry had thought about going a little out of their way to see if David wished to join them. Then he remembered that David had mentioned going out this morning to hunt for a deer. The thought made him hungry for fresh venison.

Henry, Jonas, and Theodore briefly acknowledged Will, who was standing behind the hardware counter waiting on a customer. They made their way to an empty table and ordered their long-awaited coffee from Sarah, the new Mrs. Britt. Theodore, who was already hungry again despite having eaten an enormous breakfast, also ordered bacon and eggs.

In the center of the store was a large round stove surrounded by some wooden kitchen chairs and an empty, upside-down flour barrel. Three of the chairs were occupied. In the one nearest their table sat Honus Weatherby who, by all accounts, was Thayer's oldest resident. When the younger Weatherby had arrived in town to open a blacksmith shop, his widower father had come along and helped out in the shop until his rheumatism had forced him to 'retire.' He now spent most of his days in the store acting as a kind of unofficial greeter and occasionally helping out at one of the counters if things were particularly busy. The old man walked with a pronounced stoop that was far less noticeable when he was seated. He had not gone bald but liked to joke that his full head of hair had turned prematurely white. He did not have a beard but only a neatly cropped mustache that stopped short of reaching the corners of his mouth. Unlike most men his age, he still had nearly all of his real teeth, though they were badly stained from many years of smoking. Thick spectacles enabled him to read, though with some difficulty, while his hearing remained largely intact.

Neither Henry nor Jonas knew the man who was seated in the other chair and guessed that he must be a visiting parent of one of the town's residents. The man appeared to be nearly Mr. Weatherby's age but somewhat more robust. The third chair was occupied by a boy about seven or eight years old whom Henry assumed to be the second man's grandson.

Weatherby took a long, leisurely puff on his pipe and then laid it, still smoking, in a makeshift ashtray on the flour barrel. This left both of his hands free to assist him in telling his story. This he did with a great flourish, honed from years of telling the same story to anyone who would listen. He especially enjoyed relating it to people like the young boy sitting before him who had never heard it. Henry knew the story by heart. So did Jonas, who would miss only the embellishments that had been added in the repetitions since he had last heard it. Theodore had never heard it. Both Henry and Jonas were more interested in watching his reaction than in the story itself.

Weatherby began, talking slowly and with little emotion. Henry and Jonas both knew what was coming and decided that the old man always did it this way to make the rest of the telling seem more dramatic.

"It was near fifty years ago." He picked up the pipe, took a quick puff, and placed it back in the ashtray. "I wuz a young buck back then, really good lookin' too if I say so myself n' already tough as hell. No one ever bothered me neither 'cuz any that did, knew they'd be in for a first class whoopin'. In the parts where I wuz a livin' wasn't many white folk – mostly jus' Indians but there was a lot of 'em. An' there wuz bears n' wolves – lots of 'em – more than roun' here. They was ever'where too. They'd hide behin' trees 'n rocks an' you never knew when you wuz gonna see one. They wuz mean too – bigger and meaner than any critter you ever seen. I heard o' one bear that wuz near twelve feet tall when he wuz standin' on his back legs. Never saw 'im musself but I alus' knowed he wuz out there. Heard once he took a neighbor's prize bull from its pen n' jus' picked 'im up n' carried 'im off into the woods to eat 'im. 'Nuther neighbor went a' huntin' 'im n' he never came back. All they found wuz 'is gun n' one of 'is boots. 'Reckon that ole bear jus' ate the rest. Didn' even find 'is bones."

Theodore gave Henry a questioning look. Henry simply shook his head and smiled. Jonas knew what the look was about. "Just wait," he told Theodore quietly. "It gets better."

"I wuz a' livin' down south. I don' mean Iowa either. This wuz real down south where the Rebs are now – in Luziana. N' there wuz gators – bigguns' – n' they'd come right up outa the swamp n' grab a deer or even a cow. I heared once 'bout one even tak'n a bear! I never seen 'im but they say he wuz twenty feet long if he was a foot.

The low measured speech was becoming louder and more agitated. The young boy's mouth was now fixed wide-open and his eyes appeared about to pop out of his head.

"Anyhows, that wuzn't the most of it."

Henry took a sip of his coffee and excused himself to pick up the mail. In addition to the latest edition of *Harper's Weekly*, there were three letters – all from Dr. MacDonald. There was one addressed only to Rose. Another was addressed to the entire family. The third, which Henry pocketed surreptitiously, was addressed only to him. He guessed that it would carry much the same tone as the one that he had received earlier.

"It'd been only a few years since President Jefferson had bought the land off ole Napoleon. We wuz at war with the British n' there was talk ever'where that they wuz a' fixing' to try n' take it away. Well, we wuzn't gonna let 'em do it."

The wide-eyed boy was now so close to the edge of his chair that Henry half-expected him to fall off and go tumbling against the stove.

"So ole' Andy Jackson come headin' down there with 'is army to put a stop to it. We all knew he didn' have enough men so fellas came from all over to join up n' help 'im out. There wuz us white settlers n' there wuz free colored folk n' slaves n' injuns."

The boy spoke for the first time. "There were Indians?" he asked excitedly.

"N' pirates too," Weatherby went on. "Jean Lafitte and his crew showed up extra guns n' flints n' powder. By then we knew we wuz gonna be able to give 'em a good fight. Hell, we even started to think we might win!"

By now, Weatherby was at full steam. No one in the store could help but hear him as he grew carried away in his own story. With each exclamation, his face showed more excitement. His hands flailed more widely as he started to describe the massed British army.

"They wuz thousands of 'em," he went on. "Jus' been shipped over from fightn' Napoleon. We wuz hearin' they brought hunnerds of huge cannons n' brand new muskets that could shoot over two miles jus' to aim at us. We could hear 'em a shootn' 'em off n' practicin' forty miles away. N' it was louder than any storm you ever heard!"

"Were you scared?" the boy asked. "You must've been powerful scared." The grandfather looked toward where Theodore, Jonas and, now again, Henry, were seated. He flashed a wide, knowing smile being careful that neither his grandson nor Weatherby could see. Henry replied with a slight smile and a nod.

"We wuz but Ole Hickory told us how gooda' soldiers we all wuz n' how it would all be alright n' we believed him cuz' he wuz the greatest general ever!"

"Anyhows, we jus' hunkered down with our varmint rifles 'n our six-pound cannon 'n waited fer 'um to come.

"Finally, we seen 'um. They wuz fine lookin' too. Jus' 'bout the purtiest army I ever laid eyes on. Musta' been a hunnerd thousan' er more. They all had these pretty red coats with rows of shiny brass buttons 'n white belts 'n they wuz all wearin' them tall bearskin hats. Looked like they wuz out fer a parade. They had drums 'n fifes 'n bagpipes 'n they wuz jus' a struttin' toward us like no one's bizness."

"'N that's when I see 'im."

"Seen who?" the boy asked incredulously. His grandfather leaned over and whispered in his ear. "I mean '*saw*' who?" he corrected himself.

"Not 'who'," Weatherby replied, "it. Why, the elephant, of course!"

Theodore leaned toward Henry, not wanting Weatherby to hear him. "An elephant? There was an elephant?"

"I'll tell you later," Henry replied equally softly.

"There he was, right in the middle of all of 'um," Weatherby went on. "'N he was enormous – near as tall as a house. "'Is head was this wide!" He stretched both arms out as far as they would go. "'n those big ears wuz a floppin' when he shook 'is head 'n that trunk was swayin' back 'n forth. It wuz sumpin' to behold! 'N then he stopped 'n leaned 'is head back 'n raised that trunk in the air 'n let out this awful bellow like you never heard."

Thas' when ole Andy Jackson rode up on 'is horse. There he was, on that big white horse, a wavin' 'is sword 'n sittin' there so proud 'n tall in that bright blue uniform with its gold braid 'n 'is white hair a blowin' in the wind. We all jus' wanted to stand up 'n shout but we had to stay behind our cotton bales 'n keep our guns aimed at the British. So there they were – Andy Jackson 'n that elephant – jus' a starin' at each other back n' forth – seemed like ole Jackson was jus' lookin' right through 'im. It seemed like forever. Finally, that elephant musta' knowed he wuz beat cuz' he shook 'is head one more time 'n turned aroun' 'n started walkin' the other way."

"Then what happened?" the boy asked, barely able to speak.

Henry nodded to Jonas and they both stood to leave. "Time to go," he told Theodore. "We've business to tend to."

Theodore protested slightly, wanting to hear the rest of what Weatherby had to say. "But, I ..."

"You don't need to hear the rest," Henry said sternly. I'll tell you some other time. Like I said, we have business." They walked to the front counter. Henry quickly purchased some sugar, flour, and coffee from Will and they walked out. Theodore, eager to hear more, still wanted to protest but knew it would be fruitless and followed along, saying nothing.

They had ridden in silence nearly to the bridge over Crescent Creek. Theodore finally spoke. "The elephant wasn't real, was he?" he asked. "The old man just made that part up?"

"Oh, he's real alright," Henry told him. "Not real in the sense you could walk up and touch him, but he's real. I've seen him. So have Jonas and Reverend Joshua and Will Britt and Leland Atlee. We've all seen him. So has nearly every man who has ever gone in to battle. Each one describes him a little differently but once you've seen him, he's always there. You never forget him. I just pray *you* never see him."

They rode for a while without talking again. "So, what happened next?" Theodore finally asked Henry.

"That's right. You don't know, do you? Well, that's why we left. I didn't want to hear it again. Too many good and brave men died that day and for nothing. No one there knew it but the war was already over. The British just kept marching forward in their rows and Jackson's men kept shooting them down. They would march right over the dead and wounded and get mowed down and more would come. Finally, the attack was finally called off and the British went back to their ships. But they left nearly two thousand dead and wounded all over the field. That's all you really need to know. War is ugly business."

When they got home, Henry retreated to his library with his copy of *Harper's Weekly* and Robert's letter. He tucked the letter in the back of his journal for later reading when he was sure no one else would be around. Standing at the table by the window, he made an 'X' over Milledgeville on his map and started a line toward Savannah.

That night, he crept downstairs to the library and took Robert's letter from the journal.

Atlanta, Georgia
November 2, 1864

Dear Henry,

As I asked you with my previous letter, please read this and then burn it. No one else in the family needs to see it. As I write separate letters to Rose and the rest, there is nothing here that they need to hear of.

Our hospital has been here for some time now and, from what we are told, that is like to remain the case perhaps until the end of the war. Most of the wounded from Kennesaw Mountain have either died or have been sent home or to hospitals up north. We are still caring for the more grievously wounded from the battle for Atlanta itself. The hospital is located in what had been the public library. When we occupied the building, all of the books and other contents were piled in the street and burned like so much rubbish. It bothered me greatly to see such waste. I take some comfort that our valiant wounded soldiers are more precious than books that can be replaced. With the city itself being only thirty some years old, I doubt that much of the library's collection was either particularly rare or valuable.

I have never before seen such devastation visited upon a people. From my reading of the Napoleon Wars in Europe, I have noted that those were fought largely by armies in the field. Though tragic for those involved, the loss of life and property was largely confined to the combatants and their equipment. The civilian populations and their homes were, for the most part, unaffected. When peace came, life usually went on much as before with the only changes being new rulers and different boundaries on maps.

Here, however, it is different. Much of the city has been reduced to rubble as a result of the fighting. Hardly a public or private building is without significant damage and a large number have been either destroyed or damaged beyond repair. So many livelihoods have been taken away by businesses being either demolished or commandeered by the army. Many of the city's residents have been forced from their homes and have either fled or are living on the streets with little food or shelter. Though there are many who may be deserving of such a fate by having owned slaves or mongering for a war, I feel for the innocents who wanted no part of either and simply wanted to be left in peace. I fear that General Sherman, when the army resumes its march, may order whatever remains of the city to be destroyed.

Conditions at our hospitals have improved somewhat. Food seems to be fresher and more abundant. I do not attribute this to the Quartermaster Corps. I think that most of what we are getting has been foraged from farms and plantations that the army has seized. There still seems to be a shortage of the bandages and medicines that we need in order to care for the wounded.

The Confederate wounded who were left behind when their army abandoned the city seem to fare much worse than our own. Those who are deemed well enough to travel have been moved to prison camps. I fear they will not be well cared for and that many will survive neither the journey nor the imprisonment. The ones who remain are the ones in worse condition. They are considered prisoners even though they have not been taken to camps. There seems to be little interest in their welfare. Conditions where they are kept are unsanitary. Disease and infections seem rampant. I have not seen them but am told by some of our officers who have been there that the men are purposely being under-fed. Women from the city who have volunteered are being allowed to change bedding and provide what comfort they can but are given little in terms of supplies.

I am so weary of all of the suffering on both sides and pray each night for this awful war to come to a swift end. I think I mentioned to Rose in one of my letters, but don't recall for sure, that I no longer wish to have my own medical practice after the war. I wish to spend my time instead working to heal those who have suffered so enormously. I wish to be able to do it in a peaceful surrounding that is conducive to providing real care without the burden of new wounded being brought in each day.

Pray for peace.

Sincerely,

Robert.

Henry tucked the letter back into the journal and closed the desk. Moving the table by the window, he rolled up the map and carried it to the trunk that still sat in the upstairs hall waiting for its journey to the attic.

****

Other than the food, liquor, and cigars, Stark found nothing useful in the cave. Making brief walking journeys around the plantation, he kept retreating to the cold but less bitter confines of the dugout. There was little to be salvaged. As the ashes cooled, he sifted through them and found some small tools from which the wooden handles were missing. Where the kitchen had been, he found eating utensils, a couple of cooking pots, and some pieces of Annabelle Morgan's fine china. At his old quarters, he found his coffee pot but disgustedly hurled it away when he remembered that he had found no coffee in the cave. He thought of dragging his cooking stove into the cave and fashioning a chimney but it was too heavy to move and he quickly gave up on the idea. He liked the idea of the cave's being warm. He realized, though, that the same heat that might make him more comfortable would also cause the stored food to spoil more quickly.

He decided, instead, to try building a small shelter around the stove but was unable to find any suitable materials to use. There was plenty of standing pine but he had no tools that he could use to cut logs and fashion a dwelling or to cut firewood. He then remembered the barn where he had murdered Toby. He recalled seeing numerous axes, saws, and other tools that had been abandoned there along with moldy, but intact, horse blankets and canvas.

He made his first trip to the barn the next day. Carrying the pistol with its last two rounds and dressed in Andrew's coat, he set out at first light. Reaching the stream, he found that the recent spell of unusually cold weather had caused it to freeze solid enough for him to walk on. Though he had to walk slowly in order to avoid falling, he found that he could make much better time than by walking among the branches that lined the bank. On the return trip, he carried an axe, a shovel, and two horse blankets.

It was nearly dark when Stark returned to the cave. The next morning, he returned to where Andrew's body still lay. With some effort, he managed to pick up the body and lift it over his shoulder. He slowly trudged toward the overgrown flower garden where Andrew's parents and

Annabelle lay buried. The going was slow. Several times he slipped on the snow and ice and narrowly escaped falling. The body was heavy and he had to stop twice along the way to relieve himself of his burden and to rest. Even with the sharp chill, he found himself sweating heavily from the exertion. He considered abandoning the trek as not worth the effort but the idea was short-lived and he continued on.

It was midmorning when he reached the garden. The clouds that had largely obscured the sunrise were now thicker and a mix of mist and sleet was falling. He laid the body near the flowerbed and returned to the cave to retrieve a horse blanket and the shovel. By noon, he had managed to dig a respectably deep grave in the semi-frozen ground. As he wrapped the body in the blanket, it occurred to him that Andrew had always carried a prayer book in his coat pocket. He wondered if it was still there. He reached into the pocket and confirmed that the book was still there. Leafing through the slim volume, he found that Andrew had curiously left a bookmark at a particular passage. He straightened his legs, stood over the body, and found himself reading aloud. "In My Father's house are many mansions. If it were not so, I would have told you. I go to prepare a place for you …"

Finished reading, he placed the book between Andrew's hands. Next, he wrapped the blanket around the body, placed it in the grave, and began to cover it over.

In the next week, he made three more trips to the barn.

Chapter XXIV

Henry pulled the journal from its place in the desk and began to write.

It is cloudy and gray today and very cold. I expect that it will snow heavily by evening. The day is one where one could easily become very melancholy, especially when spring seems so distant. However, I find myself and the family to be particularly cheerful in spite of it all. We are all looking forward to the arrival of the baby next summer and to Joshua and Ellie's wedding as well. In four days, it will be Christmas. Em, Ellie, and Rose have been baking special breads, cookies, and other treats. The house smells so festive!

The news from the war, if any war news can be good, is encouraging. There is word, as yet unofficial, that General Sherman has captured the city of Savannah. If that is true, and I pray that it is, one can say almost with certainty that the rebellion has failed and the Republic has been preserved. With the Confederacy split by not only the Mississippi River but also now by the army, I do not see that the South can now fight much longer. I hope that those who are determined to continue the rebellion will soon see the futility of their cause and will lay down their weapons in order to avoid additional bloodshed on both sides.

I would like to think that the end of the war will bring a great peace across the land, much as the calm that follows a great and destructive thunderstorm. I fear, however, that such will not be the case. It may take years, and perhaps more than a generation, to dissipate all of the hatred and bitterness that has been created on both sides. I do not envy the President his task of trying to re-unify the country, especially given the vindictive sentiments held by many in both Congress and within the Cabinet itself. It saddens me that Jonas holds the latter attitude but I vow not to let that come between us. I predict that the reconstruction will be a long and painful process but at least one where the issues of slavery and secession have been settled. I am mostly content to let the politicians fight it out among themselves. Hopefully Providence will guide them to whatever solutions are reached and the citizens will be largely left alone to go on with their lives as they see fit.

December 21, 1864.

The next morning dawned bright and clear. It had snowed overnight as Henry had predicted. It was a bit less cold but still not warm. Determined to accept Mary Alice's invitation to tea, Em and Rose had bundled the children as warmly as possible. With Ellie driving and Solomon pulling the sleigh, they had happily taken off immediately after breakfast. Henry and Jonas lingered over the kitchen table, each nursing another cup of coffee, and leisurely smoking his pipe. Presently, David arrived. He had explained to Mary Alice that he had little desire to share the house with five women and two babies all at the same time. What he had not told her was that his services were needed at the Hancock home for a Christmas surprise for Em. Though he trusted his wife not to tell, he had once been present when she hosted a sewing group and seen how easily secrets could be shared.

It was not long until they heard the whinny of a horse and the jingling of bells as Will Britt and Joshua came up the drive with Will's wagon. Weeks ago, he had removed the wheels and replaced them with runners in order to make the delivery vehicle usable through the winter. Sarah would be joining the others at Mary Alice's tea and, like David, had not been told of the surprise. The men all stood around the wagon as Will climbed from the seat into the bed and began to remove the canvas cover from the contents.

Ever since renting the house from the Anderson's, the only heat had been from the kitchen range and a small fireplace in what was now Henry's library. Often, the fireplace sat covered over with a wooden panel since using it seemed to pull more warmth from the room than it provided. The heat from the range made the house livable in the winter but little more. Coats or bulky sweaters were often required in order to be comfortable. Upstairs, multiple layers of blankets, quilts, and comforters were needed to provide the warmth necessary to sleep. The babies had normally been wrapped in so many layers of clothing that they appeared to be bundles with faces, rather than small people.

The dining room shared a common chimney with the kitchen and there was an opening for a stovepipe but Albert and Lucille had moved before installing a stove. Henry had planned to put in a parlor stove but the plan had been interrupted by the war and then by a lack of funds. 1864 had been a bountiful year for crops and Henry had decided that some comfort was in order.

As Will supervised, Henry and Jonas, along with Theodore, Joshua, and David, removed the wooden crate containing the new stove from the wagon. The five of them were easily able to carry it onto the small porch outside the kitchen door. Within moments, they had disassembled the crate and managed to carry the stove through the kitchen and into the dining room. Even Henry, who had seen it only as an ink drawing on a flyer from the stove company in St. Paul, was surprised by its magnificence. The stove was round, shiny, and coal black. It stood on four nickel-plated feet. The fire door and the door below it for removing ashes bore the same shiny nickel finish. Henry's pride in the stove was exceeded only by the anticipation of the look on Em's face when she returned from the tea party.

Henry's closely guarded secret had been in the works for weeks. He had planned it long before the Thanksgiving celebration. Will had sent away for a flyer advertising a number of different stoves. When the flyer arrived, Henry, Jonas, and Will had pored over it, discussing at length the merits and appropriateness of each model before deciding upon the one which they all agreed was the perfect choice. Will had mailed off an order and waited while the stove was built and then shipped overland from the factory to the store. Once it arrived, Will had wanted to deliver it immediately. Henry, against Jonas' objections that the house needed to be warmed as soon as possible, had been adamant that it be brought out to the farm at Christmastime. Henry, being the one paying for the stove, had won out, and the stove had sat in its crate in the back of the store for nearly eleven days.

It took them little time to place the stove on the brick hearth that had sat empty since the house was built and to connect the stovepipe to the chimney. Within an hour of Will and Joshua's arrival, the entire group sat in chairs around a glowing fire, congratulating themselves both on getting the stove in place and on having kept the secret.

****

Sleet pelted the canvas roof of the small log hut. Inside, Stark sat on his crudely constructed bed watching the fire in the stove and chewing on a piece of smoked ham. Due to the foul weather, he had spent little time outside recently. Even if the weather had been more pleasant, there was little to do. He did not enjoy hiking in the woods and was still fearful of encountering ex-slaves or wild creatures. He had thought about walking down the road to Milledgeville but had decided against it. As a result, he was becoming increasingly bored, ever more bitter about the turn in his fortunes, and yet more angry toward those whom he blamed.

He had long-since lost track of time. He sensed, however, that it was near Christmas, perhaps even Christmas Eve – the anniversary of his last visit from the little family whom he had murdered. The thought of a return visit made him uneasy and he turned to a half-empty bottle of Andrew's bourbon to ease his nerves.

He awoke hours later. The sleet had stopped but the inside of the hut was much colder than he remembered it being. He opened the stove and noted that the fire was as strong as when he had last tended it. Outside, the wind was howling, or so he thought. The canvas roof was whipping and the single room felt drafty. The sheet of canvas that he had hung for a makeshift door blew violently back and forth. He moved to refasten the straps that held it in place to the door jamb but when he looked outside the air was still. The clouds had dissipated and the stars were shining brightly. Moving away from the door, he again heard the howling wind and felt the drafty chill. He wanted another drink and cursed himself for having finished the last bottle without bringing another from the cave. Nervously, he crawled back into his bed and pulled the layers of horse blankets and burlap bags more tightly around him.

Anxiously eyeing the canvas door, he saw it again come loose from the straps and begin to blow. In only moments, the family appeared. They appeared just as they had the last time he had seen them. Toby still was barefoot with a large, red stain on the front of his overalls that were buttoned over only one shoulder. Celia's dress still appeared soaked and splattered with river mud. As before, her head hung awkwardly to one side. Her eyes appeared at once unseeing and, at the same time, knowing and unforgiving. The infant, whose name he did not know, had not grown and still hung loosely in her arms.

Unlike the last time, no shadowy figure appeared behind them and he did not here the ominous, 'We know,' that the figure had repeatedly uttered.

Stark sat upright on the bed. "I told you not to come back here," he shouted angrily but in vain. "You can't be here. You're dead! Go away! Go now." He hopefully expected that they would heed his command but knew at the same time that they did not hear. They remained as before, standing, saying nothing and not moving. He continued to feel their unseeing gaze. As he watched, Toby motioned slowly for him to come.

Carefully, Stark reached under the straw-filled bag that served as his pillow and pulled out the revolver with its remaining two rounds. He did not aim the gun toward his own head as before but, instead, aimed it at Toby. Without

thought, he pulled back the hammer and fired a shot.
Nothing happened. "Leave, I told you, leave now!" Again,
he pulled back the hammer and squeezed the trigger. The
shot echoed loudly in the cramped space. A puff of white
smoke obscured the trio and when Stark could again see the
doorway, they had gone. He left the bed, moved cautiously
toward where they had been standing, and felt two holes in
the canvas 'door.' Suddenly realizing that the revolver was
now useless, he hurled it against the wall and sank back on
the bed.

****

Weeks ago, Henry and Jonas had done as Will Britt
and most others had. They had removed the wheels from
their wagon and replaced them with runners made by Old
Honus Weatherby's son, Horace, in the town's only
blacksmith shop. The runners made it possible for the bay
mare and Theodore's gelding, Ned, to move the wagon
with ease through all but the deepest snow and even more
easily over packed snow and ice. Earlier in the evening,
they had filled the wagon with fresh bedding straw. The
entire family, bundled against the cold in heavy coats and
layers of blankets, had piled into the makeshift sleigh for
the trip to church services. Henry drove the team while
Jonas sat beside him and the rest of the family buried
themselves in the straw in the wagon's bed.

Since the Methodist Church was yet to be rebuilt, it
had been agreed that the Christmas Eve service would be a
joint one with the Lutherans at their church, with both the
Lutheran minister and Joshua presiding. The Lutheran
Church was a fine, new frame structure on the east side of
town two blocks away from the rows of mismatched shops
and stores that comprised the business district. It had been
built even more recently than most of the town in order to
accommodate a rapidly growing congregation. The move

had enabled the Church to donate their much smaller log structure to the Methodists but that building had burned last month when struck by lightning. As he had with the Britt's store, Jonas had assisted in building the church's interior and had even designed and built both the pulpit and the choir loft.

Henry eased the horses and their human cargo into the end of Main Street. The town did not yet have street lamps and the shop windows were dark. Intermittent grayish-white clouds drifted across the waning half-moon and stars providing a shadowy light. Among gently falling snowflakes that had nearly reached the ground walked darkly bundled-up figures of various sizes – men, women, and children also on their way to the church. Flickering lanterns swayed back and forth reminding him of the fireflies that decorated the street late on summer nights. The houses near Main Street were mostly dark. Here and there a lamp had been left burning and provided a dim glow. For the most part, the houses were invisible but for the snow-covered rooftops that reflected the moonlight but again went dark when the next cloud obscured it. White smoke curled from chimney and rose in spirals only to disappear into the lower clouds.

It seemed suddenly to Henry that the world extended only as far as the gently rounded hilltops behind the town. In this moment, its only inhabitants were his family, those carrying the lanterns toward the church, and those who had already arrived there. It felt as if his life had begun only upon making the turn onto Main Street and that anything prior belonged to someone else. In the same turn, he was singularly unconcerned about the future. He was inclined to believe that the rest of his life, and indeed, all time was frozen into what was unfolding before him. He now imagined himself as simply one of the characters in a forever peaceful and unchanging scene.

He only recalled the sensation happening to him once before. As a child, on a rare family trip to Columbus, he had found himself standing before a painting of George Washington with his soldiers at Valley Forge. He had been so drawn into the painting that he had actually begun to feel a chill even though it was June. The feeling had only left him when his father had tapped him on the shoulder and reminded him that it was time to leave.

This time, there was no tap on the shoulder and no reminder to move on. He could plainly hear the voices of Jonas, Theodore and the others. At the church, he heard Joshua's sermon and participated wholly in the prayers and hymns but the feeling remained. Back at home, he 'awoke' as he was unharnessing the horses and putting them up for the night, feeling is if someone else was standing aside and watching.

****

Darius awoke to sunlight shining through the 'windows' and through the cracks between the boards that formed the walls of the barrack. The wind that accompanied the late-December sunlight was chilling but less so to him than the dank air that had always filled the crypt. He did not recall leaving the crypt nor did he remember how long he had been there this latest time. Today, though, felt different than the other times he had been released.

Presently, he was approached by two guards. "Hell," he muttered to himself. "Already? Not again." The guards were not men he recalled seeing before and their demeanor seemed different – not congenial but less threatening than before.

The guards stood by his bunk but did not lay a hand on him. "Come with us, please."

They are actually asking? he reflected briefly and incredulously. They are actually asking?!

"Come with us, please."

"Where are we going? Back to that damned hole?"

"We don't know anything about a hole," one responded. "Come with us, please."

The sunlight nearly blinded Darius as he stepped from the barrack into the yard. Damn, it was bright after the near total blackness of the crypt. And it was cold – not the damp cold of the crypt but cold, nevertheless, and windy. His knee ached as he walked and the hand felt as if were being smashed all over again. He was pleased when they stepped back inside from the cold and even more pleased to see that they had arrived at the camp hospital. Thoughts of morphine or laudanum began to run through his head.

"You'll not be use'n the hand again, Lad." The camp surgeon appeared to Darius to be roughly the same age as his father. Tall, lean, and freckled, he seemed much healthier than Andrew had looked when Darius last saw him. Michael Reilly's hair had turned mostly white but both it and his drooping mustache both showed vestiges of the red of his younger years. "I canna' be fixin' either it or the leg for ya' wishin' it as I might. The doctor completed a thorough examination, painfully gently moving the fingers this way and that as he tried to assess the damage to their muscles and nerves. I can only be given' ya' something to ease the pain. No, you'll not be use'n them but in time they'll stop hurting ya'. It were cruel injuries ya' were given – more than a man needs to have. It must have been Billings, I'm thinkin'."

"Do you know him?" Darius asked, still unbelieving of the physician's gentle visage compared to that of his tormentor.

"I don't and proud I am to say so. But I've heard of him and that's bein' enough for me," Reilly replied. "We are at war and I know that but you've been a danger to no one since you arrived here. A cruel business war is but it needn't be so away from the fighting. Ah, yes, I heard of Billings alright but wouldn't be wantin' to know him. Such men have no place in life, even in a war. That's why the colonel in charge of the camp ordered them replaced."

"You're not one of them, are you?"

"One of whom, Lad?"

"The Minnesota guards."

"Never been to Minnesota or even this far west. A New Hampshire man I am except for bein' born in Dublin."

"I didn't think so," Darius told him.

"The Minnesotans who were here were a bad lot, especially Billings, I'll be agreein' with ya' – bad and vindictive as I heard but loyal to the Union as I am. Most were in Southern prisons and exchanged. Right they are to be revengeful but had no place here as guards. But ya' should'n be judging all Minnesotans by them."

"Oh, I will. You be damned sure of it," Darius thought, but did not say, "and the rest of the goddamn Yankees with them. Be sure of it as I'm sitting here looking at your Irish face!" He feigned contrition, fearing that anything less would result in his not receiving the prized morphine or laudanum. "I'll try to be more understanding," he lied. "Understanding, hell!" he told himself.

Darius was not merely pleased to see the Minnesota guards gone. He also fervently hoped that they had been sent into battle to be slaughtered by the Confederate forces still in the field. The vision that pleased him most was the one of Hosea Billings being run through with a bayonet and screaming in agony as he died. Only a vision that he was the one administering the fatal thrust gave him more pleasure.

Even before his most recent time in the crypt, word had constantly been spread by the captors of strings of Federal victories and of the imminent demise of the Confederacy. Rumors had abounded that Lee and Johnston had already surrendered their forces and that Jefferson Davis was under arrest. Darius had discounted all such rumors – choosing instead to believe that it was the North that was on the verge of surrendering. Either way, the general feeling throughout the camp seemed to be that the outcome of the war had been pretty much decided and that its end was nearly at hand.

The mood of the inmates at the camp seemed to have greatly improved. There was more laughing and talking. Card games had become more jovial with friendly chatter, less bickering, and fewer accusations of cheating. The food had improved, more blankets were being handed out, and the sick were receiving prompt medical attention. It all appeared to Darius to be in preparation for the surrender of the captives to the victorious South and an attempt to dispel future rumors that the prisoners had been mistreated. As skeptical as he was about the motivation, he welcomed the result. He was cautiously optimistic that there would be no more confinements in the crypt.

In addition, Darius was told by a fellow prisoner that the departed Minnesota regiment had been replaced by one from Wisconsin. The word in the camp was that the new guards had never seen battle and never themselves been confined in Southern prisons. They seemed to have less passion for revenge, to be more tolerant of minor infractions, and mostly interested in finishing their service as uneventfully as possible before going home.

The atmosphere today in the barrack was particularly festive. Here and there, small groups of prisoners were sitting about singing Christmas carols and happily pulling the strings and wrappings off packages from home. Though the guards were watchful that the packages did not contain contraband, they mostly kept to themselves and did not interfere as the prisoners exchanged candy, tobacco, and cold, but still mostly fresh, rolls and cookies. Several evergreen trees had been brought into the barrack, obviously from outside the camp, by guards who were also homesick and wanted to somehow participate in holiday festivities. The gaiety was heightened as the barrack filled with aroma of pumpkin pie and fresh, hot coffee. Though most knew that the respite from normal prison life would be a temporary one, they seemed hopeful that better days were at hand. For most, that seemed to be enough.

Though he was relieved, Darius was far from jubilant. He did not join in the festivities. There was no package from home. There was nothing to trade with the other prisoners. He had no desire to engage in the small talk and laughter. In the year since arriving at the camp, he had only been asked once to play cards. He had declined the invitation, not mentioning his fear that his compulsion to cheat might stir up unnecessary trouble. In the end, there was nothing to do but brood. And brood he did – brood and seethe and wait.

****

Isaac sat on a chair outside of his tent with his feet up on a wooden box and contemplated his future. The outcome of the war seemed no longer in doubt now that his army had reached Savannah and the Confederacy was now effectively split into three parts. But, as he saw it, the future was not a bright one for colored soldiers once they were out of the army. While the white veterans, especially those who had miraculously come through the war still able-bodied, would find many opportunities in the post-war world, most colored men, even educated ones, would find themselves doing the most menial of tasks. He knew that he would do what was necessary to survive but did not relish the idea of breaking his back as a laborer on the new transcontinental railroad. He could not see himself spending his days planting and picking cotton, even if paid in cash or shares to do it. He had seen recruiting posters advertising for men to enlist or to stay in the army after the war and go west. Posts were being established on the frontier to protect settlers seeking to settle the area for ranches, towns, and farms. All of the posts would need soldiers. Isaac did not consider himself to be a warrior and had no desire to be one. Like nearly all with whom he had served, he much preferred peace. He saw in the poster an opportunity to be an arbiter between the settlers and the Indians who presently roamed the land, and to have a real part in creating a new 'country.' The more he thought about signing up for the new duty, the more attractive the idea became to him.

****

Thayer, Minnesota
December 26, 1864

My Dearest Robert,

Well, yesterday was Christmas. But I write you tonight in strict confidence and deep sorrow. You must decide for yourself whether to burn this letter after you have read it or to keep it. Either way, I ask that you promise me to never reveal its contents to another soul – now or ever.

I can only bring myself to write you about it now but some time ago, Henry left in the early morning to go to Crestville. He left Em a note saying only that he had business there and would be home in plenty of time for evening chores. By evening, he had not returned and Em began to fret awfully. She asked Jonas to go look for him which, of course, he did. It was nearly dark by the time and Jonas, knowing that he would not hear if Henry called to him, stopped by David and Mary Alice's' house to see if David might accompany him. David was not home, having not yet returned from Thayer so Jonas went on without him.

It was well into the night when Jonas returned with Henry and Solomon. According to Jonas' account, he had nearly given up when the clouds parted enough to allow some moonlight to show through. It was then that he saw Solomon standing beside a pond along the road but did not see Henry. As he approached the pond, he saw Henry lying asleep in the grass on the bank. This is the most difficult part to write and is why I ask you to never talk of my letter. Next to Henry, Jonas found an empty whiskey bottle and a vial of laudanum. I would not have known of it except that I heard them talking as they came in. Em had worked herself into such a state that she became so tired that she could not stay awake and had gone upstairs to lie down with the baby.

I do not know what would bring Henry to take up drink but I fear that there is something awful in him that his pride will not allow him to share with the rest of us, including Joshua. I even heard him tell Jonas not to tell anyone about the drink. He said he would tell Em in his own good time but could not promise that it would not happen again. It must be such a terrible thing. I am disturbed that it might be such a torment as the one that causes Jonas to wake up in such an awful way when it has been storming. I cannot begin to comprehend his changes day to day. Some days, he seems so happy and content with his life as he did yesterday and, other days, he is so different. On those days he seems dark and brooding and barely speaks to any of us, even to Em. I believe that it would help both Henry and Jonas to talk with us about what they have locked up inside but I fear the Hancock pride that they share may forever prevent it.

I also fear for Jonas. He is such a fine and Christian man and such a gentleman but, my dear, he carries such a grudge that it seems almost a poison to him. He is so frightfully bitter toward the South and all of its people. This past Thanksgiving, we had all enjoyed a wonderful meal when Jonas and Joshua disappeared for a time. Jonas later told me that they had gone to the horse shed. Even though they are the best of friends, Joshua confided in me that they had engaged in a terrible argument. He told me not to tell the others but that he had to tell someone. Jonas had said the most hateful things, he told me. He even said that Jonas had told him it was wrong to pray for the people of the South and that, as far as he was concerned, they could all rot in Hell. When Joshua asked him about the innocents, he said that Jonas had told him that there were no innocents even among the children – that were as guilty as all the rest but just had not 'grown into it yet.' He blamed the South and all of its people for his deafness, for Henry's loss of his eye and for all of the North's widows and orphans. He said that there could never, in either this life or the next one, be a punishment harsh enough for all of the South's sins and for the misery that they have caused.

Jonas expresses his unmerciful thoughts to our friends other than Joshua. Sarah Britt told me that Jonas asked Will the other day how he could be so forgiving of the (I will not say the word he used) who had shot off his leg and killed Thomas. He told Will that it was time for him to learn the ways of the world and place blame where it was due. He even told young Theodore that he should be angrier about the way he and his family were treated in the South.

It seems that there are two Jonas' – the kind and thoughtful one that we love so dearly and the one who harbors and expresses such vile thoughts. Most who hear Jonas speak, I think, understand, even though they may not agree with him. I am afraid, however, that some will in time cease to be his friends. That would be such a terrible price for him to pay. What can one do? I feel so much pain for both of my brothers and love them both so much. I pray for them every night but have come to wonder if God isn't perhaps just as deaf as Jonas. That's an awful thing for me to say, isn't it?

I cannot write more now. It is too painful. I am convinced that it is this awful war that has made both Henry and Jonas so miserable. I think that they are suffering inside for what they have witnessed and have been called upon to do. Such suffering must be far greater for them than the loss of hearing or an eye. It must be so for thousands of others on both sides. So many, if they get to go home at all, will do it with wounds not visible but just as egregious as the loss of an arm or a leg. I so pray that you will return to me as healthy in mind and spirit as you were before the war. War is such an awful, awful thing.

Please know how fully and completely I love you. It will always be so even if you should become afflicted like Jonas and Henry. I ask only that you will confide in me and allow me to comfort you. I so wish you to be home with me and our baby.

As always in love,

Rose.

****

"My name is Keela. Mama wanted to name me Magnolia because that was her favorite tree and she thought it was a pretty name but Mastah' wouldn' allow it. He said it was a white girl name and no little n… baby should have it."

Adam had asked her name as they stood in line waiting to purchase some of the rare food supplies available in the ravaged city. An enterprising merchant had managed to get two wagonloads of flour, eggs, coffee, and salt pork from some area farms that had escaped the pillaging. Adam suspected that the farmers had paid handsomely to avoid having their goods hauled away by one of the army's many foraging parties. He assumed also that the merchant had paid additional bribes not to have his inventory confiscated when brought into town. The man had set up a tent where his store had stood only days before. A long line had formed in the cold and sleet and Adam was certain that the goods would be sold out long before he and the others near the end of the line reached the tent. He had decided, though, to brave the weather and wait his turn on the outside chance that some small quantities of one item or the other might remain.

The girl and one other man stood ahead of him separated by a short distance from the rest of the line. Shortly after, the other man decided that his wait would be fruitless and left. A few other people approached, saw the line, made the same decision, and walked off.

"I think Keela is a pretty name," he assured her quietly. He was confident that no one else in line would hear him engaging with the girl. The rest of the line moved a bit as they stood still. He was sure that the other people waiting cared much more about getting their share of the scarce food than whether the one-armed man behind them was talking to a Negro girl.

He looked down into her dark brown eyes. Her cheeks were moist but he could tell that it was due to more than just the melting sleet. "How long have you been here?" he inquired.

"I don't know," she answered softly and hesitantly. "I ain't got no watch 'n wouldn' know how to tell anyhow. I jus' know it's been a long time. I was here n' the white folks, dey jus' come up n' call me names n' crowd ahead. I know I ain't gonna get no food but I gots ta' try."

He could see that she was shivering from the cold. He took off his short coat and placed it gently around her shoulders.

"Why would you do that for a darkie girl?" she asked him incredulously. "I wuz' jus' a slave."

"Not all white folks are bad," he whispered into her ear. He was careful even though he was sure he would not be overheard. "Me and my pa and ma, we never believed in slavery."

He saw, for the first time, a slight smile. "I alus' thought that near all white folk in Georgia had slaves."

"Many are for it, even the ones who can't afford them, but not everyone. I think there may be many who believe as I do but don't say so." He realized he was talking a bit louder now but was not concerned. He was still comfortable that no one but Keela would hear or pay attention. "What are you doing here alone?" he continued.

"I ain't got no mastah' no more," she answered.

"That's not what I meant. Slavery is gone in Georgia – or it will be soon."

"I wuz jus' a tryn' to get some food. I'm hungry."

"No one came with you?" he went on.

"I got no one." She was sobbing now. "Mastah' 'n his family was runnin' south from Atlanta. Dey was in a wagon and Mama 'n me wuz walkin' hind'. Dey kep' tellin' us to keep up. Mama, she kep' up but me, I fell 'n hurt my knee. I wuz havin' trouble walkin' 'n dey kep sayin' to keep up but I couldn'. I asked if I could ride but Mastah's girls, dey said dey wouldn' ride in the wagon wid' me so he jus' left me by the side of the road. Mama, she wanted to stay wid' me but dey made her keep a runnin south wid' dem 'n I wuz alone. I don' mis dem but I shore' do miss my mama."

By the time she had finished her story, Adam wanted to sob with her. "Do to have any brothers or sisters? Did they go with them?"

"I had a little brother," she told him through the sobs, "but Mastah selled him off when he heared that the Yankee army wuz getting' close to Atlanta. Said he wasn't worth keepin' 'n takin' along."

Adam had nothing he thought would comfort her and remained silent as the sleet continued to sting his face. Word began to come down the line that the only thing left to buy was tobacco. People, cold and discouraged, began to drift away. Tobacco was the one item that could still be found somewhat easily. Besides, Adam had never used it. Following the lead of the others, he turned to leave. Keela stayed, looking bewildered, in the middle of the street. Adam had gone only a few feet when he turned back to her. He held out his hand. "Are you coming?"

"Where?" she asked.

"Home."

It took them only a few minutes to walk the several blocks to Adam's home. Keela's knee had mostly healed and, though she still had a slight limp, she was able to keep up with him. He slowed his pace to allow her to do so without feeling that she was holding him back. "Only a little further," he kept assuring her. He could tell that she was still hesitant but stayed with him since she had nowhere else to go. "We need to get warm. Ma will have some dry clothes for you and we can eat." He was sure about the clothes but much less sure that there would be food. There was little of it left in the house. They were eating sparingly, living mostly on potatoes and cabbages that had been stored in the basement, and even those were nearly gone.

As they approached the house, the sleet was letting up and the night sky was beginning to show its way through wispy, intermittent clouds. The army now occupying the city had kept the oil street lamps burning – not as a courtesy to the town's residents, whom they held in disdain, but to make it easier to patrol the streets. The light allowed Adam to see a horse tied at the gate that separated the small front lawn from the street. Hitched to the horse was a tall box wagon with red lettering on the side that read 'Artis Kendrick, Purveyor of Fine Spirits.' He wondered how the wagon so clearly labeled could have avoided being commandeered by the occupying army. He surmised that a handsome sum must have changed hands to accomplish it.

Adam's relief at being nearly home quickly turned to dread. He had met his father's cousin only once on a visit to Atlanta before the war. Nathaniel and Artis had not been close and Adam surmised that this was a business visit, not a social call. Nevertheless, Artis had allowed Adam and his mother to continue to live in the house rent-free after Nathaniel was killed in the war. For that, he was grateful. But any kind feelings that he had for Artis stopped there.

Adam knew that Artis did not share his and his parents' views about slavery. While Nathaniel had seen the war coming, he had always held out hope that it would be avoided and that slavery would someday die out on its own. Artis, on the other hand, had become a 'fire-eater.' He was a passionate defender of slavery, owned several slaves that he kept as house servants, and had been in favor of secession. Nathaniel had always kept his unpopular views to himself, aware of the consequences if they were to become known. He had left Georgia to fight in the war but had seen himself as fighting not for slavery but to defend his home. For that, he had given his life and Adam had given his arm.

Artis, though, knew of Nathaniel's views. He kept the knowledge to himself but had strongly suggested that his cousin would be wise to take his family and move north. In rebuttal, Adam recalled, Nathaniel had stated quite clearly that Georgia, in spite of slavery, was his home and that he had as much right as anyone to live there. As far as Adam knew, that conversation had been the end of it. Nathaniel and Artis had agreed that they had differences and the topic had never come up again. He knew though, that when he walked to the door with Keela in tow, the argument would begin anew.

Susan met them at the door. At first, she saw only Adam as the girl was standing behind him and in the shadows. "Cousin Artis is …"

"I know," Adam interrupted her, nodding toward the wagon. "Mama, there is something I need …"

It was Adam's turn to be interrupted. Artis came to the door. He had obviously been partaking of the wagon's contents. The man before Adam bore little resemblance to the Cousin Artis that he remembered. That man had always been impeccably well dressed and groomed. His jet-black hair was always neatly trimmed and combed. He was always clean-shaven and looked like he had just stepped out of the barber's chair. Adam had never seen as much as a speck of dirt on the man's boots. His hair now was long and shaggy, reaching well below his ears. He had several days of graying beard and wore a shirt that appeared not to have been washed in weeks. The boots were worn and spotted with red clay. "About time you got here, boy."

Artis quickly spotted the girl. "So," he said loudly with a slight laugh, "Adam Kendrick finally got himself a slave!"

Adam was tempted to lunge at him but restrained himself. "She's not a slave," he protested. "She's a free woman and we're coming into the house!"

Susan Kendrick stayed between the two men, confused by what was unfolding, but wanting to somehow keep the situation from getting out of hand.

"By God, she won't!" Artis bellowed. "If she crosses this threshold, it'll be to clear the table and wash the dishes like a proper kitchen girl."

Keela was now quivering and Adam sensed that she was about to bolt and run. "Only if she chooses to help," Adam shot back. "I told you she's not a slave – not mine and certainly not yours." He took her hand. "It's alright, Keela."

"You will do well to remember that this is my house!" Artis retorted. "There's barely room in here for decent folks. The little whore can sleep in the buggy shed but she's not coming in."

Adam again wanted to attack him but knew that, even able-bodied, he would have had little chance against the much larger man. "Very well," he answered. "Then I will too." With Keela in tow, he headed for the shed.

Susan looked back toward Artis. She appeared to be trying to make up her mind what to do next. After what seemed to him to be an eternity, she stepped off the porch and joined them.

The next morning was Christmas but Adam and Susan barely noticed. With Artis' grudging permission, they went back into the house to gather up what possessions they could manage to carry. That done, the little trio walked through the gate to the street and headed north. "I think we should go to Boston," Adam told them. "I've always thought, if I didn't live in Georgia, I should like to live in Boston."

CHAPTER XXV

Adam made his feelings clear soon after they left Milledgeville. There would be no stealing of food on their trek north. They would live on whatever nature provided – or not at all. Neither Susan nor Keela agreed but both thought Adam should be their leader. Keela argued that white folks had been stealing from coloreds for generations and that a little payback wouldn't be wrong. Susan, never outspoken or one to take a strong position, said she could see it both ways. The Bible commanded one not to steal but maybe a chicken here or there wouldn't really be stealing. Perhaps God would look the other way if they were to take one now and then. In the end, they arrived at a compromise. They would take nothing from a small farm where it appeared that there had been no slaves. Places, on the other hand, that had plantation houses or cotton barns would be fair game.

As mid-February approached, food became more and more scarce. Most plantations had been stripped bare. Those that *had* food guarded it as a commodity more precious than gold. A pumpkin or a few sweet potatoes here and there that had rotted in the field provided most of the available nutrition. Once in a while, Adam was able to snare a rabbit but that was difficult. Most of those had already been taken either by predators or by Federal forage parties for sport while scouring the countryside for larger prizes. Fish from ponds and streams provided some sustenance but even the fishing was not good. Such game as there was proved difficult to cook. Adam was reticent to light fires. Whether for warmth or cooking, they might be spotted by Federal patrols or Confederate stragglers and deserters eager to take what few possessions they had left. Their hunger, along with the lack of adequate clothing or shelter, left them all wondering whether they should have either stayed in Milledgeville or stopped at Atlanta. But that die had already been cast. They agreed that the only real option now was to press on and pray for better fortune.

They travelled mostly at night and rested in whatever cover the woods and brush offered during the day. On this particular night, the half-moon was mostly shrouded in fog and a cold mist stung their faces as they walked. Keela begged to either stop and rest or else she'd be left behind. Adam knew that she had already been left behind once before and he was determined not to let it happen to her again. Tired him, but knowing they needed to move on, he convinced her to climb onto his back and let him carry her piggyback style. It meant moving more slowly and taking smaller steps but the choice soon became fortuitous for them all.

Taking longer strides, Adam might not have tripped and fallen over what he thought was a tree root – might not have thrown both himself and his small passenger to the ground. As he pushed off on his arm to get back to his feet, he realized that what he had tripped over was a human leg. Examination showed the leg to be that of a Federal sharpshooter who had either fallen where he stood or been shot from a tree and landed below. The thought of either saddened him. It mattered not to him whether the man was Union or Confederate. The whole war was a colossal exercise in madness that never should have happened. But happened it had. Now thousands upon thousands were either dead or maimed for life – and for what? There was nothing to be done about it now. The man was dead. All that was left was to offer a short prayer for his immortal soul. There were no tools with which to bury him.

What Adam *did* do was to search the soldier's pockets. He was not looking to enrich himself but, rather, for something that might identify him. If he could find something, it might allow him a chance to do one last thing for him once they completed their journey. He did, indeed, find an envelope the man probably had received from home, along with a pocket watch. He opened the watch and found what appeared in the fog and mist to be a miniature portrait – perhaps a mother, sister, or widow. The watch was still ticking and the body had only just begun to freeze. He carefully pocketed the items, hoping to someday return them to the man's family. He made a whispered promise, requested the man's forgiveness for what he was about to do, and asked him to consider it a trade.

Adam handed his mother the bedroll. Next, he shook the fresh ice crystals from the woolen overcoat and put it on. "I'm doing this to warm it up," he looked up at Keela. "Once it's warm, I'll give it to you." She managed a slight smile and leaned over to hug him. Adam next slung the rolled-up pup tent over his shoulder and discarded his own worn-out boots, replacing them with the nearly new ones. While Susan held one of their precious few remaining small candles, he searched the man's haversack. He found fresh socks, a shirt, a small amount of tobacco, a quantity of ground coffee, a tin of hardtack, a large package of jerky, a supply of matches, a compass, and a small brass telescope.

What Adam found on the ground next to the body was the most useful item of all. Still wrapped in protective oilcloth was a nearly new Sharps carbine complete with a quantity of ammunition. His heart leapt at the thought of being able to perhaps provide himself and the women with fresh venison.

CHAPTER XXVI

Henry finished his breakfast and stepped out onto the back porch. The Late-March sky was slightly overcast but wasn't threatening rain or snow. A mild month had released the farm's assets. Every waking hour except on Sundays had been spent either preparing seedbeds or finishing the timbers in preparation for the barn-raising planned for April 17th, the Monday after Easter. Jonas and Theodore soon joined him and together they walked out to hitch up the horses and mules.

Henry and Theodore were working closely enough together that they could talk to pass the time as they moved back and forth across the field. Deciding that enough progress was being made in that endeavor, Jonas had gone back to working on the timbers. "Have I ever told you," Henry asked, "how important you are to this farm? I've really been wondering how Jonas and I are going to manage when you leave for the army and we have to do everything for ourselves. Seems to me some days you outwork the both of us. I don't suppose I can talk you out of going?"

"I'd been meaning to tell you," Theodore replied, "I've pretty much decided not to go. It looks like the war is going to be over before long now. By the time I would be able to do my part, there probably would be nothing left for me to do that would really help."

"Then you'll be staying here at the farm? I'm glad. I've really come to see you as part of the family."

"Not forever," Theodore answered. "I owe you everything I have and I want to be where I'm needed. But there's really something else I need to do."

"You don't *owe* me anything," Henry assured him. "We haven't *given* you anything. You've more than earned everything. But I'm curious. What is it that you want to do?"

"I've been thinking about it a lot and praying about it and talking with Reverend Joshua. He thinks he can get me into the seminary where he went to school in Boston. I want to be a minister."

Henry took off his hat and wiped the sweat from his forehead with his handkerchief. "I've known you for a while, Theodore. I think I know what you want to do after that but I'll let you tell me."

"I need to go back south. There are going to be a lot of freed slaves down there who are going to need a lot of help. I can help them. I can minister to them and I can teach them. I want to start a church and a school."

"I think that's a wonderful thing to want to do," Henry replied. "Just know how hard that will be. There'll be a lot of bitter white people down there who won't think it's right that colored folks learn to read and write. It's unfortunate but there's going to be a lot of hate."

"All the more reason I need to go, but I won't do it without your blessing."

"You know you have it. When do you need to go?"

"Not 'til after the fall harvest," Theodore assured him. "That should give you time to hire someone before next spring."

The dinner bell rang in the distance. "Let's see what Em has fixed for us," Henry said. "She'll be relieved you're not going to the army. She'll like that you want to be a minister. I wouldn't tell the rest of it just now.

****

419

United States Army Hospital
Atlanta, Georgia
March 29, 1865.

My Dearest Rose,

I think of you much these days as I look forward to coming home and getting on with our lives. There is little to do here now as action has for the most part ceased. Most of the wounded have either recovered as much as they will and been invalided out and sent home or have been evacuated to more permanent hospitals up north. There is still some fighting in the Carolinas but most of the wounded from those engagements are being sent to either Charleston or to Nashville.

I expect that I will be mustered out of the service on or about the tenth of next month. After that, I do not know how long it will take me to get home but suspect that it might be as much as two or three weeks. Many of the railroads leading north from Atlanta are still in the process of being rebuilt for the army's use after being destroyed by our army last summer. I don't know if I will come by way of Nashville and then up the river from Memphis or up through Kentucky and Ohio and then west through Illinois. I will try to let you know as soon as I know more and hopefully my letters will reach you before I get home. If they do not, we will be together and the letters will make no difference.

My Dear One, it is such sweet relief to no longer see our grievously wounded soldiers coming in from the field and to once again concentrate in anticipation on the gentler pleasures of life. That said, I think I no longer want to have my own little medical practice as I once did. I think it will be more satisfying to work in one of the hospitals that will be needed to take care of the many men from this great conflict who will need some form of treatment for the rest of their lives. To be able to come home every night to you and our little ones will make such a calling very bearable for me and I should still be able make a comfortable living for us all.

Kiss our baby for me. Tell her Papa loves her and will be home very soon.

As always in love,

Robert.

Army camp near Little Rock, Arkansas
March 29, 1865

Henry Hancock
Thayer, Minnesota

Dear Captain,

I hope this letter finds your family well and in good spirits. It is raining quite hard here in Little Rock today but even such a spell of weather cannot dampen my spirits. The news as we receive it from all of the fronts sounds encouraging and most are confident that the war cannot now last much longer. We are unclear as to where the regiment will go next. It is anticipated that at least a small force will need to remain here for some time in order to keep peace. There are rumors spreading about the camp that we might be mustered out. There is also talk that we might be sent south for duty in New Orleans or perhaps in Texas. Obviously, I would as soon be mustered out and return to Crestville as soon as possible to resume my work there. I don't believe that, however, is up to me. I will go where ordered and serve out my time there.

I think that there are still folks here who don't understand that the war is over and that the South is beaten. A woman – I shall not call her a lady for she did not act as such – came into the provost office a couple of days ago and insisted that we find her slave and return him to her as she needed him for spring plowing. When I told her that the man no longer belonged to her and was free to come and go as he pleased, she went into a rage and began to call me all manner of foul names. I had my aide escort her back out to the street still screaming and kicking.

That is all of the news that I have for now. Please write me at this address as it pleases you. If we have moved by the time your letter comes, I am hopeful that it will be forwarded and will still reach me. I look forward to seeing you when I return to Crestville.

Sincerely,

Lt. Leland Atlee   United States Army.

****

Stories were now spreading among prisoners and their captors alike that the war had already ended. No one seemed to have the truth. Some were saying the fighting had ended. Others were saying it was likely to go on for another year. Some were saying the South was beaten. Others were claiming that the South had won the war and that the Confederate Army was on its way to liberate the camp. Darius ignored both rumors. He was neither happy nor despondent. Both emotions had melted into his anger.

He no longer had room for rational thought. He sat on his bunk … and waited.

****

A very light fog hung over the little clearing as the sun rose. Susan and Keela were preparing to bed down for the day behind some bushes and small trees near the clearing's edge. Adam had mostly lost track of the days but from the phase of last night's moon figured that it had been about three months since they had left Milledgeville. He further estimated that they must now be somewhere in northern North Carolina or southern Virginia.

As he watched, a pregnant doe wandered into the far side of the clearing and stopped to graze. As quietly as possible, he retrieved the oilcloth sleeve and removed the always-loaded Sharps. Carefully placing the rifle in the fork of a tree so that he could both aim and fire with his one arm, he mentally issued an apology to the deer. He began taking his aim and prepared to squeeze the trigger, hoping that no human predators were within earshot. Just as he became sure of his aim, he felt the cold steel of Harold's revolver press against the back of his neck. "What are you doing?" came the gravelly voice behind him.

"I was about to shoot me a deer," Adam replied nervously, watching the now-startled doe bound out of his sight and into the woods.

"Not on this farm, you ain't," Harold growled without moving the pistol. "Them there deer belong to me and George. Now take that Sharps n' lay it on the ground n' back off."

It was then that Harold first noticed Adam's missing arm. He stared at it without speaking. Adam, seeing the stare, volunteered his answer to the unasked question. "Gettysburg." He sensed that Harold was still skeptical.

"Reb or Yank?"

Adam hesitated, guessing that his answer might determine his fate. His best odds were that Harold himself was secessionist but, in this confused world, one could no longer be certain. He hesitated and weighed his answer.

"Well?"

Adam rolled the dice. "Reb," he answered and waited. "Lost it tryin' to wrestle the Yanks off of Little Round Top. Didn't work out so well."

Harold appeared unconvinced. "The Sharps – where'd ya git it?"

Adam didn't want to dishonor the dead soldier who had generously provided the weapon but figured necessity required it. "Took it off a dead Yank about a month back. I figgered he wasn't gonna need it no more.

It was at this point that Susan and Keela emerged from the brush to see what the commotion was about – Susan with the blanket wrapped around her and Keela wearing the sharpshooter's coat. Adam watched Harold shift his view toward them. He appeared to focus on the young colored girl and the coat. "It's a long story," Adam told him. "Same Yank."

A now thoroughly confused Harold decided the little group was harmless and tucked the revolver back in his belt. "Cain't be too careful these days," he muttered, offering Adam his hand. He yelled back into the woods, "Hey, George! Guess what I found." He turned again to Adam. "Never know what your' gonna find when you step out to take yur' mornin' piss. Never you mind the deer. George 'n me got plenty of meat back at the cabin. Your' welcome to share.

What George and Harold generously called their house was hardly worth the name. Already falling into disrepair before the two had left for the war, the two room, log cabin had deteriorated further in their absence. Chinking between the logs had cracked, dried, and all but disappeared. The shake roof was rotten and had more bad shingles than good. One of the two small glass windows had broken and now was just an opening with a piece of tent canvas tacked over it. It appeared to Adam that the only repair the two had made was to re-plaster the inside of the log fireplace with fresh clay.

To the weary stragglers, the house may as well have been a sultan's palace. For the first time since Milledgeville, they felt warm, dry, and safe. Harold poured fresh, hot coffee while George prepared warm biscuits, bacon, and eggs. After the meal, Susan and Keela bedded down on the soft, straw-filled mattress in the bedroom. George, Harold, and their guest sat at the crude table by the fireplace, drank more coffee, and talked.

The two hosts lit pipes and offered Adam a cob pipe with a small amount of tobacco. Not wanting to seem ungrateful, he lit the pipe and began puffing on it but had trouble keeping it lit. "Ain't smoked before, have ya?" Harold asked, smiling. "Well, never mind. Ya' needn't do it just to be social."

"Reckon he won't be wantin' the corn liquor either," George joked to his brother. "That's alright, son," he turned and smiled at Adam. "So where ya from?"

"Georgia."

"That's a fer piece," Harold remarked. "Ya' been walkin' all winter?"

"Since Christmas."

"I kinda figgered from the look of ya. Where ya headin?"

"Boston."

"Why Boston?" George asked.

"I'm not quite certain really – just seems like a good place to go. Besides, there isn't much left of the South."

Harold changed the subject. He nodded toward the bedroom. "Your mother?"

"Yes."

"The girl? Your slave?"

"No. I met her in Milledgeville. She had nowhere to go after her owners ran off and took the rest of her family with them. Told me she thought she had an aunt that had been sold to a family in Maryland. I told her I'd try to help her find her. Besides, slavery is against the law now."

"We had a slave once before we went to the war," George offered. It was the first either of the pair had mentioned being involved. "Called him Buster. Lived here in the house and ate with us. We paid him some to help work the tobacco. He knew he was free to leave if he was unhappy and none of us would go chasin' after him. When we came back, both he n' Pa were gone. Never found out what become of either one of 'm."

"Sounds more like a hire than a slave," Adam responded. "Hope they made out OK. Doesn't sound to me like you joined up to protect slavery. I didn't either. Honestly, I didn't put much stock in it. Never seemed right. I joined up after Pa got himself killed at Malvern Hill – just wanted to keep the Federals from coming to Georgia and burning my house. So, why didn't you just sit it out?"

427

"We couldn't," George offered back. "Weeda' got conscripted anyhow. Besides, the hell raising politicians got everyone all fired up 'n we just kind got caught up in it." Then came the half-truth. "Got ourselves captured at Vicksburg 'n sent to Camp Douglas in Illinois. They offered us parole if we'd sign a loyalty oath and not go back to fightin'. We'd had enough by then 'n wuz more 'n happy to sign so they exchanged us. We made our way back here 'n been here ever since."

"So," Harold remarked, "ya thinkin' of goin' by way of Richmond?"

"We've been mostly avoiding cities and towns," Adam answered. "But yes, I guess we'll have to go somewhere near it."

"I wouldn'," George cautioned him. Whole area's full of Rebs and Yanks dukin' it out. Thousands of 'm. Last we heared, Ole' Robert's boys is takin' a real beatn'. They say Richmond's about to git taken an' that'll 'bout do it for the South. No, I wouldn' go there at all. My guess is it won't last more 'n a couple of more weeks. Yer more 'n welcome to just sit it out here with us."

****

It had been an arduous journey for the small band of colored troopers who now stood on the parade ground at Fort Leavenworth, Kansas. The trek had begun almost immediately after their regiment had assisted the rest of Sherman's army in capturing Savannah. The force had been ordered back to Atlanta, moving along the same line they had taken weeks earlier. The journey had been on foot because there were no railroad tracks or trestles left intact between the two cities. There were also no supply wagons. The regiment had lived on whatever it could forage from a countryside already stripped nearly bare during the November and December march. Though the trip had been largely uneventful, there had been occasional clashes with parties of Confederate stragglers and raiders.

Once back in Atlanta the regiment had been divided – those who wished to stay being assigned garrison duty in the occupied city, those who had opted to go west to the frontier continuing on.

As before, there were no usable railroads and few supply wagons. They had continued on past the sites of the fall campaign – Kennesaw Mountain and many others. Still foraging and fighting, they had finally reached Kentucky where they could board trains heading west toward the Mississippi. The journey, though now less tiring, remained slow. Time seemed interminable as the train sat on sidings so that trains full of troops, munitions, and supplies could roll eastward to help finish the war in Virginia and the Carolinas. Finally reaching the Mississippi at Memphis, they had boarded a riverboat headed upstream to St. Louis and up the Missouri River to Leavenworth.

"Fall in!" barked the company's newly assigned captain. "Attention! Shoulder your weapons. Lieutenant Douglass, present your orders."

Isaac stepped forward, handed over his envelope, and re-joined the line.

"Company, stack your weapons. You will not need them."

The grumbling began immediately. "Why not? Thought we were comin' here to be soldiers, not cooks and stable hands. This ain't why I signed up! I ain't gonna do it!"

"Lieutenant, silence your men. This insubordination will not be tolerated – now or ever."

Isaac issued a sharp rebuke and the grumbling ceased.

"You will not need them," the captain continued, "because they are not suited to fighting on horseback. You will be issued repeating carbines. How many of you have ever ridden a horse?"

A few tentatively raised their hands. "Plowed wid'm," several answered. "Wasn't many allowed to ride'm."

"Great God!" the captain exclaimed, looking upward, "What have they sent me? Never seen a breech-loader, can't ride. Now they expect me to take them out to fight the best light cavalry since Genghis Khan's Mongols. Great God!"

Isaac raised his hand. "Permission to speak freely, Sir?"

"Granted," the captain replied, now holding his head in his hands.

"Sir, I know these men. I've served with them since before we went into Georgia. It's true that most have never ridden and most have never seen a repeating rifle, let alone fired one. But there are two things they do very well. They learn and they fight! I saw them at Kennesaw Mountain. I watched them help rout the Rebs at Peachtree Creek and again at Jonesboro. All these men need is some teaching. They have never disappointed me and I swear they will never disappoint you either. "

"There. I've said my piece. They are yours."

Isaac's heart sank at the thought of what he had just heard and said. So we aren't sent here to keep the peace at all, he realized. We're here to make war on the Indians. Feeling misled and betrayed, he prayed silently. "God, help these men. God, help us all."

CHAPTER XXVII

With the onset of warmer weather, Stark had moved back to the relative coolness of the cave. He returned to the hut only to retrieve the few scant possessions he still stored there and to cook his meals – not that there was much left to cook. As the end of winter approached, he had used the last of the salt pork. What was left of the cabbages was now soft and moldy almost beyond description. He was not skilled at snaring small animals and he had used the last of his ammunition to shoot at the apparition of the little family that continually haunted his nights.

The apparition had not appeared last night, Saturday, but his sleep had been restless with bouts of fitfulness. When he finally slept, he had slept long. It was now nearly noon on Sunday, April 9.

Not yet fully awake, he imagined hearing gunfire coming from the direction of Milledgeville. For a brief time, and still groggy, he allowed himself the delusion that the Confederate Army that had abandoned the city in November had returned and was attempting to reclaim it. He discerned small-arms fire and cannons. There were other random smaller explosions that he could not make out. There was nothing to indicate to him that the occupiers were blowing up their ammunition depot to prevent its being captured intact. He remained unalarmed by the proceedings. If the Federals managed to repulse the Confederate assault, nothing would change and things would continue as before. If the attack were successful, perhaps it would represent a turning of the tide and victory for the South would again become possible. Neither outcome, he decided, would affect him immediately or directly.

In his desire to have fresh air in the cave as he slept, Stark had forgone his usual practice of closing the door and locking it from the inside. Now, as he lay still, mostly asleep, sunlight streamed in along with the slight breeze. As he awoke and struggled to adjust his eyes to the brightness, he failed to notice the dark-skinned, dark-clad man sitting on the bench near the barren food shelves.

"Well, well, well," came a throaty declaration from the dark corner of the cave, "if it isn't Hamilton Stark!"

Stark bolted upright from the layer of horse blankets that served as his bed. Still fighting the brightness from the door, he scanned the mix of sunlight and shadows in the cave for the source of the vaguely familiar voice. "Who's there?" He remembered all of the 'visits' from Toby and Celia. He had grown somewhat accustomed to them but this was disturbingly different. First of all, it was daylight. The vision had never before occurred in daylight. Secondly, the little family had never spoken. The only utterances had come from an unseen figure behind them, "We know."

"So," the voice answered, "you don't remember me?"

Stark hoped that he was experiencing simply a new and different vision but it seemed unlikely. It was too real. After some moments, he recognized the voice. "Big Billy?"

"Yassuh. Big Billy hisself in his big ole' black flesh."

Stark now recalled the plantation's blacksmith – large, burly, and muscular, seeming sometimes as large as the horses and mules he shod. "What are you doing here?" He saw the man emerge from the shadows and begin moving toward him. Even more menacing than the man's size, which was frightening enough, was the revolver that Billy had trained on his chest. In his other hand, he held what appeared to be leg irons.

Still training the revolver on him, Billy tossed the irons on the cave floor next to Stark. "Put dem on!"

Stark stared at him for a moment and noticed a wide but menacing grin. Billy waved the revolver slightly and repeated the order. "Put dem on."

He knew he couldn't overpower Billy but Stark briefly considered throwing the irons to perhaps disable him or, at the very least, dislodge the revolver from his grip. He slowly moved the irons toward his feet. Perhaps he could distract Billy by talking to him. It was worth a try. "So, where did you get them?"

"Oh, dat's da 'licious part," Billy answered with satisfaction. "Made dem right under ur' nose Ole' Billy did. Did it jus' as you wuz standin' der' watchin'. You figgered you wuz gonna slap 'em on some poor field hand. But Ole' Billy, he knowed different. Ole' Billy wuz plannin' right der' he wuz gonna slap 'em on you someday if he ever got hisself da chance. So when he got 'em done, you know what Ole' Billy did. He buried 'em in da groun' a'hind the cotton shed n' waited. Put dem on."

Stark reached toward his feet and nervously began to comply. "How long are you going to make me wear them?" He hoped that, once Billy had satisfied himself seeing him in irons, he would simply remove them and go on his way.

"Oh, you won' gotta wear dem long," Billy answered. Jus' for a while. Ole' Billy jus' wants to watch you fer a while. Soon Ole' Billy gonna make sure you cain't ever run off from dis plantation. Yessuh, Ole' Billy, he got plans fer you. Den Ole' Billy take dem off."

Once he was satisfied that Stark couldn't jump him, Billy retreated to the bench in the corner and sat down. Reaching into a burlap bag that sat next to him, he pulled out a large piece of smoked beef rib. He smacked his lips and began to gnaw at the rib, stopping occasionally to gulp a swallow from the jug of corn liquor that the bag had also contained. "Sorry," he laughed. "Ole Billy, he didn' bring 'nough fer you."

For perhaps an hour, neither of them spoke. Big Billy broke the silence. "By da way, Seth, you 'member Seth don' you. He was da fo'man from da south field. He wuz da last one dat Mistah Andrew let leave. Mistah Andrew dun' teach 'im to read n' write. Anyhows, before Seth leave, he tells ole' Billy dat he knowed what really came of Celia and Toby. He said he didn' tell Mistah Andrew da truth causin' he thought Mistah Andrew might jus' send you 'way. He wanna make you pay *hisself.* Anyhows, before Seth leave, he tells Ole' Billy what you done and tells Ole' Billy to give you dis." He reached in the pocket of his overalls and pulled out a carefully folded note. "We know."

"Where did he go?"

"Dunno. He coulda' gone up north or he might be holed up in da woods around here. He didn' say. But if he's out in da woods, I knows one thing. You gonna need to depend on Ole' Billy here to 'tect you. Dat's fo' sure."

****

Darius welcomed the balmy April weather that marked the real beginning of spring. It would be short-lived, he knew, followed quickly by the withering heat, the stifling humidity that he thought to be worse than that in Georgia, and the sweaty foul stench that would soon fill the barrack.

It was only the second Sunday of the month. Sunday mattered not at all to him except that he used it to mark the passage of time. The day was always obvious to him from watching the organized, and wasteful he thought, prayer meetings in the barrack. They were always the same – the prayers that he considered useless and the same gawd-awful singing. He was always glad when they ended and a sense of normalcy returned.

This morning, there was no normalcy. Just as the last prayer ended, an explosion of gunfire from outside the barrack shattered his anticipated 'peace.' He allowed himself briefly to believe that the Confederate Army had finally taken the camp. There was the rattle of muskets, punctuated by cannon fire, and a repeated popping noise that he couldn't identify. One particularly large reverberation brought him to thinking that the arsenal itself was blowing up. Had the Yankees done it to keep it from falling into Confederate hands or had his own army done it? It didn't really matter.

What he noticed next, however, disturbed him. The guards in the barrack neither shouted at their prisoners nor rushed outside to join the fight. No frantic orders were being given during the periodic pauses in the shooting. Finally, during one of the pauses, he could make out the sound of church bells ringing gaily in the distance. It dawned on him that there was no battle at all. The Yankees, with all of their noise, were *celebrating*.

Palm Sunday dawned unusually warm in Thayer. Pastor Gibbons pulled back the curtains of his room and marveled at the bright sunshine and nearly cloudless blue sky. He had been praying for exactly such weather for the first service in the new Methodist Church but also had prepared himself for whatever the Lord might choose to send. He had slept little the night before. He had worked late revising and then practicing his special sermon about the trials and tribulations of Christ. He would explain, though his congregation already knew, how those same trials and tribulations were necessary for the Easter renewal to be celebrated *next* Sunday. It crossed his mind repeatedly how wonderfully symbolic it would be if the terrible war were to end before Easter.

Sunday, as usual, began long before dawn at the Hancock farm. Henry, Jonas, and Theodore were busy with the daily chores that needed to be completed before the family could leave for church. Rose and Em prepared breakfast, while Ellie tended the children. Talk in both the house and the farmyard ranged from the weather, to things to be accomplished before the barn-raising, to what the new church would look like on the inside. Of the entire family, only Jonas and Theodore had seen the inside. They and Will Britt had done most of the finish work and crafted the pews and the altar. There was little talk of the war. There had been little news lately and work at the farm left little time for speculation about when it might end. All of them assumed that it would end soon of its own course and none of their talk would hasten it.

Jonas could not hear the compliments directed to Will and himself as people entered the rebuilt church but could tell by the pointing and broad smiles that their work was unanimously appreciated. "It's so beautiful," one said, pointing excitedly at the altar. "Oh, my!" another exclaimed as she surveyed the newly arrived stained glass windows which they had just finished installing on Friday. Will's mother rubbed her hand across the smooth finish of one the new pews and proudly gave her son a motherly hug as Sarah looked on. Mrs. Stevens stood near the choir rail and softly fondled the new piano that the Lutherans had donated for her to play at services yet to come. "Oh, Jonas, it's wonderful!" Ellie told him as she surveyed the entire scene. As Mrs. Stevens began to play her new pride and joy, families picked out the pews that they expected to occupy for many Sundays to come. For each member of the congregation, a child from the Sunday school class had placed a green paper cut in the shape of a palm frond. A small boy whose father would not be coming home was given the special honor of ringing the bell to beckon members of the congregation who had not yet arrived. Minutes later, all had been seated and Joshua, wearing brand new clerical garb, stepped behind the pulpit and opened the over-sized Bible to the passage he had earlier marked. "This is the day which the Lord has made. Rejoice and be glad in it."

The last hymn had been sung, the last 'Amen' said. Joshua stepped from behind the pulpit to indicate that the formal worship service was ended. "Next Sunday is Easter," he reminded the congregation, as if any could possibly forget. "I think it most appropriate to use that day and our celebration of Christ's resurrection to also dedicate our risen church. After everyone has had their Easter dinner, Ellie Hancock and I invite you back at two o'clock to share with us as we …"

Before he could finish, the new doors of the church flew open and a breathless figure appeared in the opening. "It's over!" he shouted excitedly. "Lee has surrendered! The war is over!"

EPILOGUE

The shadows that had reached westward toward him from the tombstones had disappeared as the sun moved overhead. They were now mostly invisible to Phillip as they had made their way eastward behind the stones and faded into the shade created by the timber. Turning briefly to look behind him, he noted a gathering bank of gray clouds rapidly closing the distance between themselves and the sun. It would be only minutes until the shadows would be entirely erased. He poured the last of the coffee from the Thermos bottle and took a sip. Finding that not even the insulated bottle had kept the remaining coffee suitably hot, he emptied the cup on the ground and shook out the last drops before placing it in the rucksack.

The pleasantly cool breeze of late morning had turned into a chilling wind against his back. The duck-canvas safari jacket that had kept him comfortable earlier no longer seemed adequate. He continued to read, holding the book in his left hand while using his right to pull the jacket more tightly around him. Presently, the chill became too much for his aging bones and the fading light no longer allowed him to read. He removed his reading glasses and placed them in their protective case in the rucksack. Next, he carefully returned the journal to its cover and slipped it back into his jacket pocket.

With some effort, he managed to get his feet to leave. His knees and back quickly reminded him that he was no longer young or even middle-aged. Finally, able to stand, he took a last lingering stroll around the cemetery, careful to reserve enough energy to make the trek back to the car. Mindful that this would likely be his last-ever trip to this cemetery, he paused pensively at Henry's grave. He turned and slowly walked away.

NEXT

IN HENRY'S LAND

The Hancock family saga continues as Henry and Jonas encounter a harsh climate, a financial panic, and old friends-turned-enemies as they work to preserve and grow the family farm. Their trials are complicated by the arrival of a vengeful Darius Morgan who comes to Minnesota seeking to carry out the plot hatched during his imprisonment. Theodore, Keela, and Adam face both resistant freed slaves and bitter Southerners as they seek to establish an educational ministry in Adam's hometown of Milledgeville, Georgia. Disillusioned with his role in trying to conquer the Plains Indians and the brutal tactics employed by the army, Isaac turns to a new life as a homesteader in western Kansas.

Made in the USA
Monee, IL
11 December 2019